"Hush," the Irishman whispered.

Johanna Elizabeth nodded in compliance. She could feel his breath beneath her ear, against her throat. The broad hand upon her mouth moved away.

She knew he was hiding. Impulsively, she whispered, "I will help ye." Standing on tiptoe, she tilted her head toward his mouth. "Kiss me, and make it look like you mean it."

He required no greater urging, and he kissed her hard, a long, rough groan rolling forth from his throat.

"If I asked, would ye give yourself to me?" he drawled, knowing he should not ask, should not dream. Still, he had to know.

"Aye," she murmured, unable to resist the way he was making her feel. Her pulse was pounding so furio
might burst. "Fo
thing."

Praise for
NANCY RICHARDS-AKERS

"A marvelous talent!"
Rendezvous

"Nancy Richards-Akers has artfully crafted a tapestry of Medieval Scotland that will live in your heart forever."
Affaire de Coeur

Other Avon Romances by
Nancy Richards-Akers

THE HEART AND THE HEATHER
THE HEART AND THE ROSE

Other **AVON ROMANCES**

ALICE AND THE GUNFIGHTER *by Ann Carberry*
CAPTIVATED *by Colleen Corbet*
FOREVER BELOVED *by Joan Van Nuys*
HIGHLAND FLAME *by Lois Greiman*
INSIDE PARADISE *by Elizabeth Turner*
THE MACKENZIES: LUKE *by Ana Leigh*
THE OUTLAW *by Nicole Jordan*

Coming Soon

PROUD WOLF'S WOMAN *by Karen Kay*
MIDNIGHT BANDIT *by Marlene Suson*

The Heart And The Holly

NANCY RICHARDS-AKERS

AVON BOOKS NEW YORK

THE HEART AND THE HOLLY is an original publication of Avon Books. This work has never before appeared in book form. This work is a novel. Any similarity to actual persons or events is purely coincidental.

AVON BOOKS
A division of
The Hearst Corporation
1350 Avenue of the Americas
New York, New York 10019

Inside cover author photo by Michael Pendrack
Published by arrangement with the author
Library of Congress Catalog Card Number: 95-96050
ISBN: 0-380-78002-X

First Avon Books Printing: June 1996

AVON TRADEMARK REG. U.S. PAT. OFF. AND IN OTHER COUNTRIES, MARCA REGISTRADA, HECHO EN U.S.A.

Printed in the U.S.A.

RA 10 9 8 7 6 5 4 3 2 1

To every soul torn between the Anglo and the Irish.

It doesn't matter how you were raised, when or where; it must never be too late. Being Irish releases inhibitions, fulfills Destiny, brings you closer to the light.

Teadam 'na baile.
Let us go home.

Acknowledgments

The author wishes to acknowledge the significant archaeological, historical, and scholarly materials contained in *Wicklow: History and Society*, Ken Hannigan and William Nolan, Editors, Geography Publications, Templeogue, Dublin, 1994; and to thank Ken Hannigan, Senior Archivist, National Archives of Ireland, and Mrs. Willie Nolan for graciously taking my phone calls and answering my questions.

Thank you also to Elizabeth Feeley, Valerie Higgins, Emily O'Connor, and Countess Sandor Karolyi, for their friendship, enthusiasm, insights, encouragement, dreams, and confidences . . . goddesses in Ireland.

Author's Note

The geographic boundaries of County Wicklow as it is known today did not exist in the fourteenth century. Wicklow was not shired until 1606, and until then the area was administered as a part of Dublin.

In medieval Ireland, what one called Wicklow and its mountains depended in part upon one's race.

If one was Anglo-Norman, and living in Dublin with a view of the shadowy mountains to the south, one might call them the Dublin Hills. The native Irish, on the other hand, did not have a generic name for the boggy maze of valleys and forested peaks, and it appears they referred only to individual mountains by name.

The Anglo-Normans referred to the mountains as *terra guerre*, land of war, and to the settled lowlands as *terra pacis*, land of peace.

The coastal land extending south of Dublin was called *Uí Briúin Cualann*, an Irish territorial and political area included in the old kingdom of Leinster, that was adopted by Anglo-Norman settlers.

Herein, I exercise an author's prerogative and use the term *Wicklow Mountains* because it is a point of reference readers can locate on modern maps. Indeed, it is an area into which many readers may have hiked or toured.

As for other place names, I use the Irish spellings from the *Suirbheireacht Ordonáis*, Government of Ireland Ordnance Survey.

Finally, my use of Irish may in some places seem archaic to those familiar with the language as it is spoken and taught in Ireland today. Because of the historical context of this story, I sought earlier usages, and my primary resource was Reverend William Neilson's *Introduction to the Irish Language*, published by P. Wogan, Dublin, 1808.

Key to Irish Names

Aislinn, pronounced *As-lin,* meaning a vision or a dream.

Bébinn, pronounced *Bevin,* meaning white lady. This was one of the more popular female names in early and medieval Ireland.

Bláth, pronounced *Bla,* meaning a blossom, flower, or gentle, smooth.

Bran, pronounced *Bran,* a raven. It was one of the most popular names in early Ireland, especially toward the end of the Middle Ages. According to the Finntales, there were two warriors named Bran in the Fianna.

Broinninn, pronounced *Brinin,* meaning fair-bosomed.

Ceara, pronounced *Kara,* meaning bright red.

Dallán, pronounced *Dolan,* from *dall,* meaning blind.

Echŕi, pronounced *Ek-ri,* very old name meaning lord of steeds.

Étaín, pronounced *Ed-in.*

Marga, pronounced *Mor-ga.*

Méabh, pronounced *Maeve,* meaning intoxicating, she who makes men drunk. It was one of the most popular female names in later medieval Ireland.

Niall, pronounced *N-ial,* also an ancient name appearing as early as the seventh century, and used by numerous high kings.

Rian, a form of *ri,* meaning king.

Ruarc, is pronounced *Rourke* as it is spelled in this text. It derives from the early Irish word *arg* for hero or champion.

Sean, was brought into Ireland by the Anglo-Normans and adopted by the Irish. It is a variation of the French Jean.

Tadhg, pronounced *Teig.*

The Heart And The Holly

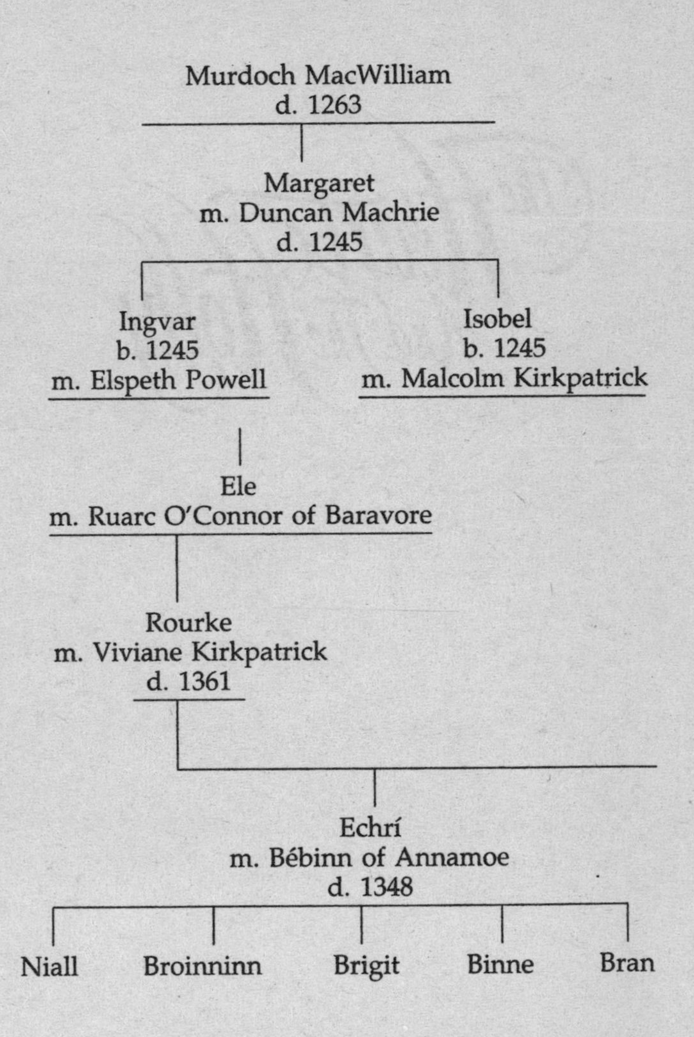
Murdoch MacWilliam
d. 1263
Margaret
m. Duncan Machrie
d. 1245
Ingvar
b. 1245
m. Elspeth Powell
Isobel
b. 1245
m. Malcolm Kirkpatrick
Ele
m. Ruarc O'Connor of Baravore
Rourke
m. Viviane Kirkpatrick
d. 1361
Echrí
m. Bébinn of Annamoe
d. 1348
Niall
Broinninn
Brigit
Binne
Bran

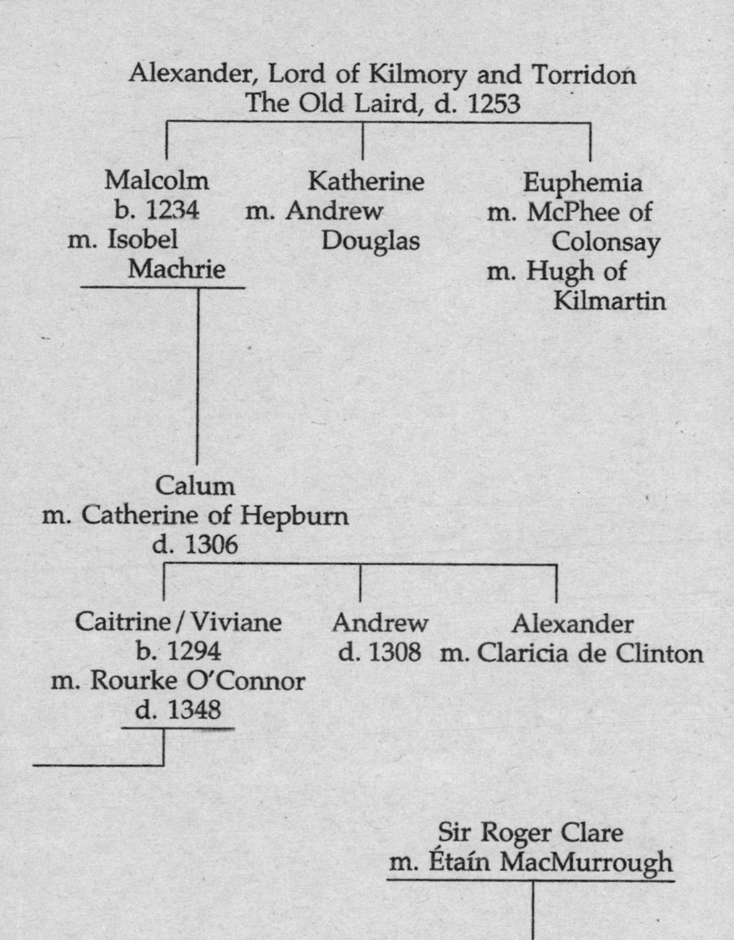

Sir Roger Clare
m. Étaín MacMurrough

Aislinn Clare

Prologue

Uí Briúin Cualann
Leinster, Ireland
Summer, 1368

Bran O'Connor was a dangerous man. Righteousness empowered him. He could do anything. An unrestrained whoop of triumph burst forth from him, and cupping hands to mouth, he raised his face heavenward.

"*Seanathair, an cluinn thu?*" he called out to the spirit of his dead grandfather. "*Grandfather, do ye hear?* I've driven one of them out of our land this day. Can ye hear me, *Seanathair*? I've sent one of them back across the sea to England." The victorious words rose above the cries of curlews, the crash of waves breaking upon the shore below him. Here was a man who was used to defeating his enemies. Indeed, he was a man who found great satisfaction in doing so.

The Irishman grinned and surveyed the familiar landscape. To his right and winding southward, the coast curved toward Arklow, where English warders kept watch from the round tower. To the southwest, the inland trails led to Kilkenny, where the Parliament loyal to their liege lord, King Edward, met. To his left and a hard day's ride to the north past the royal fortress at Wicklow, and farther north past the massive hump-backed promontory rising from the sea at Bré, lay Dublin Castle, stronghold of the English.

But the enemy was not everywhere.

Behind Bran extended the shadowy forest of the Wicklow Mountains. It was rebel territory beneath the dense canopy of ancient oak and hazel trees, and that knowledge deepened the grin upon his rugged features. Those high hills had been held and defended by generations of O'Connors. Bran knew that wilderness well. He knew its schist and granite peaks, blanket bogs and labyrinth of inaccessible, secluded glens. It was his reason to live, and his reason, if need be, to die.

That was how it should be, he thought as he pulled off his coarse woolen tunic and unbuckled the leather belt from about his waist. He removed the heavy dagger, which had been sheathed in the belt, letting it fall beside the tunic. He was a descendent of *Conchobhar mac Taidg*, ancient king of Connaught, and like his cousins in that old kingdom on the other side of Ireland, Bran's family had held fast to their land in Leinster despite almost two hundred years of English efforts to the contrary. He was the oldest son of Echrí, and had been the head of his family since the Great Pestilence of 1361, and his O'Connor blood was pure. Neither his father nor grandfather nor their forefathers before them had done as many Irish chieftains had done: The O'Connors of Leinster had not married the daughters of Anglo-Norman lords, nor wed their women to the sons of their enemy.

There was not a drop of English blood running in Bran's veins, and that was something of which to be proud. MacMurroughs and O'Fearys might intermarry, even an occasional O'Connor in Sligo, but never an O'Connor of Leinster. They did not need the political advantages derived from matrimony to protect their lands. A well-honed longsword and dagger were all that a worthy Irishman needed.

Bran stood atop a sand dune, the sea breeze tugging at his braids that were as black and iridescent as the wings of the raven for which he had been named. Sunlight glinted off the silver talisman hanging from a cord about his neck. His chest and arms were painted with woad in a flamelike pattern of bright blue that burst open like the jaws of some mythic beast across his chest. There was an aura of virility in the way he raised his painted arms to the passing clouds. Beneath the woad pattern, his shoulders and back were scarred. So, too, did his chest bear witness to the many battles in which he had fought. The most notable scar was above his heart. It was a grotesque puckered thing about the size a child's fist that drew one's eye away from the glinting silver talisman and bright blue flames. It was the only thing about this man that did not seem perfect, for that scar above his heart was a reminder that this seemingly invincible creature was, indeed, a mortal.

His lungs filled with salty air, his painted chest expanded. It was a good thing he had done this day. His family had needed to be protected, and Bran had succeeded. He had stopped his younger brother Niall from betraying their heritage for no better reason than the milky white thighs of a wench. It was a good thing Bran had done, delivering the young woman to her father at the quay in Wicklow town.

"*Mallacht ort,*" the lass had shrieked at Bran, daring to speak Irish even though the Parliament at Kilkenny had declared that the English in Ireland must not do so. *Curse on ye,* she had spat, her dark eyes flashing in anger, high color flaring upon her cheeks, and that wild black hair twisting about her face like a thousand serpents. "If I were a man I would see ye in Hell. *Druisfhear,*" she had hurled forth the insult, calling him a fornicator, a lecher.

Bran had not replied. He had acted as if he had not heard, as if he had no recollection of what she meant, and he hoped no one else had paid heed to her ranting. What she had implied was also banned by Parliament, and Bran had no desire to become embroiled in the very illegalities from which he had sought to protect his brother. Not a muscle upon his face had moved as he handed the rope with which he'd bound her hands to her father.

Sir Roger Clare had been grateful for the return of his daughter. "Thank you, sir. It appears in this matter, at least, we are of one mind. I am in your debt."

Bran had known what Sir Roger meant, and he had given a dismissive shrug. He had no desire to have an Englishman in his debt. It was best if they had nothing to do with one another; that was what the statute intended, and Bran would gladly comply. *Degenerate English.* That was what their own kind called the likes of Johanna Elizabeth Clare, and it was an appropriate name. Half-Irish, half-English, they were no better than mongrels. Sir Roger no more wanted his daughter marrying an Irishman than Bran wanted his brother dallying with a girl whose blood was a blasphemous mingling of races. The very notion went against the laws of nature and of man.

"Your family will have no more trouble from her, I promise," the father had vowed.

The young woman had jerked the rope and kicked out at her father as she spewed forth a litany of curses. They were much the same words Niall had uttered just before Bran had been forced to physically overcome him. Niall had been furious at Bran's meddling and outraged by the accusations his older brother had made against his lady fair; the younger O'Connor had proclaimed himself her champion, ready to fight for her honor, and Bran had had no choice except to knock Niall unconscious. It was the only way to prevent him from keeping his assignation in the ruins of a ringfort. Soon enough the lad would realize the folly of his ways.

After all, it had not been Niall's idea to elope with Lady Johanna Elizabeth Clare. She had manipulated him from the first. Niall was not to blame. He was inexperienced and lusty, ideal prey for a temptress with lips that begged to be kissed and a body that begged to be caressed. Niall had been bewitched. Such things had been known to occur, and Bran knew that one day his brother would be grateful for everything he'd done to protect him.

"I don't want to hurt you," Sir Roger had told his daughter as he tried to propel her toward a sailing vessel at the end of the wharf. There had been a sense of desperation in the Englishman's voice, and even now Bran found it odd to recollect how that emotion had touched a chord within him. They were each only trying to do what was right for their respective families, and it was not easy in these times. "Behave yourself," he had admonished before speaking once again to Bran. "I'm sending her to my wife's family in England where she will learn to act like a lady."

Those words repeated themselves in Bran's mind. *To act like a lady.* The phrase had echoed through his brain these past hours since he'd left Wicklow and headed for this bay. Johanna Elizabeth Clare was many things, but an English lady wasn't one of them. His mind's eye conjured up an unruly tangle of black hair framing a pale face, thick tresses that tumbled over slender shoulders to cascade down her back; his memory recreated an image of moist full lips as red as blood and a temper that could ignite as quickly as the golden light that he'd seen blazing from the dark depths of her sultry eyes. More than once she had reminded him of a sudden spring storm, and it had struck Bran that forcing her to become an English lady went against the natural order of things.

"Please, *cuidighim mi,*" she had whispered to Bran, those dark eyes looking straight into his as if she could see inside his soul. *Help me,* she had pleaded in a hushed voice, which her father could not hear over the noise of the waterfront. A voice that had been meant only for Bran.

The muscle along Bran's jaw had twitched. By St. Cieran's bones, why couldn't she accept that the distance between them could never be great enough? Didn't she understand that his winning depended on her defeat? Still she had stared into Bran's eyes and repeated herself, "*Cuidighim mi,*" and it had been at that moment that she had raised her bound hands toward him.

It had been unnerving. She was unnerving, and Bran did not like the way this memory tugged at him. She was a degenerate, one of *them*. She was a schemer whose only intention toward his younger brother had been to take advantage of his youthful infatuation. There was a name for women like Johanna Elizabeth Clare, and it wasn't lady. She was a *beadag*. A lying, enticing female.

She had used her wanton voice and stormy eyes, the feathery touch of her soft fingers, and the sweet scent of her skin to lure Niall. She had beguiled him with promises of love. She had used magic. Bran had seen the myrtle leaves hanging from a cord at her waist, and he had detected the cloying aromas of mandrake and cyclamen on Niall's breath. She had bewitched him. But all the sorcery in Christendom could not overpower a brother's loyalty. Johanna Elizabeth Clare had not counted upon Bran's determination to keep her away from his brother, and when she had tried to work her magic upon him instead of Niall, Bran had used her as she would have used his brother. He had kissed those full red lips when she had asked him to taste her; he had caressed those breasts after she disrobed and stood before him without a touch of shame. She had called him *druisfhear*, but he had done nothing more than take what she had offered him. Bran O'Connor had been empowered by moral righteousness, and there was nothing he wouldn't have done to best the scheming witch at her own game. He had saved himself from her as surely as he'd saved Niall, for she had tried to poison him as surely as she'd tried to poison his brother.

Good had triumphed this day. Why then couldn't he banish that vision of her hand extended to him for help?

Again, Bran raised his face to the sun and after another cleansing breath he unlaced his boots, then he pulled off his trousers to stand and stare out at the sea as naked as the hour he had come into this world. His buttocks were firm and as bronzed as the rest of his body, his torso was lean, and his flat stomach was corded with muscles that tightened with the slightest movement. There was not a scrap of excess flesh upon him, and very little body hair except a swirl of black that began where the woad flames coiled together between his ribs and thickened as it moved lower to his male parts.

Below the dunes, the tide was low. A wide expanse of mud had been exposed between the pebbled strand and the waves of the Irish Sea. Bran had come here several times with his grandfather Rourke. They had sat in the shelter of these dunes, and Bran had listened to the story of how his grandfather had fought the English in Scotland alongside their Highland kin. It was a great inspiration to hear how the Scottish chieftains had defeated King Edward at Bannockburn and had driven the English from their lands.

What he had done this day was right. There should be no lingering image of a hand extended for help. But there was, and Bran had to purge himself of the sentimental weakness worming its way into his spirit.

With a leap he was running down the dunes toward the water's edge. Bran ran hard and fast. His feet pounded the moist black mud, and soon his muscular legs, his buttocks and lean torso were coated by the ooze as it flew upward with each long stride. Plovers skittered out of his way. Up ahead a finger of ocean reached across the mud, and he ran through the shallow pool, kicking up the water that mixed with the mud and woad and sweat streaking down his limbs. Harder he ran, faster, thrashing through the incoming tide until the only things of which he was aware were the sensations of straining muscles, of cold water and of lungs that felt as if they were going to burst.

It was more than a full mile to the end of the strand, where mud and sand gave way to an impassable outcrop of rocks. There, Bran turned around, quickening his pace to reach his starting point before the rising sea caught him. Already the water was ankle deep, the occasional pools afloat with sea wrack leaves came up about his knees, and soon the frigid water and strips of kelp would be eddying about his waist.

Some distance before him an object cast upon the shore attracted his attention. It was large and white, and as he neared, Bran realized it was a person collapsed at the water's edge. His pace quickened. Not for a moment did he fear the poor soul might be dead. Rescue was foremost on his mind when he leaned down and grabbed hold of a bruised arm to sling the limp form over his shoulder. Just as he began to hoist the body, his movements came to an abrupt halt, and his breath caught.

His mouth dropped open as he took in the sight of the bruised and bloodied creature in a tattered gown. She had no more life than a rag doll. He exhaled a pent-up breath. It was her. Johanna Elizabeth Clare. He could tell. Although her eyes were closed and her complexion had taken on a deathly bluish hue, that ghostly condition did not disguise the rich hair and shapely mouth, nor the high cheekbones and winged black eyebrows.

An awful gurgle escaped from her. Liquid bubbled at one corner of her mouth.

She still lived, and for an instant, Bran almost gave into the impulse to drop her. There was no denying that he wanted to throw her back to the sea, to let the waves pull her beneath the surface, where the fish would feast upon her flesh. He had won this day. She was supposed to be sailing to a place far across the sea where she would never tempt another O'Connor brother again. There was that gurgling noise once more. It was a hideous, strangled sort of sound, fainter than the first one, and her skin seemed even bluer than a moment before, if that was possible.

It would have been easy to let her die, thought the Bran who wanted to win. An image of her hand reaching out for help rose before his mind's eyes, and he shook his head to toss off the vision. Still he saw her hand, and in his heart, he knew that he could not leave her here and walk away without looking back. He had been able to walk away at Wicklow, but not this time. He was not that strong. He was not that cruel.

Acting on instinct, Bran set her upon the dry sand. Quickly, he knelt beside her, rolled her onto her belly, and after positioning her arms above her head, he pressed once, then twice upon her back. With a gush large quantities of sea water were expelled from her mouth, and in the next moment, she was alternately gagging and vomiting. When the contents of her stomach had emptied upon the sand, she gave an exhausted moan and curled onto her side.

One, two, three heartbeats passed, then as if on cue her eyelids fluttered, she groaned, then coughed, and slowly, she opened her eyes to stare up at him. Any lingering doubt as to her identity was gone in that instant. There was no other young woman who had those same dark eyes, and for the space of several more heartbeats they stared at one another. At first, it was as if she were looking through him, then Bran saw the glimmer of recognition in those dark orbs. A touch of color returned to her cheeks. She knew it was him, and if he had expected pitiful tears, pleas for mercy, or a flurry of lurid invectives none of that was to happen. Instead she began to laugh, beginning with a thin whimper, then strengthening to an ugly rattle that rang with derision, and his innards churned as much at her plight as at his own. Then as suddenly as it had started the laughter stopped.

"Here we are," she said. "I found ye in Hell like I promised. But I did not know it was so wet and cold. I did not know it would be so lonely." Her ragged voice was barely above a whisper, and Bran leaned closer. The suggestion of a smile appeared at the corners of her mouth only to contort with pain when she spoke again, "Go ahead. Throw me back. There is no one who will miss me."

Her words shocked Bran. It was almost as if she had been listening to his thoughts. Memories of the past three days churned through his mind, clashing with every notion he'd ever had of what was right. That parting on the Wicklow wharf returned to him. He wanted to win, but at what cost?

Cuidighim mi, she had said. *Help me.* And he had denied her.

What in the name of Heaven had happened since he had returned her to her father? Why wasn't she on that ship bound for England?

Out of nowhere, Bran's mind conjured up the image of his grandfather frowning upon this unfortunate scene. Rourke had held all women in special affection. He had respected every female whether she was high or low born, whether she was Irish, Scottish, English, Norman, or Norse, and he had treated them with singular gentleness and consideration. It was a lesson Bran had not learned as well as he might have, and in his haste to fulfill his obligations as O'Connor chieftain, Bran had not been willing to consider any course other than returning Johanna Elizabeth Clare to her father. After all she belonged with her own kind, he had reasoned. But something had gone wrong, and Bran wondered if it was possible that one action that was right could be in conflict with a very different action that was equally acceptable in its own right. His grandfather had not counseled him on such things, and frowning, Bran glanced toward heaven.

Darkening clouds were roiling above him. A storm was blowing in from the sea, and when he turned back to the woman, his grandfather's voice rose from the recesses of his mind. He heard Rourke telling the story of how Ingvar, Rourke's grandfather, had rescued the Lady Elspeth Buchanan from her fortress in the Scottish Highlands. Lady Elspeth had been his enemy's wife, yet Ingvar had believed in Fate, and he had accepted that Lady Elspeth was his; having rescued the lady, he wed her and made a life with her.

Fate never made sense. It was always unexpected, often contrary, and it must never be denied. Bran was a Christian as O'Connors had been for more than six hundred years, yet like his ancestors that belief was tinged with shades of the old ways. Reality was not predictable. There was an arbitrary aspect to life beyond any man's control.

It must be Fate that explained what had happened this day, and in that case, Bran must take Johanna Elizabeth Clare to shelter. Of course, it didn't make sense given what he had done earlier this day, but there was no other choice for him. He dared not risk defiance of Fate. Later, he would make sense of it. Now he must act.

The Irishman scooped the young woman into his arms and made his way over the dunes toward the woods beyond the shoreline, feeling as he went not in the least bit heroic but disappointed, irritable, and thwarted. Bran was angry. He did not like to lose.

Every sliver of Bran's earlier elation had been extinguished. Nothing had turned out the way it was supposed to this day. Everything had gone wrong, and Bran O'Connor's temper was turning as black as the wild forest of the Wicklow Mountains. He cursed and hurried his pace as the first oversized raindrops fell from the sky. Bran would take her to shelter and see her well enough to be on her way, but he did not have to be nice to her.

PART 1

THE HOLLY

Chapter 1

Dublin Castle, Terra Pacis
April, 1368

"A toast to my bride!" declared Sir Roger Clare, knight and lord of Killoughter, as he rose from his chair at the high table. He was a fine-figured, vigorous man of two-score and three years, clean shaven and garbed for this momentous occasion in a cote-hardie of dark green velvet and a gold-lined ermine cloak. No expense had been spared, for while this was not his first wedding, it was certainly his most consequential, his young bride being a kinswoman of Thomas Minot, archbishop of Dublin.

Sir Roger raised his goblet to the delicate maiden seated to his right. She was an Englishwoman, born and raised in the gentle hills beyond Bristol, who had come to Ireland for the sole purpose of marrying him, and she was as fair as a Somerset rose. The faint bloom of pink upon her creamy cheeks heightened as she bestowed a shy smile upon her new husband. The bride was wearing a fitted ivory silk gown in the English style, the bodice was scooped, the neckline rested low on her shoulders.

"To Lady Alyson! To my bride!" Sir Roger toasted, savoring the thought that he would bed this comely woman before the night was spent.

The archbishop nodded his approval, and, as did the other guests who had come to celebrate in the great hall of Dublin Castle, he drank in salute to the bride. "To Lady Alyson, long life, loyalty, and obedience!" he pronounced. Goblets were emptied, and a small army of pages scurried around the hall to replenish drinking vessels before the archbishop raised his goblet a final time to Sir Roger. "Faith, sir, may your lady wife bless you with many fine sons!"

A rowdy cheer rose to the rafters of the evergreen-decked hall, and the trenchers and serving platters on the trestle tables trembled as the guests stomped their feet in exuberant approval when Lady Alyson rose to stand beside Sir Roger. She slipped an arm through his, tugging slightly so that he was forced to lower his head, then she whispered in his ear. A hush fell over the crowd.

Sir Roger's expression altered. A flicker of something like dread glanced across his features as his gaze moved beyond Lady Alyson to rest upon another young woman seated at the high table. She was as expensively dressed as his wife, but that was where any resemblance between the two women ended. While Lady Alyson had hair as flaxen as an angel's with features that bespoke a demure disposition, this other woman's hair was black as night and her exotic eyes hinted at a peril as dangerous as the countryside beyond the walls of Dublin town. Once again, Sir Roger raised his goblet. "And to my daughter. To Lady Johanna Elizabeth."

"To Lady Johanna Elizabeth," the guests erupted in unison, followed by more cheers, more stomping. This time the bright, multicolored pennants flying above the hall swayed, and even the glazed windows and torches mounted on the walls seemed to quiver before the din subdued and the musicians picked up their lutes and cymbals to play a familiar tune. It was time for the third course to commence, almond omelets with currants, honey, and saffron, after which the guests would have time to dance before the fourth course of sweet fish with dates baked in pastry was presented.

Lady Alyson faced her stepdaughter. She smiled in gentle, genuine kindness.

The object of this attention forced a thin smile. Johanna Elizabeth had never been adept at concealing her innermost sentiments and usually she didn't care. But tonight was different. She knew how important this was to her father, and she prayed that no one would perceive that she didn't share his jubilation. In truth, she was seething on the inside as the assembled guests echoed her father's toast, her name rippling through the hall.

Johanna Elizabeth. She hated the name. It was so English. So proper. So tidy. So drab.

It wasn't her.

Her spirit was Irish like her mother's, may the good Lord bless her dear departed soul, it was not English like her father's. She was restless, mystical, overemotional, and thoroughly beyond restraint, or so her father charged. Indeed, she believed her father described her to perfection, and she was proud of it despite his complaints. Her mother had called her *Aislinn*: so, too, had her father once upon a time. *Aislinn. A vision, a dream.* It was Irish, the name given her at birth, reaffirmed upon her baptism, and no matter what the Parliament at Kilkenny might say, it would always be hers.

But her father had not called her Aislinn since the

English in Ireland had been forbidden to use their Irish names. It had been little more than a year since the Parliament at Kilkenny had enacted its infamous law. The Kilkenny Statue outlawed all connections with the natives. Marriage, concubinage, and fosterage were forbidden. The English language must be spoken even by the Irish living among the English under threat of losing their land; English clothes and fashion must be maintained; English saddles must be used, and riding bareback was illegal; disputes were to be settled by English not Brehon law; Irish minstrels, troubadours, pipers, storytellers, and harpers were forbidden to come among the English. There were more edicts, all in contradiction of earlier ones that had endeavored to draw together the two races; the new policies were intended to keep them apart. In particular, they were fashioned to reform those degenerate English, who had intermarried with the natives, and at times, behaved more Irish than English.

As if from very far away Johanna Elizabeth heard her stepmother's voice filtering through the lutes and cymbals, bells and drums. Slowly, she refocused on the woman standing at her father's side.

"May you be as blessed in matrimony as I have been," Lady Alyson was saying. "It is my sincerest wish that you, our dearest Johanna Elizabeth, find a husband as worthy and handsome as your father."

Johanna Elizabeth's smile wavered. It had been little more than a year since Sir Roger had begun to search for an English wife for himself and to talk of an English husband for his daughter. But her thoughts had nothing to do with finding a husband. She thought instead of her father and how he had heeded every clause in the Kilkenny Statute to the exact letter, trying without success to make his daughter obey them as well. She thought of Ireland, and something twisted inside her chest.

She blinked away tears as she looked at her father kissing Lady Alyson on the forehead. She tried to pretend it did not hurt to watch how easily he dismissed everything that had been a part of the life he'd shared with his first wife. It was not that he had decided to wed again that hurt, but that he had imported a perfect English bride. It was almost as if he were trying to compensate for the mistake he'd made by marrying an Irish woman in his youth. This marriage to Lady Alyson Windsor was his ultimate compliance with the statute.

Sir Roger smiled upon Lady Alyson, and gave a nod of accord. It was a worthy little speech she had made to his daughter, and he was proud of his new wife. He was pleased, too, that his daughter had managed to behave so well these past few days in Dublin. Mayhap there was hope for her after all. Perhaps she would yet be a proper English lady. He grinned at Johanna Elizabeth, wanting only the best for her. She was his only surviving child, and it pleased him to imagine the security that might one day be hers once she was wed to the right gentleman. He did not notice her brittle smile when he sat down to finish his omelet.

"Lady Johanna Elizabeth?"

She looked toward the voice. It was Simon Windsor, one of Lady Alyson's brothers, executing a bow and muttering something about being honored to dance with her. A trio of yellow-haired lordlings had come to Dublin for their sister's wedding. It was their first visit to Ireland, and they hoped for a little excitement, in particular, for a glimpse of the wild Irish, perhaps even the chance to behead one or two of the savages, they had boasted. All three brothers were unwed, prone to pimples, and each was more insufferable than the other. Oliver, the eldest, had the habit of staring at Johanna Elizabeth as if she were something slimy to be avoided in the street; indeed, she could not help wondering if Oliver Windsor liked boys better than girls. If that was the case, Simon and Philip made up for their brother with an excess of suggestive stares and lewd remarks that left no doubt as to their carnal preferences.

Simon placed one hand beneath Johanna Elizabeth's elbow to assist her from the chair. His fingers were clammy. She could feel the moisture beneath the thin fabric of her fitted sleeve, and it repulsed her. She didn't move to rise. Instead, she raised her goblet and drained its potent contents, then signaled to a page for more.

"Go on, dear," encouraged Lady Alyson in her ever-sweet voice. She sounded like an older woman instead of someone whose age was, in fact, only four years more than Johanna Elizabeth's nineteen summers. In a lower, almost girlish voice, she added, "You must dance with each of my brothers and tell me which pleases you the better."

The page refilled Johanna Elizabeth's goblet with honey-sweetened wine. "A moment, sir, if you will allow. I am thirsty," she said to Simon, knowing it was a lie, knowing that she had already had too much piment this night and should not be drinking so much as another drop. But it was the only way she could think to dull the pain and ward off the tears, the only way to pretend she was not miserable. The only way to dance with Simon Windsor. She required four gulps to empty the goblet, then she allowed Simon to lead her from the dais to the center of the hall, where couples were gathering for a country dance, an *English* country dance, *of course.*

In her mind, she heard the rousing call of pipes, the strain of harps. Irish music. And closing her eyes she saw Annacurragh, motte of her MacMurrough kin, her mother's birthplace on a rise above the Aughrim. Every spring she and her mother, her brothers and father, had traveled south from the garrison at Killoughter to MacMurrough land in the wooded heights of Croghan Kinsella at the southernmost end of the Wicklow Mountains. There, they had celebrated May Day with the lighting of the fires on the surrounding hills. She remembered how everyone had held hands and danced around a May bush, the girls wearing garlands, while the pipers and harpers wore gold and green sashes, and how when the bush had been set afire, the young men had leapt through the flames.

How dull this English dance was by comparison. How silly and without meaning. She sighed, opened her eyes, and, gazing past Simon Windsor, she saw a tall gentleman leaning against the far wall. A familiar little chill tickled at the nape of her neck. It was a sign, a sort of warning to her that things were not what they appeared. She had a sixth sense, not sight into the future precisely, but the ability to discern things about the present, and at this moment, she knew the gentleman lounging against that wall was watching her. His gaze slid over her, she felt it as certainly as she would have felt his hands, and, emboldened by the honeyed wine, she stared back at him, allowing her regard to move over his face and form in equally brazen appraisal.

His features were angular, almost gaunt, with sharp cheekbones, a narrow jaw, a prominent masculine nose, and thin lips that made her think he did not often laugh. He was not handsome in any conventional sense, but Johanna Elizabeth admired his black hair, almost too glossy for a man, and she was intrigued by the deep set of his eyes that did not waver from her face.

He was dressed like the other gentlemen who mingled about the hall. Mayhap he was a guest from Bristol, or kin to one of Ireland's powerful bishops or earls, and at a passing glance, there was no reason to suspect he wasn't one of them. The English style of dress for gentlemen boasted bright colors and expensive embroidered fabrics, and he was suitably garbed, wearing a vermillion cote-hardie of embroidered velvet over yellow hose that ended with pointed shoes. But Johanna Elizabeth's glance had been more than passing, and it was his hair that gave him away. Careful observation revealed his raven black hair, glistening beneath the torch light, was not cut in the English manner of a short bob. It was long, and to hide its length it had been tucked beneath the cloak fastened at his shoulder. He was different than the others. He was Irish, and a ripple of excitement raced through Johanna Elizabeth.

The dance was taking her away from his line of vision, and she looked back until she lost sight of him, waiting until the dance would bring her around to that side of the hall again. What was he doing here? she wondered as she glanced at Simon Windsor, who did not appear to have noticed a thing. So much for seeing one of the wild Irish. Around the hall they circled with the other couples until she was once again at the spot where she had first seen the Irishman. The music stopped. The dance was ended. He was still there, leaning against the wall, arms crossed at his chest, and he was still watching her without a trace of emotion upon his face.

Across the crowded hall, his unreadable eyes held hers, and Johanna Elizabeth could not help herself. She smiled full of invitation at the Irishman, cocking her head to one side in the hope that he would ask her to dance. Surely, his hands would not be clammy, and she almost laughed aloud at the wicked direction of her thoughts. The musicians began another tune, but to her disappointment the Irishman scowled, then he pushed away from the wall and disappeared into the shadowy corridor behind him.

"Wait!" the word escaped Johanna Elizabeth before she could stop it, but it had only been a whisper. No one had heard. To her right, Simon Windsor was asking about the conditions on the King's Road beyond the *terra pacis*, or land of peace as the Vale of Dublin was commonly called. She gave a hurried reply, then added, "Excuse me, sir," implying that she required her female privacy as she went toward the shadows into which the Irishman had vanished.

On brocade slippers she dashed down the corridor, swiftly, silently, across the dank stones and finally, out a wide double door into the night. The air was crisp, her breath made a white cloud before her, and, wrapping her arms about herself against the cold, she surveyed the castle yard. Where had he gone? She glanced to the left, to the right. Had he already passed through one of the gates? Or had he slipped inside a tower? Carefully, she descended the uneven stairs, avoiding a mound of sleeping hens halfway down, and once at the bottom, she began to make her way around the yard.

Up ahead the night watch called out. The warders were changing shift.

A hand shot out from the shadows, fingers wrapping about her upper arm to jerk her into the dark recess where the castle wall met one of the towers. She let out a gasp. The enamel circlet of holly leaves tumbled off her head, her hair fell free, and Johanna Elizabeth opened her mouth to cry out in alarm. But not another sound came forth as a large palm covered her mouth, stifling her scream. She blinked, her eyes adjusted to the dim light, and looking up, she saw it was him. The Irishman. She was not certain whether to be afraid or relieved.

In the cool, quiet recess behind the tower stairs, he gazed down at her from his significant height. They stared at each other, both breathing heavily as he held her, one hand locking her arms behind her back, pressing her against his firm chest to prevent her from struggling. There was an intimacy, however unintended, in the way he held her, and Johanna Elizabeth was unnerved by her awareness of his strength and—may the Blessed Virgin forgive her—of the heavy bulge of his manhood.

Her pulse quickened, and her heart beat like the wings of a trapped bird when his eyes slowly moved from hers to the yard behind them, then back to gaze at her with a hunger that he did not trouble to disguise. It was the first sign of reaction she had detected in him, and the result upon her was devastating.

Johanna Elizabeth's heart leapt. She had seen that hunger before in many a man, both English and Irish, and most recently upon the sallow faces of the two youngest Windsor brothers, but she had never responded to it. This time, there was a languid, melting sensation radiating from the core of her. It was unspeakably pleasurable, and all thought of fear or curiosity about who this man was or why he was in Dublin Castle fled her. It was her body that was in charge, not her mind.

Behind them the watch was nearing. The great keys in his charge rattled against one another, the metallic sound echoing into the night sky.

"Hush," the Irishman whispered in English.

Johanna Elizabeth nodded in compliance. She would be silent. He leaned closer, and she could feel his breath beneath her ear, against her throat. It made no sense, but she trusted him. The passing sensation at the nape of her neck told her everything would be all right.

The broad hand upon her mouth moved away, and she watched its movement to see it slip beneath the fancy English cloak and clench the hilt of a dagger. Her gaze darted back to his, but his expression had changed, and it was once again as unreadable as it had been when he'd watched her dancing in the hall. The warder was almost upon them, and the Irishman bent his head, his lips moving close to hers in an effort to conceal his face from the passing guard.

She knew he was hiding, and when she felt the soft caress of his breath as his face turned in toward hers, something inside her came undone. Impulsively, she whispered in Irish, "Don't worry, I won't let anyone see ye. I will help ye." Standing on tiptoe, she tilted her head toward his mouth. "Kiss me, my lord," she whispered, her lips brushing against his. "Kiss me, and make it look as if ye mean it."

He required no greater urging, and he kissed her hard, a long, rough groan rolling forth from his throat when her mouth opened beneath his. He had wanted to touch her since he first saw her in the hall. He had heard the stories of the daughter born to Sir Roger Clare and his Irish wife. Bewitching, they said she was. Uncontrolled, saucy, darkly beautiful, and a festering thorn in her father's side. But he had not believed the half of it. Now he knew it was true. By the blood of the good St. Daghán, she was as alluring as he'd heard, and she was in his arms. What a pleasure it would be to have a woman such as this, if only for one night.

"If I asked, would ye give yerself to me?" he drawled as if they were lovers, knowing her answer did not matter, knowing he should not ask, should not dream. There was no time to spare. Still he wanted to know. He had to know.

Her senses were reeling, her face was hot, and her legs were unsteady. Too much piment. Had she heard him right? She couldn't think what to say, or how to keep control of herself. She had never been around a man like this before. She couldn't focus.

"Tell me true, would ye be mine this night?" he asked in the tiny space between their lips. Her breasts were pressed against his chest, her slender thighs were parted to accommodate him. She was soft, pliable, and smelled of crushed rose petals. He pushed against her, heard her tiny gasp, and he pushed again, nibbling at the edge of her lip.

"Aye," she murmured, unable to resist the way he was making her feel. She had been kissed before, but never like this. Young men had rubbed against her, but she had never felt anything as thick as this man. Her pulse was pounding so furiously she thought her heart might burst. "For a night, I would do anything," she murmured in a velvety drawl, letting her tongue run along his lower lip.

His gut lurched. A quiver of lust passed through him. The stories were true. Lady Johanna Elizabeth was the kind of woman who was bound to get some poor unsuspecting Irishman in a heap of trouble. She was delicious, *and she was forbidden.* He pulled his lips out of reach of her teasing tongue. He did not need this kind of help.

"Not yet," she said, her voice sounding not like her own, but like that of some vibrant, earthy being. She didn't want him to stop kissing her. This was nothing like the awkward caresses she'd known before. She liked the taste of him. He had been drinking ale and the strong, earthy flavor lingered upon his lips. And she liked the feel of him. He was warm and hard and alive with a power that she needed to share. She had felt him quiver, and she wanted to feel it again. *It is true. I would do anything this night,* she wanted to tell him, but instead, she merely warned, "Another warder passes by. It is too soon to stop."

"Who are ye, *cuileann*?" he asked, calling her *fair lady,* his lips once again brushing against hers as he spoke. He was glad she had not stepped away from him. "I would have yer Irish name."

"*Méabh,*" she replied in a throaty whisper, emboldened by a sense of the unknown that weakened her knees and made her heart soar. This was a game. This kissing, this dangerous flirting with an Irishman in the yard of Dublin Castle. This was a game, and as she would never see this man again, there was no reason to tell him the truth. Nor was there any reason to deny how pleasurable was the feeling of his thighs, his chest, and the beating of his heart against her. No reason to blush and act like a simpering English maid when the bulge between his legs pulsed against her. This man had no doubt heard her toasted as Lady Johanna Elizabeth, yet he wanted to know her Irish name, and this was a perfect opportunity to shed her English yoke, to be wild and free. She could behave as she wished, instead of how her father would like her to act. It only mattered that at this moment she would be *Méabh,* or *Maeve,* as the English preferred, and she was going to take as much pleasure as she might this night. She would play the game, enjoy it, and do her best to enchant this man while dancing with danger in the courtyard of Dublin Castle. After all it was what the disapproving bishops and earls expected of her. She was a degenerate, so why not?

"*Méabh,*" he murmured against the column of her slender throat, inhaling the musky female scent of her, trembling like a youth in his first encounter with a girl. "And rightly named ye were." In the ancient legend of *Tain Bo Cuailgne,* there had been a headstrong Queen Méabh of Connaught. The name meant *intoxicating. She who makes men drunk.* Sir Roger's daughter was, indeed, a reckless, dangerous, intoxicating creature. He cupped her face in his strong hands, his fingers weaving through the curls at her temples as he gazed down at her, and he angled his face to her lips to savor one final kiss. It was a long, slow kiss.

At length, he pulled away, allowing his fingertips to savor a lingering touch against her cheek. "Farewell, my *cuileann,* my lovely *Méabh,*" he said in a tone as bittersweet as the fiery longing that twisted through him. It was never to be. They were of two different worlds, and her willing answer would never matter. "*Slán agat.*" *Farewell.*

He swept her an implausible bow, low to the ground and entirely English. Then he was gone. In an instant, he had bounded up the exterior stairs of the tower, ascending three steps at a time in long powerful strides, and upon reaching the top, another man emerged from the shadows. Together, they went over the wall without making a sound and without looking back.

It was the Bermingham Tower, where prisoners were kept, at the southwestern corner of the castle, and Johanna Elizabeth knew there were no narrow lanes on the other side of the wall. At that point it was nothing but open country to the south, and she knew where he was headed. *Uí Briúin Cualann.* To the shelter of the oak and hazel mountains, and the very thought made hot tears pool in her eyes. Above all else, it was where she would rather be, for those mountains were the very symbol of all that was Irish, all that was dear and to be desired.

From the great double doors that led to the hall she heard the Windsor lordlings talking.

"Any sign of the wench?"

Johanna Elizabeth held her breath.

"It appears Lady Johanna Elizabeth isn't out here," said Oliver in a voice that gave the impression of someone trying to avoid an unpleasant odor.

"Too bad." It was Simon of the clammy hands. "I wouldn't mind catching that one alone in the dark."

Her stomach tightened.

"Alyson says she's a maid, and we must mind our manners," Philip reminded the others.

"Ah, that's our Alyson, always trusting. But who can tell the truth about our new kinswoman? She's half-Irish, and you know what they say about the Irish. Amorous, sensual, and loose to lechery above measure, that's what they say."

"Yet you would be willing to make a woman such as that your wife?" spoke Oliver, again, in that pinched, ever-disdainful tone.

"You always were the worst sort of fool, Oliver," sneered Simon. "It appears that you may also be the only man who could turn away from a chance to diddle such a delectable morsel and the right to call it his own. Perhaps 'tis true what they say about you."

"Well, I wouldn't be so certain of your possession," Oliver said with a sniff. "It's not decided which of us she shall wed. I may just surprise the both of you."

Johanna Elizabeth's stomach began to churn. The prospect of being sent away from Ireland, to be wedded and bedded by one of the Windsor brothers was nauseating. How could her father entertain such a future for her? She kneeled down. The ground was cool and hard, and she groped about her feet, searching for the circlet of enamel leaves and berries that had been dislodged from her head when the Irishman grabbed her. But she could not find it, and she swiped at the tears of frustration that had started in earnest.

If only she could make her father understand. But that was impossible. He'd always been protective of his only daughter, now he was oppressive, and the future that Sir Roger envisioned for her was bound to be her death. Johanna Elizabeth needed a plan. She had to escape. She needed to be Aislinn again, and she had to be with her mother's people or else her spirit would surely wither and die.

Chapter 2

Johanna Elizabeth's head was going to explode. Despite the blue sky and the fresh salt air blowing off the Irish Sea, she felt horrible, and she fixed a disgusted stare upon Oliver Windsor, who was mounted on horseback to her right. Philip was riding on her left, and Simon was a few lengths behind. They were heading south on the Bré to Wicklow road, bound for her father's command at Killoughter, and since leaving Dublin town some four hours before, Oliver and Philip had not stopped talking. They were running a tally of the ways in which Ireland was an inferior province relative to England. It required every ounce of tact that Johanna Elizabeth could muster to speak in a moderate tone. "Please, my lords, enough. I am sure you have proved your point, sir. Several times over, in truth. There is no reason to go on."

"And lepers," Oliver continued as if he had not heard. "Already we have passed three groups of them begging at the side of the road. In England, our religious orders devote themselves to feeding, clothing, and housing such wretched creatures so they do not offend decent folk."

"And as to the fashion in which your peasants

clothe their offspring," Philip offered this point of observation, "it is heathen. Indecent. And thoroughly without discipline."

"Have they never been taught how to properly swaddle a child?" Oliver asked in his most condescending manner.

Yes, indeed, her head was going to explode, Johanna Elizabeth thought with an inward groan, and then Oliver Windsor would truly have something about which to complain. She'd had far too much honeyed wine the night before, and not enough sleep to recover from the ill effects. Too many wedding guests had been crowded into the dormitory adjacent to the great hall, and three other women had shared the bed assigned to her. She had made a space for herself, lying perpendicular to the others, but sleep would not come as the piment kept her head spinning with worries about what the future held for her.

Now that Sir Roger was bringing his new wife to Killoughter, he and Lady Alyson could turn their thoughts to arranging the much talked about English marriage for Johanna Elizabeth. It would not be long before they had decided her future, and she needed a plan. She needed it soon. She had to escape, and be Aislinn before her father had wed her to one of the Windsors or sent her off to England to find an equally repugnant husband. That horrifying prospect had tormented her into the wee hours. She could not, would not, leave Ireland, and with that thought tumbling through her mind, she had not been able to doze off until the cock's first crow. Even then she'd had only an hour or two of fitful rest before a servant had roused her to prepare for this trip.

There had been spies in the castle the night before, Irish spies from one of the tribes in the *terra guerre*, the land of war, the archbishop had informed her father at dawn. The natives in the hills beyond the Vale of Dublin were planning something, and it would be unwise to be on the open road once the sun had set. Thus, Sir Roger had insisted upon leaving Dublin long before the angelus bells tolled over the Liffey. Perhaps he had foreseen the delays that his wife's possessions would present to their progress.

No more ridiculous sight had Johanna Elizabeth ever beheld than Sir Roger's party as it rumbled its way down the coast. It was a train of absurd proportions, if one wished to travel quickly and without incident in Ireland. Indeed, it would have been wiser to travel by sea, but the brothers insisted upon seeing the country, and thus, they were a slow-moving target for raiders, an open invitation for thieves. Six wagons were packed with massive, elaborately carved furnishings from England and France. There were coffer chests of silver and gold plates, goblets, knives, and candlesticks, plus fragile mirrors from Venice, and an assortment of Flanders tapestries and wall hangings. Twelve sumpter horses were laden with the bride's wardrobe plus assorted gifts from the archbishop and the other wedding guests. And, of course, there was Lady Alyson's traveling coach, a stately vehicle in shades of gold and scarlet, that the bride had brought aboard ship from Bristol, and in which she rode with the embroidered velvet curtains pulled closed to protect her from the Irish wind, not to mention unseen pestilence that might stalk the countryside. With the arrival of spring, any manner of evil might already be infecting the peasants, and it would be only a matter of time before the upper classes became contaminated as well, if one did not practice vigilance.

Although Johanna Elizabeth had as great a horror of plague as anyone else, she declined to ride inside the coach with her stepmother. Despite her headache and queasy stomach, despite the possibility of unseen pestilence, her horse needed to be exercised, and there was no way Johanna Elizabeth would have permitted one of those Windsor lordlings with his elaborate rowel spurs to ride her Bláth. In Irish it meant gentle, smooth, and the mare had been so named because of her swift easy strides when she galloped across the headlands and hills. Bláth was a superior, spirited animal, and an Englishman would not know how to treat her properly. It was common knowledge that the English were mediocre horsemen at best, and Bláth would not tolerate poor handling. Indeed, the mare would toss the likes of Oliver Windsor from her back as if he were of no more consequence than a flimsy creel of onions.

A rook's sharp cry was carried on the wind. Johanna Elizabeth twisted about to glance into the greening limbs of a massive, lopsided oak, but she saw nothing. There were no roosting birds, nor was there any movement of limbs as if one had taken flight from the huge, dark nests balancing between the uppermost branches.

The lumbering procession of carts and sumpter horses continued southward. They had left the ecclesiastical lands that stretched from Dublin to Bré. A few miles ahead was a place called Deilgne, where they would stop for a short rest before covering the second half of the distance to Killoughter. It was an old Norse settlement with two churches, one of them dedicated to St. Kevin's disciples, a mill, and a handful of cottages, and the travelers would accept whatever hospitality the villagers of Deilgne might offer.

Caw. Caw.

The cries rose from a weather-battered stand of oak and hazel trees about a hundred yards to the right, and Johanna Elizabeth exchanged a quick glance with her father. He understood the unspoken question upon her face, and when he gave a sober nod, she reined in Bláth. Something was amiss.

"We shall make camp here for a brief respite. Hobble the animals securely," Sir Roger called out to his retinue, motioning the drivers to cluster the wagons together. He dismounted, handed his reins to his groom, and went to Lady Alyson's coach. He parted the curtains to speak to his wife. "Perhaps you would rather remain inside, my lady. The sun is overbright, and the winds are on the rise."

None of that was true, but if Lady Alyson did not believe Sir Roger, or if she wished to exit the confines of her coach, she did nothing to indicate her own desires were contrary to those of her husband. "If you wish, my lord."

He nodded, obviously satisfied with her compliance. "I will have some cool water sent to you. Our local springs are singular in their clarity and freshness, and I am certain you will be pleased, madame." From within the coach came Lady Alyson's whisper of thanks. Sir Roger bowed, the curtains fell closed, and he turned to his men-at-arms, who had begun to form a perimeter around the encampment.

Lively bird chatter filled the air, and Johanna Elizabeth did not look to see from whence the noises came. She was observing her father as he walked among his men, and she was considering how he had treated Lady Alyson. Sir Roger was an affectionate, physical man, but that was not evident in the polite way he had conversed with his new wife. Johanna Elizabeth remembered the open affection between her parents, and had expected the same between her father and his new wife, especially the morning after their wedding night. But they had not kissed when the curtains opened and Lady Alyson leaned out, nor had her father allowed his hand to touch his wife's where it rested on the sill. They were still treating each other with a formality that seemed abnormal to Johanna Elizabeth.

A bustle of activity descended upon the traveling party as servants unhitched horses and led them to water. Another outburst of bird chatter rose above the jangle of bridles. This time, it was sharper and more high-pitched. There was nothing natural about it. Faith, it was not a bird, but a man, and what had started as a semblance of a rook's caw turned to a thin torturous shriek. Servants stopped their work, the men-at-arms grasped sword handles, and the scene froze as if it were one painted upon a wall hanging.

"By all the saints in Heaven," exclaimed Oliver Windsor. He had turned as white as a boiled egg. The ghoulish cries of many men joined those of the first, and Oliver Windsor implored Johanna Elizabeth for an answer, "What is the name of God is that noise? I have never heard anything so hideous."

A shiver chased its way over the flesh on Johanna Elizabeth's arms. The keening moans and ghastly shrieks were unearthly, but not unfamiliar. Sir Roger barked out orders to his men-at-arms, and throughout the camp weapons were drawn in readiness to repel the attack that was about to come.

Johanna Elizabeth lifted her knee from the saddle brace and slid from her horse. With a slap to the mare's backside and hastily whispered words, she hied Bláth to trot behind a clump of nearby bushes. The horse obeyed, and Johanna Elizabeth looked at the Windsor brothers, who had not budged from their saddles despite the chaos descending about them. Their eyes were wide as if fearing Satan himself had come to take them to Hell. "That is the wild Irish you were so eager to tame," she told them.

"At last, our chance to have a go at the savages," the brother Simon declared with bravado, but he failed to quell the dread in his voice as he dismounted.

Still the demonic wailing continued. It grew louder, unrestrained, and more frenzied. The horses whinnied with fright. Oliver Windsor's sword arm trembled, and Johanna Elizabeth's glance darted toward her father, then toward Bláth. Raids were a common occurrence on the King's Road in *Uí Briúin Cualann,* and although Irish warriors had little use for gold platters or silver candlesticks, horseflesh was another matter entirely. Usually it was O'Tooles, who did the raiding this close to Dublin, but whoever it might be, they were always eager to harass English travelers and add to the value of their stables.

Abruptly, the frightful cries gave way to an unearthly quiet that had barely settled upon them before the afternoon reverberated with the thudding hooves of a horse being ridden hard. From out of the trees, a man galloped at full speed, swinging an axe, and yelling an Irish battle cry. "*Fag an bealach*!" He charged straight toward the men-at-arms. *Clear the way*!

A second raider followed, then a third, a fourth, and more than a dozen followed until Sir Roger's traveling party was surrounded by shrieking, heavily armed savages cloaked in wolf skins over chain mail, their faces painted blue with woad. Blood-curling wails mixed with the clash of metal upon metal, and there were screams of pain as wounds were inflicted.

Johanna Elizabeth grabbed the dagger that was sheathed beneath her kirtle. It was not a dainty tool to use at mealtime, but a deadly weapon, and she carried it always despite her father's protests that English ladies did not do such things. It was an Irish dagger crafted of bronze that had belonged to her MacMurrough grandfather, and Johanna Elizabeth carried it not because of fear, but because her mother had taught her that a wise woman should always be prepared to defend herself.

A quick glance told her she was safe for the moment. Another visual sweep assured her Bláth was safe. Her gaze skittered over the scene, and she saw her father, a mace in one hand, a battle axe in the other, warding off one of the raiders. He was a good fighter and a respected knight, more than a match for any native warrior, and she was not afraid for him. She stood still, wondering whether to seek shelter, when out of the corner of one eye, she spotted a raider trying to open the coach door. Lady Alyson was screaming, her cries mingling with those of the warriors. The raider at the coach ripped the curtains off with a single jerk and tossed the fancy fabric to the ground. Another look told Johanna Elizabeth none of the men had noticed this. There was no one to help Lady Alyson, and without considering her actions, Johanna Elizabeth ran forward, raising her dagger high.

The raider, who was leaning sideways from his horse and pulling on the leather strap that should have opened the coach door, did not hear Johanna Elizabeth approach. But he felt her attack when she sliced his outer thigh.

"Go de an donas a duine!" the man roared. *What the plague*! It was not a deep wound, but he was bleeding like a stuck pig.

Johanna Elizabeth leapt back, but not in fright, rather in recognition of the voice, and of the angular, gaunt features of the man glaring down at her. Merciful angels in heaven, that prominent nose and those deep, hooded eyes were unforgettable. It was the

Irishman she had kissed last night. Although his sharp cheekbones were painted bright blue, she recognized him, and some perverse instinct made her cross herself. She had dropped the dagger when he shouted the vicious curse, and now she tried to back away from him. He was moving his horse straight for her. The coach was behind her. There was no place to go.

He stared down at her. His eyes did not waver as he came nearer. He sucked in his breath, and she saw the muscles along his jaw tighten. His gaze narrowed like the point of a well-honed sword as his horse walked forward until he had trapped her against the coach. Neither of them spoke, and she wondered if he had recognized her. Time stretched to an eternity. The sounds of the raid were swirling about them as if from a very great distance. It was a dizzying sensation, and of a sudden, Johanna Elizabeth heard nothing except the frantic pounding of her heart. He shifted his dark, fathomless gaze from her face to his injured leg. She watched as he touched the glistening wound, a shiver ran through her, and when his fingers were covered with blood, he bent downward and smeared the sticky, warm liquid across her mouth.

Johanna Elizabeth almost fainted. She leaned back against the coach to support herself as she gagged at the taste upon her lips. She wanted to swipe at it with the back of her hand, but she dared not move, and she held her breath, knowing for the first time what it meant to be terrified. She tried to control her expression and hide her fear, but her chin quivered. She managed to hold her head high, but she could not blink back the tears that clouded her view of his hostile face. His gaze cut through her like a blade. He hated her. The need to cry was almost a physical pain.

"O Dhia! gach an cathar," the war cry pierced the air

as he pulled sharply on the reins. *Oh, God! to each of us a fortress.* It was a bitter, tenacious motto. The horse responded with a wild snort, it reared, and with the skill only an Irishman could boast, he controlled the animal. The beast seemed to hop backward on its hind legs, and when it was standing on all four legs once again, the Irishman wheeled the stallion around sharply, swiftly, and both horse and rider galloped away to rejoin the others.

Three of the raiders had freed the hobbled horses, they called out their success, and the others fell back from fighting to drive the animals into the woods. Their mission was complete. They did not wish to massacre Sir Roger's party, merely to harass them, to draw a few ounces of English blood, and, of course, to steal their horses.

Johanna Elizabeth sagged against the coach, holding the wheel in a tight grip to prevent herself from collapsing in a heap. She swiped at her wet eyes, and took a deep steadying breath. It was almost over. The stolen horses and Irish raiders were disappearing beyond the trees. A straggler hurried to catch up with them, but stopped before reaching the trees and turned back. He let out an exuberant whoop, and before she could wonder what he intended, a chill tickled the nape of Johanna Elizabeth's neck.

She intuitively knew what had happened.

He had seen Bláth, and in confirmation of her suspicion, she watched as he rode toward the mare, reaching out to grab the reins that were dangling toward the ground. Bláth saw the approaching raider, whinnied, and shied backward.

The raider missed, but did not yield. He circled around for another pass.

"No!" Johanna Elizabeth cried out. She pushed herself away from the wheel.

An ashen Lady Alyson peaked through the window and reached out for her stepdaughter. "Nay, Lady Johanna Eliza—"

She shook off the arm that would have stopped her as she dashed into the open space. "Not my Bláth! Stay away from her!" she ordered in Irish, not caring for one instant what the law required. "Do ye hear me, ye villainous thief? *Bheir mise ort gun crean thu air." I'll make ye rue it.*

The raider made a second pass, and this time, he grabbed hold of the reins. Johanna Elizabeth whistled, but there was too much commotion for Bláth to hear the familiar call. Johanna Elizabeth took a deep breath, whistled again as long and loud as she could, and this time, the mare heard. Bláth fixed her attention upon her mistress. The raider tried to lead her away, but Johanna Elizabeth whistled a third time, and the horse broke free as her mistress ran to her.

In the next second, Johanna Elizabeth had swung herself onto Bláth. Her father's shout of disapproval rose above the thunder of hooves, but she did not turn back as she clutched the mane and gave the horse a gentle kick. They were off like an arrow from a bolt. The devil was at her heels, and she would outride him, even mounted on the unnatural sidesaddle her father insisted that she use in compliance with the statute. No one was going to get her horse, and she intended to lead this raider on a merry chase. There was a cart up ahead blocking her escape. Easily, she jumped the obstacle, and just as easily, her pursuer followed her over the cart and down the road.

Johanna Elizabeth knew the terrain well, and she galloped southwest for about a quarter mile. There was an old cow track up ahead that wended its way through a thick woods toward a glen beyond, and she hoped to lose him on the narrow path. But when they reached the woods, and she plunged into the undergrowth, he did not fall behind. He kept pace with her, zigzagging through the foliage as swiftly as she did. Indeed, she feared he was gaining on her. He was an excellent rider. No doubt he knew the country as well as she did, and Johanna Elizabeth leaned low over Bláth's neck, urging the horse with sweet promises to lengthen her strides. But escape was not to be.

A warlike whoop pierced her ears, and the breath was knocked from her lungs as the rider lunged from his horse to pull her off Bláth. Together, they hit the ground with a violent thud.

The impact was stunning. The raider grunted. Johanna Elizabeth struggled to rise, but her strength had been sapped, she could barely draw a breath, and he pinned her beneath his body. Panting from the exertion of the ride, she jerked upward in a feeble attempt to free herself, but could not move. She could not even see the raider through the tangle of black curls covering her eyes. Blindly, she clawed at him, making contact with his face, and scratching as deep as she could.

He swore and grabbed her wrists, his fingers squeezing until she winced from the pain. She cursed like a heathen, tossed her head to dislodge the hair from her eyes, and spat at him. He slapped her hard with the palm of his hand, and she froze. No one, not even her exasperated, irate father had ever touched her like that, and she stared in breathless astonishment at a young Irishman with thick yellow hair and blazing blue eyes set in a handsome face. There was woad upon his forehead and nose, blood on his cheek where her nails had broken the skin, and there were bits of dried leaves in his hair.

The raider was breathing as hard as she was. He did not trust this Englishwoman, who rode like a native and fought like a stoat defending her litter. He continued to straddle her, holding her wrists above her head, then looking down, he saw the red welt left by his hand that was rising on her cheek and the blood upon her lips.

"*Cia mar a tha thu*? Are ye all right?" he spoke first in Irish, then in stilted English. "*How fare ye*?" He could not stop himself from asking. He had not meant to draw blood. She was young, but not a child. About his own age, he guessed, eighteen or nineteen summers, and he was surprised at how pretty she was. Indeed, the sight of her comely face blunted his fury. But nothing was as unexpected as what she said and did next.

"Oh, I am fine. Quite fine. I have never been better, in fact," Johanna Elizabeth replied, her voice transforming to a ripple of unrestrained laughter. The pounding in her head was gone, and she laughed until tears began to roll from her eyes. She was not thinking of how this would-be horse thief had slapped her, or how he was holding her prisoner. She was remembering instead the expression upon Oliver Windsor's face when he had unsheathed his sword. Between giggles, she managed to say, "Did ye see their silly faces? Peacocks, that's what they are, strutting about with puffed-up chests and boasting how they would tame the Irish. Daring to tell me how Ireland was not good enough for their sister. But ye showed them. I have never felt better. *Go raibh maith agat.*" *I thank you.*

He stared at her flushed face, wondering if she were touched by the faeries or had been in the sun too long. He listened to her laughter and pondered her words, thinking that she must be mad to be thanking him and muttering about peacocks. She was dressed in an odd style that was neither English nor Irish precisely, and he ventured to guess that this astonishing creature was Sir Roger Clare's daughter. While he had never seen her, there were stories aplenty about her, of how she defied the statute, of how she rode like a native, and did as she wished, not as she was told. He knew it was Sir Roger's train they were raiding, but he had never expected to encounter his notorious daughter in the flesh. But, more significantly, he had never expected to be enchanted by her beguiling combination of spirit and beauty. She was a female worthy of admiration. She had proven it by that magnificent ride. She was courageous and entirely without fear, and it was remarkable that she had put the well-being of her horse above her own safety. Aye, such an extraordinary woman was worthy of a man's admiration, and before he had any idea what he was going to say, his sentiments went from thought to word:

"A man would be blessed to spend his life with a woman like ye."

Johanna Elizabeth stared up at him, hardly believing that the first words her captor would utter sounded like a marriage proposal. Her initial impulse was to laugh aloud and deny him, but the rebuttal upon her lips remained unspoken as his words gave blossom to a remarkable idea. Her mind sped onward faster than a crossbow, planning, scheming, and imagining a happy ending for herself.

There was no longer any need to worry about the future her father intended for her. In the space of an instant, she had a plan. Wasn't life grand? She went to bed one night plagued by an insurmountable worry, but before sunset the very next day that problem was solved. She would spend her life with an Irishman. She would wed an Irishman. Such a union would mean she could be Aislinn again. Indeed, Aislinn forever. It would mean that she would never have to fear being sent to England or being bedded by the likes of Oliver Windsor.

Aye, my handsome Irish lad, and blessed ye will be, for ye will be spending yer life with me.

But she did not say this aloud. Instead, she replied with a playful smile that lit her dark eyes with a twinkling golden light. "And who are ye to be making such claims? What is yer name?" she asked in a soft voice, thinking that no matter his name, he would make a far more favorable bedmate than any man her father might select for her. He was young, attractive, and a worthy Irish warrior. What more could she want? "*C'ainm a th'ort*? What is yer name?"

"Niall O'Connor." He swallowed in a suddenly dry throat. She was a wild thing, exactly as they said, and he had never seen a creature so pretty. He wished he might touch the flaming welt upon her cheek and make it go away. He had not meant to hurt her.

"Och, Niall O'Connor, do ye know who I am?" she asked, and he nodded. "And are ye saying that ye'd defy the statute for me?"

He blinked twice. He had only spoken in jest, but he would be the fool if he took back his words. He took a deep breath and said the kind of thing he thought would please this enchanting creature. "Aye, that I would, for I do not bow to any man, and certainly not to the earls and bishops at Kilkenny."

Johanna Elizabeth smiled. He had spoken well. "Hear me then, Niall O'Connor, for 'tis hoping that we meet again, I am. 'Tis hoping that we can be friends, I am. And, perhaps, in time, much more."

Aye, this was the man, and she could not have chosen better had she gone about the countryside searching on her own. This was the fellow who would guarantee her deliverance. He said he was an O'Connor. That was good. The O'Connors lived at a place called Baravore in the deepest reach of a remote valley in the mountains. It was several hours' trek north of the MacMurrough motte, but she would find her way there. She would find him, and she would get him to marry her. It did not make any difference if he had meant what he said, for she had learned much powerful magic from her MacMurrough grandmother, and she would use it on him. By *Domhnach Chrom Dubh*, the harvest-time festival, and before the frost returned, she vowed that she would be wed to an Irishman, and this particular Irishman was as suitable as any other.

Aye, life was grand, and it was an almost perfect moment of self-satisfaction were it not for the unbidden image of the gaunt, raven-haired Irishman that rose before her mind's eye. Her heart skipped a beat as she remembered how much pleasure there had been in his kiss. She remembered the taste of his blood, his narrow, hooded gaze, and the dark anger upon his face, and she shivered as a little chill tickled at the back of her neck. Whoever he was, he would not be kind. Niall O'Connor, on the other hand, had already proven he was capable of kindness, and that was a noble attribute in a warrior. It was nothing short of a miracle that Niall O'Connor had tried to steal Bláth this day. It had been Fate, and such a noble, kind Irishman was more than suitable for her plan.

"Do ye believe in Fate, Niall O'Connor? Can ye feel it here between us?" she asked in a voice that seemed to purr. She was determined that her plan would succeed and would stop at nothing. "Can ye feel it telling us we'll be meeting again?"

Niall swallowed hard. Now his mouth was turning dry. Fate? He sensed nothing so portentous between them. What he felt was his erection pulsing with desire for this pretty girl who was acting as if she liked him. She might call it Fate. As far as he was concerned it was damned good luck that had brought them together.

"Niall!" a man called out from woods. "Where are ye, lad?"

"*'Seudar dhomb bhi falbh*," Niall said, glancing in the direction of the voice. *I must be going*. He rose to standing above Sir Roger Clare's daughter and enjoyed one final glance at the prettiest wild thing he had ever seen. It would be nice if he met her again, but he did not think that particularly possible given his elder brother's opinion about her kind. She was degenerate English, and to hear his brother Bran tell it, there was nothing worse.

Johanna Elizabeth knew he was looking at her, and she gave a little pout of disappointment, then rolled onto one side like a contented kitten, drawing up her knee until her kirtle raised high enough to reveal a shapely leg. She smiled at him, both bold and sweet, challenging and trusting at once. Her feet were bare, and the rounded outlines of her hip and breasts were shown off to perfection. She knew the sight she presented. Indeed, it was purposeful. She did not want Niall O'Connor to forget her. She wanted him to yearn for her, to look for her, and to be glad when their paths next crossed. "*Greas ort, ma ta,* Niall O'Connor. *Haste ye, then*. Rejoin yer clansmen. But know, my fine Irishman, that we will be together soon."

After the echo of hooves had faded away, Johanna Elizabeth lay upon the ground to stare up at the passing clouds. For the first time in many days, she did not think of the future and experience the awful sensation of the life being drained from her. The parting expression upon Niall O'Connor's face told her everything she needed to know.

She had succeeded in the first part of her plan. Niall O'Connor would be looking for her, and he would be glad to see her.

Chapter 3

"Well done, lads. Ye should be proud of yerselves," Rian O'Toole congratulated the raiding party that mingled about him in a glen on the other side of the oak and hazel wood. He was a burly man in his sixth decade, the hair at his temples had long ago turned white, his ruddy face bore the ravages of a lifetime of battles against the English. There was nothing appealing about the look of Rian O'Toole. His features were rough and square, and his nose gave the impression of having been broken more than once. It was his proud stature that attracted notice, sitting as he did, erect and with a touch of arrogance, upon a mighty war horse that he had stolen twelve years before from the earl of Desmond, one of the degenerate English and justiciar of Ireland. It was such daring accomplishments that had won the O'Toole chieftain loyalty and respect among the Irish in the Wicklow Mountains. "And how are we faring, my fine lads? Do any of ye need to be sewn up?"

There were a few minor injuries among the men, came the reply, whereupon they set about tending to each other and their horses, or to rinsing the woad from their faces in the nearby brook. Twenty-nine native Irish had ridden that afternoon against Sir Roger Clare, and every one of them had survived. They were O'Tooles, O'Byrnes, and O'Connors, warriors from the rebel tribes in the uncolonized frontier south of Dublin. *Terra guerre,* the land of war. It was ancestral O'Connor land. They had been there the longest, and despite occasional differences of opinion with O'Tooles and O'Byrnes, who had been driven by the Anglo-Normans from their rich lands in the plains of Kildare into the high, boggy hills of Wicklow, they were united in their determination to keep the English out of the mountains.

It had been a fine day for a raid.

"Some moss is needed over here," one of the younger men called out, and he motioned to another man who was slicing pieces of a puffy green substance from the base of a tree. "Over here. For my brother."

"It is nothing but a scratch, Niall," Bran protested when everyone looked in his direction. He did not like to be fussed over even when a wound was severe, and he tried to reassure Rian O'Toole, who had come to inspect for himself. He was sitting on the trunk of a tree that had fallen sometime in the winter, and he stood at the older man's approach, biting back an oath and gritting his teeth at the stab of pain that shot through his leg. "It hurts like the very devil, but it's worse to look upon than is dangerous, I believe."

His legs were bare beneath his woolen tunic, and a thick stream of blood had run past his knee. Even his boot was streaked with blood that was darkening from deep red to black as it dried. Bran lifted the tunic to reveal a thin gash about three inches in length. "See, the bleeding stopped long ago."

"Aye, it's but a scratch, *ceart go leor,*" Rian O'Toole agreed. *Right enough.* He gave the wound a poke to assure himself it was not warming, then remarked, "Color is good. Appears to be all right, and if it heals cleanly and without any infection, the scar will hardly be showing. But yer brother is right to be concerned for ye, lad."

Someone handed a chunk of moss to Bran. Its long, black roots were dripping with the medicinal substances that would purify a wound.

"Go raibh maith agat," Bran thanked the fellow and pressed the moist dark underside of the plant to the wound. He leaned back against the tree trunk and secured the moss with a strip of fabric he'd torn from the bottom of his tunic.

"Ye must take better care of yerself, Bran O'Connor. *Níl luibh ná leigheas in aghaidh an bháis,"* said Rian O'Toole. *There's neither herb nor cure for death.* "Ireland needs men like ye and yer brother. Ye did fine work last night to bring us word of Sir Roger's travel plans, and ye rode well this afternoon. We could not have succeeded without yer help. Yer grandfather would be proud of ye."

Bran shrugged. This was another kind of fussing he did not like. He had never been comfortable with accepting compliments or thanks when he'd only been doing what was necessary. "Any other Irishman would have done the same. Thanks are not needed. I would do it again anytime, if need be. Ye need only ask, Rian O'Toole. Though ye must not be expecting me to dress like a plumed bird again."

Robust laughter erupted in the forest clearing. Rian O'Toole had seen Bran O'Connor in the stolen English finery, and a truly amusing sight it had been. "But, lad, did no one ever tell ye those particular shades of scarlet and yellow become ye? Did not all the English ladies swoon in surrender at the sight of ye with desire in their eyes, for I'm thinking not a one of them has ever known a real man."

Niall and the others joined Rian O'Toole in laughter while the object of this good-natured merriment scowled.

"And those shoes." O'Toole's silver eyebrows twitched with amusement. "Walking about with steer horns affixed to the end of yer feet is how they looked. Stop yer frowning, lad. Can it be ye do not wish to own such a pair of pointed wonders for yer own? Why, think on it, lad: ye would not have to fight the English, merely pierce them with your toes."

Bran could not stop from smiling at this, but he did not laugh. His leg was aching, and he remained motionless to lessen the discomfort.

Rian became serious. "I mean it, Bran O'Connor, thank ye. 'Tis getting on in my years, I am, and I am neither so crafty nor spry as I used to be." Rian O'Toole had been waging war against the English for more than fifty years, and he was glad to know there were younger men such as this one who would keep up the fight after he was gone. He passed a large calloused hand over his face, feeling the rough weathered skin and the flesh about his jowls that had not always been there. Rian O'Toole had been six years old when he watched his father's head being tossed into a basket. In that single year, some four hundred rebel heads had been sent from the mountains for the castle walls, and Rian had been fighting the English ever since. He still had a warrior's skill, but it would not be long before that was taken from him.

This time, Bran accepted Rian O'Toole's thanks. He read the older man's expression and understood the broader meaning behind his words. He would not disappoint the chieftain. "It is because men such as yerself and my grandfather taught me well, Rian O'Toole. *Go raibh maith agat.* I thank ye, but not for yer praise and confidence, but for passing yer knowledge and inspiration on to me."

The two chieftains embraced, then drank from a wine-skin that was being passed around. Bran wiped his mouth with the back of his hand. There were many more miles yet to travel until they would reach home. The sun was setting. Once night fell it was easy to lose one's way in the dense woods or to meet with an accident such as a fall in the perilous terrain or an encounter with a hungry night beast on the prowl. Soon it would be too dark to travel, and in the remaining hour or so, it was vital to put more distance between themselves and their enemy.

"We should part now," said Bran. He pushed away from the fallen tree, and with a low whistle, he called his stallion.

"Aye, lad," replied Rian O'Toole. "It is time to divide the horses amongst us and bid one another farewell. Until next time."

The English still had a penchant for decorating the gates and walls of Dublin Castle with the heads of rebels. It would not be long before Sir Roger sent a squadron to exact revenge for this afternoon's raid. The deeper the Irish went into the mountains, the closer to their mottes and fortresses, the safer it would be, the easier to hide and evade, to fight and win. They split into family groups, each taking an equal share of the stolen horses. The O'Tooles were bound for the northwest, and they set off on their own, hoping to reach their hillfort on the heights of Kippure in the last two to three hours of sunlight, while the O'Byrnes and O'Connors began their journey to the south together. The O'Byrnes were headed to a stronghold west of Glendalough, and the O'Connors, who had the furthest distance to travel, would ride with them. The two clans would make camp this night some distance down the Vartry, and at dawn, would continue together as far as the Glenmacnass River at *An Laithreach* before parting company.

"Bitheamaid a falbh," Bran said to his men. *Let us go.* Four others had ridden with him this day, and they mounted their horses for the journey home. In addition to Niall, three of their sisters' husbands, who resided with their families at Baravore, had joined the raid. One of them, an O'Connor cousin called Finnian, led the family's share of stolen horses that had been tethered together.

It rained that night, and in the morning, when the O'Connors and O'Byrnes broke camp on a rise above the Vartry a sinuous mist twisted about the whitethorn and holly bushes like the spirits of ancient pagan gods that had once roamed those woods. The river below was hidden beneath a heavy mantle of gray vapor. Only the faintest rays of sunshine cut through the thickening spring foliage. The men were cold and hungry, eager for hearth and home, and the women who would welcome them upon their return. They kept a steady pace until the banks of the Glenmacnass. There, the two clans went their separate ways.

"Soruidh uam gu d' phiuthair," said Dallán O'Byrne. He pulled his horse aside to talk with Bran before following the river north with his clansmen. *My respects to yer sister.* He took something from beneath the damp fur wrapped about his shoulders. It was one of Lady Alyson's gold goblets. He handed it to Bran. "Give this to yer sister, and tell her it is a good faith pledge that I will soon come to her at Baravore."

" 'Se bleatha sin," Bran said. A knowing twinkle lit his eyes. *That will be welcome.* He took the goblet and

grinned. Indeed, his sister Broinninn would blush to the high heavens that Dallán O'Byrne had sent her a token of his esteem. They were to be wed in the first week of May, and his sister's maidenly blushes were a constant source of amusement to Bran. Like all of the O'Connor women, Broinninn had been wed in her fifteenth summer to a cousin, but at the age of twenty and with three small children, she was a widow. Whenever Bran thought about the relationship between Dallán O'Byrne and Broinninn something contracted in his heart, and it made him smile. His sister's shy glances were evidence that although she was a woman, wedded and bedded, this was her first experience with romance, and Bran was pleased that a chieftain such as Dallán O'Byrne would take Broinninn to wife and give her happiness. It was a wonderful thing—this coming together of two souls as if Heaven had meant it to be—a rare thing that Bran did not think would ever happen to him. Yet it was enough to see the rest of his family happy.

"How about ye, Niall?" Dallán asked. "Have ye a message for my bonny sister?"

"Now which one of yer sisters would ye be meaning since they are all, each and every one of them, such comely lasses?"

It was a reasonable question. The O'Byrne women were fair, red-haired lassies with great blue eyes and charming little dimples, and Niall had been flirting shamelessly with every one of them for years. They were like sisters to him, for Niall, as was custom, had been fostered to Dallán O'Byrne's father for seven years.

" 'Tis Ceara who is asking after ye."

"The lass asks for me now, does she?" Niall was pleased. Ceara was his favorite, and although not the prettiest O'Byrne sister, his fondest memories of the years he'd spent in the O'Byrne household always included her. She was the youngest, having just turned fifteen, and unlike her sisters, she had a reserved, patient nature that he admired. "Then ye must tell Ceara that I am expecting her to save at least two dances for me at yer wedding feast."

"The wedding is a few weeks away yet. The lass will be disappointed to hear she must wait until then for a dance, let alone for the sight of ye. She misses ye, Niall." Dallán's voice softened as if he were trying to convey a special message that only he should understand.

Niall stared at Dallán without reply. He was not thinking of the sweet, red-haired Ceara, but of the wild Johanna Elizabeth Clare, and he was wondering if it could be true that somehow Fate had been at work yesterday. Rational thought told him otherwise. He did not even think he believed in Fate the way his grandfather Rourke had believed. But he could not get the notion out of his mind. She had been so certain and calm in her conviction, and it made Niall believe that anything could be possible.

"Niall?" prodded Bran. He didn't like the faraway expression upon his face.

"Have the faeries bewitched ye, lad?" asked Dallán. "Or are ye dreaming of our darling Ceara?"

Bran studied his brother, saw the scratches on his face, and he knew the truth. It was not holly leaves or a whitethorn branch that had done that to him, but a woman's fingernails, and it was not Ceara about whom Niall daydreamed but someone else. Bran had seen Niall ride after the Clare wench, and he did not like it one bit. "Come, Niall, stop yer daydreaming, now," he said abruptly. "We must be on our way."

If anyone noticed the change in Bran's demeanor, they didn't remark upon it. Although his tone was sharp, his words were true. It was time to go, and after a final farewell, Dallán O'Byrne rode in the opposite direction to catch up with his men while Bran led the way south.

They rode single file into the ever-thickening wilderness. The forest was alive with the call of birds and the noises of small creatures scurrying to hide from the approaching human intruders, who made their way through the leafy bracken, avoiding the flowering whitethorns and glossy hollies. Some of these bushes had grown to trees, their thorny branches and sharp leaves reaching to the lower limbs of the great oaks, whose greening upper branches rustled in the wind above the treetops. While they could not travel quickly, especially with the stolen horses, they maintained a steady pace for about an hour until they came upon a clearing, where there were the shallow remains of a recently dug fire pit.

"There were English camped here. A handful of men. Five. Mayhap six." Niall jumped down to inspect. The ashes were warm. "They haven't been gone long."

Bran scanned the perimeter of the clearing for any indication that this was a trap. Reassured that was not the case, he spoke to the others, "We must do what we can to evade them. I do not want to lead them to Baravore." The moraines that cut between Mullacor and Carriglinneen into Glenmalur were deep and dangerous and—to those who did not know the way—impassable. It was a dark mystical place about which the natives whispered frightful legends, and hence, the English did not enter the glen unless they were led by natives. Several military excursions in the last century had been disastrous to the English; indeed, it was said that men, who had not been wounded in battle, perished on the steep slopes from lack of breath. There had not been English in Glenmalur for eighty years, and Bran did not intend that any carelessness on his part would offer them entrance.

"Finnian, from here on, ye need not be leading the horses yerself. We shall divide them, one to go with each man, and then each of ye will be traveling alone, along a different route. Make it as round about as time permits, and if need be, leave the horses to save yerself and get within sight of the pass by dusk. But wait above, and only enter the valley under cover of darkness. Niall and I will stay here, and follow in a few hours. If all goes well, every one of us should be within the palisades at Baravore before tomorrow morning."

The brothers-in-law rode out of the clearing, each mounted on one horse and leading another. One man went to the north, the second to the east, and the third to the west. Bran and Niall lounged on the ground while their horses munched upon tender shoots of green at the edge of the clearing. The sun slipped lower in the sky until it reached the top of the great oak trees. It was almost time to leave when the sound of men talking to one another filtered out of the woods above the jangles of spurs and bridles. Niall and Bran exchanged a quick knowing glance. Only the foolish, arrogant English rode through hostile territory conversing with one another in full voice. Without a moment to spare, they slapped their horses on the rumps and sent the beasts out of the clearing. Bran's stallion knew the way into Glenmalur and down the length of the glen to Baravore; hopefully, the other animals would follow.

Bran and Niall scrambled for cover. No sooner had they crawled into the underbrush than the English entered the clearing. There were seven of them fully armed. Five of the men were on foot, each shouldering a massive longbow with a quiver full of arrows at the waist. There were two knights on horseback. The Clare coat of arms was emblazoned upon their breastplates, boasting a gold donjon tower upon a field of blue, but Sir Roger was not among them.

"We come full circle, sir," spoke a crossbowman.

"Aye, but it is not for naught," one of the knights replied. "Look, someone has been here after us."

"English?"

"Nay, the raiders it appears. Observe the nature of the tracks left behind. Not all of the horses have riders. Our quarry is nearer than we thought."

"This way," cried a knight. "Forward!"

They went in the direction in which the riderless horses had gone. A moment later, Niall made as if to crawl into the open, but Bran's hand stayed his movement.

"Nay," he whispered. "If they find the horses they'll be back. We must wait. We must hide ourselves better than this, for they will be searching more thoroughly if they return."

A few yards distant there was an outcrop of boulders. Crouching low, they moved away from the underbrush to inspect the rocks, where they found a small hole rather like an animal's den. There was enough space for both of them to sit with their legs drawn up to their chests. Together, they gathered a sizeable bundle of boughs that they used to wipe out their footprints, and then they scooted inside the den, positioning the bundle of brush to hide the opening.

"Do ye think there are more of them?" Niall wondered.

"Probably."

"Would they attack Baravore?"

"There is always a first time." There was another

native stronghold called Ballinacor at the eastern end of Glenmalur. Ballinacor had been assaulted on several occasions, and there had been fierce combat at that end of the glen, but the English had never dared to go the length of the Avonbeg to Baravore.

"Maybe we should not have stolen Sir Roger's horses."

"What do I hear ye saying now?" Bran peered at his brother in the dim light. "How can ye call yerself Irish and even be wondering at such a thing?"

"But I do not like to be thinking we could be responsible for putting Mam and the others in jeopardy."

"Have ye forgotten, Niall?" asked Bran, stricken not by the notion that his brother would question his decision to participate in the raid, but that somehow he had failed to imbue in Niall the kind of pride and commitment to the Irish cause that his grandfather Rourke had given to him. Niall was the youngest O'Connor child, born six months after their father had died in the first Great Pestilence, when Bran had been five years old. Before that Bran had been the only son among a household of daughters, and from the first, he had been as watchful and protective of his younger brother as a parent. He had always loved his brother fiercely, and had been the one to teach him to walk and ride, to hunt and wield his sword with deadly skill. But had he failed in the most important lesson of all?

"We are not the ones who started this, Niall. It is them. Their kind. The Anglo-Normans, the English, and we only do what we must. And someday, may the Good Lord be willing, we will drive every last one of them back into the sea." He stared hard at Niall to read his reaction, but his brother was not looking at him. It was the way he had been when Dallán

O'Byrne was talking with him. Bran could not help himself, and he snapped without preface, "Stay away from her."

"Stay away from who?"

"Sir Roger's daughter." Bran could not control this concern for Niall. He knew what was right, and he had to make certain Niall did not make any mistakes.

"What do ye know of her?" Niall phrased the question carefully.

"More than ye could imagine," Bran said. He had known it was she who stabbed him, although he had not given any indication that he recognized her. It had been the most peculiar incident he'd experienced to gaze upon the very same woman whom he'd kissed with such passion a few hours before, then to see his blood staining her dagger. For an instant, he'd almost lost his concentration, which only served to incite the anger that her dagger had inflicted when she stabbed his leg. *Méabh,* she had called herself. She was, indeed, intoxicating. And infuriating, to be able to surmount a warrior's defenses like that.

It was more than the fact that she had stabbed him that had made him angry. It infuriated him that when he looked at her his focus wavered. He was a warrior and nothing should distract him, but she had, and that was when he had smeared the blood on her face. He did it without any forethought. He had acted on impulse. It had seemed right at the time, but what he would have done next, if the raiders had not started to disperse, he could not begin to imagine. For the truth was, he had wanted to kidnap her, to take her to some distant, quiet clearing in the woods and kiss her again, and that yearning for her had made him want to strangle her. It had made him reach out and touch her with his bloody fingers, to wipe his hand across her lips and feel some measure of satisfaction when he left a mark upon her. "She's degenerate English," Bran said. That was everything Niall needed to know about her. "Forget about her."

"But she is half-Irish after all," Niall retorted, thinking of her bravery, of the love she'd shown for her horse, and of how she had almost managed to outride him even on that comical English saddle.

"Half-Irish, ye say, as if that were any kind of virtue," Bran snorted in disdain. "She's a MacMurrough on her mother's side, which is more like half-devil."

"I did not know."

"Well, now ye do, and like I was saying to ye: Stay away from her."

O'Connors had been fighting MacMurroughs long before the first Anglo-Normans set foot on Irish soil. They were enemies as ancient as the heather hills and bogs that covered the land. They had been raiding each other's cattle, kidnapping each other's women, and feuding over boundaries before the Vikings had built Dublin, even before St. Patrick had brought the word of Christ and the Resurrection to the island. Such feuds between ancient tribes had not been uncommon, and over the centuries many alliances had been forged between once bitter enemies, but never between O'Connors and MacMurroughs, for Diarmait MacMurrough, with a single, unforgivable act of betrayal had made them enemies for all time.

Diarmait MacMurrough was to blame for Norman colonization. The warrior king of Leinster had altered the course of Irish history, having in 1166 sailed to England and sworn fealty to King Henry in exchange for military support against the O'Rourkes and O'Connors. Diarmait of the Foreigners, they called him in mocking insult, for what he had done. The English had been happy to oblige, and King Henry wrote an open letter to his subjects, encouraging them to rally to MacMurrough's assistance. Help came from the earl of Pembroke, Richard FitzGilbert de Clare, who agreed to lead an armed force to Ireland and restore MacMurrough to power on the condition that he would give him his daughter in marriage, plus the right of succession in Leinster. In point of fact, Sir Roger's daughter was doubly cursed: a descendent of both Clare and MacMurrough could never be trusted.

"What happens to a woman like that?" asked Niall.

"What do ye mean?"

"Half-Irish, half-English. Who will accept her? Where will she have a future?"

"And why should ye be caring one way or the other? Haven't I told ye? Ye're to be staying away from the likes of her," Bran said, regretting his overbearing tone the second he had spoken the words. He did not want to alienate Niall, to make him defiant out of youthful stubbornness, and he started to apologize, but remained silent as his ears detected the crunching of footsteps in the clearing. Bran and Niall reached for their daggers.

"There's no sign of them over here." A man spoke in English. "What about there?"

"Nay."

"But they could not have gotten very far without their horses."

"Keep searching."

For well over an hour, the footsteps and voices came and went. At last, they faded away and did not return. Time passed. The brothers breathed a bit easier. Night fell, the forest darkened to black, and Bran said a silent prayer that the others had reached Baravore.

Niall dozed off, but Bran couldn't sleep. He did not dare to close his eyes, not, however, because of the English soldiers, but because he did not want to see the vision of terror in her eyes when he had smeared the blood upon her lips. He did not want to hear her velvety whisper when she said, *For a night, I would do anything*. He did not want to remember that he'd asked the question. None of it made sense. It was not good, and like Niall, Bran had to forget about her. His leg was cramping, and he passed the hours massaging the muscles to prevent it from stiffening up on him altogether.

It was about midnight when he woke Niall. " 'Tis time to be going on our way again."

They pushed aside the brush, and crawled out from hiding.

"How's yer leg? Can ye make it?"

"Aye, I'll make it," said Bran. He had no choice.

Chapter 4

From the heights of Carriglinneen, rain-swollen brooks rushed toward the Avonbeg that ran the length of the glen to Baravore. Eleven mountains circled the valley, their peaks standing sentry above the secluded wilderness, Lugnaquillia towering above them all. Passage into the glen was dangerous, and from all sides, water cut steep ravines into the hillsides. The noise from the falls was deafening, and to the knowing traveler, the thunderous roar was a familiar welcome, but to intruders it was a warning to keep away, for it was whispered that the *Sidhe* lived beneath the silvery pools that dotted the valley floor and within the hearts of the hills. There were beautiful maidens in Glenmalur, but according to legend, they were not human.

If one listened carefully, a man could hear the *feadhree* playing their flutes and harps and dancing to the music of the cascading water. If one looked, a man would see beautiful maidens beneath the moonlight frolicking along the banks of the Avonbeg. They were the *Sidhe,* a race between angel and man, cast out of Heaven as a punishment for their pride. Some had fallen to earth, while others had been carried to Hell by demons, from whence their evil spirits issued forth disguised as comely young women to tempt humans into sin. Under their influence, a man would commit any and every crime against God and man, and when his soul was blackened to the core, the evil faeries would carry him to Hell for eternity. Although the English earls and bishops might sneer and consider themselves above such superstition, the common men among them had not forgotten their own old gods, and there were few English soldiers who would dare to test the legend, which the Irish, of course, embellished to their advantage at every available opportunity.

Before descending the steep slope, Bran and Niall waited for a signal from the watch. There was always someone guarding the vale, someone ready to warn Baravore, if strangers dared to enter uninvited. Up and down the glen, clansmen watched and waited, keeping in contact with one another by whistles in the night or light refracted from bits of mirror during the day. Bran cupped his hands about his mouth and made a low hooting noise similar to an owl's call. An "owl" called back; the watch was in place. Then another three hoots rose into the night sky from a nearby crag. Farther down the valley, owls called to each other. O'Connor clansmen were positioned along the crags and ledges to stop any English soldier who dared trespass into their territory. No one would be allowed to follow Bran and Niall into Glenmalur that night. The two men scrambled down the rocky slope, and upon reaching level ground, they made their way along the cattle path that led toward a dot of light some distance down the valley.

Every evening as the sun was setting, Bébinn O'Connor went to her chamber at the top of the round tower to set a torchlight in the narrow window. When she had come to Baravore some twenty-six years before as a bride of fourteen summers, the chamber had not been hers. It had belonged to the old chieftain, Rourke O'Connor, and his wife, a Scottish beauty called Viviane. Then the nightly task of climbing the steps and setting the beacon to guide the menfolk home had been Viviane's. It was a custom as old as the first hillfort that had been built at Baravore, and this night, as always, the entire clan gathered to await and greet their returning chieftain.

Baravore had changed over the centuries from a simple hillfort to a motte with a wooden palisade, and now it was a walled fortress much in the Anglo-Norman style with ramparts and a tower rising over the gate. Between the inner and outer bailey, there was an old fosse as well as remnants of the wooden palisade. Water still flowed into the fosse that served more as a convenient source of water for livestock than a line of defense just as the old palisade was these days used as a ready source of firewood. The chieftain and his immediate kin resided in the tower above a great hall; the unmarried warriors and male cousins occupied the tower above the gate, which also housed an armory and deep well. Scattered around the bailey and erected flush to the castle wall were numerous post-and-wattle structures with turf roofs. There was the old long-house built of stone and clay, *teagh na n-aoigheadh*, the *house of the guests* in which distant kin, visitors, and servants slept, plus there were stables, a cow byre and haggard, and a tiny chapel. The chapel had been a gift from Rourke O'Connor to his wife upon the birth of their first child, and it was the pride of Glenmalur with a stained glass window depicting a band of gold-winged angels watching over Highlanders on the field at Bannockburn.

There were two doors into Baravore. The main entrance was at the rampart, and there was a postern gate at another location to allow the residents to escape, if necessary. The portcullis at the main entrance was raised as Bran's and Niall's silhouetted figures appeared, and a small door in the massive oak gate was opened to them. They slipped inside, went through a passage that cut through the base of the tower, and upon entering the bailey, they were surrounded by family. It was always a cause for celebration when warriors returned home. Finnian and the other brothers-in-law had been within the fortress walls since dusk, and now with the arrival of their chieftain, the clan could, at last, truly celebrate. The lateness of the hour did not matter. Bran O'Connor was home, the English had not entered the glen, and there were five new stallions in the stable.

"Bran, *machd,* it is a fine welcome home to ye, *son,*" said Bébinn, the widow of Echrí O'Connor and mistress of Baravore. She smiled in gratitude and affection at the sight of her two sons. "A blessing it is that the Lord's everwatchful angels bring this night upon our home."

Bran strode toward his mother. Her beauty was remarkable. He was always struck by that when he saw her after being away, and he thought how strange it was that he could ever forget such a thing. *Bébinn* meant *white lady,* and a fitting name it was, for she was tall and fair of complexion with great blue eyes and flaxen hair as white as the finest sun-bleached linen. It had been nineteen years since his father had died, leaving her a widow at the age of twenty. She was still vibrant and lovely, and Bran wondered why she had never remarried. From time to time, chieftains had made the trek to Glenmalur to court Bébinn, but she did not leave. It must have been a very strong love she'd had for Echrí O'Connor.

"It is good to be home," Bran told his mother.

Bébinn embraced her elder son feeling, as always, the same pang of sadness that there was no else to greet this bold, handsome man. His sisters mingled about the yard arm-in-arm with their husbands; soon Broinninn, her children tugging upon her skirt, would be wed again; and it was only a matter of time before Niall decided which girl—among the many who wanted him—he would marry. But there was no one for Bran.

"It went well?" Bébinn asked, not having the vaguest notion where they had gone. Of course, she could guess that it had something to do with harrying the English, but beyond that she knew nothing. Bran never told where he took the men when they left or what they planned to do. Her husband never had, nor had the old chieftain, Rourke. It was best, Rourke had explained, never to tell the women. If there was trouble, and the English came to question them, then they could answer truthfully. Bébinn never knew. Indeed, she did not want to know, for she loathed the hatred and the fighting, and so she never asked.

"Aye. It went well. We were successful, and nothing more than a few ounces of blood were lost."

"Ye're favoring one leg. *Céard a tharla*?" she asked. *What happened*?

" 'Tis naught but a scratch, and Niall has already made certain I had attention for it. Ye would have approved of the poultice. It was moist and black as a peat-bog."

"Good for yer brother to be taking such care of ye." Bebinn slipped her arm through Bran's as they went across the inner bailey. "But many is the man who has died from less than that. Is it causing ye much pain? Is it warming? When was the last time ye were checking the color? Will it need stitching?"

"Fear not, Mam, ye'll be getting yer chance to fuss over it like a worried hen once we're inside. *Le so,*" he said, digressing to a more neutral, pleasant topic. "*By the by,* Rian O'Toole was sending his best to ye."

"Did he, now? *His best,* was it?" Bébinn surprised her son with a blush that was almost maidenly. "That's mighty fancy talk for an Irishman with a price hanging over his head. What was it that he truly said, if I might be asking?"

Bran grinned. "He asked if ye were still the fairest lady in all of Ireland, and when I told him it was true, he swore like a devil and said it was a piece of rotten luck that he was not young enough to be riding south and claiming ye for his own."

"Some people never change," she said on a ripple of laughter.

"And who would want it otherwise?"

Bébinn stared at Bran, but could not speak. In truth, that was her wish for her eldest child. He was a fine son in every way; he had never let her down, and she did not fear he ever would. And he was a worthy chieftain, loyal and brave. He was trusted by their clan; the men would do anything he asked of them. But there was in Bran an almost zealous harshness that she worried would hurt him some day. After Echrí's death, Rourke O'Connor had raised the lad, and the older man's influence had been profound. Bébinn knew that her son shared his grandfather's intense pride in the purity of their blood, and she knew he lived to fulfill Rourke's vision. Bran lived to drive the English out of Ireland as they had been defeated in the Highlands. He would stop at nothing to do this. It was noble and worthy, yet Bébinn could not deny the sadness it caused her. She did not like the unrelenting determination she saw in her eldest son. It reminded her of her own father, and she remembered with sorrow how it had blinded him and caused much unhappiness.

Thus it was that each time Bran rode out of Baravore, Bébinn wished that he would return changed. He was too harsh on himself, too unbending, and at times, unreasonable, and she feared that unless he were different there would never be anyone waiting for him when he came back. A clap of thunder echoed between the mountains and down the length of the valley.

"*Thigibh astigh. Come ye inside.* There's fresh venison on the spit, and a hearty cheese soup with onions that will warm ye after being out on a night such as this. *Tá faitíos orm go bhfuil an drochaimsir chugainn.*" She hurried them along. *I'm afraid the bad weather is coming.*

Niall, who had been to check on the horses, came up from behind. "And how's my lovely mam this night?" He gave her a hug and kiss.

Bébinn smiled brightly. This was her baby, the lad who flirted with the lassies, the daring imp who had once spread his arms like wings to fly from the fortress wall. She had never worried that Niall was too hard on himself. She worried that Bran was too hard on him. "How did it go between the two of ye?"

Niall shrugged. "Och, there were a few rough moments."

"Aren't there always?" this came from Bran.

"And don't we always manage to slide on through?"

"What was it this time?" Bébinn was not going to let them push this aside. Something had happened, and she wanted to know what.

The brothers exchanged a glance.

"Now what was it?" said Niall, ruminating aloud.

"Seems like I've forgotten already. But if I remember, Mam, I'll be sure to tell ye." He gave his mother another quick kiss and hurried ahead, bounding up the stairs that led into the hall.

Bran and Bébinn both knew he had lied. His mother assumed it was because he didn't want to fight with Bran in front of her. Bran, on the other hand, suspected it was because Niall, far from forgetting any of it, was probably thinking about the Clare wench at that exact moment. Indeed, tonight, his brother would probably dream about her. It was a good thing they were not planning to ride toward the coast any time soon.

"And how about ye, Bran?" Bébinn stared up at him. She was a tall woman, but her son loomed above her, and she had to tilt her head to get a closer look at the expression in his eyes. "Have ye forgotten what happened between the two of ye?"

"Nay, I have not." Nor had he ever lied to his mother.

"And will ye be telling me?"

"There's no reason not to. Am I not always honest with ye?" he said. "It was a woman."

"Ye disagreed over a woman?" There was relief in her voice, and she smiled a sort of mother's smile that made one think she knew a secret, a very pleasing secret. Maybe something different *had* happened after all.

Bran scowled. He did not like the hopeful expression that lit his mother's features. "Nay, Mam, it was not what ye're imagining."

"And how would ye be knowing what's in yer own mother's mind?"

"Believe me," he said with gentle persuasion. "I know. We did not argue over a woman's affections."

"How was it then?" Bébinn held up the hem of her

kirtle as she ascended the slick wooden stairs to the hall.

"I told him to stay away from someone."

"And why was that, I'm wondering,?"

"Because the woman was Sir Roger Clare's daughter."

At the top step, Bébinn stumbled.

Bran took hold of her elbow to help her regain her balance. "Are ye all right?"

"Oh, how clumsy I grow," Bébinn said, blathering on in a fashion that was most unlike herself. "How silly and clumsy. It was the wet steps, you see. I must get one of the girls to scrub them down. Much too slippery, this time of year. Of course, I am fine. There is nothing to concern ye. Nothing at all," she said as she entered the torchlit hall.

But when the beautiful widow raised her face, there were unshed tears sparkling at the tips of her eyelashes.

There was a walled garden at Killoughter. A full acre of tidy pathways winding between pruned hedges and artistically clipped bushes. The flowers had been planted in perfect rows, separated by color and type, and undulating from low growers to high growers like waves of a rainbow sea. Although it was early in the season, the garden was already alive with color. The blues were first in this striking spectrum with broom, and cowslip, and whorls of bugles; next came the purples, the standergrass and valerian, then the red-purple spikes of betony; yellows followed with ladies' mantle and celandine; and finally, were the whites of the sweet-scented madder, briony, sanicles, and arbutes. Johanna Elizabeth supposed that such order and precision were hideously, absolutely English. But she loved it nonetheless, and she hummed a lilting tune as she followed the seashell path beyond the rose bushes to a tiny cottage at the rear of the garden. A small lidded basket woven of rushes hung from her forearm, and she carried several gardening implements in one hand.

Killoughter had been built by one of her Clare ancestors more than a hundred years before, and control of the castle had passed back and forth between the English and Irish several times. Sir Roger had led its liberation from Irish hands, and as a reward the young, unmarried knight from Carlow had been given the moated castle to command and defend for the crown. Killoughter was reinforced as a ward, an outpost of Dublin in *Uí Bríuin Cualann*, and the garrison under Sir Roger's command included twenty-two men-at-arms, eleven mounted soldiers, and two hundred foot. In addition, the settlements at the Grange and Castletimon, and the priory of Lllangony were placed under his administration. Sir Roger had become a man of much consequence.

The first months at Killoughter, however, had been bleak ones for Sir Roger, especially the first winter, and so he set about finding himself a wife, an Irish wife to be specific, for he had intended to make peace with his neighbors and hold fast to that which was his. Since the castle had been constructed by a Clare, it was his by ancestral right, and he was determined the Irish would never control it again, at least, not in his lifetime. Besides, being a fifth son, there was nothing for Sir Roger in Carlow. His fortunes were to be made and held at Killoughter, and being ambitious, he did as so many other young warriors had done and wed the daughter of a native chieftain. At that time, marriage between the Anglo-Normans and Irish was an accepted avenue to harmony, and it had been more than a shrewd political move, for Étaín Mac-

Murrough bore him six children and transformed the cold garrison into a bustling home.

Étaín had loved the walled garden. She had spent hours there, tending her herbs and watching her children play as the seasons changed, and it was where she had asked to be buried beside her sons. It was where Johanna Elizabeth went to remember how things used to be before her mother had died, and her father had started to change. It was the one place on earth she could still be with her mother, and she had come this day, in part, to say good-bye.

At the far end of the garden, the cottage was the same as when her mother had been alive. Johanna Elizabeth had made certain of that. There were several bricks of newly cut turf on the roof, and there was a fresh coat of whitewash on the shutters and door. She opened the door and, stepping inside, was cloaked by the myriad aromas of herbs and the sweet scents of flowers.

Everything was as it had always been from Johanna Elizabeth's earliest memories. The only furnishings were a table in the middle of the room with a rough-hewn bench on each side. Several mortars and pestles rested there, above which hanging from the ceiling beams were an assortment of dried herbs, and flower blossoms, branches, bits of bark, leaves, and vines. Johanna Elizabeth knew where everything was stored, for she kept it exactly as her mother had, and she began to fill the little basket hanging from her arm with byrony root, myrtle leaves, and the dried yellow blossoms of St. John's wort that she had gathered the summer before. She also took the smallest mortar and pestle for later use.

Exiting the cottage, she went around to the back, where a small plot of plants was circled by a ring of glittering gray and white stones. Setting down the basket and implements, she knelt on the dark ground. More rain had fallen in the night. It was damp beneath her knees, and she could feel the cool moisture penetrating the fabric of her tunic. Carefully, she sorted through the plants. It was still early in the season for everything that she would like to have had, but at least there were cyclamen and marigolds.

"It has always seemed odd to me how anything so pretty can also be so powerful," Lady Alyson remarked from behind her.

Johanna Elizabeth startled. She had not heard anyone approach, and raised a hand to shield her eyes when she looked up at her stepmother. "Hello, Lady Alyson. You are familiar with such things?"

"Of course. We are not that different in England. There is an herb garden at my father's manor."

Johanna Elizabeth did not want to hear about England, especially not anything that might make it seem less than the foreign place she believed it to be. She looked away from Lady Alyson and paid an excessive amount of attention to the orange marigold blossoms she was snapping from their stems and placing in the basket. Several moments of silence passed between the two women.

"Your father has sent me to speak with you," Lady Alyson was the first to speak.

"I am sorry to hear that." Johanna Elizabeth bit her lip, and continued to stare at the orange flowers. The distance between her and her father filled Johanna Elizabeth with despair. Before the trip to Dublin, she had pleaded with her father not to turn away from her, to try to understand why she could not bear to do as he asked of her, and while Johanna Elizabeth did not blame Lady Alyson for any of this, she could not help thinking that her father's new wife was making it easier for him to avoid her. They used to talk face to face, sometimes raise their voices at one another, but, at least, they had been able to talk, and if they disagreed, there had been a measure of respect between them. Now he sent someone else. "To send you in his stead is to act the coward."

"How can you speak thusly of your father?" Lady Alyson asked in the voice of one who had never dared to have an opinion of her own. "I thought you were a better daughter than that. He loves you very much."

"That is unfair. I am a good daughter, and I have always loved my father."

"Then why do you resist his plans for you, Johanna Elizabeth?"

Of a sudden, that sensation of not having enough air enveloped Johanna Elizabeth. It must have been the way Lady Alyson had said her name, so English, so controlled and proper, and she struggled to remind herself that it did not make any difference what her stepmother called her, no difference what future her father intended for her. There was no reason to panic. She had a plan. She was not going to England. This interview would be ended soon enough as would her days at Killoughter. She inhaled a deep breath, and looked up at Lady Alyson. "I am a good daughter as long as blind obedience is not a requisite."

"But what else is there for a daughter?"

Johanna Elizabeth took another breath. How odd was this conversation. It was not in the least bit the way she had imagined that talking with another young person would be. She had often yearned to share secrets and wishes and hopes with someone her own age, but this was as if she were talking with a much older person, and she could not help wondering if Lady Alyson had ever had any fun. Indeed, she could not help wondering if Lady Alyson had ever laughed with her father. Probably not, and that was truly tragic to consider.

"You must realize the compromising position in which you placed yourself the other day."

"What do you mean?"

"When you chased after that horse thief."

"I could not let him take Bláth."

"And thus it was that you gave him your virtue, instead. That does not seem a very equitable trade."

Johanna Elizabeth gasped, indignant. "I did no such thing."

"Ah, you know that to be true, and while I believe you speak the truth, it does not matter what you or I believe. It is the appearance of things that matters more than what actually is, and what was observed is that you disappeared into the woods with an Irish savage—without an attendant, mind you—and that you were absent for a long time. Time enough for *something* to have happened."

Johanna Elizabeth was going to choke. Her breathing had become shallow, and she required several moments before she could speak. "And is that what my father believes?" she asked in a voice that was barely above a whisper. She waited for her stepmother's reply.

"It is what my brothers believe," Lady Alyson said, seriously.

Johanna Elizabeth exhaled. *Thank God, I am no longer good enough to be the wife of a Windsor,* she almost cried aloud. Perhaps, she would not need her plan after all. Perhaps her father had changed his mind, and was going to let her remain unwed and at Killoughter.

"My brothers are gentlemen, and as such they are willing to keep your indiscretion a secret. Indeed, they know how much I wish to please my husband, and as a favor to me, they have agreed to escort you to

England, where my mother will arrange a match in your behalf."

"What did you say? I am to go to England after all?"

"Of course, and your father agrees it is the best course when all is considered. He had hoped that you might have decided upon one of my brothers before leaving Ireland, but now that is no longer possible. Instead, you will sail to England with my brothers when they return to Bristol. What better way could there be to find a suitable husband?"

"But what if—" The look upon Lady Alyson's face stopped Johanna Elizabeth from finishing the sentence.

"Yes?"

She swallowed and asked, "What if I do not wish to do this?"

Lady Alyson stared at her, impatient. "Not *wish*? And of what importance, pray tell, is *wishing*, if a profitable union can be arranged? You should be extremely grateful, especially to my brothers. Of course, it is not an easy thing to consider being sent from home to a strange land. But it is for the best and will turn out for the best. Why, look at me. Do you imagine it was not a frightening prospect to know that my husband was old enough to be my father, and my new home would be in the middle of a savage frontier?"

"I am sorry. Has it been bad for you?"

"No, and that is the point. It has been nothing compared to the horrendous visions I allowed my mind to conjure up. Your father is a gentleman and a good husband, and my mother would never arrange for you to wed any man who was less than your father. Do you not dream of a husband and home and family to call your own?" she asked.

"My dreams are forbidden," Johanna Elizabeth answered with blunt honesty. "I dream of my mother's people, of this land called Ireland, and of the people who call it home. I dream of the stirring music of pipes and harps, of dancing barefoot round bonfires, and of a place where one's soul can be forever young. And I wish for a man who would cherish me for no reason save the unseen bonds between our souls. My dreams are rooted in Ireland. If any of this is ever to be, it will happen here, not across the sea. I do not want to go to England. I cannot go." She knew she sounded like a petulant child. Either that, or a woman possessed by faeries.

"You have no choice."

Oh, but to the contrary, I do. She thought of Niall, plucked another vibrant marigold blossom and took a deep breath. "Perhaps you are right, Lady Alyson," she said aloud. "Nothing could be as dreadful as the tormented wanderings of my mind." She stared at the marigolds and imagined the steam rising from the infusion she would boil from the flowers. She had a plan, and it was going to work. She was not going to England, but—in the meantime—she must not let anyone suspect her. She stood and looked her stepmother straight in the eye. "I will do as you and my father wish."

Lady Alyson embraced her. "You will not regret this, I promise."

How right you are. I do not intend to have any regrets in my life. Johanna Elizabeth smiled at her stepmother. "When I am gone will you tend to this garden? Keep it up? It was my mother's favorite place, and I could not bear to think it did not thrive. She is buried there alongside my brothers." Johanna Elizabeth motioned to the corner of the walled garden that was closest to the mountains.

"Sir Roger had other children?" She looked in that direction, and saw for the first time the row of carved grave slabs.

"You did not know?"

"He said nothing. No one did."

"My father had five sons. They were all taken by the plague as was our mother."

"I should be delighted to keep up this garden," Lady Alyson said without hesitation, and then, as if imparting a secret, she added in a quiet, solemn voice, "I shall do it for all of you. For all of us: the women of Killoughter."

Johanna Elizabeth's nose burned with unshed tears, her eyes misted. "Thank you," she repeated this several times, and then embraced Lady Alyson. Perhaps, they were not so different after all, and for the space of a heartbeat, Johanna Elizabeth could not help wondering if in another time and place, she might have been friends with this young woman.

That night, Johanna Elizabeth climbed the tower steps in search of her father and found him walking the rampart, looking to the west where the silhouette of the high hills edged the night sky.

Sir Roger saw her and stopped, bracing himself for the worst. "Daughter," he greeted her slowly, cautiously, expecting an outburst of oaths. His lady wife had told him that Johanna Elizabeth had agreed to travel to England, and he did not believe it could have been as simple as she'd made it seem. What had transpired in the walled garden this afternoon did not sound like an encounter with his daughter. Indeed, he would not have been surprised if she had reduced Lady Alyson to tears.

"Good evening, Father," Johanna Elizabeth began with equal restraint. "As you must have been informed, Lady Alyson spoke with me this afternoon, and I have come to tell you that I will do as you wish. I will go to England. I will endeavor to become a lady and behave in a way that will make you proud, and I will endeavor to be a good wife to the gentleman chosen for me." She did not like to lie to him, but there was no other way to advance her plan; she had to make him believe that she intended to be docile and obedient.

"I have heard this favorable news from Lady Alyson, but to hear it from you makes me most happy, indeed."

Johanna Elizabeth winced. She saw the affection upon her father's face and did not like to think how disappointed he was going to be when he realized what she had done. But she had no choice, not if she wished to remain in Ireland. "I do have one request, if you please, sir. A favor, if you will allow it."

One of Sir Roger's eyebrows arched. This was more like it. Things were not going to proceed as easily as Lady Alyson had predicted. His daughter was going to dictate her own terms, and there was no telling what that might entail. "If I can, I will grant it."

"I would visit with my mother's family before leaving. I ask that you allow me to make one final trip into the mountains to see my grandmother at Annacurragh."

"But the statute—"

"The statute!" She tossed her hands upward. "The statute. Must I hear of it day in and day out as if it were some model of perfection and goodness? It is no harmless thing, this statute of Kilkenny, that grown men should dictate how others must dress and talk, and name their offspring. But that is not the worst of it. That they should dare to divide families, to outlaw the comings and goings between the English and Irish, even those who share blood and kin, is cruel. And to dictate that the future must fit their pristine racial mold is unreasonable. You know that as well as I, Father. Why can you not admit that?"

"It is not mine to admit. I am a knight, Johanna Elizabeth. I must obey my liege lord."

"But, Father, did you not hear the gossip in Dublin? There are many who defy the statute, and it is said their number grows daily."

"Aye, daughter, I heard the talk. But disobedience does not produce happy endings. Do you think the king will ignore his subjects in Ireland who openly flaunt his wishes? Aye, I heard a great deal of talk. Indeed, I heard that it may not be long before England sends an army to this land to impose the crown's will upon those who would disobey. If that happens, I do not want you in the middle of such a war. It will be brutal and ruthless; no one will be spared from suffering. You will be safest in England, and I will not discuss this any further. I've already begun to make arrangements for you to travel under the escort of her brothers."

"How soon did you plan to send me away?" She had vowed to wed an Irishman before summer's end, and she needed time to get to Annacurragh and find Niall.

"In about five weeks."

"Then I can still make my proper farewells. Please let me visit *Seanmhair*. You know as well as I do that if I go to England, I will probably never return to Ireland—at least, not while Grandmother is alive—and I do not think you would make me leave without seeing her one last time. You may have forgotten my mother's family, but I have not, and no matter where you send me, I will never forget." She spoke in impassioned tones.

Sir Roger shifted his weight from one foot to the other and glanced away from his daughter to stare blindly at the mountains. He wanted to curse and scream, but he set his palms deliberately against the cold stone rampart, then balled his hands into angry, impotent fists. Christ's nails, he had not forgotten, not for one minute. And may God forgive him for his blasphemous thoughts.

The truth was he hated politics and war. He loathed the statute. He missed his family with such intensity that the pain was a great cold spot upon his soul. And he regretted having married both his wives.

He looked at his daughter and saw Étaín. He remembered her passionate nature and the way her eyes had flashed with a reckless golden light when she laughed. Truth to tell, that was why he was sending his daughter away. He could not bear the memories. He could not bear the guilt. He was married to another now and should not care, should not remember, but Johanna Elizabeth was a constant reminder of everything that Lady Alyson was not and never could be. He should never have cared so deeply for a native Irish woman. He should have listened to those who were older and wiser; he should have believed them when they told him that kind of love was doomed from the start.

"Will you, Father?" Johanna Elizabeth crossed the allure, and when she had reached Sir Roger, she touched his arm, almost in supplication, but more in hesitant affection. Her voice was rich with hopeful expectation, "Will you let me visit *Seanmhair* before I must go to England?"

He could not refuse her, and gave a mighty sigh. "Aye, my child, that I will. You can have six weeks.

I will not send you to England until the first week of June. I would like to know that you have safely crossed the sea before the worst of the summer storms."

Overcome with elation, Johanna Elizabeth sagged against her father and hugged him as she had not done in a long time.

Two days later, she rode out of Killoughter for the MacMurrough motte overlooking the Aughrim Water. There was no train of sumpter horses, only Johanna Elizabeth mounted on Bláth, and a single escort, a young warrior, who knew the way through the mountains. Johanna Elizabeth did not need wagons laden with trunks. Everything she would need was in the lidded basket that was tied to the saddle horn.

Chapter 5

"Have a care, *ogha*. It is a dangerous game ye play," Marga MacMurrough warned the younger woman whom she called *grandchild*. Marga, seated by the light of an open window in the women's bower at Annacurragh, was spinning wool about her distaff. She was a very old woman. Her hair was pure white, her wrinkled skin had an ashen bluish tint, and she squinted, for her eyesight was poor whether she was trying to focus on something near at hand or far away. Indeed, she drew the fibers through her fingers, twisting the length between her thumb and forefinger without looking. The sunlight was for warmth. Despite the season, the old woman was always cold these days. "Ye're right, *ogha,* yer father's decision to send ye to England is not right, and how glad I am that ye chose to come to Annacurragh. Ye'll always have a home here. Besides yer pleasant company is better medicine for my aching bones than even the best mistletoe and valerian. But there is no pleasure in hearing ye tell me of this scheme of yers. Ye must take care," she warned again.

"It is no game I play, *seanmhair,*" Aislinn replied. She, too, had been spinning, and she paused in her work to wipe her greasy fingers on her kirtle skirt. The wool was unwashed, oily, and still smelled of sheep. Sir Roger Clare's daughter had arrived at Annacurragh seven days before. No one had used her English name in all that time. She was among her mother's people and was no longer Johanna Elizabeth. She was Aislinn as her Irish mother had named her. "I would not risk my future with game playing."

Grandmother MacMurrough turned her face toward Aislinn and smiled while her fingers kept twisting and threading the wool. "Ye're a bold lass—that ye are—and I'm seeing more and more of yer mother's determination in ye with each passing year. I'll never forget how it was when my Étaín made up her mind to marry yer da. The chieftains and their families were invited to celebrate the feast of St. John with the English earls. There we were in the great hall at Black Castle, Wicklow, and '*Mam,*' she said to me, pointing to a handsome young knight seated at the head table, '*'Tis my husband I've set my eyes upon this day.*' "

" '*Yer husband,*' I exclaimed in wonderment. '*And how do ye know he'll have ye?*' I asked, most curious. '*Well, I've made up my mind,*' yer mother, she said to me, as if no other explanation was necessary. She could feel in her heart that it was right, she told me, and being right it would come to pass. So tell me, young Aislinn, do ye have that same feeling? Are ye that certain of the path ye follow?"

"Aye, *Seanmhair,* I am that certain of what I do," she said. The awful suffocating feeling was gone. It had not bothered her once since leaving Killoughter, and with every new dawn at Annacurragh, she became more confident that her future would never be in England, but here in the Wicklow Mountains. She sensed it in the depth of her soul, and in the rush of her blood when she walked the green hills to stand on a rocky precipice, the wind tugging at her hair, and all the creatures of the bard's "Song of Summer" appeared before her. She knew this was where she belonged when she heard the dust-colored cuckoo calling to its mate, when she watched swallows encircling the peat mounds, and saw speckled fish leaping from silver waterfalls. She knew this when she gazed across oak forests that the English had not felled with their axes, and her heart swelled with joyful pride and satisfaction.

"My mind is made up. I'm going to marry Niall O'Connor. It will come to pass, and very soon, in fact. He is bound to be at the wedding, and once I see him again, I will be able to make my ambition one step closer to reality." The clans were gathering in the first week of May for the wedding of the O'Byrne chieftain to the widowed sister of the O'Connor chieftain, and a group of Aislinn's cousins had been invited to attend—two MacMurrough wives being sisters of the groom. Aislinn intended to accompany them. She had made a vow to see herself wed to an Irishman, but this chance to see Niall—so soon after her arrival at Annacurragh—made her think that she might fulfill that promise in shorter time than she had dreamed was possible. "Do not worry, *Seanmhair*. I have brought a plentiful supply of marigold and other herbs that can be used to secure a man's affection. I have not forgotten the lessons ye taught me, and I intend to be making good use of them when Niall O'Connor and I meet again."

The old woman laughed, a healthy rosy tint rising on her sunken cheeks. "Ye speak with much conviction, yet ye're not going to leave anything to chance. A wise girl, ye are, and if I did not know better, I would believe the pestilence never took my Étaín away. Och, it is good to have ye here, and good to know ye're not willing to let yer da send ye out of Ireland." She stopped twisting the wool and reached out a thin hand to pat Aislinn upon the forearm. "But why an O'Connor, lass?"

"Because Niall O'Connor said he would not bow to any English law. He said he would defy the statute for me, and once we are wed his family will protect me."

Marga frowned. "I would not be depending on that."

"What do ye mean?"

"O'Connors only wed pure Celt. Don't ye remember? It has always been that way and much trouble it has caused up and down the glens and hills for generations of lovers. Even if Niall were so bold to marry ye, I can't imagine their chieftain would accept ye."

"*Muir, air Muir*!" Aislinn exclaimed with indignant contempt. *Marry*! Somewhere in the back of her mind there was a dim recollection of an old and uncompromising O'Connor chieftain named Rourke. "Surely their chieftain has too many years and too many aches and pains of his own to meddle in the affairs of his clansmen."

"Nay, the O'Connor chieftain is young and very much involved in everything his clan does. Like his grandfather and countless generations of O'Connors before him, he has not forgotten it was a MacMurrough who brought the English to Ireland. I do not believe he would allow any O'Connor to marry a MacMurrough, let alone one whose father is English."

"The man ye describe must be as arrogant and pigheaded as the Parliament ever could be." Her features sharpened with the same scorn that tinged her voice.

"Of course, ye're right. The English are not the only bigots in Ireland, and it is well known that the

O'Connor chieftain is a bigot and a bastard. But that does not make it any less true. Bran O'Connor is a determined and dangerous man. When ye find Niall O'Connor again, the lad may not be as eager as ye'd like him to be. And if that happens, ye must not despair, *ogha*. There are many others who would be proud to take ye to wife. Would not one of yer MacMurrough cousins do? It would be much less complicated. Did ye not regard how pleased yer cousin Sean was to be seeing ye?"

"Och, *Seanmhair*, are ye telling me it was marriage on his mind when he greeted me with that devilish twinkle in his eyes? I think it was more likely that Sean was pleased to see me because, at last, he'll have the chance to get even with me for the time I blackened his eye."

Grandmother MacMurrough squinted at Aislinn. "Sean is a grown man, *ogha*, and he does not think of blackened eyes when he looks upon the likes of ye. There are other things on his mind."

"But, *Seanmhair*, I cannot consider Sean and such *other things* in the same thought. Sean is my first cousin. It is not seemly."

"That's the English in ye, sounding so prim." The old woman made a clackiting noise of disapproval with her tongue and shook her head. Her eyes were closed, and her mouth formed a frail smile. "There's nothing wrong with passion, *ogha*. It is healthy and pleasurable. Indeed, a man and woman should not marry unless the enjoyment between them is fervent and enthusiastic. There is an unquenchable fire between ye and Niall O'Connor, is there not?"

Aislinn was taken aback by this question. She stammered in reply, "Of—of course."

In truth, passion was not something she had considered when thinking about Niall O'Connor, and she tried to recall the details of their encounter. He was handsome, she had noted that, but how, she tried to recall, had he made her feel? She remembered relief that he had not hurt her, relief that the plan had started to form in her mind. But what of more intimate feelings? She could not recollect any. Instead, it was the dark Irishman in the courtyard at Dublin Castle she envisioned, and she trembled. This was not the first time his gaunt, masculine face had risen before her mind's eye. Her memories of him were sharp. She remembered how his arms had held her, how he had kissed her, the earthy taste upon his lips, and how she had enjoyed the way he felt, enjoyed the way he had made her feel. The sensation of his fingers upon her mouth and the taste of his blood came back to her. His touch had been rough; the taste had been salty sweet. Her mouth went dry, and her lips quivered as her hand rose to touch them. Slashes of bright red stained her complexion.

Her grandmother opened her eyes, took one look at Aislinn, and gave a bawdy wink. "Och, Aislinn, do not be worrying, lass. It is a fine thing to flush and tremble at the thought of the man ye will marry. It appears there is, indeed, fire between the two of ye, and in that case, I can do no less than wish ye luck and success. *Soirbheas leat, ogha,*" she bid her farewell with best wishes. *Good luck with ye, grandchild.* "Ye're to be having a wonderful time at the wedding feast, and when I see ye next, I expect to be hearing nothing but good news."

The clans met on the shore of a high mountain loch at a place known as Dysert, where an old monastic community clustered at the water's edge. Here and there, the dense oak forest had been cleared away to make space for massive granite crosses. More than twenty of them, carved with Celtic designs, and dedicated to one Irish saint or another, dotted the clearings around the loch. It was a sizeable settlement that had been built over more than seven hundred years, boasting several churches, a priory, and three holy wells. In a valley that dipped behind the priory, several mountain paths intersected, making Dysert accessible to the clans, especially for the O'Connors and the O'Byrnes—the families that had protected the religious community over the centuries, first from the Vikings and now from the English.

The wedding had been at midday on the steps of St. Finnian's Church, and the feasting and dancing, which had already been going on for several hours, would continue well into the night. Bonfires blazed against the darkening sky, woodsmoke flavored the air, and the music of flutes and drums, harps and pipes rippled between the mountains. Aislinn sat on a stump, a reserved onlooker in the crowd of several hundred men, women, and children, but it was not the bride and groom dancing about one of the bonfires that she watched. Instead, she scanned the sea of faces in search of Niall, and in the waning light of dusk, she caught sight of him. He was standing with a young woman, who was surely kin to the groom with the cream fair skin and coppery hair for which the O'Byrne women were well known. The redhead tugged upon Niall's tunic sleeve, but Aislinn could not hear what was being said, and she stood to get closer to them.

"Ye haven't heard a word I've uttered, Niall O'Connor," said Ceara O'Byrne, unaware that she was being watched. She gave his sleeve a second tug.

He mumbled something, but did not look at her.

"Niall," Ceara said in a firm voice. She hesitated as if she might berate him, but instead, her elfin face dimpled with a smile. "Niall," she said, gently, sweetly, "would ye marry me, Niall? And would ye find yer way beneath the hills to steal the faeries' gold for me?"

"Tá," he replied, vaguely aware that she had asked him a question. *Aye.*

"And would ye be getting me a stable of horses faster and sleeker than ye have at Baravore?" Her dimples deepened. She had never seen anyone as distracted as Niall was at that moment, and although she would rather have had his undivided attention, this really was amusing. "And would ye be telling my brother ye wish to live with me without the blessing of the church?"

"Anything ye want, Ceara," Niall spoke a bit more distinctly this time, but he was still looking beyond her. Lines furrowed his brow. His lips were tensed together as he stared across the bonfire at an empty stump. Sir Roger's daughter had been sitting on that stump. He was certain of it, and his eyes searched the crowd.

"Niall O'Connor!" Ceara gave him a jab in the ribs. "Do ye have any notion what it is ye've agreed to do?"

Niall startled, and turned to Ceara. He ran the fingers of both hands through the thick blond hair that threatened to tumble across his brow and eyes. A repentant, almost boyish expression softened his handsome features. "Sorry, Ceara. What were ye saying? Do ye want to join the dance?"

She laughed. It was impossible to get angry at Niall. She had known him too long and too well. "A dance would be nice, if I thought I had yer attention."

"I saw someone I knew, or, at least, I was thinking I did." He apologized again as they joined the line of men and women holding hands and moving in a giant serpentine pattern around the bonfires.

The tempo quickened. The dancers moved faster, and Niall thought he had another glimpse of Sir Roger's daughter. He imagined she was standing, this time, and staring at him through the blue-gold flames, her long, black tresses curling about her shoulders like a luxuriant cloak, shimmering in the firelight.

He had not forgotten her. He could not forget her as his brother had said he should, and this was not the first time he had conjured up her image. If someone laughed, he heard her. If a horse galloped across a meadow, he thought of how she had ridden like the wind. Indeed, he had developed the habit of comparing every other female to her. None of his sisters were as pretty, nor as self-assured. No one's hair was black enough, nor long enough. No one's eyes were as enchanting, as exotic. No other woman was as daring or as bold. Ceara was too fair of complexion, her hair too bright. Her sisters were too thin. There was no other female to compare to Sir Roger's daughter.

Around the second fire the couples coiled, faster yet, and then around a third fire, and a fourth. An outburst of merriment rumbled forth from one of the dancers, and the playful yelp was repeated up and down the line of dancers. Feet were skipping, hopping, entwined hands were held high, and bodies were twisting to the frenzy of flutes and drums. Then the music stopped. Just like that. And just as abruptly, the dancers stilled, speaking not a word as the final notes echoed across the glassy loch and into the silence of eternity. Only when the night sounds drifted out of the forest—crickets chirping in the bracken, frogs croaking at the water's edge, leaves rustling in tree tops, and the creak of great oaks bending with the wind—only then did the couples begin to disperse.

"Thank ye," Ceara, breathless and flushed, said to Niall. The crowd was moving toward a trestle table set with refreshments. "Are ye coming? There's chilled cider over there." But again, he did not acknowledge her. He was staring in the opposite direction, and although Ceara tried to see what he was watching, she was swept along with the others and saw nothing.

The crowd divided on either side of Niall, who was tall enough to see over most of their heads. There she was on the other side of the fire, and this time, he knew it was no figment of his imagination as he watched her come toward him, slowly, gracefully. Floating out of the darkness, wisps of smoke swirling about her, she was a goddess of the *Tuatha de Danann*, forever young, forever beautiful, possessing powers no man could resist. She was wearing a kirtle dyed the light blue tint of bilberry, a fox pelt was draped over her shoulders and slender arms. The blue fabric hugged her hips and waist, the bodice dipped low, and in the hollow between her breasts there rested an amulet of dried wildflowers entwined with colorful satin ribbons.

"Should I be believing my eyes?" he asked when she stood before him. "Or should I be begging the faeries to be kind to me, this night?"

"Believe yer eyes, Niall O'Connor, for I've never broken a promise," she said, her quiet words sounding like a whispered caress. "Don't tell me ye've forgotten about me already?"

"Nay. It would not be possible to forget ye." He took her hands in his. Thoughtfully, he turned them over, and stared down at them for a moment as if to reassure himself that she was flesh and bone before looking up to gaze once again into her dark eyes. "But how do ye come to be here and not at Killoughter with yer father?"

She explained the connection between her mother's family and the O'Byrnes. "Even if there had not been this wedding, I would have found ye while I was visiting my grandmother. I spoke the truth when I said we would meet again. I would have found ye and come to ye. Wherever that might have been."

"Ye would have crossed the mountains on yer own?" he teased, prompted by a sudden need to diffuse the unusual intensity he was feeling. He was right. She was not like the other young women. There was something about her that was almost mystical.

"*Ó tá,* Niall O'Connor, I would have done that for ye. *Aye.*"

"I've never known a woman like ye before. Ye're truly remarkable, Johanna Eliza—"

"*Ní hea*!" She set two fingers against his lips. *Nay*! "Ye must not be calling me that. My mother named me Aislinn, and that is what I have always preferred. It is what my MacMurrough kin call me, and is what ye should call me."

"Aislinn," he tried it out, thinking that the name proved that what he'd told Bran was true. She was more Irish than anything else. She was not one of them. "Aye, that's a perfect name, for I have dreamed of ye."

He gazed upon her with a gentle smile, but his expression abruptly altered when he saw his brother out of the corner of one eye. He tried to remain calm. "Come let us walk by the loch."

Aislinn readily agreed, for she, too, had seen him, no more than ten paces away, and her heart nearly stopped. In part from shock and surprise, and in part at the impressive sight he made. He was dressed in a tunic of the finest linen that brushed his knees. It was embroidered at the sleeves and hem with golden threads befitting a man of rank and wealth, the belt at his waist was of heavy leather, and the dagger sheathed therein was ornamented with two blood-red gemstones. He wore sandals that laced up his long, bare legs.

Evidently, he was a chieftain, and the notion tantalized her. She could not stop staring at him. He stood at an angle, his face in profile, and when he threw back his head in laughter something hanging about his neck attracted her eye. It was the upper half of a crucifix, specifically, a sculpture cast in silver of Christ's drooping head with the crown of thorns. It looked costly, heavy and old, and resting as it did against the muscled outline of his chest, it enhanced his overall appearance of being a man who wielded much power.

He was talking with a stocky older man and a woman with yellow braids. Aislinn knew the man. It was Rian O'Toole—everyone knew the oldest chieftain in Leinster—but she did not recognize the tall, flaxen-haired woman. She was beautiful, and she was flirting with Rian O'Toole.

"A walk by the loch?" Aislinn faltered, wishing that she had not wasted precious time with such a foolish reaction, and when Niall threaded his fingers through hers she found herself holding him tight. She wanted to get away before *he* had seen her. But it was too late. The woman was saying something, and he was turning toward her.

"Look, over there with Niall. *Cia hi an cailin sin?*" Bébinn asked. *Who is that girl?* "I'm not recognizing her."

Both Bran and Rian O'Toole glanced in the direction she indicated.

"I can't be telling ye her name, but a pretty lass, she is, *tá, cinnte,*" Rian O'Toole replied. *Aye, certainly.* "Though I seem to have some recollection of seeing her before, I can't be placing where it is that might have been. She came with the MacMurroughs which makes her some kind of kin to Dallán O'Byrne."

Rian O'Toole and Bébinn resumed their conversation, neither of them noticing the way Bran's expression was changing.

Bran's jaw locked with tension. What was Sir Roger's daughter doing here? He wondered if there was about to be some kind of retaliatory attack for the raid. Were English soldiers poised beyond the trees waiting for a signal to swoop down upon the merrymakers? His glance darted around the shore, over the bonfires and the crowd, along the edge of the dark woods, and back to her. He saw nothing suspicious except for the degenerate English creature with the wild dark curls talking with his brother.

Aislinn watched his facial features contort. He had seen her, and she did not like the way he was looking at her. The flames of the bonfire cast demonic shadows across the gaunt angles of his face, and she imagined that he was thinking about killing her with his bare hands. Her breath caught. Her heart was pounding. He stared at her as if she had done something wrong. Indeed, she had. She had stabbed him, and it did not matter what had gone before in Dublin. The darkening expression upon his face told her that he was going to exact retribution for using her dagger on him. That was his only memory. The animosity in his gaze burned as bright as one of the bonfires, and she knew that she had to leave. He was disturbing her in a way she did not understand, at once repellent and enthralling, and she turned to flee before he could reach her.

She raised a hand to her forehead. "Och, Niall, while I would love to walk alone with ye, my head is pounding something terrible. I would be a poor companion this night. Can we not be alone tomorrow? *Truly alone*?" she ended on a coaxing, and what she hoped was suggestive tone.

He swallowed his disappointment.

"There is an abandoned motte above the path that leads south to the Aughrim. Do ye know it?" asked Aislinn.

"Aye, I do. I will meet ye there."

"At noon," she said, and he agreed.

They hesitated as if they might kiss, but did not. Instead, they briefly clasped hands, and then she hurried into the crowd. He went toward the refreshments.

Bran saw her turn into the crowd, and for a moment, he was not sure whether to go after Niall or her. Reasoning that he had already warned Niall, he went after her to do the same. At the edge of the gathering, she moved out of the light of the bonfire, and began to make her way down a gentle hillside. He followed, lengthening his strides. She was not going to get away before he had his say. He saw her glance over her shoulder, and, sensing that she was about to bolt into the woods, he ran the final paces that separated them, and reached out to grab her. He seized her wrist.

"No!" she cried, struggling to free her one hand while she tried to reach her dagger with the other.

He saw what she was trying to do and spoke harsh and hard, "Don't ye dare try yer knife on me again."

"Let go of me then." Her voice was amazingly steady, defiant.

"Quiet," he ground out, and yanked her to him, pulling her up against his body. He stood behind her, his arms locked about her waist, walking her into the shadows of the black woods. The fox pelt had fallen to the ground somewhere behind them. She smelled clean and fresh, and he could not stop himself from inhaling as he forced her legs to move with his. The sweet scent of crushed rose petals filled his nostrils, and he became aware that she was trembling. His mind drifted. He remembered the first time he had touched her, and his body reacted to the memory. A jolt of lust exploded in his loins, engorging him, tempting him, enraging him. In anger, he halted, and jerked her sharply as if it would shake off the memory and extinguish the desire warming his blood. "Don't move or make a sound."

"What do you want?" she asked, finding it very hard to speak. Her breath was unusually shallow. The aura of him was overwhelming. Indeed, it frightened her. She could not see his face, but she felt his breath upon her neck.

"Stay away from Niall O'Connor," he whispered from behind. His lips were very close to the sensitive flesh below her ear. She trembled, and he sharpened his voice. "Did ye hear what I said? Stay away," he hissed. "Ye don't belong here."

She had never heard such hatred. Surely this hostility was not because of the wound she'd inflicted upon him; the dagger probably had not penetrated deep enough to require stitching. But his anger was a palpable thing, and she tilted her face to search his eyes for another reason. He had deep-set, hard eyes. She inhaled sharply. Demon eyes. Blood thrummed through her, and a dizzying tension crackled between them. She should get away. It wasn't safe here. But his arms held her captive.

"Ye should not be among us. Go away." His lips feathered against the corner of her mouth that was so close, too close to his, and he shut his eyes as if to deny the tremor that wracked his body. His arms tightened about her waist. He couldn't stop himself. He rocked forward into her buttocks, splayed his hands across her stomach, and he ran them down the front of her thighs as he leaned his face into the column of her neck, letting his mouth brush against her soft skin.

Aislinn gasped. It was more of a little moan of pleasure at the quiver of sensation flickering through her. His massive manhood was pressed against her, and there was no stopping the languid melting that radiated from the core of her. It was so new. So strange. So powerful. Her legs weakened, but she wasn't afraid as she gave in to the unknown. She had heard of the uncontrollable passions a man could ignite in a woman, and she surrendered to the natural. Her head fell back, one cheek resting against his shoulder, and her lips parted in expectation as his mouth hovered closer to hers.

"Damn ye," he whispered. His lips caressed her bare skin with each syllable. He was pulsing, aching. He had warned his brother against her, but he had not warned himself. She had haunted him, and now here she was in the flesh to torment him as she had been doing in his dreams. "Damn ye," he murmured, one hand slid up her torso to hold her chin, his fingers brushing against a silken black curl that had tumbled across her cheek. She was deliciously warm and soft, and he angled her face away from his shoulder.

Their eyes made contact again. She sucked a deep gulp of air and moistened her lips with a lick of her tongue. She heard him swear beneath his breath as his fingers moved from her chin to her shoulders, and, spellbound, she did not resist when he twisted her around in his arms until they faced one another.

Up the hill, the musicians began another song. This one was not a lively dance, but a lilting ballad. The rhythm was deliberate and carnal, the drummer striking his *bodhran* in an unhurried, pulsating cadence, the harper producing a thin, high vibrating melody, and, holding her waist with both hands, Bran began to sway to the sensual tempo.

Aislinn moved with him. She had forgotten all about Niall. She forgot everything except the way his muscled thighs pressed against hers, and the way the music wrapped about them. He leaned to one side, she went with him, smoothly, deliberately, and with each erotic strain of harp song, his arms about her waist tightened by increments as they seemed to melt into one another. His heart was pounding against her breast, and she heard the wild beating of her own. It was so natural. Their bodies were pressed together tightly, and she was acutely aware of the masculine bulge pulsing between her legs. She raised her head, and their eyes locked together.

"Damn ye to hell and back," he ground out. It was a cry of surrender, wrenched from him as if in great pain. He didn't want to do this, but there was no way to stop himself any more than he could stop his lungs from taking the air they needed. "Damn ye," he repeated on a moan.

"No!" she cried out, but she was not certain whether she was denying his words or his touch. She did not want him to say such things to her. Not now. It wasn't right. No man should touch a woman with such intimacy while giving voice to such contrary thoughts. "No!" she said a second time, but it was too late.

His mouth swooped down to claim hers.

There was nothing tender about his kiss. It was hard and bruising as if he sought to punish her. His mouth plundered hers, his tongue forcing her lips apart, tasting, delving, stroking as he molded the full length of his body against hers. His loins pressed harder, more insistently against her. He felt her arch against him, heard her moan. Her hands were in his hair, her tongue was meeting his, and still, he needed more.

He moved them toward a tree, where he leaned her back against the massive trunk. Her legs were parted, slightly bent, and he positioned himself between them to rock his straining desire up against her female parts, still kissing her, still delighting in her moans and eager, willing responses. He moved against the cradle of her, simulating the sex act, and wondered if beneath the material that now came between them she was ready for him. One hand moved downward to caress the length of her thigh, then slipped upward beneath the hem of her kirtle. The garment had rucked about her knees, and when he touched bare skin she moaned again.

"A mhorair, bheagan a bheagan, tha tighinn fodham," Aislinn murmured in a throaty, impetuous whisper. *My lord, little by little, I am resolved.* The meaning of those words in Irish implied that she was *under his command.* She was not certain what to do next, but she would do whatever he asked. The longing within her was unbearable.

Like a sudden, unwanted awakening from a wonderful dream, Bran heard her sultry, ardent words and crashed to earth. He pulled his mouth from hers. They stared at each other. The only sound between them was their rapid, shallow breathing, and he remembered what she had said at Dublin Castle. *For a night, I would do anything,* and he knew that it was as true now as it had been then.

He could have her here up against the tree, beside

the pebbled beach, or on the bracken-covered forest floor. He could have her panting, moaning, thrashing beneath him, and he took a backward step for a fuller look at the sight of her wide, passion-clouded eyes, her heaving breasts, and bruised lips. She would do anything for him, and it was not right. She was not one of them, and he should not be kissing her, nor touching her with the intimacy of a lover. What was wrong with him that he had so little control? He disgusted himself.

With the back of his hand he wiped away any trace of her kiss from his mouth.

Aislinn gasped. He could not have insulted her more deeply. The message was clear, and she raised a hand to slap him.

He caught her wrist. "Nay, just leave. And don't come back." He stepped aside from the tree to let her pass.

Scalding tears threatened to spill down Aislinn's cheeks. She could not let him see her pain, and quickly, she glanced downward as her shaking hand straightened her kirtle hem in readiness to leave as he'd commanded.

Her heart was aching when she fled. She did not know his name or by what right he gave her such orders. She knew only that she hated him for his cruelty, and although she would never see him again, she would never be able to forget him.

Chapter 6

"At last, ye arrive, Niall!" Aislinn greeted. She had been waiting for him in their trysting place, a pretty clearing beside a waterfall.

"Were ye worried?"

"A little," she confessed.

"I'm sorry." Niall had seen Aislinn like this before and did not like to think he had made her worry when there was no reason to be concerned. He smiled in reassurance.

"It does not matter. Ye're here." She offered him a wine-skin that had been in the pool below the falls to chill its contents. "Ye must be thirsty after yer long trek. This will quench ye. Come sit beside me and rest yerself, now. *An òl thu so?" Will ye drink this?*

"Olaidh." I will drink. Niall nodded his thanks. He accepted the plump pouch, and sat down. Stretching his lanky legs before him, he tilted back his head, and drank long and deep of the golden liquid that streamed from the skin.

At last, Aislinn was able to relax. She smiled, especially pleased to see Niall imbibing so generously of the beverage she had prepared.

He wiped his mouth with the back of his arm.

"Were ye worried I would not make it today?"

"Nay, ye're a man of yer word, I know that," Aislinn replied. She had arrived at this secluded glen almost two full hours before Niall, and in anticipation of his arrival, she had spread a woolen blanket at a relatively dry distance from the misty falls. There was cheese and bread and berries, which she had carried in a small sack and had set upon the blanket. "I know ye'll not let me down," she said as much for herself as for him.

While Aislinn had not worried that Niall wouldn't meet her as they had agreed, she was concerned that their relationship was not developing quickly enough. They had been together twice while the clans were at Dysert, and since then they had been meeting every three or four days at this spot, situated a little less than two hours' distance between Baravore and Annacurragh. By now, Aislinn had hoped Niall would have proposed marriage.

Her plan seemed to be advancing well. She had succeeded in making him remember her when they were apart; she had succeeded in making him desire her, but somehow she had not got quite right the way one makes a man think of marriage and romance in the same breath. Indeed, with each visit it seemed Niall became more and more interested in one thing and one thing only. Carnal pleasure.

Ultimately, he would propose to her. Aislinn could not allow herself to doubt that, but she was not pleased with the time this required. Within a sennight her father would send an escort to Annacurragh for her, and she must be wed before then. She must be gone. There was no time to waste on matters of the flesh. Thus it was that she had prepared a special cordial of cowslip for Niall this day. The sweet golden liquid, while generally used by housewives to cure memory loss, was known to have other unique affects upon a man's mind. It took one's mind off distractions; it was even claimed to make a man amenable to actions he might usually avoid. To enhance the potency of the wine, Aislinn had added a touch of cyclamen, and lastly, a pinch of powdered briony root—not too much, for its bitter taste could be easily detected—to guarantee that Niall would focus on nothing but her, in particular upon any suggestions that she might impart to him. Now she encouraged him to drink some more.

"Pleasant taste, it is. Sweet, but refreshing," he commented as the liquid went from cold to warm in his mouth, and then to hot as it went down his throat, producing a sensation of well-being that spread through his chest, and then burst upward into his head. It was strong stuff, and Niall, feeling thoroughly untroubled by anything beyond this precise moment, leaned back on bent elbows to admire Aislinn.

Her moist red lips were parted slightly, he was certain, in invitation to be kissed, and the column of her throat—so slender, so smooth, so unblemished—begged to be caressed. She was the loveliest creature he had ever seen, and it was a wonder that she wanted him. "Ye're looking particularly luscious today. Might I be having a kiss from a lass so fair?"

She smiled, then gave in to a ripple of light laughter born of sheer delight. Flirtatious and happy and entirely satisfied with this turn of events, she was. This morning, she had sewn three silver coins in her kirtle hem. *One for pretty praise,* the charm claimed. *Two for a kiss, and three for a wish.* And as her grandmother had taught her, Aislinn had recited the spell each time she had sewn a coin into the hem.

One was hers already; he had offered her pretty

praise. Two was soon to be reality; he had asked for a kiss, and she would allow it. So Aislinn concentrated on number three, wishing for a marriage proposal from Niall O'Connor as she shut her eyelids, puckered her lips, and leaned forward to brush her mouth against his.

"Och, lass, 'tis a real kiss I'm wanting from yer pretty lips," Niall said. He rolled toward Aislinn, taking her with him so that she lay on the woolen blanket beneath him. He stared down at her, and murmured, "A real kiss, and much more than that, my vision, my dream, my lovely Aislinn."

He kissed her eagerly, his hands framing her face, his fingers caressing her skin. There was nothing harsh or demanding in the way he nibbled the soft flesh of her neck, his mouth moving lower to the expanse of skin exposed above the bodice of her kirtle. One hand left her face to fondle her breast, and his mouth worked its way nearer as if he might kiss her there.

"I am a maid, Niall," Aislinn protested quietly. Niall aroused none of the sensations she'd experienced when the dark Irishman kissed her. It was easy to keep her wits and stay focused on her purpose this day. She tried to get away from Niall's embrace.

"Have a heart, Aislinn." His voice was hoarse. He lay atop her, and rested his forehead against hers. His breathing was ragged. "Ye're such a fair wonder, and I ache for ye. Do ye not feel how I ache for ye?" He took her hand in his, and, slipping it between them, he cupped her palm along the length of his swollen arousal.

Aislinn snatched her hand away. She would not, could not let Niall take her until she was certain that her future with him was secured. What if all he wanted was this? She could not take the risk that once he'd had her the attraction would diminish, and he would become bored with her. She knew men could be like that. Potions and infusions, incantations and magic aside, such disinterest had been known to happen even when ordinarily reliable spells were used. His thick blonde hair had fallen forward to touch her face, and she threaded her fingers through it, pushing it off his brow. She tilted her face and leaned upward a tiny bit to whisper in his ear, "Ye must be patient and understanding, Niall. Do ye not remember what ye said to me when ye chased after me and pulled me off my horse?"

"And what would that be?" he asked, although he had not forgotten. Indeed, he remembered far too clearly while he had hoped against all odds that she had forgotten.

"Ye said a man would be blessed to spend his life with a woman like me."

He closed his eyes momentarily, cursing his foolish tongue for getting away from him. While he had not lied, it had been stupid to speak of things that could never be.

"And ye said that ye would defy the statute for me."

He raised his head and gazed at her, wishing that she would understand. He did not want to hurt her. "And am I not doing so as we speak? Are we not meeting in defiance of the statute? Is this love-making between us not forbidden?"

"But—but," dared she speak aloud what was in her mind? Had the cowslip achieved its full effect? Would the third coin deliver its magic promise? She had no choice. She thought of England and the future that her father intended for her. She must speak. "But I want more than trysts and love-making, Niall. I have been saving myself for my husband, and I would like that man to be ye."

"Ye're saying ye want to marry me?" He had been afraid of this since that first afternoon they'd met near Dysert. There was an intensity about her that he found both enthralling and disturbing. He was flattered that she was attracted to him, but at the same time, it was unsettling. She was different from Ceara and the other young women who had sought his favors. She lacked their youthful quality, and instead, there was an intense determination about her. While being the object of such undivided attention was enjoyable, he couldn't deny the suspicion that from the start she had wanted something from him.

"Aye, Niall O'Connor, I wish to make a life with ye."

Something in his chest constricted, and he rolled off of her. Of course, she would be a fine wife, and he would be the envy of many a man with a beautiful woman who bore him healthy children and gave him happiness as well as loyalty and pleasure. But marriage with Sir Roger Clare's daughter—no matter what she called herself—was not possible. He took a deep breath, and forced himself to look at her. "I cannot marry ye, Aislinn. And it is not the statute that prevents me."

"What is it then?" She moved into a kneeling position, sitting back on her legs, which were folded beneath her. "Why can't ye marry me?"

"My brother would not allow it."

Her lips pursed together in a thin, tight line. She tried to remain pleasant, but could not keep the cross tone from coloring her speech. "This is not the first time ye mention yer brother. Who is this paragon to be lording over yer life? Is it not yer own to live as ye wish without a brother's meddling?"

"He is my elder brother, and the head of our clan." Niall pushed himself up in a similar kneeling pose in order to speak with her face to face. "But most important of all, he is the O'Connor chieftain."

Cold dread washed over Aislinn even though she was thinking of that warm afternoon in the women's bower at Annacurragh with her grandmother. "He is the O'Connor chieftain who hates the English?"

"Aye. And MacMurroughs. And degenerate English," he added in a voice so low she had to lean toward him in order to catch what he said.

"Am I lost then?" the question was torn from her in quiet desperation. Could the coins have played her false? How could the cowslip and briony have failed? She had one last ploy, and she searched Niall's eyes, hoping that it might work. If it didn't, then she was doomed, for she had run out of both ideas and charms. The quiver in her chin was genuine. Niall was her hope for the future, and she could not bear to consider the alternative. "Are ye saying there is no future for us?" Her voice was pitiful, verging on desperate. "For me? Have I no hero to champion me?"

Of a sudden, Niall's resolve faltered. By the blood of the holy martyrs, he had been trying to remain aloof. He had been trying to do the right thing by his brother, trying to live up to what was expected of him, but those woeful words too easily pierced his defenses. More than the promise of a wedding night of sexual bliss with a woman who had saved herself for him, it was the appeal to his sense of fairness that swayed him. In this regard, Niall was much like his grandfather, Rourke, who'd always had a protective, tender consideration for the weaker sex. With that wretched little speech, she touched that same chord within Niall, and it rekindled the concern he'd voiced to Bran, and which lingered in the back of his mind whenever he thought of her.

What happens to a woman like that? Who will accept her? Half-Irish, half-English. Where will she have a future?

"Is there no place in Ireland for me?" Aislinn sensed this strategy was getting through to him, and she drove the point home. "For us? Is there no place where the English and men like yer brother do not reign all powerful?"

"There is the west," he said, playing into her plan. "There is Connaught."

On the other side of Ireland, it was different from Leinster, where the Irish were at war with the English, and very different from the Vale of Dublin, where intolerance prevailed. It was a place where the two races got along rather well. Indeed, it was the sort of place that had posed such a threat to English rule that the Parliament at Kilkenny passed their infamous statute.

"What kind of life would we have there?"

"A better one than here."

"And what would we do there?" she asked very deliberately.

Time slowed in that instant. Niall saw Aislinn's hopeful, expectant face, and the golden sunshine and blue sky of the afternoon faded away; the rapid tattoo of his heart pounded against his chest, it resounded in his ears. The dizzying sensation from the beverage returned.

This was a moment he would remember for always. He did not hear the crash of the nearby waterfall, he heard only her bleak question, *Am I lost?* The prospect of Aislinn being abandoned and alone without a hero—as she phrased it—was a tragic thing to consider. One had only to watch her wade through a stream, skirts rucked about her knees, the wind blowing her hair, to hear her infectious laughter or her pretty voice singing an Irish lullaby, or to ride with her across an open meadow to know that she had a spirit that could never be caged. A spirit that needed fulfillment, that needed to savor and taste and enjoy the whole of life. To put allegiance to his brother's bigotry before her future made him think of plucking the wings from a magnificent butterfly.

Aye, here was a moment Niall would never forget, for it would define him from this time forward, distancing him from the world he knew best. Slowly, thoughtfully, he made his choice, and the words came out of him:

"We would have a life as man and wife. We could elope, and go to Connaught, where my O'Connor cousins would welcome us."

There, at last, it had been said! Aislinn exhaled a pent-up breath. Praise be to all the virgin saints, she would be marrying Niall O'Connor as she had hoped, as she needed to do. She would not be leaving Ireland, and Aislinn started to cry tears of relief.

"What is wrong?" he asked, bewildered.

"There's nothing wrong. Everything is right. Perfect. It couldn't be better. Ye've made me happier than ye could ever know. There is nothing I would rather do than elope with ye, Niall, and go to live with yer cousins in the west. And since I take it this is yer way of proposing, my answer is aye. I will marry ye, and thank ye for making me so happy, for giving me so much."

Niall couldn't believe his ears. He had brought this woman such happiness that she cried as she thanked him, and a great sense of masculine power swelled within him. He was doing the right thing. "We could set out in three or four days' time," he said, thinking that he needed to explain this to his mother, who was certain to give them her blessing.

"Why not tomorrow?" she asked.

"Why so soon?" he rejoined.

She could not tell him that she was afraid he might change his mind. "There is no one else to include in our plans. Why should we wait? What is there to delay our wedding night?"

Niall grinned, his head was swimming with visions of kissing her once they were wed. Visions of much more. Her eagerness was pleasing and contagious. This was the kind of woman of whom most men only dreamed, and she was going to be his. "Tomorrow then, it will be," he said quickly, committing himself before some dark image of his brother could rise up to argue with him.

They made plans to meet before noon at an abandoned ringfort that was some miles northwest of Croghan Kinsella. Niall gave her detailed instructions on how to get there and told her that since it was a greater distance for him and through more rugged terrain, she should not worry if he was late again. He would not let her down; he would be there.

"Should we not seal our betrothal with a kiss?" she asked when it was time to part. Niall O'Connor was a kind man, and she would be a good wife, Aislinn vowed as she remembered her parents, and how they had always been at each other's side through both the joyful and the sad. Aislinn recalled how deeply they had valued their family and children; how they had shared such joy and satisfaction in the life they had built together. She could make a worthy life with Niall as her parents had done. He deserved no less, for he was offering her a future worth living. She would devote herself to him, and standing on tiptoe to kiss him on the mouth, she silenced the little voice whispering from the darkest recess of her mind.

What about a man who would cherish ye for the unseen bonds between yer souls?

She scolded herself not to be greedy. She would not be going to England. She was going to stay with her mother's people. She was going to have the music of pipes and harps, the joy of dancing barefoot around bonfires in a land where one's soul could be forever young. That would be more than enough. It had to be, she told herself.

Niall returned her kiss, and when they stood he helped her fold the woolen blanket.

"Would ye wear this tonight?" she asked, pulling an amulet of dried flowers from the pocket of her kirtle. She had prepared, been clever, thoughtful, and wise in her plans to wed Niall O'Connor, but nothing would come of it if she did not have good luck. There was a saying, *It is better to be lucky than wise,* and Aislinn intended to heed that adage this night. The amulet, shaped like a star, was made of the marigolds she had plucked in the walled garden at Killoughter, woven together with strands of her hair. A man could not forget a promise to a maid if he wore such a token containing her hair, and made by her hand. "It will keep ye from harm through the night, and bring ye safely back to me."

"*Rachaidh, go deimhin, le cuidiu Dé.*" Niall accepted the amulet. *I will, indeed, please God.* It was attached to a strip of leather. He slipped it over his head. "There. Now nothing will stop me from returning to ye."

"Ye must not be too hard on yer brother," said Bébinn. It was late afternoon, six hours since they had realized Niall had gone without apprising anyone of his plans, and it was not the first time in the past weeks that he had disappeared without a word of explanation. Bébinn and Bran were in the women's bower, where she was taking advantage of the last hour of good light to finish weaving the basket she'd started that morning. "Please for my sake, Bran, can ye not go easy on him?"

Bran scowled. He did not like to disappoint his mother, but he resented it when she took up for Niall, which seemed to be more and more frequently. Niall was Bébinn's babe, the youngest, her last child, and it had always seemed to Bran that she had protected Niall more than she ever had him. Niall was like her other children, fair-haired O'Connors with blue eyes and a square Irish jaw. Bran was the only one of her offspring to have the looks of their Scottish kin with high cheekbones, gaunt features, deep brooding, green eyes, and ink-black hair that were distinctly Kirkpatrick characteristics. Somehow his different looks set him apart from the others. It was, he always thought, the reason he had been his grandfather Rourke's favorite, for he bore a resemblance to his beloved wife, Viviane, and his cousin, Alexander, who were both Kirkpatricks. By that same token, Bran had reasoned his dark features were the reason why his mother treated him differently.

"I do not ask of Niall anything that I do not expect of myself," Bran said brusquely.

"Perhaps, then, it is that ye're too hard on yerself. Perhaps, yer standards are too high."

"A warrior's standards can never be too high. *Bi sambach, st!*" he admonished her. *Keep yer silence*! This was one of those times when he was worlds apart from his mother. He swore at her beneath his breath. "What does a woman know of such things? Especially a woman who would flirt shamelessly with Rian O'Toole. It was a mighty spectacle ye created of yerself at Dysert."

Bébinn stared at her son. He had a tender heart—somewhere deep inside—and she despaired of ever discovering how to release it. "I am a woman, not a nun."

"Ye're a grandmother!"

"And ye're unfair and mean-spirited. Have ye never given any thought to my widow's lot? What it must be like for me? How it must pain me to be surrounded by others who have what I lost when I was but twenty years old?"

"Forgive me, Mam." Bran had the grace to be ashamed. "I do know of what ye speak. Indeed, I have wondered why it is ye never remarried. But O'Toole? And why now after all these years? He may be respected, but that's only because he's feared, and he may be powerful, but that's only owing to his reckless nature. I do not picture ye with a man such as that. Besides, he is too old for ye."

"Who else, then? Oh, Bran, don't be so serious," she quickly amended, knowing not whether to laugh or frown at her son. "My question is no more real than was there any serious intent in the flirtation. It was all in good fun. Nothing more. I was merely enjoying myself." She smiled, in part at the pleasant memory of her daughter's wedding, and in part with satisfaction at the basket she had just completed. She set it aside, and began to make a frame for another one in the same low oval shape. They would be perfect for serving loaves of bread, fresh from the ovens.

Bran watched her for a few minutes before speaking. "Will ye back me up with Niall?"

"*Ciod rinn e air dhochair*?" she asked. *What fault has he committed*?

"As sure as a granary attracts rats, he's been sneaking off to meet Sir Roger's daughter somewhere in the hills. By the rood, think on it, Mam, he might already have planted a little bastard in her. Part English, part Irish. What then, Mam?"

"As ye have reminded me I am a grandmother, and I have always loved each of my grandchildren equally. Thus it is that I should love this one as much as the others."

He swore again, this time in a louder voice. "How can it be that ye're willing to let him ruin everything?"

"Surely, this is not as dire as ye make it out. I do not see mountains crumbling to the sea, or devils rising up from the loch."

"What about English marching down the length of Glenmalur?"

Bébinn was silent for a moment, thoughtful. "I do not think Sir Roger would do that."

"And what pray tell do ye know of the workings of Sir Roger's mind?" he rejoined in contempt.

She glanced at her lap, concentrating on twisting the shiny green lengths of supple water reed about the twig frame. When she spoke she did not answer his question. "No matter what ye have to say, the fact is that I can't refuse one of my children, if there is love involved."

Bran stared at his mother in disbelief. He knew what Sir Roger's daughter was like, and he suspected there was not much *love* between her and his brother. "I know about women like her, Mam, and I've no doubt there is much lust, where she is involved, but not love," he said in a bitter scornful voice. "Mayhap Niall has been foolish enough to have mistaken such emotions for love. Indeed, that is my fear: that Niall will be losing his head to the wench."

"Men lose their heads in love," Bébinn said as if it were the most natural thing in the world. "Indeed, that is the way of love, and sometimes there is a happy ending, sometimes there is tragedy. But the worst tragedy would be to turn away from the chance to know real love."

"Even if that love is against everything a man has been taught to uphold?" the question was torn from Bran in a weary voice. He wanted to be the kind of chieftain that Rourke had been. He wanted to instill the same sense of pride and commitment that Rourke had imparted to him in his brother and nephews, and maybe, one day, in his sons.

Bébinn knew what Bran meant, and she wanted to comfort him. She did not want to argue. Above all else she wanted him to understand and to change; she wanted him to have someone who would miss him when he was gone and who would be waiting for him to return. "I was not raised an O'Connor. I do not believe those things are more important than love. I think a body must know love—must surrender to the powers of love—before he can accomplish other things. Does that shock ye, now? Do ye think me a bad person? A Judas in yer midst for all these years?"

"Sometimes, Mam, I do not know what to think." He stared at nothing in particular as he spoke, a strained expression making his features sharper, more gaunt. "Ever since I can remember I have wanted one thing: to make certain that the O'Connors did not surrender to the English, that they were at the fore of the fight to drive them out of Ireland. It was what Rourke wanted, and he passed that burning ambition on to me. There are two things I must do: protect the O'Connors, and drive the English into the sea. I consider that a sacred trust, a vow not only to Rourke, but to future generations of O'Connors. Yet each time I think of Niall, all I can see is that I'm failing."

"Och, *ni hea*! My son, ye must not be talking like that. *Nay*. It near tears my heart to breaking to hear ye talk of failure." She lay a maternal hand upon his cheek and spoke very softly. "Yer grandfather Rourke was a remarkable chieftain. They will be singing ballads about him for a hundred years or more, and I can think of no higher ambition than to strive to match his footsteps. But there were other things that were important to Rourke."

She stroked his cheek, wishing that he had not come to this. "Rourke was well satisfied. He died a contented man, owning a rare inner peace, and while he knew his work was not done, he believed he'd done his best. Above all else, he would want ye to have that same satisfaction. Yer grandfather wanted yer days on this earth to be rich with fulfillment. He would not want one of his grandsons to be an incomplete and miserable soul. He would not want ye to be troubled with self-doubt. Such a tormented man is no good to anyone. A man must be true to his heart first, then he is ready to serve his clan."

"But what of the statute? If we allow Niall to follow his heart, he could be putting Baravore in jeopardy."

"To that I have no answer. But what value is there in life without risk? What value do ye have in family, hearth, and home, if there was never any struggle to gain or hold it?"

From the woods beyond the fortress walls there came a series of hoots, the signal that someone was approaching. Bran rose. It must be Niall. He had been away all day. Too much time. Enough time to get himself in trouble. The last thing they needed was Sir Roger bringing a party of men-at-arms into the glen in search of his daughter. What was wrong with his mother that she did not understand this?

Bébinn set her hand on Bran's forearm. "Be fair with him."

"I'll try," Bran said, wanting to make her happy. If

there was anyone he loved, it was Bébinn, not only because she was his mother, but for all the things that she was and that he could never be. While he had the tendency to be negative, she always saw a positive aspect to anyone or any situation; she moved with grace and laughter; she was generous to a fault. Most of all, she was forgiving, something which he found extremely difficult, if not impossible, to be. For those reasons he loved her, and loving her, he wanted to please her. But as Bran stepped into the bailey he thought of how Niall had intentionally defied him, and it was impossible to control his anger.

"Niall!" he roared. The portcullis was being lowered. Niall had entered, and since there was no sight of him in the bailey, there could only be one place he might have gone. Swiftly, Bran ascended the stairs in the gate tower, calling out his brother's name. He went to the chamber above the armory, where the unmarried clansmen lived, and there Bran found Niall, sorting through a pile of furs and blankets.

"What do ye want?" Niall asked in a cold, impersonal voice. He did not look up from what he was doing.

Bran crossed the chamber, grabbed Niall's tunic collar, and jerked him upright. "For starters, I want ye to look at me when I'm talking." Niall glared at him, hostility burning like a fire in his eyes, and although he did not open his mouth to speak, Bran smelled the cloying scent of cowslip and briony upon his breath. He swore violently. "In the name of St. Cieran, ye were with that witch, and she has drugged ye!"

"Curse ye, Bran, *sios dh'ifrinn is abair gur mise a chuir ann thu!*" he growled. *Down to hell, and say I sent ye.* "Ye'll not be talking of her like that."

"What have ye been drinking?" Bran demanded, and then an odd thing happened. The scent of cowslip and briony faded to be supplanted by the unbidden sensorial memory of crushed rose petals, of luxuriant hair, and warm, soft skin. Had she bewitched him, too, that his memory might sense her with such vividness? He scowled at his brother.

"Nothing. Ye smell nothing," Niall mumbled, trying to avoid eye contact with Bran. He did not like the control his brother could exert over him, and knowing that he made the right choice, Niall wanted nothing to taint his determination.

"And I'm King Edward, and ye're the Holy Roman Emperor," Bran retorted in mockery. "Are ye an idiot, Niall?"

"This is none of yer affair."

Bran thought of how easily she had widened her legs for him, how she molded herself to him. Had his brother had her? Had Niall taken her in the forest against a tree? The thought incensed him, and he snarled, "It will be my business when ye get her belly swelling up with a little bastard."

"It is not like that between us."

He found that impossible to believe. He knew how quickly she responded to a man, how ardent she was. *"Cha 'n 'eil innte ack an dearg shiùrtach,"* he condemned her with the cruel bitter words. *She is nothing but an arrant whore.*

"Nay, Bran, she is no whore. She is saving herself for her husband, and there will be no bastards. We are going to marry."

Bran felt as if the air had been sucked out of his lungs. There was a ringing in his ears as Niall's declaration echoed over and over. *We are going to marry.* He shook his head to stop its repetition. "Marry her? By God, ye'll be doing no such thing," he ordered.

"We will," Niall shot back as Bran again grabbed hold of his tunic and jerked him sideways twice before Niall managed to break himself free of his hold and moved out of reach.

"*An raibh sé chomh maith sin, anois*?" came Bran's insult. *Was it as good as that, now*?

Niall refused to acknowledge his implication. "Aye, we will marry. And ye'll not be telling me what I can and can't be doing."

"But ye're wrong, Niall," Bran said, his low voice steady and full of threat. He advanced toward his brother and shoved him hard against the chest with the flat of his hand, throwing him off balance and forcing him to take a step backward. "I *can* tell ye what to do, and I will." Bran gave Niall another short, hard shove. "Ye'll be listening to me, Niall, and ye'll be listening well." With a third shove, he had pushed Niall up against the wall. The marigold amulet fell from the leather cord, and crumbled into pieces as it dropped to the floor. Neither of the men noticed it beneath their feet. "Ye can't marry her."

"I can, and I will."

"I won't let ye."

"How do ye propose to be stopping us?" he demanded, standing square and defiant, almost provoking.

Bran's response was quick and powerful. He punched Niall in the stomach.

Niall doubled over with a groan.

"Don't make me do it again," Bran said. "I want a promise from ye, Niall, a solemn oath that ye'll stop this foolishness. For the sake of Baravore and everyone living here. Stealing horses is one thing. Why it's almost accepted; certainly, it's expected of the Irish. But stealing daughters is another thing altogether. Could ye live with yerself, let alone die with a clear conscience, if the heads of yer clansmen decorated the town walls of Dublin? And for nothing more than a whore?"

Niall bellowed like a wounded beast as he straightened up, and swung an arm, his fist impacting on Bran's jaw. "Call her whore again, and I'll kill ye. Brother or no, I'll take yer life with my bare hands."

Bran delivered another punch, stronger than before, this time to Niall's face, and the unmistakable crunch of bone reverberated through the chamber.

"Aargh," Niall sputtered. "Ye broke it! Damn ye!" Blood was gushing from his nose.

The brothers faced one another, bent arms poised for a fight, fists clenched, moving warily from side to side, each eyeing the other with caution, and waiting for the moment to make the best move.

"I want to hear ye tell me ye'll stay away from her. Tell me that ye won't marry her."

"Never. By this time tomorrow we'll be wed."

Bran made a sudden move, punching Niall first in the face, then in the belly, then the face again. They were not evenly matched. Bran, having won the warrior's prize three years running at the harvest festival, had repeatedly proven himself a better fighter than Niall. By now, Niall could hardly hold up his head. He was swaying from side to side on unsteady legs. Bran stood over him, and, taking hold of his hair, he pulled his brother's bloodied face close to his. "Where will ye be meeting her?"

Niall's eyes were swelling closed, his nose was broken, and one of his teeth was loose. There was a burning in his torso where Bran had pummeled him. His head was throbbing, he could barely think except for one thing: he didn't want to fail Aislinn entirely. "I cannot fail her. She will be waiting for me."

"Waiting for a man who's in no shape to travel?" Bran scorned. "I'm thinking that most unlikely."

"Ye may not understand my concern for her. But I would not want her to believe she'd been abandoned or to worry that some ill had befallen me. She will be there and must not be left waiting without explanation."

"Then tell me where it is ye'll be meeting her," Bran said.

"Nay," Niall mumbled. He could barely move his lips.

"Ye will only be worse in the morning, and unless ye tell me, she will be left waiting."

"If I tell, ye will not hurt her will ye?" asked Niall.

"Of course not." Bran was taken aback. Was the distance between him and his brother truly so great? "How could ye even ask such a thing?"

Niall gave a resigned nod. "The ringfort northwest of Croghan Kinsella. She will be waiting there," he said.

Bran knew an awful relief. He did not feel good about what he had done. There was a churning in his stomach. Carefully, he set Niall on a pallet, then he called to one of the clansmen to chain Niall to the wall. His brother would not be allowed to leave the armory until Bran gave permission.

Chapter 7

Aislinn did not make any farewells at Annacurragh. When her father came looking for her, she did not want anyone to lie for her. Besides, farewells were too final. Aislinn preferred to think that in two or three years she could visit Annacurragh—mayhap, her father would be reconciled to her choice, the statute would be repealed, and she could show off a brood of babies to her cousins and grandmother. She merely gathered up the necessary supplies for a long journey, and after a restless night's sleep, she rose at dawn, took Bláth from the stable, and headed to the ringfort to wait for Niall.

The site was not difficult to locate. Niall's directions had been excellent. Each of the landmarks was where he had said it would be, and the ringfort was exactly as he had described. While it was called a fort the site was actually an old farmstead, encircled by a series of ditches. Almost nothing of the farmhouse remained. Here and there a few toppled stones or a rotted post were visible beneath ferns and moss. The only structure was a stone hut nearly hidden beneath a tangle of vines. It might have been a *teach alluis*, a *sweathouse,* although it hardly looked large enough to accommodate an average man's full height.

She tethered Bláth by a stream, where the water ran clear, and there was a nice clump of sweet grass. Finding herself in need of a rest, she lay upon a large flat stone. There, stretched out on her side, and resting her face on the pillow of her arms, she fell asleep. It was several hours later when a large raindrop, landing upon her nose and another upon her eye, awakened her.

The day had turned dark, the sun now hidden by a heavy mass of black clouds. The temperature had plummeted, and the wind had turned fierce. Twigs and dust and bits of dried leaves were blowing every which way. Thunder rumbled in the distance as the rain became heavier, drenching Aislinn. She jumped off the rock, ran to fetch Bláth, and then led her horse into the shelter of the stone hut.

There were no windows in the hut, only a single opening of a low, narrow door through which Bláth's girth barely fit. The roof was made of a large stone slab, and in the poor light, Aislinn saw that a triangular stone bench had been built into each corner. There was a fire pit in the center. It was definitely a sweathouse, and as such was the perfect place to be secure from the storm.

At first, she hovered at the entrance, worrying about Niall and staring out at the storm for some sign of him. There was more thunder, followed by lightning, and even more thunder, so loud and close that the ground trembled. The storm was fierce. The rain turned to hail, and the wind drove the hard, frozen particles into the hut.

Bláth whinnied, and Aislinn moved away from the doorway to pat the mare's nose as much for her own comfort as for the animal's. There was another bright flash of lightning. It was near. The deafening crackle of impact followed immediately. Too near. The horse emitted a shriek of fright. A tree had been hit, and there was another sharp explosion at the exact moment a man ducked beneath the lintel and entered.

"Niall," she exclaimed, sending up a silent prayer of thanks. "Praise be that ye've made it safe to me through this vicious weather." She threw herself against him. "How good it is to feel my arms about ye. Just hold me for awhile. Hold me."

Every nerve in the man's body jolted at her embrace, and to his horror, he did as she asked. His arms went about her shoulders, and he held her. Her hair was damp, making the scent of crushed rose petals sharper, sweeter, and for the moment, he lost all sense of who he was and why he was there. He was only a man, seeking shelter in the arms of a woman. He inhaled deeply, closing his eyes and resting his chin on the top of her head.

"I've been frightened, Niall, and worried for ye. Come, let me warm ye."

Her voice, tender with promise, brought the man crashing back to reality. *Let me warm ye.* Her meaning was all too clear, and he struggled to control himself. His arms fell from her shoulders. He set her away from him.

A thunderbolt ripped across the sky, and in that gleam, their faces were revealed to each other.

"Oh, my God in Heaven!" Aislinn gasped as she took in the black braids, the deep brooding eyes, the straight masculine nose, the severe mouth, and gaunt face. Water beaded on his brow, dripped from his hair, streaked his cheeks, and in the quick flash of silver, he was a savage sight. "It is ye," she said on a breathless whisper.

They stood only inches apart. Lightning radiated

the darkness, and she watched as his gaze moved from her eyes to linger upon her mouth. She could imagine what he was thinking, what he was remembering, for her own memories were unforgettable. She thought of his lips devouring hers, his tongue probing her mouth while his loins surged against her. A pang of desire rippled through her, she swallowed hard, then there was a pain in her chest, and scalding tears flooded her eyes.

"*Smi,*" Bran said, detached. *Aye, it is me.* His regard was wintry when he looked from her mouth back into her eyes, yet a thin, controlled smile came to his lips, for he was pleased. He was winning, and he liked to win. He didn't like to fail. He had stopped Niall from making a mistake with this scheming *beadag*. Now he had only to keep his body under control until he had gotten rid of her once and for all.

"What are ye doing here?" Aislinn took a step backward, and tilted her face to watch him. His head grazed the stone ceiling. He was far too tall, much too big and broad in that little hut.

"I am here instead of Niall."

Aislinn eyed him warily. "But where is Niall?" she asked experiencing a first prickle of panic.

"Where he belongs. Just as ye shall soon be."

"I-I don't understand." Her voice wobbled. The panic was spreading, warming, seeping through her.

His cold eyes bore into her, relentless. "At Dysert, I told ye to leave, but ye didn't heed me. And more than once I warned Niall to be staying away from ye, but he's always been hot-headed, and I should have known he would defy me."

He had warned Niall. This man, whose name she did not know, but whose memory was imprinted upon her for always. *He* had warned Niall about her. Of what concern were Niall's affairs to this man?

Aislinn squinted at him. He bore no resemblance to Niall, yet could it be that this man was Niall's brother, the O'Connor chieftain? He must be. It was the only explanation that made sense, but knowing who he was did not quell her unease. It tore at her. It terrified her, and she glanced beyond him toward the door. She wanted nothing more than to run as far and as fast from that hut as she could. She wanted to hide from him, but she could not even look away from him. She felt like a doe cornered by a pack of wolves, transfixed by the sight of her attackers as they surrounded her. She'd lost that one fleeting chance to break away and run to safety.

"Why is it that ye hate me so fiercely?" she asked. There were a hundred other things she wanted to know, but this was the first question that popped forth. A clear sign that she was not thinking straight.

"It's not that I hate ye." The question caught Bran off guard, and he replied before he had fully considered what he was saying. He tried to be more exact. " 'Tis yer kind. Ye're not one of us, and it's for yer own good—as well as for ours—that I'm doing this. Someday both ye and Niall will be thanking me for stopping the pair of ye from making a terrible mistake. I've come to take ye back where ye belong."

"Where is that?" She was finding it hard to concentrate in the confines of the hut. *Terrible mistake.* The words were repeating themselves in her mind. She had to remind herself to take a breath.

"To yer father." For some strange reason his voice softened, and he caught himself before he called her *cuileann* as he had once before. He knew better. Despite her physical appearance she was no fair lady; she was a temptress, a witch who intoxicated men. She was named Méabh for a reason, and he should not be affected by the bewilderment working its way over her features; it made her appear vulnerable when he knew that was not the case. He forced himself to frown, and was surprised when she covered her ears with her hands.

Terrible mistake. It was that phrase and not mention of her father that distressed Aislinn. She stared at Niall's brother, the words repeating themselves in her head, and as if to stop them, she clapped her hands over her ears, unable to make any sense of what was happening.

"Ye know nothing of where I belong," she managed to whisper before her throat dried up on her. The awful suffocating feeling had returned, but not due to the prospect of being returned to her father and from there being sent to England with Lady Alyson's brothers. Something far worse was making her feel as if she couldn't get enough air in her lungs.

Outside, the storm was passing. The rain had stopped, mist was rising from the forest, and the late afternoon sun bathed the gray mountains in pale light. Inside the hut, Bran could see the full extent of confusion and misery upon her features. Did she actually love his brother? The notion made him uncomfortable. Abruptly, he turned away from her, and occupying himself with mundane matters, he set about leading her horse to the door.

"What are ye doing with my Bláth?"

"The hut is far too small for the three of us, and I don't wish to sleep with a horse. My stallion is out there. The storm has passed. It will be safe for yer mare."

"We are staying?"

"The night, at least. The streams and rivers will be swollen. There will be flooding in the glens, and it would be dangerous, indeed, foolhardy to travel in the dark," he said, then ducked his head and exited the hut with Bláth.

Aislinn watched them go. Of course, he was right, but she said nothing when he came back.

Bran did not like her silence. "Do I have to tie ye up?"

Her eyes widened. The last trace of color faded from her cheeks. "I am yer prisoner?"

"It is not as harsh as ye make it sound." Once again, he was compelled to comfort her, and his jaw clenched with a sort of angry frustration the second he'd spoken. He loathed the weakness that was making him say such things, and to counteract this failing he hardened his tone of voice, making it flat and resolute. "There is purpose to my actions. One goal. I am going to return ye to yer father, and I can't be letting anything prevent that. If ye ran away, I would go after ye. I intend to make certain ye are returned to Sir Roger. Nothing will stop that." But the gruff voice was no use. She looked thoroughly dejected, and Bran could not stop himself from saying, "Ye must not feel so bleak. Certainly yer father will forgive ye."

"It is not that." She stared straight into his eyes as if she were speaking to the deepest, darkest corner of his soul. Her voice was very soft. "Ye do not know what he plans to do with me."

"He will beat ye?"

"Nay, my father has never beaten me," she whispered across the hut.

"What could be so awful?" His voice, too, was low and quiet as if they were sharing secrets.

"He will send me to England to wed an Englishman."

Bran was surprised at the loathing in her voice. After all, she was half-English. Marriage to one of her own should not be a bad thing. "Ye do not like the man yer father has chosen for ye?"

"I do not know him. Indeed, my father has not picked him, but it would not make any difference who he was. Any Englishman would be disgusting."

He stared at her. It was not what he would have expected from her kind.

"Ye don't understand, do ye? Ye look at me and see a half-breed, something lower than contempt. Well, did ye never think that is how I could feel about the English?" A touch of color returned to her face, and her voice was growing louder, vibrating with conviction. "My father may have passed some of his Norman blood into me, but not much, I swear to ye, not much. My soul is Irish. It is my mother's blood that courses through my veins, that makes my heart beat and gives me life." Her voice began to thicken with emotion, and when she finished a tear escaped from one eye. "I love this land, these high bogs and mountains, the night winds and misty dawns, the noisy rooks and thieving stouts, the sagas of *Tain bo Cualnge* and *Fled Bricrend,* our customs and old ways, and to think of leaving Ireland and everything that encompasses is to think of being torn from the breast of the mother who gave me life and nourishes me yet."

Bran could never have imagined such an impassioned speech. It touched a chord within him. He knew of what she spoke, and he knew she spoke the truth. "I am sorry," he said, bewildered to discover how easily he was feeling her sadness.

"*Naile, air Naile!*" She swiped at the tear with the back of her hand, and glared at him in contempt. *Marry!* "So sorry that ye're willing to deliver me to my father when ye know it will surely be the death of me?" she asked in disgust.

He did not answer right away. When he did, his words were pensive. "I begin to understand."

"What is it that ye think ye understand?"

"Ye and my brother. I begin to understand how and why it was that ye were going to marry Niall."

She glared at him with a defiant tilt to her chin as if challenging him, daring him to go on.

"Ye were using him," he accused, condemning her.

"It is not that ugly."

"Do ye deny it?"

"*Ní hea*. But it was not as cold-blooded as ye think. I would have been a good wife to yer brother. I would never have forgotten what he did for me, and I intended to spend my days repaying him. I have done nothing of which I am ashamed."

"Did Niall know any of this?"

"I am not cruel."

Bran's mouth twisted. "My brother was an easy victim."

"It was not like that, *ar m'anam*." Aislinn protested. *Upon my soul.*

"It seems that way to me. Ye would not try to convince me of yer undying devotion, would ye?" he sneered, thinking how she had gone from Niall's side into his arms at Dysert.

She fought the urge to lower her eyes. "I would not try to deny anything."

He grunted a sort of satisfaction.

The sun was sliding behind the mountains, and it was getting colder. Bran set a fire in the pit, glancing every now and again at her as he worked, knowing that she must be as chilled and uncomfortable as he was. Someone else had recently taken shelter in the hut, leaving behind a ready pyre of twigs and turf in the pit. Using the flints he always carried in a small leather pouch, Bran struck them together several times. Sparks jumped, and soon there was a fire.

He warmed his hands, and motioned for her to do the same. But she did not move from her spot on the other side of the hut, and he gave an indifferent shrug when he took off his tunic. He lay the wet garment near the fire and began to strip off his leggings. That done, he proceeded to set out the leggings beside the tunic when he heard her tiny gasp.

"Certainly, ye've seen many a man before," he taunted when he caught a glimpse of her staring with astonishment at his nakedness.

Aislinn flinched slightly, then squared her shoulders, and held her head high. She had never seen a naked man, but did not bother to tell him the truth. He would not believe her, especially not with the way she was gaping at the phallus between his legs. It was huge, and she knew it could get larger. Something erupted inside her. Her hands were suddenly clammy, her face was getting hot. She could not turn away, and she gulped, then moistened her lips with her tongue. A bright red flush crept up her neck and face as she thought of what it would be like to reach out to touch it. She wanted to feel it beneath her hand, to wrap her fingers around it, to know how it would react when—

Her hands flew behind her back where she clenched them together. May the good Saints Fáelán—all fourteen of them—give her the strength to stay away from him. He was her enemy, he held her in nothing but the lowest contempt, and to have these thoughts about him could only result in disaster. Had she not learned at Dysert how this man could hurt her? Surely, she did not wish for more of his ill treatment? Had she no self-respect?

Bran saw the way she focused on him. He watched her blush and noted how her tongue had darted out to swirl about her full red lips, and it almost killed him. He crouched to rummage through the pack he'd dropped by the door upon entering. He pulled out a woolen length of fabric, stood and wrapped it about his torso, securing it at the waist. He tossed one at her.

"Here. Yer father would not be happy, if I returned ye to him with a running nose and hacking cough. Take off yer wet things and wrap this about yerself." He turned away so that he would not have a view of her as she disrobed. No matter what he told himself, his loins stirred for her. No matter who she was and what he knew of her, he wanted her, and that wanting was more than wrong. It was dangerous. Truth to tell, he'd wrapped the blanket about his waist not for modesty or warmth, but to hide the evidence of his arousal. Between his legs, he was hard as a rock, hot and pulsing upright for her.

As much as Aislinn did not want to follow his advice, he was right. She was wet to the skin and would surely sicken if she didn't take off her clothes and warm herself by the fire. She stepped backward into a shadowy corner, and slowly, began to pull off the overtunic that she wore like a top layer over her kirtle. Beneath her kirtle, however, there was no other layer. There was nothing about her breasts or privates as an Englishwoman would wear beneath her outer garments, and Aislinn was acutely aware that her sodden kirtle clung to every line and curve, every pucker and valley of her female form.

He heard her moving, and his mind tormented his body, drawing up images of what it was she was doing. Were her legs bare yet? Was the skin of her thighs as bewitching to gaze upon as her slender, creamy shoulders? And her breasts? Would they fill his open palms? He tried to think of other things. Unfortunately, his *other thoughts* were no less troublesome. Visions of her taking off her clothes and lying with Niall crowded his mind.

There was something he had to know. "Was there ever passion between ye and Niall?" he spoke harshly to cover the thickening hoarseness in his voice.

His voice startled Aislinn. She dropped the kirtle hem that she had raised halfway up her torso. Right away, she knew what he meant, and she moved deeper into the shadow. *Passion like there is between us.* She swallowed, but could not reply. A chill was working its way up her spine to the base of her neck, and she began to shake as the most unspeakable idea clutched at her mind.

Terrible mistake. The words returned, this time taking on a wholly different meaning. It had been a terrible mistake to consider marrying Niall, but not because he was an O'Connor and she was degenerate English. It was a terrible mistake because there was no unseen bond between their souls. There was no passion that pulled them together like there was with this man, his brother, her enemy.

The prickling at the nape of her neck told her this explained why she had acted as she had in the castle. This was why she had kissed him, said those things, and acted with such abandon. Her soul had known what her heart and mind did not, and stunned by the force of this unexpected revelation, she had to lean back against the wall for support.

She could not bear to look at him, crouching on the other side of the fire pit with his back to her. He had not even bothered to face her when he asked that question. Perhaps, however, that was something for which to be grateful, and she closed her eyes, knowing that she had never been more utterly alone than she was at this moment. This shocking knowledge should have filled her with joy, but it didn't. She heard him rise, and knew he was waiting for her to speak.

Bran did not like the way she was avoiding his question. It goaded him to ask, "Was Niall yer first?" He scowled. It annoyed him that he would even speculate upon such a thing, and he got even angrier because imagining her with Niall made him feel as if he'd been cheated. That anger forced him to add, "Or have ye whored yerself with scores of other men?"

Ní hea! she wanted to cry out in denial. *Nay!* But she did not trust herself to speak, and pressed back against the wall as he started to walk around the fire.

"Was that what ye were trying with me?" he demanded, tension deepening his voice. He walked toward her, but was stopped short a little more than an arm's distance away by what he saw.

With her back to the wall and her arms spread out like wings on either side of her, her breasts were fully revealed by the clinging wet kirtle. They were perfectly round with large nipples that puckered beneath the fabric like flower buds, and they seemed to swell higher, rising and falling with each agitated breath. No wild imagining could have been more explicit than this. The tightening in his groin was excruciating as his gaze lowered down the length of her stomach to where the fabric cleaved to the vee between her legs. He shifted his stance slightly, his swollen shaft was pulsing against the woolen fabric, and he hated himself for not being able to control his body. He hated himself so much that he wanted to blame her. He wanted to hurt her, anything to be in control.

"Were ye hoping to bewitch me? Is that what ye were trying with me? If Niall did not succumb to yer potions and spells, then mayhap ye could seduce me.

Ye were working on the both of us at the same time. Is that it, now?"

Aislinn heard his words, and wanted to cry. The emotion came out of nowhere, rendering her immobile as the familiar chill tickled at the nape of her neck. Everything was becoming clear. Hideously, awfully clear. Just as she understood the terrible mistake, she understood that his pain was hers, and unless they could have harmony between them, neither of them would ever have a day's serenity on this earth. This was their Fate.

"Answer me! Were ye trying to seduce me?"

She stared at him, but the tears would not come. She wanted to explain, to try to comfort him, but words would not come. He would never understand.

"Answer me, damn ye." Bran was seething with anger.

"Nay, I was not trying to seduce ye." An actual physical pain tore at her heart.

"What then?"

Again, there was that prickling sensation as she came to understand more of what was happening. She did not need to ask why he was acting this way. She knew, but could hardly believe it herself. It did not seem possible, but the chill at the nape of her neck which signaled her other-worldly understanding beyond that which was evident, had never failed her. "*Ead ata ort*," she whispered, incredulous. "*Jealous ye are*. Ye're jealous of Niall. That's what this is about. Ye're jealous."

"Jealous. Me?" he sneered. His anger was on the verge of boiling over to rage. She quickly realized she'd better watch what she dared say to him. "Never. And especially not when it involves a degenerate English harlot."

"*Mallacht ort*," she hissed, her own anger rising to

match his. *Curse ye.* "I am no harlot, and ye'll best be remembering that, ye self-righteous bastard!" Aislinn swung her arm, her palm open, and she aimed at his face.

Bran caught her wrist, and yanked her away from the wall. He stood over her, glaring into her upturned face. "I'm thinking that ye've tried that once too often."

Aislinn met his gaze and gulped. "And what will ye do?" she jeered, twisting her wrist in an attempt to free it. Oddly, she was not frightened of him. "Will ye punish me?"

He looked at her wrist, and squeezed until she stopped moving. He heard her whimper, knew the pressure must be painful, and as if in a trance he stared at his fingers wrapped about her wrist, saw the red streaks already rising on the creamy skin, and deliberately, he relaxed his hold. But he did not let go. He loosened his grip so that instead of hurting her, his fingers began to stroke the underside of her wrist. He heard her sharp intake of breath, sensed her trembling reaction to his caress, and refocused his gaze upwards. Her face was framed by a mass of abundant black curls, and there was a sultry expression in her eyes. Her moist red lips were parted in an invitation he could not refuse.

He enveloped her in his arms, his mouth crushed down on hers, and she responded to him. Her arms went about his neck, fingers entwined in his hair, pulling him closer as her mouth opened beneath his, her body seeming to try to make itself dissolve into his. His blanket slipped away from his waist, and Bran cast it aside as the wet kirtle worked its way up her thighs until they were both naked from the waist down. His shaft slid between her bare legs, brushing against the nest of curls, where he felt her honeyed moisture. He lodged himself between her upper thighs, rubbing back and forth until his full length was slick with her juices, and she was moaning, and straining against him.

With both hands he grabbed her buttocks to steady her, and spread her legs, opening her to him. He would take her here as he should have taken her against that tree, and bending his knees, he quickly tilted his pelvis backward, then forward to position his feverish manhood at her damp female lips. The engorged head slipped inside her. She was ready for him, and he quivered at the awful beauty of it, forcing himself to go slowly, for he was larger than most men and did not want to hurt her when he slid his full thick length into her.

"Oh, my God, no!" Aislinn cried out. The fear that she had not earlier experienced now claimed her. She pushed against his chest, dislodged him from between her legs, and managed to make a space between them.

"Are ye a teaser?" he asked, a taut, rough edge sharpening his words. "Is that the sport ye play, now? Bait and provoke? Were yer silky words in Dublin nothing more than a lie? And at Dysert when ye whispered, *A mhorair, bheagan a bheagan, tha tighinn fodham,* when ye called me *my lord,* would ye have denied me then when it came to this?"

She could not bear to meet his gaze. She heard the raw yearning, the anger and confusion in his voice, and she did not want to see it in his eyes, nor did she want him to see her dread and loathing. There were a thousand things she feared. She was frightened of being hurt by this man; he had wounded her before, and instinct told her that if he did it again, it would be worse than the last time. She did not want to give him something of herself that he would not value.

But most of all, she was afraid of never having this

kind of passion with another man. Each time they were together the erotic force between them was extraordinary, and long after she had been returned to her father, years after she had been sent to England, and her memories of Ireland began to fade, this would remain bright. Indeed, it would be against this that all other men would be compared and fail. She knew this was true, and it filled her with sadness to think of never experiencing the whole of love-making with this man, whose body and soul were meant to meld with hers.

But she could not have it all. She could not protect herself against everything. She could not save her heart and mind, while letting her body know the fullness of perfect physical ardor between a man and a woman. She would have to make a choice.

"Ye've taken me too far to stop," he leaned closer and murmured against her ear, hardly believing his desire was so intense that he was going to beg this woman. His hands dared to brush against her upper arms, softly, tentatively, his fingertips trailed up and down in a tempting caress. "Tell me what ye want. Anything. Tell me how ye like it, and I'll do it." When he ended his voice was scarcely more than a whisper, yet his final word rumbled forth from his throat with urgency. "Anything."

Aislinn could not help it, the husky timbre of his voice made her shudder. She took a deep breath. She had come to her decision. "Would ye pretend ye love me?" came her unsteady whisper.

She would give herself to this man who was her enemy because if she did not, she would spend the rest of her days in regret, wondering what if; with a future as bleak as hers looked, that was an untenable prospect. She would spend this night with him, do anything for him, and she would return to her father with a sustaining memory. The imprint of his passion upon her soul would make England bearable. There was one thing she needed, and since he offered, she asked with wistful longing, "Would ye make love to me as if ye cherished me more than life itself?"

Bran was not one for games, but such melancholy was the last thing he had expected to hear in her voice. It reached inside his chest to clutch at his heart. He sensed his own loneliness more keenly than he wished to acknowledge. He saw his own emptiness reflected in her, and a tight knot of pain and grief began to unravel inside him. It was driving him to the brink. He clenched his jaw as if it might give him the control he needed to stop before it was too late. He was about to do something that he knew was wrong.

She watched his jaw tense in the glow of the turf fire. He was looking at her strangely, hesitating, and she held her breath, knowing that she had asked for too much. Then he lifted his hand, and very gently, he touched her face, tenderly, his thumb stroked her jaw.

"If 'tis love that ye desire then that is what ye shall have this night. But can ye be doing the same for me, *cuileann*? Can ye pretend to love me more than life itself for the space of one night?"

Her heart leapt. She was not certain if he played with her, but she promised yes, for this night, at least. "Aye, anything for the space of this night," she said, stepping closer to him, brushing her lips against his. "Taste me," she urged him, beguiling, tempting, her voice was as soft as satin. Her breasts skimmed against his bare chest, her thighs touched his legs, their breaths mingled. "Taste me, my love, for I will be sweet as nectar for ye."

Her words sent a jolt of pure pleasure to his groin,

and the realization that she was his to do with this night as he wished was powerful. He needed to touch her, to feel her, taste her, and aye, he needed to have her touch him as if she meant it, as if there was no other man for her.

This time, there was aching, sweet tenderness in their kiss. He drew her into his embrace, and kissed her slowly, thoroughly, with unbearable longing. Her lips opened beneath his, and their tongues met and fused as his hands began to caress her breasts, lush and full, straining against the wet kirtle.

"I want to see ye," he whispered against the column of her throat. He inhaled the musky female scent of her. "I can feel yer beauty. Sense it with every nerve of my body. Now I want to be seeing yer lovely body, to be worshiping it with my eyes."

He helped her slide the kirtle from her shoulders, over her hips, and down her legs to the dirt floor, where it pooled about her feet. Then he stepped back to look at her. Her breasts were lovely, round and uplifted, and he shuddered at the perfect beauty of her plum-colored nipples. Her waist was small as he had imagined it would be, her hips were curved, the skin pure of tone and flawless, and above slender legs was nestled the source of her sex, shadowed in black against the creamy fairness of her skin.

"How I have longed to see ye like this," he groaned. With the back of one hand, he brushed her cheek, and smiled. "I've never known a woman as glorious as ye. Ye're a true beauty in spirit and looks."

Shyly, she took his hand from her cheek, turned it over, and kissed the palm.

Neither one of them said anything for a long, drawn-out moment. They simply drank in the sight of each other, knowing but never admitting aloud, that this night would never come again.

At last, he murmured, "Come to me, *cuileann*," and she glided into his embrace.

Aislinn moaned at the pleasure of his bare flesh against her skin. Her hands tangled in his hair, holding him closer while he caressed her naked breasts. Beneath his palms her nipples stiffened, and to her delighted astonishment, he bent to kiss one breast, his tongue swirling about the nipple before he took it into his mouth, nipping about the tip, then sucking upon it. She was vibrating with awakening sensations, and greedily, she bowed herself up to him, wanting more. His lean muscled body thrilled her. She ran her hands over his shoulders and back, down to his waist and over the curve of his firm buttocks. In the years ahead, she would remember how he'd felt beneath her hands, how he'd tasted and smelled, and how he had groaned from deep inside his throat.

He took one of her roaming hands in his, lowering it between them, and when she encountered his erection, she caught her breath. It was hot and hard, yet the skin was smooth and soft. But it was the size that surprised her the most. Her fingers barely reached around it, and the length was longer than her hand. "Ye're a big man," she said.

"I will be gentle," he promised with the tenderness of a lover, guiding her hand to stroke him in a long up and down motion. "Nothing will hurt ye, my love, my own *cuileann*. This night is for naught but pleasure. And for love. Don't be afraid, now."

She caressed him with a trembling hand, felt him quiver, and understood that this was a special sort of power she wielded over him. "I could never be afraid of ye," she said.

Her words came so softly that he felt rather than heard them, and looking into her dark eyes, Bran experienced a totally unfamiliar ache in his heart. Carefully, he lowered them both to the ground. He lay her upon the discarded length of wool, positioned himself between her bent legs, and then leaning his weight forward on his arms, he pushed into her with a single, even stroke. She cried out as he entered her. He was almost too big, but she was wet and accommodating, and he went only part of the way inside her. It usually required several strokes for a woman to take all of him, and he had promised to be careful with her.

"Ye were made for this, *cuileann.*" Her velvet sheath closed about him, and as he grew even larger inside her, she seemed to pull him in deeper, tighter. A rough moan came from deep within him. "Ye were made for a man's body."

"*I was made for yer body,*" she said, knowing it was the truth. Her grandmother had warned her that there could be discomfort in the act of coupling, sometimes excruciating pain, but with the right man, she had assured Aislinn, there would be ecstasy, and Grandmother was right. The pain of taking him inside her was fleeting, and it had been replaced by white-hot pleasure.

"How sweet ye are. How intoxicating, my Méabh."

She heard him call her Méabh, but couldn't speak to correct him. An exquisite thrill of excitement coursed through her. It was the most wonderful feeling imaginable, and her breath was coming in deep, amazing gulps as she began to rotate her hips beneath him, fascinated and aroused by the way she could sense herself moving on his shaft.

While her eagerness was pleasing, Bran didn't want to go too fast. He still had not penetrated her entirely, and was afraid that once he had done so it would be over. He wanted to stay inside her for as long as possible, and he worked in and out of her with sustained, unhurried strokes that produced as much ecstasy as torment. "Easy, *cuileann,* easy. We'll make it last all night."

"I'm yers," she cried on a little moan, part pleasure, part frustration. Something was humming inside her, singing along her nerves, and she spread her legs. They were wide, but she wanted them wider, as wide as she could to take every inch of him deep inside her. She wanted to be filled with the maleness of him. The rippling sensation that was building in her was about to be released, and she could not get enough of him. She writhed beneath him, awestruck with yearning, pleasure, and she clawed at his back, his buttocks. "I want ye to fill me like no other man ever will. Let me take all of ye inside me. Harder. Deeper. Love me."

No woman had ever spoken to Bran like that. It was intensely erotic, and thoroughly mesmerizing, and he thought that he would have believed her if she'd said she loved him more than life itself. At that moment, he would do anything for her. With a long, quick thrust, he plunged the full length of him into her, and she expanded perfectly, then tightened about him. He could feel every muscle inside her, stroking and caressing him, and when the undulating contractions began within her that was his undoing.

A sudden tension grabbed the length of him, and for a second, his muscles and nerves seemed to suspend themselves upon some other plane of reality. But it was only momentary. In the next heartbeat, they jumped to life as a burst of energy hurtled through him. It was part agony, part bliss. A lusty groan was wrenched from deep inside him as he rammed hard and quick to the very hilt of her velvety, moist sheath, beads of moisture were flecking his back and shoulders, a clammy flush was running up his arms and legs.

Aislinn cried out, arching upward to meet his final wild thrusts. She was not aware of how his fingers twisted and pulled at her hair, and she hardly heard his earthy groans as her own impassioned exclamation, a long, sweet keen, rippled forth from her.

"Lovelier than heaven," Bran started to mutter, but the words were lost as his final release seized him, and he struggled to retain a shred of lucidity. There was one thing he must do. Swiftly, he withdrew from her, not a second too soon, nor too late, and in that instant, his thick, hot seed shot between them, and onto her belly. It was over. He shuddered, then cradled her in his embrace, his heart racing, his breathing returning to normal.

Aislinn floated back to reality as a feather drifts to earth. The first thing of which she was aware was how heavy and bulky his body seemed to be, then it was the sticky substance smeared across her stomach and down the curve of one hip. Her heart twisted. She knew what he had done, and she knew that no matter how he might have pretended, he had never forgotten that she was his enemy. Certainly, not at the end. That would have been an impossible lie to maintain.

The truth hurt, and it was a long time before Aislinn could fall asleep.

But Bran could not sleep at all. Of a sudden, the distinctions between reality and charade were not as apparent as he would have liked them to be, and his brain was telling him things that he did not want to hear.

He had spoken truly when he'd told her that there was no other woman like her. He'd never before known a woman with such passion of body and soul, with such perfect lips and breasts, such soft black hair and amorous dark eyes, such an earthy voice, and such a provocative, uninhibited response. It was all the truth, and his only lie was in omission. What he had not told her was that he did not think he would ever find a woman to compare with her, and delivering her to her father was going to be the hardest thing he had ever done.

Chapter 8

Sunlight fell across Aislinn's face, rousing her. Inside, the hut was dim, the ground beneath her was cool. Outside it was bright with the promise of a new day. She could see the lush, green canopy of the forest. She could hear the wind in the leaves, and the caw of ever-present rooks, the rush of a waterfall, the lowing of cattle grazing on a nearby hill. Propping herself up on one elbow, she shielded her eyes from the early morning glare and saw him standing a few feet from the door.

He was naked, with his back to her, one leg on the rocky ground, the other propped on a rock. For so lean a man, his body was a powerful sight. She could make out the muscular lines of his buttocks and thighs, and his torso and shoulders were as solid and hard to gaze upon as they had been beneath her fingers. A savory warmth melted over her, causing her flesh to tingle as she remembered the passion their bodies had shared.

Last night had not been a dream. It had been real, and with one exception it had almost been perfect. She closed her eyes, and the memory of his final action returned to her as did the pain that had clutched at her heart when he had withdrawn from her. Of course, she should be grateful for his caution. She could ill afford to find herself increasing with the bastard of a native chieftain. But it was not a question of legitimacy that had motivated him—the Irish did not care about such things in the way the English did—and that was why his action pierced her heart. It was her blood. She was not good enough for his seed, she was his enemy, and that hurt Aislinn almost as much as the prospect of being sent out of Ireland.

It was a crime only to the English to mingle the races. There were generations of offspring from the two peoples, and more often than not, those children grew up to be more Irish than English. Indeed, wasn't that what concerned the English? And why the statute had been passed at Kilkenny? Irish blood was stronger than theirs. The Irish were a more beautiful and virile race, more poetic and creative; they lived longer, were better warriors and their loins were more fertile than the Anglo-Normans, and whenever the two races mixed it was the Irish spirit that customarily prevailed.

What was it, then, that made this man's intolerance so unyielding? Aislinn did not know whether to admire or to pity him. Opening her eyes, she stared at the lean, rugged Irishman, his black braids hanging over strong, broad shoulders. She would never forget. Their parting was inevitable, and if there was a way to make it so, she did not want them to go their separate ways as enemies.

"Go mbeannai Dia duit ar maidin," she called out to him in a gentle voice. *Good morning.*

"Dia's Muire duit," he replied as he returned to the hut. On the threshold, he paused to glance down at her, and there was an immediate quickening in his loins. She was reclining on bent arms, her bare breasts

thrust upward were luscious in their perfect, firm roundness, and the sight of the rose-colored nipples was inviting. The end of the woolen blanket lay across her belly and covered the joining of her legs, but the slender length of one shapely leg was revealed to him. He could not look at her without wanting her, and he wondered if what had happened between them the night before had been predestined. He did not like to think that destiny had anything to do with himself and Sir Roger Clare's daughter. But he could think of no other explanation, and he supposed he could accept that destiny had brought them this far, since it was soon going to take them apart.

"*Ciod an uair a th'ann*?" she asked. *What kind of weather is it*?

"*Tha e bláth*. The day is fair and not a cloud in the sky. *It is warm*," he replied, unable to control the husky timbre in his voice. He was trying not to react, yet his body was betraying him.

Aislinn saw the evidence of his arousal, and smiled. She knew that while his mind might try to deny her, his body had come to understand their Fate. Maybe it was wrong, crazy, dangerous, destructive, but she didn't care. She wanted more of the previous night's passion. There would be nothing for her after she was returned to her father, and she wanted to live every last moment to its fullest. Maybe there was even time enough that he might come to understand. It was a risk she had to take.

"*Tha e moch. Throthad an so*," she said on a beguiling whisper, beckoning him to join her on the floor. *It is early. Come hither*. But he did not move from the doorway. She tried again. "'Tis obvious that ye would like to be lying beside me again. What is stopping ye? Was it not good between us? Did I not please ye, my lord?"

He shivered when she called him *my lord.* "Aye, ye pleased me greatly," he murmured, and entered the hut to kneel beside her. *Just this one last time, then she would be gone,* he told himself. He would be careful again, and there would never be any reason for anyone to suspect how he had betrayed his clan.

"I am glad," she replied, tossing aside the blanket and opening her arms. She was glad to have pleased him, and glad he would join her now.

Bran lowered himself toward her, and it was then that he saw the dried blood between her thighs and smeared upon her stomach. Tenderly, he set his finger tips against the dark red marks. "Did I hurt ye?"

"Is it not normal?" she asked in a quiet voice, unable to add *for the first time.* He had without question assumed her to be a woman of much experience, and the memory of that opinion wounded her now as it had before. She forced herself not to look away from his confused regard. He was trying to make sense of what she'd said, and she could not control the blush that fanned across her cheeks.

"Ye were a virgin," he said, appalled.

"*Tá,*" she whispered. *Aye.* His unexpected anger made her stiffen. For the first time, she noticed the color of his eyes. They were green, and she watched as they darkened from a pale hue to a shade so dark it made her think of dragon's wings. Her heart sank. She could not bear to see this evidence of his animosity, nor to hear it in his voice, and taking hold of the woolen blanket, she focused upon her hands as they secured the fabric about her lower body.

Bran stared at her, provoked by the contempt she was able to kindle within him as quickly as passion. *She's saving herself for her husband.* The recollection of Niall's words were at once as shocking and numbing as if he'd stumbled into a frigid mountain loch.

By the bones of St. Cieran, did she imagine he was that man? Her future husband? Had she, despite her denials, aimed her wiles at him, and, in a last frantic effort to avoid going back to her father, had she given herself to him? Why else would she have done it? As she had tried to trap Niall, she now tried to ensnare him. Bran was not flattered. He ran a hand across his eyes.

"Why did ye deceive me?" he asked, taut with rage, his eyes observing her keenly.

Aislinn's voice was as low and tense as his. "I did not deceive ye."

"That's a matter of interpretation," he retorted, each syllable sharply spoken.

"I am inexperienced in these matters," she said in a clear, distinct manner, trying to sound far braver than she was. "Is there some sort of protocol that says virgins must proclaim themselves?"

"If I had known—"

"Ye would not have had me," she cut him off and finished his sentence. Her voice was dripping with mockery. "*Muir, air Muir*! I think ye deceive yerself. Which makes ye the worst kind of liar and a fraud."

A grimace etched lines upon Bran's forehead. She had seen inside his soul. She was getting near the truth.

There was nothing that would have stopped him, and that was the sin of it.

There were too many reasons why he should not have lain with her, but he had done so anyway, and thus, he had failed. For the first time, he had failed, and she was the instrument of that failure. All the care in the world to prevent any betraying evidence would never erase the fact that he would always know. He stared at her, and the loathing in his eyes was as stark as the black spot growing on his soul. He had no right to be a chieftain, no right to call himself an O'Connor. "Cover yerself," he growled, tossing a second blanket at her. "All of yerself."

She heard his despair more than saw it. Perhaps it was guilt that was eating at him. Perhaps he imagined he'd cheated his brother out of something that was his. "Ye must know that yer brother did not love me. Nor did he have any true claims to me. Ye did not wrong him in any way last night. We did not wrong him."

"Is that what ye imagine?" Bran clenched his teeth together. He did not like the way she had used *we*.

"I do not know what to think."

"Don't waste yer time trying to figure it out," he snarled. "It's of no importance one way or the other. Soon ye and I will be going our separate ways, and although coupling between a man and a woman usually marks a beginning, *we* are at an end. Come, get up and be dressing yerself. There's no time to waste. I intend to cover a great distance in the next two days." He was gathering up the blankets as he glanced over his shoulder. He spoke in what was more of an afterthought than anything else, "And do not try any more of yer foolish pranks."

She found her tongue, and her voice rose at his insult. "Foolish pranks! Nothing I have done was foolish or intended to be a prank."

"Don't tell me ye expected to succeed," he sneered.

"I almost did." Her chin came up defensively.

"*Dia ar sabhail*!" he exclaimed. *God protect us*! "There's the only proof ye need of yer foolishness."

"How so?"

"Did ye truly think I was yer only impediment? If not for me, then yer father would have come after ye. Mother of God, lass, did ye imagine Sir Roger Clare—the knight who defended Killoughter against the seige of '58—would have stood by while his daughter flaunted the statute and ran away with one of the savage natives?"

She turned away, but not quick enough. He glimpsed the misery upon her face, and it struck him like a thunderbolt that she had, indeed, imagined that very thing. Indeed, she had believed in her success. She had not reckoned with the odds, nor with reality. Bran could not stop himself from saying, "I am sorry." Still he could not trust her, and he bound her hands. He was sorry for that, too.

"It does not matter," Aislinn replied. The weariness within her soul was too great to repress. The end was near. He was right. Her great and wonderful plan had been nothing more than a childish, ill-conceived fantasy. Married to an Irishman by harvest time? Nay, it would never happen.

Niall lay on a pallet in the chamber above the gate at Baravore. His injuries were not serious, and were it not for his one hand being shackled to the wall, he would have been up and about the morning after his fight with Bran. It was the afternoon of the third day, and he lay on his back with his free hand beneath his head like a pillow, his temper seeped in a frustrating boredom that alternated with consuming anger for Bran and himself.

He could only hope that he'd done the right thing in telling Bran where Aislinn was waiting. He had not wanted her to think she'd been forgotten, and at least, Bran's arrival would have offered some explanation. But that was where any notion of Bran and Aislinn confronting one another ceased to be of comfort. Unfortunately, when he imagined the pair of them Niall envisioned naught but violent discord between two such strong-willed individuals. Perhaps Bran had met his match. Mayhap she had bested him in a verbal war of wits, or had already managed to elude him. Such was Niall's only consolation during the long hours of tedium.

Footsteps echoed in the stairwell, drawing him out of his thoughts. Someone was ascending the tower, and by the light tred, Niall discerned it must be a woman. He averted his face to the wall. He did not want to see his mother again. She had already lectured him on the importance of fraternal loyalty and the evils of defiance, and he'd been shocked. It had been a long time since she had reprimanded him as if he were still a small lad, and even longer since she had taken Bran's side. But she had done so on both accounts, and that was another reason for Niall to be in an irritable humor. There really wasn't anyone he wanted to see.

A forced cough came from the doorway. Whoever stood upon the threshold wanted his attention and would not enter otherwise. Something told Niall it was not his mother, and he turned. It was Ceara O'Byrne. Her elfin face was pale. There was a tremulous, overbright smile upon her lips.

"Hello," Ceara said as if there was nothing out of the ordinary about her presence at Baravore. Without waiting for a reply, she crossed the chamber to kneel beside him.

Niall saw her fresh face, those bright, guileless eyes, and that warm smile, and he was humiliated. He did not want her to see him like this. Chained to the wall, dependent, chastened. He closed his eyes, and pivoted his head toward his shackled hand. Maybe she would leave if he was rude.

"Yer mother said I would find ye here," Ceara said in her sweet voice.

"What are ye doing at Baravore?" he demanded,

wondering, but not asking how much she knew about what had happened to him.

"I accompanied my sisters," she said, aware that this answer explained nothing. But she could never tell Niall that her sisters, having seen him in a forest clearing with another woman, had told her that if she harbored any hope of a future with Niall O'Connor, she must be bold. Ceara and Niall had been playmates from her earliest memories, and, of late, she'd thought something different had started to grow between them, something of a more romantic nature. That was what she wanted from Niall. Romance. She did not envision them being friends forever, nor could she picture herself gladly watching him marry another. Instead, she dreamed of lying in his arms on her wedding night, and of bearing his babies, of being his wife. Her sisters had said there was no time to spare, and so they had come to Glenmalur on the excuse of needing roots for their garden, and along the way, the O'Byrne sisters had instructed Ceara in much detail on what it was she must do when she was alone with Niall.

"And why are yer sisters here?" He did not recall any mention of an upcoming visit from the O'Byrne women. He still would not look at her.

"I am not certain," she mumbled. "Something about the herb garden, I think." She looked at him lying before her, recalled everything her sisters had told her, and taking a deep breath, she rested her hands on his chest. His head jerked in her direction, his eyes were wide with surprise, but this did not deter Ceara as she leaned forward to kiss him on his split lip.

There was a stirring in Niall's loins. A low moan escaped his lips.

"I did not mean to hurt ye," came Ceara's soft exclamation.

"*Nil, maise,* ye did not hurt me. *Indeed, it isn't so.*" He met her open blue gaze. How could he have forgotten that blue? Her eyes were the color of iris that grew at the edge of the bog, vibrant, almost purple, and he returned her smile. " 'Tis good to see ye."

"I am glad." She exhaled a tiny nervous breath. Her hands were fluttering up and down his legs. With light strokes, she caressed his whole body, running her fingers along his jaw, across his shoulders, and chest. "I had started to think that ye did not care for me anymore, Niall. Ye were so distant during the wedding celebration."

"That seems like a very long time ago," he said.

Ceara sensed his tension, and her fingers drifted across his brow, through his hair, then down his neck. "Ye must relax and think of nothing but my touch. I've come to be making ye feel better. Ye would not think to resist me, would ye?" she teased, leaning nearer until her lips brushed his ear when she spoke.

Niall swallowed hard. His pleasant, tolerant, elfin Ceara had never acted like this before. They had kissed many times until they were breathless; he had cupped her breasts through the fabric of her tunic; and once she had even let him lie atop her, the both of them fully clothed, kissing and rubbing against each other. More than once he had thought she would make him die from the agony of unfulfilled yearning; and more than once, after they had said good night, he'd found release with a willing girl. He had never expected this from Ceara. Indeed, it was spellbinding. "*Ní hea,* I would not resist ye, lass," he murmured.

She began to unlace his leggings, slowly, methodically, her shaking fingers removed the leather cords, and with each row undone, the material parted to reveal a thatch of blond hair that got thicker as she worked her way lower. The hair was soft, his belly was hard, the flesh was warm, and she trembled. Her saucy, sensuous sisters had gossiped of their romantic trysts in explicit detail, and she stared knowingly at the bulge between his legs. It was straining for release against the thin fabric, and she knew what she must do.

Her heart was thumping with such intensity she was sure it would explode when she pulled the final length of cord free. Her throat was dry, forcing her to gulp, and to take a steadying breath before she parted the leggings and freed him.

Niall arched upward as cool air touched his throbbing erection. He moaned as her delicate, warm hands encircled him. Her fingers caressed him, and he was afraid that he was going to shame himself at any second. He tried to sit up. He wanted to see her face, but a wall of glossy red hair swung forward to hide her from his view, and the chain restrained his movement.

Ceara leaned forward on purpose. Her sisters had assured her such things were healthy and normal, but it was new and strange, and she was certain that her face was an unbecoming shade of crimson. Furthermore, sisterly assurances aside, she was afraid that her delighted curiosity with Niall's sex was probably unnatural and would appall, if not revolt him, and he might send her away.

She could not help thinking it was lovely. It was long and straight and slender, and knowing what a man did with it did not frighten her. She thought it was handsome, and hoping that it would one day delve into the secret woman's place between her legs, she bent to kiss it. Niall moaned. His engorged sex quivered beneath her lips, and Ceara paused an instant to assure herself she had not hurt him. When he did not complain her lips began to nibble up and down the length of the hot, rigid shaft. She remembered what her sisters had told her, and her tongue darted out, it swirled about the rounded end, and finally, her lips closed over it. A strange new taste filled her mouth. Niall gripped her shoulders, his fingers digging in hard and sharp. She heard him cry out, and wondered if she had gone too far.

She sat up, and glanced at him, worry and uncertainty upon her face. "Was I wrong to do that?"

Niall required a few moments before he could reply. His breathing was ragged. "Ye must never imagine such a thing. What ye did was fine and wonderful." He grinned at her with undisguised satisfaction. "But why did ye do it, Ceara?"

She took a deep breath. Although she had climbed the tower steps at her sisters' urging there was another reason why she had dared to touch him in such a way. "Why?" she repeated his question. A rosy blush colored her dimpled cheeks, and she peeked at him from beneath lowered eyelashes. "Because it is what I have always wanted to do."

His heart swelled. "I am glad. Now ye must lie beside me." To Niall's delight, Ceara lay on her side, facing him as he instructed. "Now raise yer top leg and hook it across me," he whispered.

She hesitated.

"Come, it's all right. I will do ye no harm. In fact, I intend nothing more than fair play. Ye had yer turn with me, now it's mine to do what I have always wanted. Ye do trust me, do ye not, Ceara?"

She nodded.

"Say it then. Tell me ye trust me."

"I trust ye, Niall," she whispered, raising her leg to place it over his body. As she did so, the kirtle slipped away, and exposed her sex. She knew Niall did not have much freedom of movement, and she held her body still, wondering what he intended.

"Relax," he whispered against the sensitive flesh behind her ear. His free hand grazed along the back of her thigh and up her buttocks. "Relax. Close yer eyes."

Ceara did as he urged, her eyelashes fluttering against her skin as his hand moved down the cleft of her buttocks to her sex. She gasped when he caressed her there. It felt good, all tingly and achy. With one finger he trailed along the seam of her, and she understood now why he had wanted her leg raised in this fashion, for it allowed his finger to slip easily inside her. Her sisters had told her of such things, and she moaned, enjoying his ministrations, imagining that she was floating on a wave, cloaked in a perfect dream from which she would never awaken.

"Do ye like this?" he asked.

"Mmmm," was her best reply, for while his one finger was stroking in and out of her, he had positioned his thumb to massage the little nub nestled in the hair at the apex of her legs, and the sensations this produced were most distracting. How did he expect her to speak? Soon she was moaning as the wave upon which she'd been floating spun her upward, and an unfamiliar energy convulsed through her. A few minutes elapsed while her heart slowed. He withdrew his hand, and rearranged her kirtle skirt. "Do ye want me to leave?" she asked.

"I do not think that will ever happen, *ceistean*." He called her *sweetheart*, and wrapped one arm about her shoulder. Angling Ceara to him, he kissed the top of her head. Niall did not understand what had happened except that he had found his way home, and holding her fast, he drifted to sleep.

* * *

The journey from the ringfort was difficult. The path had been washed out in several places, forcing Bran and Aislinn to make numerous detours. Toward the end of the day, they came to a crossroads below Kilmacrea Hill, and there, as dusk settled over the forest, Bran helped Aislinn dismount, then he secured the long end of the rope that bound her wrists about a tree. A man stepped out of the forest.

"Greetings, Bran."

Aislinn's head turned sharply in their direction. *Bran*. It was the first time she had heard his name, and she did not know what was the odder. That she had never asked his name in the time they'd been together, or that if she had been given the task of naming him, she would have selected Bran. The raven with glossy black wings. She would never forget. Nothing could have suited him better.

"Greetings." Bran walked toward the other man as if he had expected him. He was Irish and heavily armed. "Ye had no trouble?"

"No trouble. The guards let me pass on the Wicklow trail, and I was able to make it all the way to Killoughter."

Aislinn's heart leapt. She listened carefully.

"Ye got into Killoughter?"

"*Tá*. Sir Roger himself received me."

"And—"

"Ye're to take the lass directly to Wicklow town. Sir Roger will be expecting ye at the quay, midday on the morrow."

Bran nodded, thinking of the myriad dangers of entering the English town. It could be a trap. But he had no choice. There were many perils in being Irish in Ireland, and he would face and conquer them all. Or, at the very least, die trying.

* * *

Shortly before noon the next day, Bran and Aislinn paused to rest and water their horses. They had reached the coast, and, looking northward through the early summer haze, they could see the outline of Black Castle, the English royal fortress at Wicklow that was situated on the rocky headland outside the harbor.

"Must ye take me to my father?" she asked. "Is there no other way?"

Bran stared at her. It was the first thing she had said since they'd ridden away from the ringfort.

"If I promise to stay away from yer brother will ye set me free?" she said, thinking that if she returned to Annacurragh, her grandmother would certainly shelter her. After that, she did not know what she would do, but, at least, she would have delayed this voyage to England.

"And what would I be telling yer father?"

"That I escaped."

"*Ní hea,* lass, there is no way. He knows I have ye and am bringing ye to him. There is every chance that he's had us watched, and it would not go unseen, if I simply let ye go on yer own. I cannot break my word," Bran said, unwilling to admit aloud that it was more than that. He was not safe from her any more than Niall had been, and he had to know she would be leaving Ireland. It was his only hope of winning, his only hope of doing what he must as chieftain of the O'Connors. Bran turned away from her, signaling there would be no more discussion between them.

Tears flooded Aislinn's eyes. "If ye will not be merciful with me, will ye at least save my Bláth?"

"What do ye mean?" he asked, but did not face her.

"I do not want her to be sold to some English lady

who will not know how to treat her. Even my stepmother, I suspect, would not be a good mistress. Will ye take her when ye return to the hills? Give her to one of yer sisters."

"Aye," he replied. "I can do that much for ye."

"*Go raibh maith agat,*" she whispered, *thank you,* and closed her eyes to hold back the tears threatening to spill down her cheeks.

Bran took a pouch from his saddle pack. He sat down with his back to a tree, placed a flat rock on his crossed legs, and from the pouch he poured a fine black powder onto the rock. It was a dye made from the leaves of woad, dried, fermented, and crushed. He mixed the powder with a small amount of water, and stirred it with a pointed stick until its consistency was thick and even. The color was a startling, bright blue. Carefully, so as not to upset the flat rock, he took off his tunic, and using the same stick, began to paint patterns down his arms and across his chest.

"*Beannachd do t-anam is buaidh, Ardchuraidh nan ciar-bheann,*" he sang a warrior's lament. *Blessing to thy soul and victory, high chief of the dusky hills.*

Aislinn knew what he was doing. The use of woad was an ancient Celtic practice from the time of the Druids, and it was not often that a warrior used it these days. He was going to enter Wicklow town as a warrior chieftain, empowered by the spirits of his ancestors, fierce of body and soul, and ready to battle his enemies. He was preparing to die, and when the tears trailed down her face, she cried for the both of them.

The harbor town located at the mouth of the Vartry had been settled by the Ostman, who had named it *Vikingalo.* Now called Wicklow, it was much like any other Anglo-Norman colonial borough in Ireland, dominated in the center by a market cross, where the cries of merchants mixed with the shrieks of noisy gulls and squealing pigs rooting among the refuse for discarded dates or figs, or perhaps, some moldy pastries or lamprey that had gone bad. The smell of privies filled the narrow lanes between wicker houses. The only stone edifices were two three-storied residences, one belonging to Wicklow's only barber surgeon and the other to the Italian wool merchant, and the third was a sprawling abbey at the north end of the town. The lanes, not but six or seven feet wide, were congested with wandering pigs, chickens, sheep, cattle, all their excrement, plus a rag-tag mendicant populace of vagrants and lepers that, while officially outlawed, was nonetheless visible and vocal in their efforts to acquire enough food to stay alive.

There were two castles in Wicklow. Black Castle, seen from the coast, was at the harbor, and White Castle, built on the foundation of an Ostman stronghold, was at the south end of the settlement, serving much as a town gate might have, if Wicklow had been walled. The High Road ran from White Castle to the abbey.

A warder on the rampart of White Castle announced Bran's and Aislinn's approach, and by the time they reached the High Road a goodly portion of Wicklow's five hundred plus townspeople had swarmed out of their cottages and from their garden plots to stare at the Irish chieftain leading a young woman.

Despite her reputation, Aislinn was a splendid sight, a true beauty, and many a woman it was that day who cast a warning eye at a husband. She was, after all, half-Irish, and it might be that faerie spirits accounted for her once-reputed, now proven, wildness. A man might wither from looking too long upon those unruly black curls, spinning about her face and trailing all the way to her waist. She was a shameless creature to have such a ripe red mouth and such exotic eyes—certainly, no Englishwoman was ever so wanton. A man might indeed be troubled by the likes of her, and it was of no comfort whatsoever that her hands were bound to the saddle, for the fellow that held the other end of the rope was a savage from the hills. A ferocious expression cut sharp lines into his gaunt face, his eyes were menacing, probing as if they could see through a woman's kirtle and into her soul, his bare arms and chest was painted in a heathen design, mythic creatures bearing giant teeth. There was some sort of talisman hanging from his neck, and it glinted in the sunlight as did the lethal dagger at his his waist and the battle axe secured on his other side. It lost no one's notice that the hand—about which he'd looped the end of the rope attached to the woman's wrists—was poised above the dagger handle.

"Is it her?" A grimy child in a knee-length brown tunic, filth and matted hair preventing strangers from distinguishing whether it was a boy or a girl, tugged its mother's hand in query.

"Aye, the disobedient creature," replied the mother. "In the flesh, and not a shred of shame about her."

"Whore," jeered another woman. She spat on the ground as Aislinn passed.

"Traitor," yelled several men.

"Sir Roger should send her to Kilkenny."

"Aye, for a finish the same as Dame Alyce."

Aislinn did not flinch at mention of the first woman in Ireland to be tried for witchcraft. Although it had happened more than fifty years before, no one had forgotten, and whether the woman had actually been responsible for the deaths of her husbands was still a frequent topic of gossip. Dame Alyce had been burned at the stake. Although Aislinn's bound hands had turned cold and clammy, and she was certain her complexion must be as gray as a ghost's, she was amazed at how easy it was to stare them down. Their words could not hurt her. She did not care what they thought, and she started to sing an Irish song.

"I arise today
Through God's strength to pilot me:
God's might to uphold me,
God's wisdom to guide me . . ."

Bran slowed his horse until she caught up and edged alongside him in the narrow lane. "*Na deanaibh sin,*" he spoke in a low, urgent whisper that no one else could hear. *Don't ye do that.* It was an anthem as Irish as the winds that stunted the trees that gave roost to the great dark rooks. It was "The Deer's Cry," and had been sung around turf fires long before Diarmid MacMurrough had brought the Normans to Ireland, even before the Vikings had first sailed up the Liffey, or the Book of Kells had been illuminated. It was said that St. Patrick himself had chanted the hymn upon his approach to Tara in the year 433. Indeed, it may have been that she selected this song with eerie purpose, for it was claimed that when St. Patrick had tried to come ashore at Wicklow, the populace had driven him away. Surely, it would incite this English rabble to mayhem. "*Bíodh ciall agat,*" he said. *Have sense.*

But she did not heed him. She had a resonant, musical voice, and it carried above the crowd.

"God's eye to look before me,
God's ear to hear me,

God's word to speak for me,
God's hand to guard me . . ."

"Are ye trying to get the both of us killed?" When Bran raised his voice, he spoke English. It was required of him. He wanted to leave Wicklow town alive and in one piece. He wanted to return to Baravore.

"Ye brought me here, don't ask any favors from me," she answered him in Irish, defiant, her dark eyes ablaze with flecks of golden light. A brash glow of color had returned to her face. "As for the good people of this borough, they expect this of me, and I'm merely giving them something to talk about when the season chills and they're huddling about their meager fires. Long will it be that they remember the day Sir Roger Clare's degenerate daughter was delivered to Wicklow by a wild Irish chieftain to be sent out of Ireland."

They had neared the end of the lane that led to Water Street, the quay was in sight, and she began to sing again, her back straight as an arrow, her eyes focused ahead.

"God's way to lie before me,
God's shield to save me
From snares of devils,
From temptations of vices,
From every one who shall wish me ill,
Afar and anear,
Alone and in a multitude."

Bran had never seen a more joyless, nor more noble sight, and he would not, nay, he could not say another word to dissuade her. He did not understand her, yet he was willing to admit she was a remarkable woman.

This was, indeed, the hardest thing he had ever done. Pathos overwhelmed him. He would always remember how proud he had been to ride at her side through the lanes of Wicklow town.

Chapter 9

The crush of townspeople parted and stood back. Aislinn stopped her song. Here, High Street intersected with a lane that sloped toward the quay. Lads dashed every which way with laden wheelbarrows, merchants haggled amongst each other, and piemen called their wares. There were sacks of raw wool, and bundles of hides, cages of hawks, barrels of lard, herring, and salmon, plus vast quantities of timber waiting to be loaded onto ships for export to England, Flanders, and Italy. Sir Roger stood in the midst of this, flanked by the Windsor lordlings, who presented a grim, disapproving front. Bran and Aislinn continued onward, and when they were about twenty feet in front of the crowd that had followed them through town, Bran stopped to dismount.

Only a single second was needed for the bustle of the waterfront to come to an abrupt halt. In an instant, the din of voices and the shove and thud of cargo stopped. There was no noise except the cry of gulls, the clank of rigging against masts, and an occasional ship's bell. This was the moment everyone from ship's mate to harbor master had been awaiting since dawn when the knight had arrived from Killoughter, and word had spread that his runaway daughter would be returned to him this day. Hundreds of eyes and ears focused on the imminent reunion.

"*Mallacht ort*," Aislinn said when Bran lifted her from Bláth. She did not care that they had an audience. *Curse on ye*. The end was near, and it was going to be harder than she had imagined. She wanted to be stoic and noble and brave, but her quiet, almost controlled desperation was—to her dismay—giving way to outrage. She was angry at him, at her father, at the unseen strangers who ruled over people, who broke their souls, and destroyed their lives with edicts and statutes. She directed that resentment on Bran O'Connor. "If I were a man I would see ye in Hell for what ye're doing to me. *Druisfhear*." She called him *fornicator*.

Bran acted as if he had not heard. To call him *druisfhear* was a serious, potentially lethal accusation. He was a rebel Irishman in a royal borough, and he doubted the good citizens of Wicklow would care that he had done nothing more than take what she'd willingly given him. He prayed no one else had heard as they walked the final distance down the lane. Sir Roger stepped forward at their approach, and nary a muscle upon Bran's face moved when he passed the rope to him.

"Thank you, sir," Sir Roger extended his formal appreciation, and gazed upon his daughter with a mingling of relief and frustration. He had heard her voice raised in song, recognized the Irish hymn, and he knew a distinct measure of gratitude that she was now silent. It was good to see her, good to know she had not been harmed, but he could not disguise his disappointment that she had behaved in such a willful and outright illegal manner. Of course, it was precisely what he would have expected of Johanna Elizabeth—had he not listened to his lady wife. He should have known better when he let her go to Annacurragh that circumstances were not what they appeared to be on the surface. They hardly ever were when Johanna Elizabeth was involved.

There was also tender compassion in his regard, for he could not help wondering if her love for the O'Connor lad was true. Or had it been a passing fancy soon to be forgotten? It was going to be hard for Johanna Elizabeth to leave Ireland, and he did not like to think of her enduring a double heartache. Sir Roger was not a cruel man, and like any father he wanted to make a good marriage for his daughter. He wanted the best for her, and these days that meant anything and everything that was English, including an English husband. Being degenerate English was to be out of favor in the eyes of the Crown, and if Sir Roger was to secure a good future for his daughter, he must make certain she obeyed the statute and avoided everything, and everyone, that was Irish. Praise be, there was at least one chieftain who could be relied upon to uphold the statute's ban on mingling between the races. He extended a hand to the Irishman. "It appears in this matter, at least, we are of one mind. I am in your debt."

Bran shrugged, and kept his arms at his side. He did not like to be rude, but he liked even less the notion of an English knight in his debt. The last thing he wanted was Sir Roger beholden to him. He wanted nothing to do with Sir Roger or any of his family from this moment onward.

"Your brother is well?" Sir Roger inquired, remembering his own youthful folly.

"As well as can be expected." Bran did not wish to discuss his brother with Sir Roger. He wanted this to be over. He did not like speaking English. He wanted to deliver the woman and get out of there.

"Good. That is good," Sir Roger muttered more to himself than to Bran, wondering if this interview was as uncomfortable for the Irishman as it was for him. There was no need to prolong it. "Your family will have no more trouble from my daughter, I promise. Thank you, again." Sir Roger gave the rope a gentle tug to compel his daughter to follow.

Aislinn responded with a litany of Irish curses. She jerked the rope hard as if to unbalance her father, then tried to kick his shins. Her dark eyes flashed with golden anger, that wild black hair twisted about her like a thousand serpents, and as he watched, Bran could only think how there was no resemblance between father and daughter. He could almost feel sorry for Sir Roger and whatever young Englishman found himself by her side at the altar.

"I don't want to hurt you. Behave yourself," Sir Roger admonished, unable to keep the desperation from his plea. It was bad enough that she had tried to run away with the O'Connor lad, but now to be delivered to him in such a public setting, bound like a common felon, and to behave like this, he could only think it was a miracle there was any decent prospect for her. He dared not look at his brothers-in-law. As a result of this escapade, his spirited daughter had finally alienated herself beyond redemption from the English in Ireland. There would be no marriage proposals for Johanna Elizabeth here, and her future would be altogether lost if the Windsors withdrew their offer to welcome her into their home across the water, introduce her to proper society, and find her a suitable husband.

"Cuidighim mi," Aislinn said to Bran, her dark eyes fusing with his, searching for any hint that his soul had awakened to hers. But there was no sign, and she

did not think she was brave enough. *"Help me,"* she pleaded in a hushed voice. Her emotions had swung full circle. They were not unseen strangers facing one another without recognition; together, they had partaken of the most intimate bond two people could share, and it was not right that he would do something that would destroy her soul. "Please, help me."

Bran stared at her long and hard.

Please, her heart whispered, *don't forget me.*

A muscle along the high, sharp plane of one cheekbone twitched. *It has to be this way,* but Bran said nothing aloud. He held the words inside, and cursed those long-ago moments in a darkened corner of Dublin Castle. This never should have started in the first place. Still she stared into his eyes. He wanted to look away, but couldn't, and he knew he was doing the right thing. He had to save himself from her as surely as he'd saved Niall.

"Cuidighim mi," she repeated as she extended her bound hands toward him. *Help me.* Her eyes were wide, her lips white with rising terror.

Bran's chest convulsed with an actual physical spasm. He wanted to push her hands down, to tell her to act with more dignity, with the dignity he knew she possessed. Instead, he looked away. "What will ye do with her?" he asked Sir Roger, in accented English that was thick and lilting.

"I'm sending my daughter to my wife's family in England, where she will learn to act like a lady."

Bran almost broke into laughter. There was nothing remotely funny about this, but to imagine Johanna Elizabeth Clare as an English lady was so implausible that his tightly leashed nerves nearly cracked. To think of her schooled to the ways of a lady induced his mind to concoct the most improbable vision of the world turned upside down. Churches skewered into the earth by bell towers, and rows of English gentlemen, their heads in the ground, and their feet, encased in those pointed, brightly colored shoes they liked to wear, aiming skyward, waiting to be plucked from the soil like some bizarre root vegetable.

He emerged from this most peculiar reverie when he heard Sir Roger address his daughter.

"Come, Johanna Elizabeth. We must not tarry. Again, thank you, sir." Sir Roger bowed to the Irishman, then started toward the quay, but Aislinn did not move.

"Wait, Father, a minute, if you please." Her voice was remarkably composed. She spoke English.

And Sir Roger, who had always found it next to impossible to naysay his only surviving child—indeed, the child he was about to lose forever—paused and gave a permissive nod.

Aislinn moved as far away from her father and as near to Bran as the length of rope allowed her to go.

"Please, there is something ye must know," she said to Bran in Irish, quick and frantic.

He did not budge. Despite his every instinct to turn away, the urgency in her voice secured his attention.

"Ye must know that I am Aislinn, not Méabh. And ye must know that I did not deceive ye in the hut. There was no trickery on my part to make ye think I was not a virgin." Her eyes skittered over his face searching for his reaction, some softening in his expression, anything to indicate he was listening and believing. This was her very last chance. "Making love with ye was not part of some scheme to trap ye; nothing I said or did that night in the hut was a lie. I will admit to some fabrication in the castle. But it was innocent, I swear, when I said my name was Méabh. I did not tell ye my true name only because I did not understand then what I do now. And I am most deeply sorry for that. I was not trying to deceive or trick ye in any way." She paused, half-expecting him to ask her to explain what it was she had come to understand that could make any difference, and she worried that he would not believe her if she spoke of Fate's role in bringing them together, and of the unseen bond between their souls. He might very well laugh in her face. But it made no difference, for he said nothing, did nothing.

Her last chance was gone.

She stood tall, shoulders drawn back, chin high, her bound hands clasped at her waist. Serenely, bleakly, she ended, "I am Aislinn, and if ye ever think of me, I hope ye'll remember that. *Beannacht agad,* Bran." She called him by his name for the first time. *Farewell.*

"*Beannacht Dé leat,*" he replied. The words were a farewell with God's blessing said to one who was departing. The moment of his success was at hand, and a kind farewell could be of no harm. She had told him how she loved Ireland—that much he believed—and he was sorry for her. But not sorry enough to put her before him, before his clan. He had failed at the ringfort, but never again. He knew what he must do. He had always known, and as in most of life's episodes, one man's triumph was another's loss.

Bran O'Connor was going to win today.

He had stopped Niall, had delivered the scheming creature—who would have poisoned the O'Connor blood—to her own kind, and he was going to return to Baravore.

Without another word Bran turned, and went back up the slope. He led the animals through the crush of townspeople, and left Wicklow town.

That was it.

* * *

Aislinn watched as he strode up the hill to the horses. It was done. Over. Barren relief washed through her.

"Am I to leave right away, Father?" she asked, resigned. The resistance and spirit were gone from her. She would not struggle or argue, raise her voice, or kick, or try to run away. "Am I to travel without you?" she asked, bereft.

"Aye to both your questions. I will see you only as far as the end of the wharf. Once your ship leaves the harbor, I must return to Killoughter."

"You are in haste then?" she inquired.

"Aye. But it is in no way owing to any eagerness to be rid of you, daughter."

Her concern, however, was not alleviated. "I trust that you do not plan to ride against the O'Connors. They did nothing wrong. If you wish to punish anyone, it should be me."

"Nay, there will be no retribution. It is Lady Alyson. She is not well."

Not well. How easily the implication of those guarded words made a crack in Aislinn's own misery, causing a dramatic shift in her thoughts. *Not well* could mean something as normal as a woman's monthly course or a calamity as devastating as the plague. Aislinn had been a babe the year the first pestilence struck Ireland, and had no memories of that horrendous time when more than fourteen thousand souls perished in Dublin alone. But the second Great Pestilence had only been seven years ago, and had it been seventy or seven hundred years past, Aislinn did not think she would ever forget how her mother and brothers had died frantic with the pain in their heads.

Aislinn still dreamed of that frightful time. In her nightmares she saw the flames of the funeral pyres, smelled the smoke and decay, saw the oozing, black blood, and heard the screams of anguish. The memories engulfed her. She still wondered why she had been spared. The priest at Killoughter had no answer, nor had the friars at Llangony offered any explanation, and thus it was that she had devised her own rationalization. Fate, she had decided, intended something great, something special, wonderful and different for her. She had found comfort in the belief that her life was meant to be unlike that of any other knight's daughter. She was destined for something remarkable, something of accomplishment. Now, it was pitifully clear how wrong and foolish she had been.

"Not well, you say. Is it pestilence?"

"Nay, daughter, I believe my lady wife finds herself with child."

Aislinn was actually able to smile. "I am happy for you, Father."

It was not often that Sir Roger feared he would cry, yet this was one of those times. He embraced his beautiful, willful daughter, overwhelmed by the memory of her as a baby, and of his other children. He heard their laughter and sweet voices, remembered when his sons had learned to walk and ride, and his heart ached, for he knew that no matter what the future offered, a man could never start over. It would never be the same as the first time. He held his daughter at arm's length, smiled at her, and thought that England was unprepared for this child of his. She was going to break men's hearts, if she had not already done so. He untied the rope from her wrists, and gave her a sad smile. "There is a fresh gown set out in your cabin. It belonged to your mother. The blue one you always liked so much. Do you recall it?"

"Aye," she replied. There was a lump in her throat. Aislinn wanted to tell her father she loved him no matter what. She knew it was a rare thing, this love between a child and parent, especially when the parent was a dedicated warrior and liege man to the English crown, but such affection had been natural when her mother lived, and so strong, it had survived her death. Aislinn wanted to ask how it was that a father could love a child, yet still send her away, but she knew it was pointless to try to understand her father any more than she could unravel Bran O'Connor.

Sir Roger escorted his daughter past the Windsors and toward the small craft waiting to ferry passengers to a broad, low cargo ship moored in the harbor. Aislinn did not look at Lady Alyson's brothers, but she could feel their eyes upon her, and could only begin to imagine the abominable thoughts that must be boiling about their brains.

At the end of the wharf, the captain stepped forward. "Lady Johanna Elizabeth." He greeted her with a formal bow and made some small conversation about the accommodations set aside for her, and the anticipated weather conditions for the journey. Despite her misconduct she was still a lady.

She responded with a nod and a pleasant smile. If nothing else she could at least make her father's last image of her a favorable one.

The captain urged them to hurry, and the Windsors, who had caught up, were the first to step into the waiting boat while Aislinn lingered with Sir Roger.

"God go with you, daughter, may his blessing be upon you all the days of your life, and may you know that you will always be in my heart."

Aislinn did not know what to say, and instead of speech, she embraced her father a final time, then joined the others. She sat with her back stiff, hands folded upon her lap, and her head turned at an uncomfortable angle to watch her father as the boat skimmed across the water. When they reached the cog, its single square sail half-hoisted and snapping in the wind, she climbed a rope ladder, and once on the deck, she looked toward the quay. Her father was still there, and she waved, actually more of a tentative little movement with her lower arm than a true wave. He could not have seen, but he could certainly see her standing at the rail.

"Excuse me, my lady, I'm to show you to your quarters," said a lad of not more than nine or ten years. His complexion was a dark olive tone, and he spoke English in a funny accent that added a little dip at the end of each word.

"Not yet, thank you. I prefer to remain here." She stayed at the railing for almost an hour, during which time her father never moved, and only when the ship hauled anchor to come about in a tack toward the open sea did she move. There was no point in being there any longer. He could not see her. The ship had turned.

The olive-skinned lad took her to the stern of the vessel, where three steps led beneath the castle deck and into a cabin. It was small and narrow, dark and musty. There was a bed of sorts built into the stern, and a plank with a raised edge was suspended by chains from one wall for a table. A great pile of leather-hinged chests containing her belongings was stacked against the other wall. She had not known she owned so many things, nor had she ever imagined her whole life could be crammed into five or six chests.

"There is not much light," she remarked, and the lad opened the shutters above the bed. There was a hook in the ceiling to which he fastened them.

Sunshine and salt breeze filled the cramped space. Although it became no larger, it was more tolerable, and after the lad left, Aislinn doused her face in water from a laver on the suspended table. She took off her tunic, and used it to wash her body, then ran wet hands through her hair, untangling it as best she could. Lastly, she slipped on her mother's gown. It was clean and soft, smelling of the crushed rose petals her mother had taught the servants to fold into garments when they were stored away.

With a sigh, she lay on the mattress. It, too, was clean, and smelled of fresh-cut straw. She closed her eyes and listened to the slap of waves against the wood, and was almost asleep when the door opened.

It was Lady Alyson's brothers. They crowded into the cabin. Oliver, being the last to enter, closed the door behind, and then leaned against it, looking rather pale and stupid as Simon and Philip approached her.

"What do you want?" She sat bolt upright. This intrusion was not entirely unexpected. The Windsor lordlings were obnoxious, arrogant, and rude, and no doubt they had come to insult her and deliver a scathing lecture on her behavior. Her measuring glance darted between Simon and Philip, and an awful prickling at the nape of her neck alerted Aislinn that something far worse than a lesson on decorum was afoot here. A clammy chill crawled over her flesh, and terror skirled through her as she scooted backward. But there was nowhere to go, no way to escape.

She opened her mouth to scream, but she was not quick enough.

Simon lunged toward the bed, grabbed a handful of long black hair by the root and yanked her hard. "I wouldn't make a sound, my lady. If you're a good girl and cooperate, this will be fast and easy, and relatively painless. Hold her legs," Simon ordered Philip as he swung onto the bed and pinned her torso with his body.

Aislinn clawed at Simon's face, and he hit her with his fist. Her head slammed against the mattress. Her eyes closed of their own accord, and across the black of her lids she saw shots of silver as if comets were streaking a night sky. The smell of burning peat filled her nostrils, and she forced her eyes open. Simon's spotty face hovered above her, his legs were clamped on either side of her, and lurching upward, she spat at him. Again, he struck her.

Tears sprung to her eyes, blurring her vision as she felt a momentary sensation of something thin and cool sliding about her neck. How peculiar. She heard the faint tinkle of a bell. Even odder. And then she experienced scorching, searing excruciating pain. She smelled burning flesh. It was her skin, and she screamed in agony and fear only to have the cries muffled by Simon's hands. He covered her mouth, pushing her head down into the mattress to silence her, still her.

"Enough of that," he whispered, low and menacing. "We'll not have the good captain asking too many questions. Or we'll have to punish you, and if you didn't like that, I assure you, any punishment would be far worse."

Stunned and confused, Aislinn lay there. She had no idea how much time elapsed as throbbing waves of pain swirled and ebbed about her. Slowly, her body seemed to be calming of its own accord. Her pulse stopped racing, and her breathing became more even. When she opened her eyes, Simon took his hand away from her mouth.

"Good girl."

"What have you done to me?" she asked, barely able to force the words between her quivering lips as uncontrollable tremors wracked her. Her teeth began to chatter.

"See for yourself." Simon took her shaking hand and set it on a chain about her neck. It was short and tight, hence the need to fuse together its heated ends, rather than slipping it over her head.

With trembling fingers, her hand moved along the length of chain he had secured about her neck. Dangling below the middle of her throat there was bell of the kind one would hang from a cat. The ends that had been attached together were still hot, and she held it away from her neck in a feeble attempt to protect herself from further injury. "I d-d-don't understand wh-why you have d-done this to me."

"What better way to keep track of our little pussy?" drawled Philip.

Bile rose in her throat. "Your mother will not approve."

"She will never know. Did you think we would foist a slut on our mother?"

"But why? What is your intention?"

"Our parents will be told you perished on the journey, and we will all mourn your loss with much remorse," Philip said with feigned sadness that gave way to a short sneer of laughter. "In truth, your loss is our gain, for you see, my lady, we have already made arrangements to sell you as soon as we anchor in Bristol."

"This is our insurance," said Simon who, still straddling her, flicked the bell so it rang, and Aislinn winced at the agonizing shot of pain as the chain rubbed against the welting burn on her neck. "We've no intention of losing such a valuable piece of merchandise as yourself, my lady." When Simon said *my lady* it was with mockery and disrespect. He swung off her, then leaned back to grab one of her breasts.

He pinched the nipple, and leered down at her, his expression arrogant, lusty. "By the by, we intend to enjoy this trip. Once you've had time to rest, we'll be back for a longer visit, and if there's anything the savages didn't teach you about pleasing a man, we'll make certain to further your education."

Then they were gone.

Aislinn heard a bar being slipped across the door, and she needed no time to consider what she must do. She rose to kneeling on the straw mattress: her trembling legs were weak as jelly, and her hands were shaking as she grasped the window to look out. Ireland was a long, rolling line on the horizon. Without thinking past the moment at hand, she pushed her neck and upper torso through the window.

She made the sign of the cross. *"Credim andia a tuir uilecumactac,"* Aislinn began to recite the creed. *I believe in God the Father Almighty*. And then aiming her head toward the swirling water, she slid into the sea.

On board the vessel, no one saw or heard anything.

The salt made the wound at Aislinn's neck sting, but the cool water counteracted that. Soon she felt nothing, not even the energy or will to stay afloat. Indeed, she was lucky that she had not already drowned, for she had never been good at swimming, and it was a difficult undertaking wearing her mother's blue gown. She spread her arms and legs like a star to float upon her back.

It would be best to let the current take her where it might, be it down to the kelp beds or cast upon some hermit's rocky isle, she did not care.

INTERLUDE

In Paradisum deducant te Angeli

"Mo nighean, trothad an so," an ethereal voice beckoned through the roll of waves. *My daughter, come hither.* "Come to me, my child."

Aislinn heard her mother calling, and she tried to swim toward her, but the sea was strong, the current fast, and the blue gown strangled her legs. Slowly, she began to sink into the cool, silent darkness of the sea.

"That's right. *Greas ort, ma ta,"* the spirit lovingly encouraged. *Haste ye, then.* "We're waiting for ye, now. Only a little further, only a wee bit more time, and then we can be together again."

From far away, the friars at Llangony were chanting in Latin, *"In Paradisum dedicant te Angeli."* Strands of kelp entwined about Aislinn, something wound about her waist, her neck, a ragged rock sliced at her foot, her leg, and the requiem comforted, *"May the Angels lead ye into Paradise."*

"That's it, my darling child, *gach eagal fograibh.* Come over. Come over. *Banish every fear.* There is no pain here. No sorrow. No regrets. Haste ye, now. Come over."

Aislinn opened her mouth to answer, and sea water filled her lungs.

PART 2

THE HEART

Chapter 10

Sand.

That was the only thing of which Aislinn was aware, the rough grains against her nose and cheek, the grit between her teeth. The rest of her body was numb. In fact, she saw it crumpled on a strand, waves rolling over her legs, rinsing away the bright red blood that streaked from several long cuts.

It was the most peculiar thing. She was watching this from somewhere above a stretch of shore, and she wanted to tell herself to get up and crawl to higher ground. The tide was coming in. She must not let herself drown in three inches of water. But she couldn't.

Looking down, she knew with a dreadful sense of calm that she was dying, and as she watched herself, Aislinn floated higher, farther from the shore. Closer to the clouds.

There was no sound where she was going. No pain. No sensation. Absolute hollow nothingness. Higher she drifted, mist encircling her, warm or cold she could not tell, and were it not for the blue speck of her mother's gown, she would have lost sight of herself. But her eyes stayed focused on that spot of blue, and she heard her mother's voice.

"Gach eagal fograibh, trothad an so," Étaín whispered through the clouds. *Banish every fear, come hither.*

No matter how she missed her mother, nor how she yearned to be with her and her brothers again, more than that, Aislinn did not want to lose sight of herself. She did not want to die. It was not time.

Nooooo! came her silent scream, and it was at that precise moment that she saw with exacting clarity a figure kneeling above her on the strand.

Whoever it was touched her, and with that contact a massive heave wracked her body. Aislinn hurtled toward the earth. Another heave. Extreme speed. She was vomiting up the briny contents of her stomach. Over and over, down, down she plummeted, out of control until she hit the sand, soul merged with body, coughing weakly, but alive. She could breathe again, and with an exhausted moan, Aislinn curled onto her side aware once again of the world around her.

The water at her feet was cold, curlews and gulls were making their usual seaside ruckus, her cheek throbbed where she'd been struck by Simon Windsor, the burn on her neck still ached with agonizing pain, and someone was hovering above her. It must be an angel, she thought, my guardian angel, who heard me, reached out to me, and brought me back from the edge of death. Slowly, she opened her eyes.

The world was too bright. She could see nothing, and had to blink several times before discerning a silhouette looming over her. She made out the fuzzy outline of a man, lean and broad-shouldered with long hair. She couldn't tell from his clothes whether he was English or Irish, for his chest was bare. Not entirely bare, she corrected. There was something hanging from a cord against his chest, and a chill passed along the nape of her neck as she fixed on the upper half of a molten crucifix, saw the remains of a woad design. Her gaze flew upward, and his gaunt, masculine face came into focus. She saw hooded eyes disclosing no emotion, and thin, unsmiling lips.

This was no guardian angel. It was a mortal, and not just any mortal, it was him. Aislinn thought of Hell. How could it be that she had given herself into the abyss only to come full circle? Was the torment to start anew?

She laughed, an ugly rattle. Merciful Lord, it hurt her throat. But to laugh hurt no less than the effort required to speak, and there was something she must tell him, this devil in angel's guise.

"I found ye in Hell like I promised. Didn't I, now? But I never knew it was going to be so wet and cold. I didn't know it would be so lonely." Her whisper was rasping, laden with self-derision, but, at least, she had gotten out the words. A mockery of a smile twisted her mouth with renewed awareness of pain. There was nowhere on her body that didn't hurt. "Go ahead. Throw me back. There is no one who will miss me. No one who will come after ye to seek retribution."

His lips curled in displeasure, but he didn't abandon her. Instead, he scooped her into his arms, and carried her away from the water, and Aislinn, hardly able to care, let alone resist, slipped into blessed unconsciousness.

Hands.

The second time she regained consciousness Aislinn was aware of hands. Indeed, it was the sensation of being touched that awakened her, and peeking no more than a hair's width between barely opened lashes, she saw that she was lying on the ground in what looked to be a cave. Outside, she heard the wind and rain, and inside, she saw hands. His hands.

They were moving along her arm, upward, toward her shoulder, gently probing and massaging. It was strange that she had never noticed how beautiful they were in shape, how slender, yet strong were those long, sensual fingers. She shuddered. Those battle-scarred hands had killed men, yet they had given her unspeakable pleasure, they had touched her in ways that no man ever would again. Her eyelids scrunched down against the onset of tears. This was not right.

"Don't touch me," Aislinn implored in a voice pitifully weak, barely loud enough to be heard. "Please."

Bran's hands stilled, but only for an instant. "I have to check yer bones and joints."

"No, ye don't." Her voice wavered to a stop. She could not bear this, could not bear to be reminded of everything that was never to be. To have bid farewell in Wicklow had been hard, but never so hard as being here with him now. So near, yet so far. She might as well have been across the sea in England. His soul was beyond reach. He had not understood, and never would. It required every ounce of her energy to speak. "Please, stop. Ye don't have to do anything."

"I have to know what's ailing ye."

"No, ye don't. Please stop." There was a hint of desperation in her voice.

"Ye should not be wasting yer precious energy arguing," he said with a smile. It was impossible to stop himself from being kind. He'd finally understood this when he carried her over the dunes, and her small, cold hands had clutched his forearm. She might try to reject him, but she needed him as no one had ever needed him before. It was an awesome, powerful thing for a man to realize, rather like confronting one's own mortality, which for a warrior was—in point of fact—far less daunting. He'd rather face death than this. But, as on the strand, he had no choice. "I've rescued ye, and for the time being, ye're in my care. While I'm in charge what I say prevails."

"Is that supposed to reassure me?" she asked. The irony of this situation was not lost upon her. She exhaled on a long, tremble of exhaustion. "Of all the people who could have found me, why did it have to be ye? Considering what ye've already done in my behalf, I'd be a fool to trust yer care."

"Ye don't have much choice."

"If ye hadn't taken me to Wicklow, this would never have happened," she said, slowly, precisely. It was the only way to get the words out, and none of the resentment she felt came across, none of the anger, only the despair. "If ye'd let me go on my own like I asked, we wouldn't be here now."

"Och, lass, this started long before Wicklow. Think on it. If ye hadn't concocted that plan to marry my brother this would never have happened." He fell silent. It was easiest to blame her. None of this made sense except to believe that somehow she had conspired with Fate to bewitch him as surely as she'd put Niall under her spell. Bran had been faithful to everything that being the O'Connor chieftain entailed, yet, this one woman had the power to undermine the very purpose of his journey on this earthly plain. This force over which he had no control could not be Fate. He had to believe, that, otherwise he could no longer stand before his clan and call himself chieftain. It had to be her fault. It must be sorcery, and as soon as possible he must once again put a safe distance between them.

"When ye're well enough to get up and leave without any help then ye can have yer own way. In the meantime, ye'll be obeying me. Now turn over, *mar a dhéanfadh cailín maith, like a good girl*. I would check yer back."

To his surprise, she obeyed, tilting onto one side. Her thick hair fell forward to reveal the ghastly open sore upon her neck.

Bran swore, long and harsh at the shocking sight on the side of her neck. Above the collarbone was a festering wound, oblong in shape and about the size of a badger's paw. The skin had been rubbed raw, and the exposed area was oozing. With gentle caution, he parted the hair for a better look. There was a chain lying against her neck, and he ran a fingertip along it to the bell. He swore again. Bran had heard of this belling a woman to prevent escape, this marking a wife or mistress as one's possession. It was loathsome. It was English.

"Christ's bloody nails, what manner of man is yer father to be doing such a thing to his own daughter?"

"My father did not do this."

"If not yer father, who then?" It needed salve, but he had nothing to blunt the pain, or stave off infection. He had naught but the clothes and dagger he'd retrieved from the dune. He set his tunic across her like a blanket. "I am sorry I cannot tend to it properly. Will ye tell me what happened?"

Those tender words taunted Aislinn. He was treating her as he would any other wounded creature, she knew that, yet it was too easy to pretend there was more behind it. Aislinn could not maintain the distance she should, and in a soft voice, she told him how her father had believed his wife's brothers were taking her to their family home. She saw pity in his eyes. Her shame was profound, and of a sudden, all the effort that she had required to awaken and speak seemed to have drained her. Her whole being drooped with tiredness as she averted her eyes from his. "They called this their insurance. They said they would not foist a slut on their mother. Instead, they were going to—"

"Do not say another word. *Sin deireadh anois.*" Bran was deeply moved, and a fierce protective instinct rose up in him. He set a finger to her lips. *That's the end of it now.* He sensed her humiliation, and wished to spare her. "I do not need to hear of their treachery, and ye should be putting it from yer mind. For now, ye must sleep, and when ye're better, I will try to remove it. I will try to help ye erase the past," he promised, thinking that it was both the strangest and most perfect thing he had ever said.

She slept for two days during which time a ferocious tempest tore away at the dunes and battered the coast until every tree and hedge, every gorse thicket and marsh reed was brown from the salt and collapsed from the wind.

Bran and Aislinn were in an ancient grave. The stone cairn, hidden on a hill above the bay, beneath a mound of earth, had a deep chamber, making it an ideal place to be secure from the storm, or to hide from one's enemy. Bran's grandfather had taken him there as a lad many years before, and since then he'd used it to elude the English on more than one occasion. There was a ready supply of turf for circumstances such as this, and with a small, glowing fire, there was light and a little warmth in the chamber.

But Aislinn was not getting better. As time passed, her body became stiffer, colder, and her moments of consciousness were fewer and shorter. She needed nourishment and warmth, and Bran could do nothing but hold her off the floor on his lap and wrap his arms about her in the hope that some of his body warmth would transmit to her. There was no fever, nor any infection, and her inability to rebound frustrated him.

It was an appalling prospect to think she was going to die, and there was nothing he could do to prevent it. Surely, it was not too much to expect that he might be able to keep one small woman alive.

Hours passed, while he whispered to her, rocking her, and even singing, anything to provide a link with the living. He had once heard that herbs and infusions alone were not sufficient medicine, that the human voice was equally vital to recovery from the sort of traumas she had sustained. So, Bran recited the legends of Oisin; he told her of the exploits of Brian Boru, and of the Voyage to the Other World of Bran, son of Febal, who with twenty-seven companions sailed forth in the time of dawn fire to find the Land of the Maidens. Still she did not improve. He rambled on about his childhood at Baravore to little avail. And he spoke of why she must get better.

"Ye must come back, if for no other reason than to berate me for ruining yer plans," he cajoled. "There's too much life in ye, *cuileann*. 'Tis not right that such vitality should be snuffed out. Ye're here in Ireland as ye would wish, and ye must awaken to see for yerself." He thought of everything she had held important and added, "If I called ye Aislinn, would ye return to the living? Would ye return to—"

He had almost said, *Would ye return to me*?

Was that what he wanted? Aye, it was. He would hear her speak again, and see the fire that dwelled within the depths of those sultry dark eyes. But he did not know what that meant. His mind was spinning, vague and exhausted, playing tricks on him. He, too, was cold and hungry, and he wanted to sleep, but knew he must stay awake. The rain was slackening; he must go out in search of food.

"Aislinn," he whispered her name. "I'm remembering yer name, *cuileann*, as ye asked me to. I didn't forget. I haven't forgotten anything. Now would ye be doing me one favor in return? Can ye hear me? 'Tis time to stop dreaming, Aislinn. 'Tis time to come back. Can ye do me a favor? Can ye come back?"

Her eyelashes fluttered open. Although there was no trace of recognition in her gaze, this little bit of movement was better than nothing. She must have heard him, and he continued.

"I must leave ye for a while." Was that a responding flicker in her eyes? More than likely it was nothing more than his imagination. Nonetheless, he went on, "We need food. The rain is letting up, and though there's likely more to come, now is the best time to hunt. I will be back, Aislinn, I promise. I'll not be leaving ye for long."

She had heard him, especially when he called her Aislinn. Indeed, it was that which had brought her back, and now, her mind awakened. She didn't want him to leave. She didn't want to be alone, but her brain couldn't instruct her mouth to open and form the words she needed to say. It couldn't tell her eyes to stay open, and once again, she drifted into sleep, which was how Bran found her when he returned.

By the bones of St. Cieran, she was cool as granite, and colorless. Her face was so pale that her feathery lashes looked like smudges of ash against her skin. Bran kneeled beside her. Although her lips were like ice, he detected a tiny puff of air. She lived, praise be, and he took her hands in his, rubbing them briskly to create some warmth in her.

"I've good news, *cuileann*. Fortune has smiled upon us this day," he said. "We're going to have a decent meal this night. Hot and glorious food. Roasted boar, it will be, if ye can imagine such a feast in this humble setting. Though ye must not credit my hunting skills. The poor creature perished in the deluge, caught in a rock slide, he was. Open yer eyes and look for yerself. And there's more good news. I found my stallion and yer Bláth in the ruins of an abandoned cottage. Lord be praised, the beasts are safe, and we've got my supply pack. And so it is that we'll be dining like the old kings at Tara this night."

Aislinn heard this, and knew it must be a dream. Roasted boar. The finest food of all. Tara. The realm of kings. *Dining like the old kings.* It could not be real, nor could she imagine such fanciful speech coming from Bran O'Connor. She had been asleep so long she didn't know what was real and what wasn't.

Some time later, she smelled the aroma of roast pig. It had to be real, and she opened her eyes.

"Hello," Bran said. He had been watching her and waiting for this moment, and he knew genuine elation when he saw the light of awareness in her eyes. She was truly awake, and with time and nourishment, she would recover. He would not fail at this. "Ye're feeling better?"

She nodded. "A little." Her throat was parched, and the words were nothing more than odd little croaks. Her hand rose to her cracked lips.

"Ye've been without water for quite some time. How long I'm not sure. Two days, at least. Maybe more. Maybe less. Who can tell with such a storm raging above us that turns day into night. Here." Bran lifted her to a sitting position, and set a gourd with water in her hands. He helped her raise it to her mouth. "Ye must go easy, now. Not too much. Nor too fast."

She took a few sips, then closed her eyes. "Thank ye."

"Are ye hungry?"

"Aye, famished."

"It won't be long." He propped her against the

great upright slab of rock that formed a wall in the burial chamber, and returned his attention to the meal.

As Aislinn watched him slice the meat, she wondered if it had been a dream when he called her Aislinn, or if it was as real as the roast boar. She wanted to know, wanted it to be true, but she would not ask. This little moment was so pleasant after so much horror, she did not wish to ruin it.

Bran came to her side again, and crouched down, offering a serving of meat on his open palm. "Here. *Ith so,*" he said. *Eat this.*

But she could not steady her fingers to take the food, and she stared at him, eyes wide, revealing her total helplessness, total reliance. She was at his mercy.

"That's all right. Don't worry." Those last words could mean so many things that even Bran was not certain of their meaning. With his free hand, he pushed a mass of stray curls back from her face and gave her a gentle smile. "Relax, *cuileann,* and let me feed ye."

She nodded, and opened her mouth for that first piece of meat. It was delicious, warm and juicy, and she thought she'd never tasted anything as wonderful. From this moment onward, she would always associate the succulent flavor of roast pig with tender care, well-being, and survival. She returned his smile with a shy one of her own while he fed her tiny, moist bites of boar. Soon her belly was full. She thanked him, and closing her eyes, she dared to ask what was on her mind.

"Why are ye doing this?"

"We had to seek shelter from the storm. Ye had to eat in order to get better, and I had to eat in order to keep up my strength to help ye get better."

"Ye know that's not what I mean," she chastened,

mildly. "Why didn't ye leave me for the sea?"

He didn't answer right away, and when he finally did, he put a physical distance between them. He went back to cut more meat off the boar, and did not look at her when he spoke. "I have struggled with that question myself."

"Ye must have a reason," she said softly, sensing his turmoil.

"Honor," he replied at length, not daring to talk to her of Fate and sorcery. What Bran said was true, but truth, in this case, was a shield. "A chieftain can do no more than face each moment of each day as it comes, and he must try to act with honor in every situation. To rescue ye was honorable, just as it is honorable to care for ye. There's nothing more to any of it than that."

Aislinn bit her lower lip. What he really meant was that he would have done the same thing for anyone else. But that wasn't what she wanted to hear. She wanted to be someone special in his eyes, and she could not stop herself from asking, "Tell me, do ye know my name? Do ye remember?"

Silence filled the space between them. Bran knew the answer, but did not speak. He fiddled with the dagger, slicing more meat than he would be able to eat. Why was it so hard to admit?

"Do ye remember?" she persisted.

"Aye, I do," he said, the words being wrenched from him as if it were a confession.

"And can ye call me that? Can I hear ye say my name? And I, in turn, will call ye Bran since we are not strangers."

She was right. They were not strangers, and he stared at her in the glow of the fire, thinking that most of what he knew of her was sadly superficial. Indeed, he had been determined to deny anything other than what he wished to believe, or what he saw before him. He was no longer sure of any of it. Despite her ordeal and the loss of some weight, she was as beautiful as ever. But there was something else upon her features, a sort of a suspended, hopeful quality, a vulnerability that he had never seen before. It touched him deeply, and he was moved to whisper, "Aislinn."

Like a burst of light, her features transformed into a radiant smile that brought golden accents to her dark eyes. Her soft voice reverberated with the same pleasure. "To hear ye call me Aislinn pleases me greatly. I have always preferred that, and 'tis especially good to hear it from ye, Bran O'Connor, for while ye may not understand the reasons why, I would not like it if ye called me anything but Aislinn."

"I am glad," he responded with simple elegance. It was a funny, awkward moment as if something momentous had occurred, but he wasn't sure what it could be.

She stared at him as if she'd sensed the same thing, but she said nothing.

Bran turned away. He heard her sigh, and compelled by the dual needs to stay busy and do something more for her, he said, "I'm going to try to remove the chain now."

He sat cross-legged, positioned her head upon the pillow of his lap, and proceeded to work in silence. First, he spread warm boar grease over the wound, in part to soothe it, and in part to protect her neck from the chain. Then he examined the chain, link by link, until he found a break where the metal was not fused together completely. Carefully, he inserted the tip of the dagger into the link and twisted it in an effort to widen the gap.

"Don't move," he said, applying more pressure.

The chain tightened against her neck. She tried to bite back a whimper.

"I'm sorry. I do not want to hurt ye."

"Do what ye must," she whispered.

"This will not take much longer," he said as he tried again. Then it was off. He slid the chain free, and tossed it into a dark corner of the cairn. There was a thin red line about her neck where the chain had rubbed against her, and gently, he applied grease along it.

"Thank ye," she whispered. He had released the chain, yet she was not free. He had control of her destiny. "When will ye send me back?"

"I'll not be sending ye back."

Her heart leapt. Dare she believe him? Dare she hope? She stuttered, "Why?"

"It would not be honorable to let ye go back to people who would do such a thing as this. I cannot do that."

"But I told ye my father did not do this. He is not a cruel man."

"But he is a careless man. He put ye in the care of cruel ones. And that is something I would never do."

"What is it that ye intend to do with me then?" she asked quietly, feeling suddenly cold and alone.

For several minutes, Bran did not speak as he massaged the grease into her neck, and a wonderful calm settled over him. He knew—with a sense of righteousness the likes of which he'd never before known—exactly what he was going to do, and he knew that she was going to be stunned.

"I will take ye to Baravore, Aislinn," Bran said, experiencing at that moment the most intense kinship he'd ever shared with his grandfather. Rourke was seven years dead, but at that moment, it seemed the old chieftain sat with him in that cairn and nodded with satisfaction at his grandson's decision to take Aislinn to Baravore.

Her dark eyes widened to stare at him in astonishment. She was not certain what she had expected, but it had not been this. "*Go raibh maith agat,*" she whispered as an agonizing spark of hope coursed through her. Perhaps he was not as far away as she imagined. *Thank ye* for more than you can ever know. *Thank ye for this sliver of hope that yer soul might be coming to understand what yer intellect denies.* Her eyelashes closed, but not soon enough. Tears escaped to trail down her cheeks. Once before she had hoped for too much, and she could not help herself from doing so again. She knew it was fool's business to hope, but she could no more extinguish hope than stop the sun from rising.

Bran wiped at her tears. "Sleep now. This has been a long day. There is much that has happened, and ye must rest. But when ye next awake, ye'll be even stronger, and soon we will travel."

Later, when she was asleep, Bran did something he'd been yearning to do since he'd told her that he would take her to Baravore.

He took her hand in his and brought it to his lips.

The foundation of his world had been undermined. The arbitrary, fluid forces of the universe were wrecking havoc with his life. He was not sure anymore if she was to blame. To the contrary, it seemed she was the only reality to which he might hold. Indeed, he could not let go, and because of that the future *terrified* him.

Chapter 11

"We must be leaving for the mountains as soon as possible," Bran announced when next Aislinn awoke. He was organizing the contents of his sack and paused to explain, "There isn't adequate food for the horses on the coast. Every bit of foliage has been damaged by salt spray, and the beasts will not eat the fouled leaves and grass."

"Bláth is here?" Aislinn sat up, vaguely recalling his having told her the horses had been sheltered in the tempest. Much of what had been said or had happened over the past days was a muddle to her.

"Aye, she's outside with my stallion. I fetched them while ye slept."

"*Bhfuil se fear tainn*?" she asked. *Is it raining*?

"*Ní hea*. The storm is ended. Truly ended. Are ye strong enough to see for yerself?"

"I'm an entirely new being since ye fed me so royally and removed that wretched chain from about my neck." She stretched her arms and yawned, then rubbed her eyes. "A full belly not only provided me with nourishment to regain some of my strength, but I had a blissful sleep without the gnawing, noisy pangs of hunger to interrupt me."

He nodded, knowing firsthand exactly what she meant, and extending a hand to help her stand, he asked, "How's yer head? Not spinning about in circles, is it, now?"

"I've never been the fainting type," said Aislinn, rising to her feet.

"Only the drowning type," he rejoined as if it were the most natural reply in the world. With an arm wrapped about her waist, he led her out of the burial cairn.

"Was that a jest, Bran O'Connor?" she asked, surprised and pleased at his easygoing demeanor.

"Aye, I believe it was," he admitted, the sound of his own astonishment ringing clear in his voice.

With each step toward the exit, it became brighter and warmer. Aislinn's footsteps became surer, quicker. At the opening, she halted, momentarily dazed by the sunshine, and, shutting her eyes against the glare, she drew a deep breath. A gentle breeze filled her lungs. It billowed the hair off her shoulders in a sort of caress, and a sensation of serenity settled over her. At such a moment as this, it did not seem possible that the future held no hope. She was vividly aware of Bran standing at her side, and she was afraid that if he said anything to her, especially anything nice, she would burst into tears.

Aislinn looked in the opposite direction. There was Bláth, a few yards away. She whistled. The horse raised its head, saw its mistress, whinnied, and ambled to Aislinn, who spoke in low, soothing tones to the animal.

"Do ye think ye could travel now?" Bran moved alongside her again. "Only so far as we would have to go until there was adequate vegetation for the horses, and then we would rest another day—or whatever time ye needed—before covering the final distance to Baravore."

Baravore. Aislinn's heart did a flip-flop. He'd said it again, and part of what had been nothing more than a muddle in her brain began to take the shape of reality. He was taking her to the O'Connor stronghold, she had not imagined that, and the possibilities that that implied were boundless. Indeed, hope was as bright as this cloudless, balmy day, and tears prickled her nose. She blinked hard, and buried her face in Bláth's mane. "I can travel a short distance," she said in a voice just loud enough to be heard.

"Is maith sin," he replied with a sort of blunt male noise of satisfaction. *That's good.* "Now, why don't ye take a few minutes to ready yerself while I clear out the cairn."

She nodded, but still did not look at him as she tried to compose herself. She heard him reenter the passage grave. Already she was feeling a bit better, and while he was inside, Aislinn attended to her private needs. It did not take long for either of them to be done, and in a matter of minutes, they were on their way.

The damage from the storm was extensive. The wind had been violent. Everywhere, torn limbs and uprooted tree trunks were scattered, making a sort of obstacle course through which the horses had to pick their way. The rains had been torrential, and the lush green countryside had taken on a dark brown hue. There was mud where sweet grass had grown, the sun was burning tan spots onto vegetation coated in salt spray, and the water in the pretty, silver-blue brooks swirled downstream in mad, brown whirlpools. Bran and Aislinn made their way over the hill that faced the sea, and down into a valley, where the gullies and vales were littered with mounds of debris left behind when the flood waters had receded. Great black flies buzzed noisily about these piles of wreckage, and from one or two there emanated the unmistakable stench of decay.

They passed over the next ridgeline, and into a second valley that was only slightly better.

"I did not imagine the storm had reached so far," said Bran. He glanced at Aislinn, sitting tall but pale upon her Bláth. "We must be going higher. I am sorry."

"Do not worry about me," she answered, urging Bláth onward. " 'Tis only too pleased, I am, to leave this awful place. I do not like to be reminded of death."

It was all around them. Death. And there was not a soul in *Uí Briúin Cualann* or the hills who did not know the significance of a storm such as the one that had swept across the land these past days. With such destruction, the crops would be ruined, and there would be famine; and with famine in the hills, there came war, and then disease.

Slowly, they ascended a third hill. Only after they had attained the summit and were winding their way down the other side did their surroundings begin to improve. It was greener. The way was not as littered. For the first time, Aislinn realized she had not heard a bird since riding away from the cairn. Now the day began to fill with the familiar caw of rooks and the chatter of smaller birds, all flocked inland in search of seeds or berries, small rodents, or insects for a meal.

They stopped at a clearing beside a stream with a pool that was exactly the right size for bathing. There was grass for the horses, and a wild apple tree with every one of its half-grown apples lying upon the ground. Aislinn had been told that green apples could make one sick, but the idea of a crisp, juicy bite of fruit was irresistible, no matter how tart. She ate two, offered some to Bláth and Bran's stallion, but the animals were much more interested in the yellow gorse flowers they had found.

Aislinn went and stood at the bank that sloped sharply downward to the pool. "It is too steep for my unsteady legs. Could ye help me down?" she asked. "I would have a soak to remove the sea salt and grit from me."

"It will be colder than usual with so much rainwater these past days," Bran warned.

What he said was true, but he did not warn her so much for her sake as for his own. Of a sudden, he was not as comfortable in her presence as he had been earlier in the day. The relaxed, almost companionable atmosphere was gone, and in its place, there was the slow-rising heat of passion. The thought of her bathing made him think of flesh. The image of flesh made him think of how she had stood naked before him in the sweat house, and that memory caused a quickening in his loins. He no longer was thinking of her as a helpless wounded creature, but as a sensuous, desirable woman. This wasn't prudent. While they had been in the cairn, there had been no passion. When he had announced he'd take her to Baravore, he hadn't reckoned with reawakened arousal.

"The water, cold? I don't care," she declared. There was a healthy touch of color on her cheeks, making her appear for that instant like the young woman about whom so much gossip had been whispered. "Come, help me. I do not want to fall, and I intend to have my bath."

"Are ye daring to order me—a chieftain—about as if I were a *betagh*? If this is how ye treated yer father, 'tis no wonder then that the poor man was sending ye to England."

"That's not fair."

"I didn't say it was."

She pouted, then said, "I'm sorry. Would ye please help me? I would be most grateful for yer hand, but I will not beg for it."

He could not help smiling. "I did not think ye would." Bran supported her elbow in a clumsy, yet oddly tender way. He wanted to help, but couldn't risk making contact with more than her elbow. He had no intention of letting his hands touch more of her than was absolutely essential. He did not think he had the will to resist what would happen. As she moved, her musky scent wafted about him; his forearm accidentally brushed against the swell of one soft breast. He could not help her down that embankment fast enough. At last, she waded into the pool, and when the water reached her waist, she submerged herself in one quick motion.

"Och!" she gasped, breaking the surface of the water for air. " 'Tis frigid as ye predicted, but refreshing." She ducked beneath the water again, then rose to standing.

Her back was to Bran. He could not see her breasts, but it was an impossible sight nonetheless, and his breath caught in his throat as the water sluiced off her shoulders and arms, the blue gown affixing itself like a second skin to her slender back and waist. Beads of water glistened on her creamy arms, her hair when wet became longer and trailed past her waist in ink-black curls, and it made him think how he'd like to taste that glistening skin, to smell that hair and caress those arms, that waist, and pull her against him, into his embrace. The desire in his loins tightened. His heart was beating as loud and hard as a *bodhran,* and his palms were too clammy for a grown man. He must get away before he did something that both of them would regret.

"I'll be back," he said, hoarse and abrupt, as he turned to walk out of the clearing with little idea as to what he intended except that he must occupy himself for as long as it required a woman to bathe.

Aislinn took off the gown to scrub it against the gentle gravel in the shallows of the pool. While she had never owned an extensive wardrobe, neither had she ever worn anything soiled or damaged; her mother had taught her how to care for her clothes, airing and brushing them daily, checking for spots and repairing tears as soon as they appeared. Now she cared for Étaín's blue gown with the meticulous attention to detail and sense of pride in household skills that Éatín had imparted to her. A few of the stains disappeared—there was nothing she could do about the tears—but, at least, the gown would be clean, and after wringing out the excess water, she hung the garment over a low branch to dry in the sun and breeze.

Again, she submerged herself, reveling in the sensation of the water closing over her head. She had been lying on the hard, cold floor of that cairn for far too long, and her entire body was sore. Using the fine sand, she scrubbed her arms and legs and scalp, and then floated on her back to rinse the grains from her hair. It was wonderful and revitalizing to recline in the water, her limbs floating weightless. She rested her head on a rock, and turned her face to the sun.

Time passed. The sun was dropping closer to the mountains, and with a quick glance to reassure herself that she was still alone, Aislinn got out of the water. It was not difficult to climb up the embankment without aid, and upon reaching the top, she dried herself with a handful of soft, fragrant leaves before slipping the gown over her head. It was slightly damp, but that didn't bother her as she sat cross-legged to comb her hair with her fingers.

Bran was watching. He had returned to see her adjusting the blue fabric that clung to her. It did nothing in the order of modesty to conceal her alluring form. He could see her breasts, small waist, and the curve of her hips and thighs. She sat down, but the sight was only a little less tempting, and he suspected that no amount of time away from her would be long enough to make it safe to be near her. His absence from the clearing had been for naught, for he wanted her as he had from the first time he set eyes on her in the great hall at Dublin Castle, and without announcing his return, he stood at the edge of the clearing to watch her untangling her hair, eyes closed and face raised to the late afternoon rays of sun as she ran her hands through those glorious black curls.

Aislinn froze. There was a telling chill at the nape of her neck. Someone was in the clearing, and she looked. "How long have ye been there?" she asked Bran, curious why it was that he had not announced his presence.

"Not long," he murmured in reply, making his feet move toward her.

"Is there any more of that boar grease?"

"A little," he said, knowing with an awful sinking sensation that she was about to ask him to take care of her wound. He went to the sack and retrieved what appeared to be nothing more than a wadded-up rag, and turning around, he folded away the corners of the material to reveal a glob of grease. He handed it to her.

"It would be much easier if ye put it on for me," she said, then added a sweet, "if ye please."

Bran stared at her dumb, but not numb. His fingers were itching to touch her.

"I must hold my hair up, ye see," she said when he neither said or did anything. "Is there something wrong?"

"Ní hea." What else was there to say? He wondered if he stammered, or if she heard the overloud beating of his heart, or if she saw the swelling bulge between his legs.

"Gab anall anaice liom," she said. *Come over near me.* "Here, sit behind me in the same fashion I do, and we will be done in no time. Please."

He could think of no way to refuse. So he sat behind her, his crossed legs making a space into which she scooted, fitting rather nicely. Something twisted in his gut. There was a cramp in his loins, and he nearly moaned aloud when she lifted the mass of hair off her back and leaned closer to him.

Gingerly, he applied a tiny bit of grease to the badger-paw scar with the tip of one finger. That was safe enough. *Pat. Pat. Pat.* He barely touched her. Besides, he should not apply too much pressure to the scar. Two more little pats, and he was done. He wanted to stop, but the chafe mark where the chain had rubbed against her needed attention. Lightly, he applied the moisturizing substance, and little by little, more than a single fingertip touched her. One finger became two, then three. Now the palm of one hand rubbed above the scar, then both hands were massaging her neck.

Aislinn's heart was racing. His hands were wonderful, soothing and provocative. She gave a tiny sigh, but she could not relax. She wanted to touch him, kiss him, but she worried he would suspect her, reject her, and she slipped her hands beneath her bottom to prevent them from reaching back for him. It wasn't enough.

"Once when I was a little girl I went with my mother to the linen market in Dublin town," she began, knowing that she must talk in order to deflect the yearnings that were building within her. She was babbling, uncertain where this discourse would take her. "I had never been before, and my mother had told me of the beautiful linen the women of Ulster made, but it was not linen in which I was interested. I had heard of the foreign merchants who docked at the Liffey quays, and I had spent many an hour dreaming and wondering what those foreigners would be like. They would come from Italy and Spain, my mother had said, the places from which oranges and Venetian glass had come, and the people would be splendid, exotic, if not enviable.

"In truth, they were a dingy, sad sight. But that disappointment was not the worst of it. There was a little girl with a Cordovan merchant. She had dark eyes the same as me, curling black hair the same as me, and she was my height, my age—I fancied to guess—and similar in so many other respects, yet she was speaking a strange, foreign tongue, I could not understand, and she was being beaten by a man who onlookers said was her father. In my childish mind, I could not imagine how we could seem so similar, but be so far apart, and I found myself wondering how it might have been, if I'd been born someone else. It frightened me. How was it that she was that little girl and I had come to be me, instead of her? I asked my grandmother those questions, and she told me I was a foolish child. But, tell me, Bran O'Connor, have ye never done that yerself? Wondered what life would be like if ye'd been born someone else?"

"*Ní hea*. I have not." Although Bran was grateful

for the distraction of conversation, he was not certain he liked this probing topic. It was taking his mind down paths he did not like.

"But what if ye were not Irish? If I were not half-English?"

"We would not be the same people," Bran said by way of dismissal. In truth, he could not help speculating on that very point.

"Would ye treat me differently?" Aislinn had to know.

"Differently?" He had to lie. "Aye, lass, everything would be different. Ye wouldn't have schemed to wed my brother, and I would not have been determined to return ye to yer father. *Sin deireadh anois,*" he said. *That's the end of it now.* But whether he meant he'd finished with the grease, or there was nothing more to be said on the topic of what if they'd both been Irish, Bran would not have been able to clarify, if asked.

"Thank ye." Aislinn twisted around, and found him staring at her with a kind of speculation as if he were endeavoring to unravel a mystery. The notion that he might be thinking about her in a fashion that was in any way reflective was unnerving. Likewise, the notion that he could be wondering if there was any situation in which a future might be possible between them was exhilarating. Her tongue played across her lower lip.

Bran gave a fidgety cough.

Aislinn, not knowing what to say or do next, blurted out, "Would ye help me plait my hair so it does not rest against the scar?"

He should move away. But he didn't. The prospect of threading his fingers through that soft hair was too enticing, and he found his hands reaching out in response. A slow, sensuous smile warmed his hooded eyes, softened the gaunt lines of his face.

Without speaking, they set to work. She divided the hair into three equal lengths, then held one length while he started the plaiting process with the other two. Together, they alternated the sections back and forth, and passing each to the other before weaving them across another time.

His fingers brushed against hers. Once, twice, again and again. With each braiding motion there was a fleeting instant of sweet contact, his hand against her hand, his forefinger trailing down the edge of her hand, his warm flesh against hers, and a tremor passed along her arm. She was sharply aware of his virility, and when their fingers brushed against one another again, she had to swallow, for while she could not see his hands, she could visualize those long, lean fingers, their sensual, masculine shape, and her mind began to conjure up images of the things he could do with them.

At last, the plaiting was completed. He secured the end with a strip of leather, and laid the length against her back. She took a steadying breath, then cautiously tilted her head around to thank him. His earlier smile was gone, and, wondering if she had done something to make him angry, her tongue nervously darted out to lick her lips.

Bran almost groaned out loud. That visual effect of this little motion was too much. It had been torture to feel her soft hands, her silky hair, to smell her, and sense her warmth, but now to see her tongue swirl out to moisten those delectable red lips was too much. To feel her move between his crossed legs, her arms brushing against his inner thighs, was highly arousing. There was another, stronger surge in his loins, and without thought he twisted her around in such a way that they faced each other, the dress rucking up above her knees. One of her legs extended beneath his slightly bent knee, her other leg lay across his straight one, and he put his arms about her shoulders to hold her against his chest as he set his lips to her brow, her eyes, the tip of her nose, and then upon her mouth to kiss her with unbearable longing.

Aislinn's lips yielded instantly. This was what she wanted. Their breaths mingled, their tongues touched.

"Ye know I want to make love to ye," he murmured, his voice husky with passion. His eyes were very green, very intense and smoldering with emotion. They swept over her face to fix upon her mouth. His embrace tightened, his stiff arousal straining against the material of his breeches.

His lingering gaze was disarming, but never so much as the slight pressure he exerted to press her closer to him, causing an aching need to ripple through Aislinn. Moisture burst within her. She relaxed in his embrace, rocked into him, feeling with a sense of exaltation the swelling between his legs, and remembering how that hard, hot maleness had filled her. Maybe this time, he would not leave her at the end.

"And I would let ye love me," she murmured. Her fingers slid inside the opening of his tunic, and another wave of need pulsed through her at the sensation of the firm, muscled lines of his chest beneath her fingertips. She spread her palms wide to feel as much of him as she could.

Bran reached up and grabbed her wrists to stop her hands.

Right away, she knew what this meant. "Ye want to make love to me, but ye won't," she whispered, soft and mournful. Deliberately, her wrists pivoted in his grasp until the fingers of each of her hands grazed the top of his. She sensed his grip loosen at this contact, but he did not let go.

"I can't." His expression clouded with reluctance, and his regard slid from her face to their hands. Still he did not let go. He merely stared as their touching hands began to move in tandem.

Slowly, their hands shifted in a caressing motion, lightly brushing the sensitive inner flesh between each other's fingers. They each held their breath as they watched the exotic, alluring dance that culminated in their fingers being entwined together.

"Are ye so sure it is wrong?" Her soft whisper was laden with passion as she took one of his long slender fingers and kissed the tip. She sensed the tremor that ran through him, and let her lips close over the end, taking it into her mouth to run her tongue up and down its length.

"Ye make it very hard for me, *cuileann*." His voice was harsh, raw. In truth, Bran no longer knew if it was wrong, but he couldn't afford to be ambivalent, and so he pulled his hand away from her mouth and made a small space between their bodies. He was altogether unprepared for this. Nothing had changed; she was still an intoxicating poison. He reminded himself of why he had warned his brother against her, but with her so near, so willing, so warm and lovely, it was torment to do the right thing. The night before, he had admitted to himself fear of the future, and now this heart-pounding, gut-twisting passion only made it worse.

"Is it wrong?" she asked again.

"All my life I have believed in one thing. My grandfather fought against the English at Bannockburn, he shared in the Highlanders' victory over King Edward, and it gave him hope that one day the English could be sent out of Ireland. He struggled for that every day as surely as he defended the purity of O'Connor blood, and I wanted nothing more than to be like him. To carry on his noble cause. When he was alive, everything I did was to please him, and when he died and the clan made me chieftain in his place, I was determined to be like him. There would never be any reason to doubt that I was his grandson, his heir," Bran said, but the usual pride and certainty that accompanied this speech were gone from his voice. Instead, there was a hollow quality that made his words sound automatic.

"Was he always right?" It was not a challenge, merely a question.

"I thought so," he said with a catch in his voice as if he wanted to be reassured.

She looked at him, and the space he had made between them. *So near and yet so far*. There was an ache in her heart. Would there never be anything more? It was not comforting to realize one's entire future rested on the legacy of a dead man. For that, Aislinn wanted to resent the old chieftain, but couldn't. Indeed, she wondered what manner of man he had been. "I would know more of this grandfather of yers. Tell me about the woman he married."

"Och, that's a tale, indeed. She was a Scottish lass, his cousin, in fact. Rourke's grandfather, Ingvar, was a Highlander who had been adopted by a Norse King. He had a twin sister named Isobel, from whom he'd been separated as a babe, who went on to marry the Kirkpatrick laird of Torridon and Loch Awe. Rourke's Viviane was that Isobel's granddaughter, Caitrine. But neither of them knew this when they met. Rourke had been wounded by the English in a pass above Loch Awe, and his body was washed upon the shore of a hermit's isle, where Caitrine lived in isolation. She nursed him back to health, but she'd lost her memory, ye see, at the cruel hands of the English. She did not know she was actually Caitrine Kirkpatrick, sister of the laird, and so she called herself Viviane after Queen Guinevere's tutor, the Lady of the Lake in the tale of the Grail Maidens. My grandfather always said the name suited her far better than Caitrine, for she was a rare beauty, wild and dark-haired and—" His voice faltered.

Much like yerself, he'd almost said. Is that what he believed? Was it true? Could it be that somehow there was a link between his grandmother and this young woman who had been thrust upon his life?

"And did ye know this Viviane, yer grandmother?" she asked, completely unaware of what it was that Bran had almost said. In fact, she did not know that she had drawn from him more than anyone—man or woman, friend or foe—had in years. She did not know that she had taken him another step down the path to questioning his reality, a step closer to a future that would contradict everything he held dear.

"Aye, I knew her, but not as well as Rourke, for while my grandfather lived into his seventh decade, Viviane did not survive the first pestilence. Both my father and grandmother died before I was six winters old, and my memories of them are hazy at best. I've always regretted their loss before I might have known them. I've even wondered if things might have been different if Rourke had not devoted so much of his energy and time to me. My mother has often told me how I resemble his grandfather, Ingvar, and his cousin, Alexander, who was Viviane's brother, and as Rourke got older, I sometimes thought my grandfather was trying to recapture them through me. He was never a man to engender pity, but there was a melancholy that came upon him from time to time."

"The plague," she said in hushed voice as if that

one word explained all. "There is no one it has not touched, no corner of Ireland, nor recess of any man's heart that has not been changed beyond recovery. It was never the same after the pestilence. Never the same. At Killoughter everyone in the garrison and all my family, excepting me and my father, perished that second time. For weeks it was a keep of ghosts, and moldering bodies, and while it did not kill my father, his spirit was much blighted. He hardly ever called me Aislinn after that, and that was when I started thinking about how important Ireland was to me."

Bran listened, enraptured, spellbound.

"While my mother lived I took Ireland for granted. Only after she was gone did I realize that while I was caught betwixt two worlds, I only felt a connection with one of them. Indeed, the very one that seemed to be fading beyond my reach. I knew then as I do now that I do not want to die in a cold, English fortress, to be buried within sight of the high, boggy hills as my mother had been. When I die I want to be buried in the earth of those hills," she said, the depth of her emotion making her voice quaver. There were tears in her eyes. After the space of a few heartbeats, she asked, "Did ye never wonder why ye were spared?"

"Never," he replied, somber. "It was always obvious to me. I was meant to be chieftain. Which is the reason why I must not fail. And how about ye, Aislinn?" This time, her name did not flow easily from his tongue. "Do ye know why it was ye were spared?"

"Cruel whim."

"Cruel to survive? To live? *Cén fáth sin*?" he asked. *Why so?* He saw the tears she tried to blink away. Dewdrops in the sun. His heart was aching for her.

"How could ye believe such a bleak thing? Why not something special?"

"Once I believed I was meant to fulfill some greater destiny, but it was nothing more than a childish device to deal with loss, to explain an evil I could neither understand, nor conquer. These past weeks the truth has been revealed to me. Indeed, ye've helped me see it." She laughed, a short, hard sound saturated with pain. "Neither yer world, nor my father's wants me. Is it not farcical to imagine such a forlorn creature could possibly be destined for anything special?"

Bran felt the burden of guilt she attributed to him, and he could not look at her. She was right. He was, in part, responsible for the bleak spot on this woman's spirit. He had never meant to hurt her. But she had seemed indomitable, and he had been determined to protect Niall, determined to win. Now he wondered who would protect him.

"After we reach Baravore what will ye do with me?" she asked. He had moved farther away. He put his back to her, and was taking out his flints for a fire.

Bran did not reply right away. If he might, he would ease her anguish, but it was impossible to imagine what he could do beyond what he had already promised. He would not return her to the people who treated her so cruelly, so carelessly, and implicit in that was the pledge that he would treat her with honor and respect, but beyond that there was naught but uncertainty. Bran was eager to reach Baravore, for his mother, whose counsel was generally sound, would know what he should do next.

"My mother is a wise woman," he told Aislinn. "She will know what is best for everyone."

"Ye're going to rid yerself of me somehow."

He opened his mouth to deny this, but couldn't. "Ye know that is what I must do. Only this time, I'll be careful," he said, unaware that by his words he was becoming the champion Niall had fancied he might be in her behalf. "I won't do anything that might put ye in jeopardy, and I'll never let anyone send ye out of Ireland."

Those were the kindly words she had dreaded. She put her hand over her mouth to muffle her little sob, but she could not stop the tears that streaked her face.

Chapter 12

It was twilight when they entered the valley, and the beacon from Bébinn's tower chamber drew Bran down the length of Glenmalur. An owl hooted, another answered, and Aislinn glanced upward to regard the steep, wooded cliffs.

"My clansmen are watching us, and signaling to each other," said Bran. "We will be expected."

Up ahead loomed the fortress with two stone towers, positioned on the higher ground above a ford from which it took its name, Baravore. They crossed the stream and went up the incline as the portcullis was lifted and the gate opened.

"It is not what I expected," said Aislinn, slowing Bláth to marvel at the massive stronghold.

"How so?"

"I had expected Baravore to be more traditional. Similar to Annacurragh with its wooden structures and palisade of thorny hedges."

"Ye do not approve?"

"That was not my meaning," she said, detecting a tension in his voice, and a distance he seemed to be creating between them. This strain had clung to the air about them since they'd stood on the crest at Ballyteige to gaze into the valley before commencing their descent. Aislinn feared the arrival at Baravore was not going to be easy. It had seemed such a miracle when he had said he would bring her here, now she saw that it was probably a serious mistake. With the diplomacy of a court envoy, she qualified, " 'Tis only that it seems modern." Although what she actually meant was *It seems Anglo-Norman,* but dared not utter it aloud.

"My grandfather called it Scottish. Whatever, it is well fortified against the English. They have never subdued Glenmalur, and have always known better than to dare an assault against Baravore."

Before she might reply, a pack of dogs raced through the gate, barking and leaping in excited welcome. From the rampart above, one of Bran's clansmen bellowed the O'Connor battle cry, "*O Dhia! gach an cathar.*"

Bran held his hands to his mouth, and responded with a deep, earsplitting rendition of the same. From the other side of the wall, the motto was echoed by others, and the air filled with wild yells and the howling of dogs.

Bran and Aislinn went through the gate tower, past the old fosse and remnants of a wooden palisade, and into the bailey. The yard was teeming with curious children, more barking dogs, indignant, clucking hens, confused, bleating sheep, and men and women come out to greet their chieftain. Niall stood apart from the crowd with two women; one was a tall, older woman with pale hair, and the other was a copper-haired girl. Aislinn recognized both of the women from Dysert.

Bran slid off his stallion, handed the reins to a waiting lad, and turned to help Aislinn dismount. But his younger brother was already at her side.

"Aislinn, welcome to Baravore," Niall greeted her in circumspect tones. He was more than a little uneasy, and plainly confused by her arrival with his brother, who had been so determined to keep her away from the O'Connors. Bran would never have brought her here unless something was terribly wrong. Niall studied her in concern and trepidation. He saw how tired she was. There were apprehensive lines about her eyes, and a general lack of color in her complexion. Her shoulders sagged with exhaustion, while she valiantly held her chin high. Her lustrous black curls, pulled off her neck into a plait, revealed an ugly, partially healed scar on the side of her neck and a chafe mark that circled her slender throat. "God's blood," Niall exclaimed in horror, confusion giving way to outrage. He spun around to confront Bran. "What have ye done to her?"

"Keep back," Bran said, his jaw rigid, his lips compressed in a tight, bloodless line. "I left ye in the gate tower. What are ye doing walking about? Who was it dared to disobey my orders?"

Niall did not answer these questions, instead, he faced Bran with his shoulders squared, and his feet set apart as if in a battle stance. "Ye said ye would not hurt her. *Se do beata, Bran. God save ye, Bran,* for what ye've done." He ignored Bran's order to keep back, and reached up to assist Aislinn.

"Don't be touching her," Bran spoke in a sort of snarl. He did not like Niall's implication any more than he liked the depth of concern in his voice. Nor did he like the easy way his brother had said *Aislinn* when he greeted her, especially when he himself found it impossible to use her Irish name. He still thought of her as Johanna Elizabeth, although he did not call her that. Truth to tell, he avoided calling her by any name at all. Quickly, he lifted her off Bláth before Niall might do so. He did not want Niall to touch her in any way.

"What happened?" Niall asked neither of them in particular. He spoke aloud the question that was on everyone's mind. " 'Tis more than two weeks since Bran left. What happened?"

"The weather has been a problem," Aislinn heard her own voice. What she said explained nothing, she merely hoped to diffuse some of the rising hostility.

"But where have ye been? I do not understand. How were ye injured? What has my brother done to ye?"

"Yer brother did not do this to me, Niall. He saved my life."

"Tell me what it is that I can do." When Niall looked at Aislinn, he did not see a woman with whom he'd once fancied himself in love—Ceara had forever erased all others from that place in his heart—he saw only a woman in need. It was impossible to envision Bran saving her, not after everything he'd accused her of doing. "How can I help?" Niall asked her. "Do ye want me to take ye home to yer father?"

"I said keep back. She is in my care," Bran snapped at Niall, then he scowled at Aislinn. In bringing her to Baravore, he had merely intended to pursue an honorable course. Why were they making it difficult for him? "Both of ye, heed me, now. Stay away from each other."

Niall swore a nasty Irish oath at Bran, while Aislinn cast a startled below-the-lashes look at him. The only other time she had seen him this angry was when he'd accused her of deceiving him about her virginity. Surely, he did not suspect her of some further deception, or that Niall must still be protected from her.

"*Gab a leit, a cailín.*" The older of the two women who had been standing beside Niall stepped forward and spoke to Aislinn, "*Come hither, girl.*"

Bewildered by Bran's contempt, Aislinn glanced toward the friendly voice.

"Pay no heed to them," Bébinn said in as composed and quiet a tone of voice as she could manage. She knew who the girl was without being told, and she knew from the moment that Bran had told her of Niall's involvement with Sir Roger's daughter that this young woman would come into their lives and nothing would ever be the same again. Perhaps punishment was to be rained down upon her children for her secret. She did not want them to suffer because of her. Or could it be atonement? Was it possible that they might learn from her past? She struggled not to reveal any of this inner turmoil, for surely Fate was at work this day, and there was nothing mortals might do to reverse what had been started so many years before. She forced a bright smile. "Ye know how brothers can be. I am Bébinn, their mother, and I can assure ye this squabbling between the pair of them is nothing new. I apologize that ye should be subjected to it."

Bran glared at Bébinn. She was probably the one who had unshackled Niall. If it was not bad enough that his mother was another meddler, she was now speaking as if he were a lad who was in need of a sound thrashing behind the falcon shed.

As for Aislinn, she twisted her fingers together, and did not know where to look, nor what to do. When she had thought of this coming to Baravore she had been selfish. It saved her from leaving Ireland. Baravore meant going into the hills, away from the coast where ships set sail to England, and that was all that mattered to her. She had not given any consideration to the O'Connor clan, and how they would react to her. She had not thought of Bran, and what bringing one of the degenerate English into his stronghold might imply. And may the sweet, virginal St. Daghain of the Leinstermen pardon her, she had not even thought of Niall, and how he might react to seeing her again, to knowing that she had not truly loved him, and to discovering—pray, God forbid—that she had coupled with his brother.

But it was Bran, not Niall or any of the other O'Connor clansmen, who was troubled by her presence at Baravore, which was why Aislinn did not move toward Bébinn as she'd encouraged. It would only make him angrier than he already was, and Aislinn did not want that. She stood there clasping and unclasping her hands as her conscious mind acknowledged what she had tried to deny. This was not right. Bran should not have brought her to Baravore.

"Why don't ye come with me. *Tarr liomsa.* The night wind is rising. There is a fire in the hall, and I am sure after yer journey a bowl of oatmeal would be a comfort." Bébinn stepped forward to take motherly charge of Sir Roger's exhausted daughter. *Come along with me.* She slipped a consoling arm through hers.

Aislinn managed a wobbly smile of gratitude as every gentle memory of her own mother rushed back to her. She wanted to go with Bran's mother and let her take care of her; perhaps she would comb her hair as her own mother had done, and while she ate, they would indulge in womanly talk. She remembered how her mother had taught her Irish lullabies, and how in the end, she had sat beside her mother, singing quietly, tearfully as the pestilence took her away. Tears prickled her eyes, and for a moment, it seemed to Aislinn that she might find in Bran's mother a part of the past she had so desperately missed.

"No, she comes with me. I brought her here. I'll care for her," Bran declared.

His harsh voice dashed Aislinn's vision of sitting beside Bébinn before a fire.

"But—," began Bébinn, sensing the way Aislinn tensed when Bran spoke. She saw the sheen of tears shimmering in the girl's dark eyes. "There is food in the hall."

"This is none of yer affair, Mam." Bran pulled Aislinn away from Bébinn, realizing with a profound sense of shock that he was jealous. He did not want to share her with anyone, not even his mother. "If she's hungry, she can eat in my chamber."

His grip about her upper arm was painfully tight. Aislinn's head jerked up. Her gaze fused with his, and her breath caught. She had seen that smoldering light before. It was more than anger, and she did not resist when he pulled her against his chest right there in front of his entire family. She could not resist when he stood over her, glaring down at her from his height, and his hand cupped her chin, tilting her face upward as if he might kiss her. She heard the shocked gasps from the women. A bright red flush heated her cheeks, and she cast her eyes downward, breaking the connection with his penetrating gaze. Still he held her hard to his chest.

From the corner of one eye, Aislinn saw the young woman whisper to Niall. She imagined hearing the words, *Help her,* and Niall started to move, but Bébinn put out an arm to block his way.

"I'm glad to see all of ye haven't lost yer heads. It appears that, this time, at least, Niall, ye've managed to show some sense in yer selection of female company," said Bran on a savage underbreath of barely controlled rage. Then he led Aislinn away from the gaping onlookers.

* * *

" 'Twas quite a scene ye caused," said Aislinn. While she spoke in a soft voice, her anger was revealed in the stormy light of her eyes, the tight lines of her mouth. She had not uttered a word when Bran escorted her from the bailey and up a tower stair, but now that they were out of sight and sound of the others, she could no longer keep silent.

"A scene? How so?" Bran pierced her with a mean, narrow stare before he propelled her through an open door. They had reached the second level in the tower.

Aislinn was exhausted, emotionally and physically, but she had to get this said. "Ye might as well have declared to yer mother and Niall and yer entire clan that ye've had carnal knowledge of me. Was it yer intention to make them believe I'm yer possession to do with as ye will? If so, I cannot fathom why ye, the great protector of the pure O'Connor blood, would admit to such a thing with a half-breed such as myself."

"Ye don't know what ye're talking about," he shot back while an inner voice told him that of course, she did know, and the problem was that he didn't. When he had pulled her to him in that suggestive fashion, he had been compelled by the same force that had made him smear his blood across her lips. Both times he had been angry, almost beyond control. Both times he had been overwhelmed by a sense of the world spinning out of its natural boundaries. Both times he had needed to do something to assert his authority, especially over her.

"Och, but I do know of what I talk, and foolish is the man who denies it."

"Watch yer tongue!"

"What will ye do?" she asked with challenge in her voice.

Bran clenched his teeth against his fury at her insolence. He saw his anger reflected in the golden lights that flashed from the depths of her eyes.

"Will ye beat me?"

Bran did not reply. He turned his back on her, for indeed, he feared that she would push him beyond tolerance, and that he would raise a hand against her in anger. That was something he had never done to a woman, and, with the grace of the Lord, he would never do. There was much she might make him do, but never that.

Taking even, deep breaths, he puttered about the chamber they had entered. It was a simple room with a narrow, rectangular window recessed in each of three walls, one facing Mullacor Mountain to the north, one looking to the east, and another with a view of Lugnaquillia to the south. The shutters at the windows were hung with leather hinges, and this night, they were closed against the chill. The door through which they had entered was in the western wall, in which a garderobe was also situated. The wooden floor was covered in fresh rushes mixed with creamy white meadow-sweet blossoms, and when they walked upon it the smell of sunshine wafted about her. Those were the only trappings of comfort. There was no brazier, no draft excluders upon the walls, and the furnishings were scant. A low bed covered with skins was positioned in the middle of the floor with a chest at the top and bottom ends of the bed, and by the middle window, the one facing east, there was a heavy, carved chair. Bran knelt upon the rushes, his back to her, and raised the lid of one of the chests to rummage about inside.

Aislinn did not like the way he busied himself to avoid talking with her. Determined to draw him out, and to have a response, she stated, "I do not belong here."

It worked.

"Aye, ye don't belong at Baravore," he spoke, but did not look at her. He withdrew a tunic and pair of breeches from the chest, tossed them on the bed, and rose to standing.

"That's true," she agreed on a convulsive gulp. He was going to change clothes. Right in front of her. She swallowed again. "But what I meant was that while I'm here I should not be in yer chamber."

"Where else then?" He pulled off the soiled tunic, walked around the bed to the second chest where there was a laver filled with water. Quickly, he doused his head and face, and used the discarded tunic to dry himself before donning the clean one, then he removed his breeches. The fresh tunic reached his knees. Nothing was revealed. He faced Aislinn. "Where else would ye belong? With Niall?"

"No, of course not. With the other women. In yer mother's bower, perhaps."

"While ye're at Baravore, ye'll stay here." His low voice was heavy with resolve and deeper meaning. He pulled on the breeches.

"Ye do not trust me."

He stared at her much as he had in the great hall at Dublin Castle. His facial muscles froze, for he could not afford to reveal the truth to anyone, most of all not to himself. He stared, and his eyes could not take in enough of her. She was so beautiful of body and soul that it was actually physically painful for him. Beautiful and forbidden, and he wondered for what crime he was being punished with this unholy trial of endurance.

"Ye don't trust me, do ye?" she repeated so softly he felt more than heard the sorrow in her voice.

Rationally, he did not doubt her, but his emotions were a jumble of incertitude, and in this instance, suspicion and misbelief overruled reason. "I'm trusting ye no less than I trust Niall or any of the other men of Baravore around a woman like ye."

Whatever Aislinn had intended to say withered in her throat, and she turned away in a futile attempt to erase the pain caused by his words. He might as well have called her a whore.

"I must leave Baravore. In my absence ye're to be staying in this chamber." He took two lengths of wool from the chest, and rolled one inside the other, making a sort of pack.

"Where do ye go?"

"I ride north to the O'Toole motte. If the storm damage extends into the northern hills and the length of *Uí Briúin Cualann*, we must be preparing to ward off famine this winter."

"But ye might be away for days," she complained, struggling to disguise her exhaustion. She could sleep without interruption for as long as he might be away, but she did not tell him this. "What ye ask makes me a prisoner. Will ye post a guard at the door?"

"Don't beg an argument with me. I'm tired and must travel far this night. *Ní hea,* I will not post a guard unless ye force me to do so. I want yer promise that ye will stay here." He threaded his fingers through his long black hair. The braids had been undone for days, the unkempt hair kept falling across his face, and he pushed it away in a gesture that manifested his weariness. "It would mean much to hear ye promise to honor my request."

"Why?" She was stunned.

"I can't truly say," he replied with such a look of uncertainty that he had never seemed as mortal as he did at that moment. He was bleak and lost, and could not hide it.

Honesty was a disarming thing. It reminded Aislinn how difficult this return had been for him. He had brought her to Baravore because it was honorable. That, however, did not erase the possibility that he had done so at the expense of his peace of mind, his principles, and perhaps, even at the cost of his reputation in the clan. Despite his unreasonable request that she stay in this chamber, there was much for which she should be indebted to him, not the least of which was her life.

"I promise to wait here. I can do no less in partial thanks for what ye've done for me, and when ye return, I will repay ye by leaving Baravore. Ye're right. It was a mistake to bring me where I do not belong. Ye may have saved my life, but that does not make ye responsible for me."

The sensation of being punched in the gut slammed into Bran. She did not speak sharply, yet her words cut him to the marrow. Indeed, this reaction was disconcerting, alarming, and perhaps, the only proof he required that she was right to speak as she did. He should be gratified that she was offering to leave. Still, he did not like to hear it.

"We can talk about the future later," he said, wishing that she would not look at him so intently, knowingly. It was as if she was peering into his soul, and he did not like to think that she might witness what a weak creature he truly was. He buckled his belt about the tunic, sheathed his dagger and sword, and, tossing the pack over his back, left the chamber. The door closed behind him, silently marking his departure.

Only after he was long gone did Aislinn dare to go to the bed and lie down. She slipped beneath the mound of fox pelts and wolf skins, and was fast asleep before her head touched the rush-filled pallet.

* * *

In the morning, Bébinn fetched two vials—one of wort, the other kings-spear oil—from the medicinal alcove in the kitchen, and went to the chamber in the tower on the level beneath hers. She knocked on the door, which swung open, and she glanced inside. Sir Roger's daughter was awake. The young woman was sitting in the chair by a window, the shutters were opened wide, and she was staring north in the direction she must have known Bran had ridden when he left Baravore. Sir Roger's daughter was waiting for her son, and Bébinn's heart soared with warmth.

"May I come in?" she asked.

Aislinn looked around. She had heard the door open, but she had not turned to see who entered. If it was Bran, he had returned too soon, for she was not ready to leave. If it was Niall, she did not know what to do, for while she was under no compulsion to please Bran, she did not want to do anything that would enrage him, which visiting with Niall was bound to do. It was going to be difficult enough to bid him farewell when she left Baravore, and at the very least, she did not want her parting memories to be ones of confrontation.

But it was neither of the men. Aislinn relaxed, and answered Bran's mother, "Please come in . . . if I am allowed visitors."

"My son did not say anything to the contrary." Bébinn entered and smiled. "Here, see, I have brought some oils for yer wound. It is a burn, is it not?"

"*Tá*," Aislinn replied simply. She did not want to talk about what the Windsors had done to her, and gladly sat where Bébinn indicated on the bed beside her.

"This is crushed wort stems mixed with the oil of olives from Italian traders, and this is oil from the leaves of the kings-spear plant."

"I am familiar with the remedies."

"Then ye know they can be warm, at first, but that they will soothe yer wound and encourage new skin to grow." Bébinn used a tuft of wool to apply the oils, first to the burn, and then along the chafe mark that was beginning to look better. After a while, Bébinn spoke, "I have wanted to meet ye, Aislinn Clare, for a very long time. I did not trust what my son had to say about ye, and I am pleased to see for myself that ye're as lovely as yer mother."

"Ye knew my mother?" Aislinn asked in amazement, and wondering to herself why this woman could have wanted to meet her.

"Aye, I knew Étaín MacMurrough. *Dob i an bean a bailne dreac,* and ye're the very image of her at the same age. *She was the most beautiful woman.* We were playmates as girls, ye see, for our mothers were kin by marriage, and I often visited Annacurragh when my parents went to the market fair, or my brothers moved our cattle to and from the high ground. Indeed, it's still hearing yer grandmother, Marga, I am, scolding us for tumbling into the Aughrim in our search for faerie gold. Selfish little thieves, she called us, and told us we would be blessed, if we were not cursed by the *sidhe* for our troubles."

"Faerie gold. That jogs my memory, indeed now. I do know of ye," Aislinn said, some of the mystery revealing itself to her. "My mother talked of ye, she did, and I am sorry for not recalling yer name sooner. It was often that she spoke of her friend who could not visit us at Killoughter." Aislinn fell into an awkward moment of silence, for she did not like to acknowledge the enmity the O'Connors held for her kind. But she was curious, and could not stay silent for long. "Ye've met my father, too, then, for my mother said it was ye, who was bold enough to walk up to the high table at Black Castle and ask that the lord of Killoughter be so kind as to spend a moment with two Irish girls from the hills."

"*Ó tá*. I have met yer father. Indeed, I knew him before that night. I knew him when he was only a young knight with no prospects from Carlow." She set aside the vial of wort oil, and looked at Aislinn, of a sudden her countenance taking on solemn, pale expression. "Do ye know what my eldest daughter was named?"

A chill skirled up the length of Aislinn's backbone to the nape of her neck.

"She was named Aislinn like yerself, for the moments—," Bébinn faltered. She closed her eyes for only a second, took a fortifying breath, and then rushed onward in speech before she lost the nerve to tell the story that must be told. "She was named Aislinn for the moments yer father and I shared. I named my first-born child Aislinn because she was conceived of a time that was nothing more than a dream. Exquisite in its pleasure, but fleeting and unattainable."

"*Ní tuigim tu*," Aislinn whispered on a frightened hush. She wrapped her arms about herself for warmth. *I do not understand ye*. The chill was spreading from her neck along her shoulders, and down her arms. The physical manifestations of her premonitions had never been like this before, and she began to tremble, knowing she was about to learn something of great importance. Indeed, her whole notion of the order of her world was about to change.

"*Tá*, now is the time, and 'tis ye who must hear, because I think ye will understand." She glanced for a moment at her hands, then looked up, and began, "I was young, only fourteen years, and betrothed to Echrí O'Connor, when I met yer father. Mind ye, we did not meet in any formal sense, for we were not introduced, nor did we even come to know one another's names until months later.

"A fair day, it was. So much of it remains clear in my mind. The rustle of the leaves, the smell of overripe berries burst by the sun, and the stiff fabric of the newly dyed tunic I wore for the first time. I was in the forest gathering mushrooms when our paths crossed, and in a single moment, I knew what the older girls meant when they spoke of starlight and earth-trembling when they set eyes upon a man, for I could scarcely speak when I saw yer father. Such feelings had never coursed through me when I looked upon Echrí, and I was at once as frightened as I was spellbound. He was my betrothed's enemy—that much I knew by his manner of dress and the heavy saddle upon his great war horse—yet I had never set eyes upon a man of such fair face and form, and when he spoke I had never sensed the kindness of soul and spirit he possessed. He was the most gentle man I have ever known, and when he kissed me—"

"*Ní hea,* stop. Do not tell me any more." Aislinn's hands flew to her ears. "Do ye accuse my father of seduction?"

"To the contrary, there was no seduction. What happened was right and natural, and to this day, I remember standing in that clearing, my basket of mushrooms spilled upon the earth, and thinking that the moment must have been ordained. We must have been destined, and yer father must have thought so, too, for afterwards, he searched for me, though he did not know where I lived, nor my name, and it took many months for him to find me."

"What happened?"

"Nothing. By the time yer father found me I was wed to Echrí, and my belly was swollen with child. Although yer father dared to come here to Baravore in search of me, he was a gentleman, and told no one of his purpose. He would never cuckold another man, nor put me in jeopardy by betraying what had passed between us. He made some feeble excuse about what business had brought him so deep into the mountains, and then he left. I did not see him again until that night at Black Castle, where English and Irish together were celebrating the feast of St. John, and Étaín declared she would marry him. By then so much had changed. He had become Sir Roger, lord of Killoughter, and I had several children. Étaín did not know my secret, and when she declared her interest in him as a husband, I thought that if another woman must have him then it was only right that it should be my dearest friend." She paused. Great silver tears spiked her eyelashes, and she tried to smile at the bittersweet memory, but failed. "Och, how Étaín giggled and lauded me for being brave enough that night to walk up to the Lord of Killoughter and ask for an audience. Verily, she never knew the half of the bravery it entailed."

Bébinn was crying, very quietly. Her hands remained folded upon her lap, she sat very straight, and did not wipe away the tears as they trailed down her face.

"Yer eldest daughter," Aislinn broke the silence, "she-she is my sister?"

"She was." Bébinn's hands moved now, and trembling she took Aislinn's in hers to hold them tight. She raised them to her own tear-wet face in a gesture that spoke of maternal affection and need. "My own dear, little, precious Aislinn is herself no more than a dream. Succumbed to a fever, she did, before she ever took her first step."

"Is truag liom e." Aislinn started to cry as quietly as Bébinn. *I am sorry for it.* She cried for Bébinn and her

dead sister, and for her father. "Why did ye share this with me?"

"Do ye love my son?"

"Niall?" Every time she was reminded of him, Aislinn knew a rush of shame at how easily she forgot him again.

"Nay, my older son. Do ye love my Bran?"

For a moment, Aislinn's final shred of composure almost fled her. "Does it matter?"

"It should," came Bébinn's reply as she wiped away the tears. "For many years I have been wishing that there would be someone at Baravore waiting for Bran. Now there is someone, but I fear he will never know why it is that ye were willing to wait for him."

"It does not matter. When he returns I am going to leave."

"Why? Do ye not feel anything for him?"

"What I feel is of little importance. By staying I can only hurt him, and I do not want that."

"Where will ye go?"

"Back to Annacurragh. I should never have wished for more from the start. I wanted an Irish husband, and I am told my cousin Sean might be willing to take me to wife. 'Tis welcomed there, I am, and I should never have tried to manipulate the future."

"I do not think Bran will like that, if ye leave."

"Bran does not know what he likes."

"That is true, and while yer staying might cause pain, it would pass. Indeed, any pain out of yer staying would never be as bad as the pain of separation. That kind of pain never heals. I know." She looked at Aislinn, ran a maternal hand down her cheek, and gave a little wistful smile. "I was only twenty when I was widowed, and do not mistake me, I loved my husband, but, in truth, my mourning was not for him, but for what I never had. Once Bran asked me why I never remarried, and he supposed it must have been because no man could replace Echrí. What stopped me was knowing that to marry again would be to make another mistake. There was no passion of the souls between myself and Echrí, and although I came to love him, and could not imagine life without our children, my secret is this: The icy, empty spot on my heart is not for my dead husband, it is for a handsome, young stranger in a forest glen, and the most beautiful, yet most despairing afternoon of my life. It was nothing but a dream."

Aislinn was astonished at such depth of emotion, and while she did not want to hurt Bébinn, she did not like to imagine her parents' marriage had not been what she believed it to be. It was impossible to stop herself from saying, "My father adored my mother."

"And rightly he should have, for Étaín was lovely and bold and clever and witty, and if he had taken a wife and failed to cherish her, he would not be the man I thought him to be. In truth, I never imagined yer father had given me much of a passing thought in all these years until I heard that he had named ye Aislinn, and then I could not help but hope and wonder, if somehow he might have cherished a memory of that afternoon, if somehow our souls had shared that same dream."

This was the most tragic thing Aislinn had ever heard. This exquisite woman had lived with lonely dreams, and the secret of her dead daughter and lost love for all these years. "But surely if yer feelings were so sharp, so strong, surely they must have been shared, reciprocated—"

"That is not always how it works."

Aislinn knew that Bébinn was right, and she could not help wondering at the heartbreak Bran's mother would suffer if she learned her father had wed a young English bride. Did she already know?

"I tell ye this, Aislinn Clare, not to place the weight of my grief upon yer heart, but I tell ye this tale because I do not want the same to happen to ye, nor to my son. I do not want yer passion and love to become nothing more than a dream. Ye cannot let that happen."

Chapter 13

"Aislinn," Bran called out. He took the stairs to his chamber in great long strides, several steps at a time. There was elation in his voice, for having hastened his way through the ravines and passes, he was finally returned, and did not feign to hide his satisfaction. He had been lonely on this journey. Indeed, he had been lonely for a long time, years, perhaps, and only this past week in his absence from Baravore had Bran realized how one unlikely woman had filled that empty space inside him, beside him.

Much too conveniently did Bran brush reality to the back of his mind. The prospect of homecoming was much too alluring. He ignored the fact that she was half-English and had vowed to leave Baravore, the fact that there could never be another homecoming such as this. It only mattered that now she would be in his chamber, where he had left her, and he rushed through the door, a smile of greeting upon his face, only to come to an abrupt halt at the sight of her kneeling before one of his coffer chests. Every muscle in his body convulsed in a reaction that was a harbinger of the anger that began to coil through him.

Aislinn heard Bran enter. She had heard him use

her Irish name. There was delighted astonishment on her face when she glanced up. She was astonished by this exuberant arrival, the unexpected ease with which he had called her Aislinn, and she was equally amazed by what she had at that very moment uncovered on the bottom of the chest. It was her missing holly circlet. She straightened to stand, clutching the wreath of enameled flowers to her chest.

"Why are ye going through my things? *Go de tá tú ag iarraig*?" he demanded, slamming the door closed with his foot before stepping inside the chamber. *What are ye seeking*? His smile had faded. His expression was darkening, sharpening. He unclasped the leather belt about his waist, releasing his sword and dagger. The weapons hit the floor with a thud. "I'll be hearing what it is ye have to say for yerself, if ye please."

"I-I was bored, and thought perhaps there was some m-mending that n-needed to be done." She could not stop herself from stammering. His mood had dramatically altered in the space of seconds. There was something strange in the way he looked at her, and the beard stubble upon the angular planes of his face made his expression all the more obscure.

"Ye're not my servant, nor my mother or wife. Ye've no right to be pawing through my things." He covered the distance between them in two strides, and snatched the circlet from her hands.

"But it's mine," she said weakly, reaching out to reclaim it.

"Oh?" He pretended that he did not know.

They were both holding it, each slightly tugging as if to free it from the other's grasp.

"It fell off my head. Don't ye remember? In the courtyard at Dublin Castle. I was wearing it the night my father wed Lady Alyson." It seemed like a hundred years before, but her vision of that night was as clear as if it had been yesterday. "And when ye pulled me into the shadows it fell off. Surely, ye have not forgotten?"

"*An abraimse breug*?" Bran asked. The pent-up loneliness and the anger collided within him. *Do I tell a lie*? He had tried to resist the truth, to fight it, and now she had begun to uncover it, to unravel his pretense. How could he possibly protect himself if she knew? Indignation and denial were his only weapons to pretend he had not seen his Fate that night in Dublin. A Fate that he had failed to evade. Even now he could not remember exactly how he had come to carry the circlet away with him. He recalled sweeping her a low bow of farewell, his fingers grazing against the ornament he had seen nestled in her ebony curls, yet when he had found it in his pack the following morning, its presence was a mystery. A warning. A confirmation of what he had sensed in the castle courtyard. The circlet had been a sign that some external power was exerting its force over him, and be it Fate or magic, it made no difference. He was determined to resist. She was not one of their kind. He was an O'Connor, and it must not be.

Roughly, Bran yanked the circlet from her hands, and tossed it into the far corner of the chamber. He should never have kept it, and silently he cursed himself for not having discarded it sooner. The metal made a clinking noise when it skittered down the stone wall. The only other sound in the chamber was their agitated breathing. He was angry at her, insanely angry, viciously angry, and he was not even certain of all the reasons why as he stared at her, wishing that he had not seen her dancing, that she had not followed him into the dark yard, that she had not been so warm and willing, and most especially, that his foolish, overly romantic brother had not brought her further into their lives.

He studied her, standing before him, her chin tilted upward, and he knew that she struggled not to flinch beneath his wrathful glare. Her dark eyes were bright with challenge. There was flattering color upon her cheeks, and she stood with her shoulders flung back, arms akimbo. She was a vision of defiance. His regard moved from her face, down the slender column of her throat to her heaving breasts, and again, he experienced the sensation of every muscle in his body tensing before another rush of anger coursed through him, even stronger, and more violent than before.

"How dare ye?" he asked, fixing his attention on another item she had taken from his chest. There, resting against her kirtle bodice lay a pendant of polished green stone. It was carved in the shape of a heart, suspended from a frayed velvet cord. "Are ye a thief, too?"

"*Ní hea,* I-I . . ." Aislinn tried to speak. His fury hit her with the force of a physical blow. Her chin quavered, and her charade of bravery began to collapse. She had to force herself not to look away from him. "I could not resist putting it on. It was nothing more than that, I swear."

"Take it off," he shouted. " 'Tis not yers."

She removed the pretty pendant, and held it out to him.

But Bran did not accept it from her. Instead, he ordered, "Put it back where ye got it."

She did so, then faced him. His face was haggard beneath the dark beard stubble. His mouth was twisted. There was no trace of the man who had tended her in the cairn, nor the man who had spoken of honor. "Why are ye acting like this? What could I have done that is so wrong?"

"That pendant is for the woman who will be my wife," he told her. His mother had worn it, and his grandmother, Viviane, before her. His jaw tensed, a nerve in his cheek twitched. An odd light flared in the depths of his hooded eyes with some unknown emotion. "And since ye will never be that woman I do not want ye touching it."

Aislinn's breath caught at the pain his words inflicted. One of her hands flew upward to rest upon the place above her heart, the other clamped across her mouth, but not quick enough to stay the gasp of despair that escaped her. "Ye're cruel," she whispered. Tears clouded her eyes, and she blinked, but could not dispel them. Two silver droplets slid down her cheek. "Ye are a cruel, mean-hearted man, and I do not understand why I care. I should never have stayed here, no matter what the debt I owe ye. This is not worth my dignity. Perhaps not even my life. What have ye done to me that I scarcely know myself?"

Gazing into her teary eyes, Bran was stunned into momentary speechlessness at the realization that those very words could have come from him. He looked at her, and saw his loneliness. He looked at her, and saw his own suffering, his own confusion and desperate need. Bran could not help it when he pulled her to him, and the moment he touched her every bit of anger, every bit of uncertainty turned to scorching, mindless desire. Fierce, desperate longing jerked through him, shaking him as he felt her heart beating against his chest. Brutally, his hands gripped her buttocks, his fingers digging into her flesh. He could not stop himself, and he rammed his swollen shaft against her.

Instantly, Aislinn jolted, agonizingly aware of the massive knot of his manhood. She dared not move.

She did not like to be touched like this. His fingers were hurting her, he had nearly knocked the breath from her with his roughness, and the way he thrust himself against her was crude and insulting. But that did not stop her body from reacting to his. Her skin flushed, her legs weakened, her breathing became shallow, and inside, she was roiling, teeming, swirling with melting desire.

He rubbed against her. There was nothing gentle about this contact. It was rough and dominating, and he moved his pelvis in a circular motion, exerting an almost unendurable pressure with each grinding movement. His hands released their bruising grip upon her buttocks and slid over her hips, down her outer thighs, then up beneath the kirtle along her bare skin, lifting the fabric higher as they went. He sensed the muscles of her inner thighs quivering beneath his touch.

"I'm dying to be inside ye, *cuileann*. I'm needing yer velvet cloak, yer tight warmth," he murmured. His fingers had reached the apex of her legs, they brushed against the downy nest. He groaned, ragged and needy. Deftly, he turned her around, bent her over the chest. The smooth creaminess of her flesh stimulated him. He liked to look at her slightly parted legs, the roundness of her buttocks, and her exposed sex. It begged his caress, and he skimmed a single finger along the glistening, swollen cleft. He did not need to touch her to know how ready she was for him, but he could not resist the sensation of his fingertip slipping into that slick heat, of tantalizing himself with a hint of how dewy she would be when there was more of him inside her.

"*Ní hea,*" Aislinn gasped, breathless. "Not like this." She struggled to free herself, to stand and get away, but he held her against the chest with his powerful thighs. "Please, not like this," she pleaded. She did not want a broken heart. She was determined in her decision to return to Annacurragh and marry Sean, if he would have her, and she would not return with a broken heart, bruised, mayhap, but never broken.

"Och, how could I be forgetting?" he said in harsh mockery, almost a sneer. "Ye're one for games, aren't ye, now? *Pretend ye love me.* Is that what ye want?"

"What woman does not dream of such a rare treasure as love?" Aislinn tried to speak slowly, evenly, when in truth her heart was racing, her senses thrumming. In truth, she could not deny her own awful aching for him to fill her. To feel the tip of his finger barely touching her was agony, and she struggled to subdue her wild desire to press against him until his finger glided all the way inside her. She must keep her head, and she shifted her legs in an effort to make herself inaccessible to him. She was going to leave Baravore. This must not be allowed to happen.

"Aye, love is a rare treasure, indeed, especially between the pair of us. This is not love, but lust, pure and simple." He sensed the way she tried to maneuver away from him, and his voice hardened. His finger lifted away, but only for an instant. "Ye push me too far," he said, thrusting two fingers deep inside her. She answered with a low keening moan, and he did not care what she said in denial, or how she squirmed to escape from him. Her body spoke the truth, relaxing and opening to his finger as he stroked her deeply. "There is nothing more than lust between us, *cuileann.* There never has been and never will. Nothing more than unholy, animal lust. Our bodies are perfect for each other."

"But what does that tell ye?" The words were torn from Aislinn as his delving fingers sent shivers of pleasure through her body. Ecstasy and torment. Passion and misery. She could no more have stopped her tiny moans of pleasure than stopped her lungs from taking in air.

"It tells me nothing. I'm no romantic fool to be imagining that any sort of gentler sentiments derive from rutting like a pair of beasts in the stableyard. Our races are enemies. There can be nothing more than this, and 'tis how it shall always be," he said readily, unrepentant, and without a shred of remorse. Then like a man who had lost his soul, he added, "But there is no reason we should not take what pleasure we may while we can."

"*Take*?" Aislinn's body stiffened. Her limbs seemed drained of every ounce of blood, for she feared in that second that if she refused him he would, indeed, take what he wanted by force. His fingers were stroking her faster, harder. She swallowed to speak, rushed and breathless. "Is this what ye like? This antagonism? This bitterness? Tell me how ye love to hate me," she taunted, trying to sound as tough as him, but the catch in her voice betrayed her. She ended on nothing more than a harsh whisper. "Tell me ye could take from me against my will and still live at peace with yerself in the years ahead."

Bran inhaled sharply. His hand stilled inside her. The words got through to him. He had heard her pain, and the truth was he could hardly live at peace with himself now, let alone in the years ahead. The truth was that he did not hate her. He'd already told her that weeks ago, but he couldn't find the words to explain how he really felt. For a long, frozen moment in time, light and sound and sense seemed suspended about him. The breath seemed to thicken in his chest. Somewhere in another realm, he heard his mother. *A man must be true to his heart before he can ever serve his clan*. But that conversation had been about Niall, not him. Not him. Hadn't it? Bran could not make sense of it anymore.

There was an unaccountable dampness in his eyes, and acting on instinct, he leaned forward to kiss the base of her spine, gently, almost tentatively.

"Och, *cuileann*, ye're right. Taking is wrong. Will ye be *sharing* with me, then? Will ye take pity on this poor empty wreck of a man, and share a bit of sweet pleasure with him?" he asked, thinking that if she refused him something special would be lost to him forever.

"Aye," whispered Aislinn. He played upon her heart like a poet. "Aye, to share is good." It was the most she could say without surrendering to tears, and she arched her back in response to his tender caress, feeling that somehow she had arrived at a crossroads, but did not know where she was headed, only that she must continue onward.

Bran's lips feathered up her back, kissing, nibbling. His tongue swirled out to taste. Her skin was as soft as lamb's wool, delicious as fresh cream, and the musky scent of her excited him. His hands slid around to fondle her breasts, his palms grazing the nipples beneath the fabric of her tunic. The buds tautened, and he rolled them between his fingers. He heard her tiny, soft moans, watched the way her back dipped and arched, those long black curls tumbling over one shoulder, and knowing that she was ready for him in both body and spirit, he released himself from his breeches.

It was easier for a woman to accommodate him in this fashion, from behind and bent over the chest as she was. Bran positioned the swollen head of his shaft against her moist female seam, and instead of entering her by increments, this time, he held her hips, and sheathed himself inside her with a long, single stroke.

Aislinn tried not to scream at the pleasure of him filling her in this way. She felt the muscles deep inside her conform to him, and she pressed backward against him, tilting herself to allow even deeper penetration. She moved in slow, sensual tandem with him. The pace began to build, swaying, pumping, pounding, until it crested into a rocketing, final crescendo of sighs and mighty groans, and damp, spent bodies.

It was over. And as before, he spilled his seed between her thighs.

Nothing had changed.

Aislinn drifted to the bed, lay down, and curled beneath the mound of furs. Her heart was well and truly breaking.

Bran could not look at her forlorn figure, and hastily, he gathered up a few of his most necessary personal possessions. He would stay in the men's tower above the gate until he had decided what to do with her.

It was not green reeds for weaving bread baskets that occupied Bébinn in the women's bower this afternoon, but embroidery. She was stitching an elaborate design in golden threads along the hem of a man's fancy linen tunic, and she glanced up with a smile when her eldest son entered. It was Bran's practice upon returning to Baravore to hear from Bébinn what had transpired in the glen while he was away. Sometimes it was news of a dispute over cattle, or a wall that needed mending, a birth, a death, a wife-snatching, or faerie spirits troubling the hens. This time, it was an impending wedding.

"Niall and Ceara have expressed their wish to wed on the eve of the next full moon, and I have given them my blessing as has Dallán O'Byrne. The clans will be gathering at Dysert."

"Wedding plans, is it now?" Bran sat opposite his mother, noticing as he always did how beautiful she was. There was a basket of fruit on a nearby trestle, and he helped himself to a plum. "I'm gone less than a sennight to see Rian O'Toole, and come home to discover my brother, whose heart is as fickle as a randy stag in mating season, is to be wed. While I suppose I should be breathing a sigh of relief that Niall has decided upon a good Irish girl and will not be chasing about after Sir Roger's daughter, I wonder if it is not too sudden."

"Do ye question the ways of the heart?"

"I know nothing of the heart," Bran retorted, and to his consternation, to his utter displeasure, his mother nodded her head in agreement. He looked at her with what could only be termed suspicion, and asked, "Now, Mam, perhaps ye'll be telling me what is it that ye really wish to discuss with me? Or did ye wish to make certain that I am the same callous man who shackled Niall in the gate tower to prevent him from eloping with the daughter of a degenerate English knight?"

Bébinn gazed upon him, indulgent, patient. She'd anticipated that he would act like a ruffled cock, and could not stop the tiny smile edging up at the corners of her mouth. "It is about Aislinn Clare."

"What about her, now?" He tossed the plum pit into the rushes, and wiped his sticky hands upon his breeches.

"I would like ye to allow Aislinn Clare to attend the wedding."

Bran gaped at his mother. Her request was ludicrous. He was astonished that he managed to remain calm, that he did not dissolve into outright laughter.

He did not know what he had expected her to say, but it was not this. "Sweet Jesu, Mam, Sir Roger's daughter at Niall's wedding? Have ye asked the bride about this? Do not tell me that ye're imagining Ceara will welcome her betrothed's former lover at her wedding."

"Ye know that was not the way it was between Aislinn and yer brother. Aislinn is no *strípac*, no *whore*, and I dare ye to tell me otherwise." When Bran did not speak, Bébinn continued, "As for Ceara, she is secure in her relationship with Niall, and I am certain she will welcome another guest on her special day. It is not natural to keep Aislinn in yer chamber. She has respected yer wishes in yer absence, and now ye must act in kind toward her. *Toward Aislinn*," she said with significance. "That is her name, ye know. Not *Sir Roger's daughter*. And do not be thinking it has gone unnoticed how ye treat her, nor that there has not been speculation about what has passed between the pair of ye." She paused for added meaning, then said very softly, "I pray ye were gentle with her upon yer return."

Bran stretched his legs out before him, a feigned sign of composed indifference. Actually, this conversation was making him most uncomfortable. He had never lied to his mother, and could do no less than reply, "I do not think you would be approving of what I did."

"I was afraid of that." From her chamber on the level above his, Bébinn had heard Bran's voice raised in anger. She had heard other noises as well. "I pray that ye have done no harm either in body or soul to Aislinn. She is a lovely young woman. I have come to know her over these past days and like her very much. She is in need of someone to intervene in her behalf, and I am happy to be that person. Indeed, perhaps, it was meant to be that she would come under my maternal care, for her mother was one of my dear childhood friends."

It was a struggle for Bran to maintain his nonchalant pose at this disclosure. Only one raised eyebrow revealed his surprise. "I did not know."

"Och, my son, there is much ye do not know. And someday, mayhap, I will tell ye a portion of it. Now, however, there is nothing more to be said than that it would hurt me, if ye harmed Étaín's child."

"I cannot help it, Mam. I cannot help what I say or do with her. Suffice to say, I do not know myself anymore. She is a witch, I think. It must be sorcery that makes me act as I do."

"Sorcery!" Bébinn exclaimed on a bubble of laughter, but managed to control herself from a full-fledged outburst. She uttered not a peep of amusement, nor did a single muscle upon her face twitch. Bran was, after all, being serious, and she did not wish to belittle him, misguided as he might be.

"What else could it be?"

"Love," she stated with certitude.

"*Diabal lib,*" he cursed his mother. *The devil with ye.*

"Do not be speaking to me in that way, Bran O'Connor." It was not often that Bébinn raised her voice, but she did so now. "And do not be telling me that ye imagine love is something ye can control anymore than 'tis possible to govern Fate. Love is Fate. Ye can't avoid it, Bran. Ye can turn away from it, and then suffer for it, for that is the way of love. Sometimes there is a happy ending. Sometimes there is tragedy. But the worst tragedy is to be turning away from the chance to know real love. Then there is naught but suffering."

"Let me see if I understand. Ye're telling me that I'm in love with one of the degenerate English, a woman of mixed blood, and although it is against the laws of man, and contrary to the foundation of my beliefs, it would be a tragedy if I turned away from that love."

"*Tá*," she said, more of a soft hush than an actually spoken word.

"We've had this conversation before—albeit a slightly different version—and this is where ye're going to talk about fulfillment and tell me that the goals I've set for myself can be set aside for a mere woman. A woman who embodies everything I should want to conquer and destroy."

Bébinn rested her sewing on her lap. Torn between the contrary impulses to shake him senseless for his stubbornness on the one hand, and on the other, to comfort him for his confusion, the best she could hope was that he would, at least, listen to her. "Please, no more disdain, no more anger. I think ye want my advice, and ye will find it in my words, if ye listen to what I must say."

"*Go de is mian leat a ragia liomsa*?" he murmured. *What do ye wish to say to me*? "I will listen."

"It is this. Ye cling to a singular notion of how this world is ordered. Right and wrong. Ye seem to think it's clearly divided. Them and us. All neatly arrayed to be played out by a set of rules that never changes. But it's not like that, Bran. Life is not like that. There is no perfection, and the little bits of perfection that we are ever blessed enough to encounter become like flecks of gold sifted from the riverbed. If I were to tell ye a mere fraction of my secrets, ye would be shocked that I have not yet been carried off to Hell, for it's guilty of much imperfection I am."

Bran stood. His mother had touched a chord in him, and with his back to her, he rested the palms of his hands on the trestle. His shoulders slumped forward. He stared at the basket of fruit, but saw nothing as his mind whirled backward in time. He was a lad, hardly strong enough to lift his father's longsword above his head, and a terrible darkness had descended over the valley. He had heard the words pestilence and black death. He had seen the fires burning on the hills, some to ward off the evil spirits, some to burn the bodies of the plague dead. His father's corpse had been devoured by flames one night. Bran remembered the fear and terror, the uncertainty and nightmares, and he remembered it was his grandfather who had restored security and hope to him.

"Ye're my heir now, and must be taught everything there is to know of the O'Connor legacy," Rourke had said, somber, yet proud. Bran recalled how his grandfather had always been confident. Even in the face of rampant death, Rourke had never wavered. He had wrapped an arm about Bran's shoulder in an embrace that offered comfort to a child, while hinting of fraternity between warriors. "Some would say I'm too old to be starting over with a pup such as yerself, but we'll be doing it together as I did with my sons, and one day, the clan will be appointing ye chieftain. Life at Baravore will be as it has been, and will continue to be."

The precise meaning of his grandfather's words had eluded Bran, but he had believed in him, trusted in the infinite righteousness of his wisdom. Whatever Rourke had meant, Bran had believed that calm and order would derive from following in his footsteps. If he could be like Rourke, live up to Rourke's example, then pestilence would be vanquished, and health, glory, and prosperity would abound.

Bébinn's voice drew Bran out of the past. He was still leaning on the table, his hands had clenched into fists. He glanced sideways to listen.

"Ye talk of ideals, Bran. Indeed, ye cleave to them,

and that is noble. But ideals are only half of what makes a man worthy. What of people? Of hearts? Should not a man be judged by how he treats others, both friend and foe? Ye talk of honor, but should not a man be judged at how honorable he is with himself? Ye cannot be honest with others, but fail to be so with yerself. Tell me, do ye recall the whole story of how it was yer grandmother Viviane came to own the pendant?"

He straightened, and spun around. Bébinn spoke of the green heart on the frayed velvet cord, and an image of wild black curls and sultry, gold-flecked eyes flashed before his mind's tapestry. "*Ní hea,*" he admitted. "I did not always listen." It had seemed trivial, women's nonsense. He had preferred Rourke's tales of the victory over the English at Bannockburn and how his great-great-grandfather, Ingvar, had been raised by Haakon, king of the Ostmen.

"Then I will be telling the tale once again, and this time, ye'll be listening. Sit, now," she instructed. " 'Tis a long story, and I will not be hurried." Bran had returned to the bench, and she began. "The pendant is over a hundred years old, and the woman ye wed will be the sixth bride to wear it. The first was Isobel, yer great-great-grandfather Ingvar's twin. It was a gift from a Highland warrior, who had saved Lady Isobel from bandits and then lost his heart to her. Theirs was a forbidden affection, for they were both already wed. Both their marriages, however, were real only in name, each of them having been separated from their respective spouses by years of war and politics. There was no intimacy between them, no children, no companionship, not even a polite acquaintance. Yet they were both honorable, and had respected their unions until their hearts were touched by love. It was a kind of miracle, ye see, for the lady whom the warrior had rescued was his wife. But the fact that their paths had crossed was not enough to make a difference. They never would have deviated from their separate lives, if they had not listened to their hearts, and each allowed themselves to do the forbidden and love a stranger.

"It became an heirloom, a tradition to be passed down by the Kirkpatrick lairds, father to son for their brides. Rourke's cousin, Alexander, gave the pendant to his wife, who was as unlikely a choice for a Highlander as ye could imagine. His lady love was Claricia de Clinton, English like Sir Roger's daughter, but worse than that, she was the niece of Alexander's most bitter enemy. During the years of the Scottish War for Independence, Aymer de Clinton had destroyed or seized all of Alexander's ancestral holdings; de Clinton's men had murdered Alexander's mother, executed his father, and kidnapped his younger sister. Vile loathing for de Clinton was the blood in Alexander's veins, yet, his heart could not turn away from Lady Claricia, and he loved and wed the Englishwoman, who the world had called whore. Yer grandfather Rourke knew Lady Claricia, he fought alongside Alexander, and in the end he wed Alexander's sister, Viviane, and brought her home to Baravore.

"The pendant was Claricia's farewell token to Viviane, a symbol of the message she wanted Viviane to remember always. Never be looking back. Viviane, ye see, had lost most of her childhood memories after being kidnapped by de Clinton. Indeed, she had survived only because of Claricia's intervention, and Rourke's unquestioning love." Bébinn paused. She had heard Viviane recite this story many times, and these were almost her very same words. "Viviane never regained her past. Indeed, it was a blessing to have been able to erase every memory of what the English bastards had done to her, but the greatest blessing of all was that her future was not in the past, but with Rourke. Viviane always smiled when she recalled Claricia giving her the heart, for it seemed impossible to her that Claricia ever feared the memories might return to drive her mad with doubt and guilt. Viviane was certain of the future, but she wished to reassure her dear friend, and so she held the heart in her hand, gazed upon its flawless perfection and pledged to one truth above all else: the past is never so important as love, and one must always look ahead, not behind. One must never hold to the past, nor be its hostage, but listen to one's heart and accept what the future offers."

"How convenient," Bran drawled at her conclusion. "Yer little tale can be perfectly drawn, and applied to any and all circumstances."

"I wish ye were not so bitter," said Bébinn, fearing that she had spoken for naught.

He shrugged.

"What will ye do with Aislinn?"

"I was hoping ye would be telling me."

"I think ye should marry her."

"Never," he declared.

"Don't ye want her?"

"Wanting has nothing to do with it," he said. Of course, he wanted her. He wanted her as he would never want another woman. It was a wanting of heart and soul. It was the wanting of destiny he had sensed that night in Dublin Castle. "No matter what I might want, I would never marry Sir Roger's daughter."

"Then ye've heard nothing I said."

"Och, ye're wrong. I heard that ye pray I've done no harm to her either in body or soul." What Bran actually meant was that was the only thing upon which he could act to his mother's satisfaction. He must send her away before he hurt her beyond recovery. Both she and his mother were right. He was not a nice man. He had been punishing Aislinn for his own weakness, and the only way to make amends would be to send her on her way before he did anything worse. "She will not be attending the wedding. I intend to send her back to Annacurragh before we leave for Dysert."

Chapter 14

"Would ye be willing, Aislinn, to tell me what it was like for yer mother at Killoughter?" asked Bébinn.

Together, they sat in Bran's chamber as the sun set behind Conavalla, the guardian peak at the western end of Glenmalur. A single torch upon the wall lit the chamber; one of Bébinn's rangy hounds was curled at her feet. From the hall below, where the rest of the household gathered for their evening meal, drifted the rise and fall of muted voices, an occasional outburst of laughter, a baby's wail, the rattle of tin, the knock of wood, or the yelp of a dog. The rest of the world could have been an ocean away as the two women nibbled at a light repast.

"I have always wondered if being the wife of a lord and chatelaine of an English fortress was as grand as our girlish imaginings had envisioned it to be."

Aislinn smiled at the vision of her mother so dark and Bébinn so fair wading in the Aughrim, two pretty Irish lasses kicking up the bottom in their search for faerie gold, and wondering between themselves how life was for the English girls who lived in great stone castles. "I would be happy to tell ye anything, but ye may be disappointed, for my mother's days at Killoughter were much the same as yers in most respects, I imagine. They were filled with the constant hard work to which the mistress of any large household, whether Irish or English, must attend. Most of the actual differences are unexceptional, if not outright peculiar.

"Did ye know the English serve at their high tables vegetables that we feed only to our livestock? Peas, for one. They boil the wee things, and then smother them in milky sauce, and foreign spices such as nutmeg and ginger. And, of course, their clothes are more elaborate, more colorful, but not so comfortable as ours, and the English way of riding is also more constricted than the Irish.

"All in all, my mother's life was probably not that much different from yers. When she was not occupied with her home or husband, she was with her children or in her garden," Aislinn concluded. But in her next breath, she knew how wrong she was. Of course, Bébinn's life had been different; she had been a widow for more than nineteen years, while her mother had never been alone.

"Och, a garden," mused Bébinn. She noticed Aislinn's sudden silence, the slight embarrassment in the way she was paying unusual attention to the slice of meat upon her trencher. Bébinn did not like to think that she was the object of pity, and she spoke in a bracing, seemingly unaffected tone. "Tell me about Étaín's garden, will ye, now?"

Aislinn told Bébinn about the walled garden with the herb cottage and seashell walkway, and how in the end it became Étaín's eternal resting place. "Above all else 'tis her death that strikes me as the most English aspect of her life at Killoughter. She adored that garden, especially with its view toward the hills in which she had been born, and when she knew death was near, she pleaded with my father not to let her remains or my brothers' be consumed on the plague pyre. She wished to be buried alongside her sons within sight of the hills, and so my father hid their bodies. He dug their graves himself, working only at night, and buried them on his own. I was the only witness, and it was not until the next summer when he bribed a priest that the ground was consecrated, after which he commissioned graveslabs with elaborate, near-perfect images of my mother and brothers. Two stone carvers came from England, and when they were done my father wept, for they had captured the unique slant of my mother's eyes as he had described them, the curls that would not stay bound in the meticulous, English style, the exact shape of her mouth, and the tiny, slender fingers of her delicate hands, holding a large cluster of flowers."

"Ye must miss them terribly," remarked Bébinn. It was too late for consolation.

"Oddly, what I miss more than any one of them individually is the sense of a family we had together. Now that I think upon it that was what was different at Killoughter: we were an English fortress with a family that knew itself as one. Now 'tis all gone as rain evaporates on a stone after a storm."

"But I am told yer father took a young wife this spring." Bébinn tried to sound natural, as if she had not been wounded at the thought of Sir Roger with another wife, a younger woman, when she remained alone. She smiled, pleased that her words did not seem as brittle upon her lips as she felt inside. "Perhaps there will once again be a family at Killoughter."

Aislinn studied Bébinn for any hint of how this made her feel, but the older woman revealed nothing except a composed, pleasant smile. "My father's marriage will not change anything. Surely, ye know a family does not simply happen as does a marriage or children. There must be special affection, and sadly, I do not think my father possesses any such consideration for Lady Alyson, other than what is expected of a respectful husband." Then out of the blue, Aislinn surprised them both by saying, "Do ye know what I wish? I wish that ye might one day see my father again."

"Och, child, that is a lovely, generous wish, but like all else, 'tis no more than a dream." For the first time, Bébinn angled her face away from Aislinn. There was a sudden warmth in her cheeks which she did not want her to see. "I thank ye for yer sweet aspiration in my behalf, but there would be no point in it, and I do not think I could endure my own sadness. Thus far, I have managed to avoid bitterness, but if that were to change, I would not want to be living with myself."

She nodded. "I understand."

"That is where the tragedy in all of this lies." Bébinn set her food aside. Her meal was hardly touched. "Children should not be condemned to repeat their parents' mistakes. Ye and Bran should not revisit our heartache. But it appears my son will never understand why he is in such a state of confusion and misery, while ye, on the other hand, are destined to suffer as I have through a lifetime of lonely, secret despair."

Aislinn wanted to protest, but she knew Bébinn was right.

"I thank ye for yer company this night," said Bébinn, knowing that she sounded more like a stranger than someone who had confided her intimate confidences. In truth, she no longer had any appetite for food or company, and she went to the door. On the threshold, she paused, and glanced over her shoulder.

"Do ye believe in the powers of the old ways?"

"I don't know," replied Aislinn, unprepared for the question. She thought a moment. "Until recently I believed in many things. Or, perhaps, 'tis more accurate to say that I was unwilling *not* to believe in the powers of Fate and Destiny, in cyclamen and Witch's Thimble, Lady's Smock, and clover." She smiled, a little wistful, somewhat wise. "Yer son has accused me of sorcery, but I fail to see any benefits deriving from my spells."

Bébinn returned her smile with one just as perceptive, just as melancholy. "In that case, I shall visit the chapel this night, light a tallow dip to the Holy Virgin, and recite two score Hail Marys for ye. After which, I shall be slipping a four-leafed clover into Bran's tunic, and we won't be telling any of it to him."

In the morning a commotion in the yard drew Aislinn to the window. She opened the shutters. The O'Connor clansmen were gathering, armed not for battle, but for a hunt. Bran was at their head, and she watched as they filed out the gate to disappear up and down the valley. She had no visitors that morning except a young girl who brought fresh water and a boiled egg. Toward midday, the girl came with fruit and cheese, and Aislinn asked for a selection of rosemary, wild thyme, hyssop, hawthorn blossoms, yarrow and valerian flowers, plus materials for sewing. The girl scurried off, and returned shortly, having gathered together the requested items without question.

Aislinn spent the afternoon making sachets from bits of leftover fabric, and filling the tiny pouches with mixtures of crushed herbs and dried flower blossoms. They were to be a gift for Bébinn, the sort of English luxury that Irish lasses wading in the Aughrim might have fancied. Although the beds at Baravore were not curtained as they were at Killoughter with heavy bed-hangings to which sachets were attached, Aislinn knew Bébinn would appreciate the gesture, and make good used of the fragrant sachets.

Piecing together triangular shapes of red and gold fabric, Aislinn made a pouch that formed a sort of star pattern once it was filled with the perfumed mixture, and knotted at the top. She was admiring her creativity, and beginning to sort more pieces for another pouch of similar design when there came a knock upon the door. She had lost track of the passage of time, and on her way to the door, she discerned by the sunlight's shift upon the floor that it must be late afternoon.

Upon opening the door, she was surprised to see Bran. He was standing on the landing as if it were not his chamber to enter at will.

"May I come in?" he asked, polite and formal.

"It is yer chamber. *Tar asteac sa tseamra.*" She stood aside to let him pass. *Come into the room.* As he went by, Aislinn noticed that wherever he had been this day, he had taken care with his person upon his return. She could smell clean-scrubbed skin. He had shaved the shadowy stubble from his face, and his damp hair was combed and pulled back at the nape of his neck. His tunic was fresh. His legs and feet were bare. He wore no breeches, and there were no weapons sheathed in the leather belt about his waist.

"Is there something ye need to get?" she asked.

He halted at her question, and stared about him. It was his chamber, but it wasn't. The air was unusually aromatic. She had rearranged the furnishings, and was engaged in some kind of woman's work. He had interrupted, and could not help feeling like an intruder. "*Ní hea,* I have not come to fetch anything.

Rather it is wishing to talk with ye, I am. But not to interrupt." He waved toward the tidy piles of colored wool, and the cluster of plump packets tied with ribbons atop the nearby chest. "Please, continue with whatever ye were doing."

She resumed, sitting in the chair near the window, where she had pulled one of the chests to serve as a makeshift work table. He leaned against the stone wall, folded his arms across his chest, and watched for awhile as she sorted, crushed, stuffed, and stitched. He enjoyed the sight of her graceful fingers moving swiftly, skillfully. She concentrated upon her work, and did not seem bothered by his presence.

At length he spoke. "Niall and Ceara plan to wed."

"I know." She continued to work, and did not look up. "Ceara has been to visit me several times, and was eager to tell me of their plans."

Bran could not help blinking against the improbable mental image of Aislinn and Ceara having a friendly chat. What, he wondered, did they have in common? Niall? He shook his head, and knew he would never comprehend women, no matter what their race. "My mother has asked that ye be allowed to attend the wedding, but I have decided, instead, to let ye return to Annacurragh before then." He saw her hands still. She set aside the mortar and pestle with which she had been crushing pink and crimson yarrow blossoms. With an unusual aura of calm, she looked up at him, and he was struck by the satisfaction he saw upon her face. But there were other emotions as well, flashing so quickly before him that he could not grasp their meaning. "Ye're pleased?"

"Of course."

"Then ye go to Annacurragh on the morrow. That is, if ye're certain of yer welcome there. Ye must know that I have not forgotten my pledge to keep ye safe from those who would ill treat ye, and while we may be in agreement that ye should not be at Baravore, I must be reassured that Annacurragh is the place for ye. If ye harbor any doubts, I could arrange for my kin in Connaught to take ye in."

"Annacurragh is fine," she said wondering if this Connaught offer had anything to do with the fact that Annacurragh was not far enough away. "My father believes I'm gone—dead at sea, perhaps. I do not know what story he has been told, but it does not matter. He will never suspect I am at Annacurragh, and my kin will not tell him otherwise."

"Then we are in agreement."

Looking up at him, she was reminded of how he had lounged against the wall at her father's wedding feast. For a second, she heard the music. She felt her soul's first awakening, and remembered how she'd waited to circle round the great hall for another glimpse of his startling masculine features. She would never forget, and she started to cry.

"Why the tears? Is this not what ye desire?"

"I was thinking of the first time I saw ye. It was yer hair, glossy and black as a raven's wing, that made me look twice. And, of course, the way ye looked at me," she confessed on a breathless murmur. "Ye did not fool me with yer long hair hidden beneath the collar of yer fancy English disguise. Och, how tall and dark and handsome ye were, and I could not take my eyes from ye." A charming blush colored her face. Another tear slipped from her eye to cool her warm cheek.

Bran's gut turned inside out, and he swayed forward from the wall as if to comfort her, but he held himself back. "Can ye not smile, and be pleased?"

She sniffled, and tried as he asked, but it only made the tears flow harder. Between little gulps of air, she said, "I had made a vow to be wed by harvest time. Is it not ironic that Niall will be wed, but not me?"

"I thought acquiring a husband was nothing more than a means to yer end."

At that, she swiped away the tears with the back of her hand. "Can it be that ye truly believe I'm totally without conscience? I am capable of romantic feelings, ye know. 'Tis as I said, I'm no different from any other woman who yearns for a treasure as rare as love. Somewhere, there must be someone who might hold me in regard. Surely, I am not the scheming *beadag* ye accuse me of being. Surely, ye have seen some tiny shred of goodness in me." Despite repeated attempts to wipe them away, tears streamed down her cheeks without cease, and she jumped up in a sort of frantic attempt to control herself. Ribbons and fabric, crimson petals and dried herbs tumbled to the rushes.

"Ná bi gal," he entreated. *Do not cry*. It was hard enough for Bran to see her tears, but to hear her speak with such anguish, and to know that he must shoulder the blame for her self-doubt was intolerable. "Ye must not be saying such things. Ye're mistaken as to the opinion in which I hold ye. To the contrary, there's much about ye to admire, and ye should be proud, for ye've much to offer the right man." Bran's words came forth of their own volition, sounding as startling to his ears as surely they must have been to hers.

His voice softened, "I should have told ye long before that ye're the most beautiful, and the bravest woman I have ever known. Indeed, I will never forget that day we rode into Wicklow town. How tall ye sat upon yer Bláth, haughty and defiant in the face of that crowd, and when ye raised yer fair voice in song and dared to sing 'The Deer's Cry,' I knew there was no Irish warrior more courageous nor steadfast than ye, and I knew then that ye had never meant to deceive me. I knew then that I could trust ye with my very life, if I had to do so."

Aislinn stood motionless, listening to his words, and staring at the bits of ribbons mixed with yarrow and meadow-sweet at her feet. She heard the thickening in his voice, trembled when he said *I knew then ye never meant to deceive me.* She felt herself melting and hoping in the same heartbeat. When at last she glanced up at him there was undisguised desire gleaming in her eyes.

He moved away from the wall, she floated toward him, and they stopped with less than a single footstep between them. He reached out to her, and she sighed when his long fingers skimmed down her cheek to linger at the corner of her mouth. Bran saw her tears mixing with steamy passion in her eyes. Her lips parted, and he felt her breath upon his fingers. She was lovely, and vulnerable, and deserving of the best, to be cherished by a man who could give himself to her each and every day of her life. He could never be that man, and he had no right to say what he did next.

"I'm going to kiss ye, and not because I have to hide, or because ye want me to pretend, but because I want to hold ye in my arms, and adore ye, taste ye, know ye as a lover should. Will ye allow such trespass?"

"Tá." The word was no more than a soft breath of air.

They melted into one another's arms, and when Bran bent his head to kiss her, Aislinn met his mouth, her lips already parted to receive his tongue. It was no slow, lingering kiss. There was too much bottled passion between them. He kissed her wet and open-mouthed, and when their tongues met, the kiss accelerated with a feverish tempo. In a frenzy, her fingernails dug into his arms, her mouth pulled at his, and she suckled at his tongue as he possessed her with deep, exploring strokes.

Even while they kissed their hands worked to free themselves from their garments. His tunic was quickly gone, hers slid about her ankles, and in that moment, Bran lifted his mouth. He wanted to look at her breasts, to see the downy hair at her sex, and let his eyes roam over the curves of her thighs and hips.

She stared, too, but with a bit more reserve, starting with his legs, shyly working upwards. But her gaze went no higher when she saw the scar on his thigh that had been left by her dagger. It was not a horrible scar, but she had made it, and thus it seemed only fitting to Aislinn that she should kneel before Bran to caress it with her mouth.

A guttural noise rumbled from Bran's throat. He had never expected this from her, and his head reeled at the intensity of sensations she excited within him. His teeth were clenched in a desperate attempt to maintain control. The caress of her breath, and the wet, silky, smoothness of her tongue upon his thigh were stimulating beyond any erotic pleasure he had imagined. The tendons in his legs quivered, his manhood jumped and pulsated, and he reached down to take her hand.

"Cuir do lam form," he murmured. *Put yer hand over me.* To his delight, she allowed him to move her hand to his throbbing erection, and when her fingers made contact with him, he groaned anew. The light touch was agony. It was sheer delight. He circled her fingers about him.

Aislinn had forgotten how huge a man he was. Her hand barely cupped the swollen helmet, and she stared upward in fascination at the blood-dark color of the turgid organ beneath her pale fingers. It did not seem possible, yet he got hotter, harder, and wanting him to be inside her, Aislinn rose up on her knees until her mouth was at a level with his groin.

His naked, male flesh jutted against her chin, her cheek, and acting on instinct, her lips parted to slide over the slick head and take him into her mouth. He expanded even more. She heard his groan. There was a slight discomfort in her jaw, for he was large, and she could not relax, owing in part to a sort of shock. What she was doing was unknown to her; perhaps it was evil, but when he did not protest, she began to move her lips in imitation of the suckling motion he had used upon her breast. She was not certain whether she liked it, but what she did like was his reaction. She loved the way he moaned, "*Cuileann,*" deep in his throat, and how his hands tangled in her hair, slightly tugging, almost desperate for her touch.

Gently, he held her head still, and backed himself away from her. " 'Tis time now for me to be returning yer gift of pleasure," he murmured, and knelt before her, folding her into his embrace, thigh to thigh, his engorged flesh straining to her female apex.

His hands dragged down her back to her buttocks, gripping, kneading, holding her to him, and she did not resist when he delved into her damp, heated hollow. Willingly, she widened her legs to him, and she heard her own tiny moans as his fingers moved in and out of her female place while his manhood prodded at the outer lips. Together, they slid to the rush-covered floor. She smelled honey in the dried flowers, sensed the warmth of sunshine in the rushes, and inhaled the distinctly male scent of him.

Bran's fingers caressed the trembling flesh of her inner thigh, higher, he folded her open, and his mouth went where his fingers had been. She bucked at the sensation of his tongue flicking in and out, and when she did not think she could keep herself from screaming he moved over her.

They kissed again, this time each tasting themselves upon the other when their tongues met.

He bent her legs, preparing her for his entry, and little by little, he eased into her. There were beads of perspiration on his brow from the effort of restraining his desire to plunge into her, but he held back, wanting this loving to be long, wanting there to be nothing but pleasure for her. As before she was hot and wet, opening to him like a glove, clinging to him, taking him in deeper, tighter, and as before, she begged aloud for him, for all of him. And when she cried for him to fill her, to possess her as no other man but he could, Bran was unable to control himself, and he buried himself to the hilt.

"*Ceol ne naingeal,*" she cried in soft awe as more tears trailed down her cheeks. She twined her legs about him, exalted in his power. "Och, such pleasure 'tis frightening. I hear the music of the angels."

"Ye're not going to die, I swear."

"*Parratas,*" she whispered into his lips, scoring her nails along his back. "Ye're right. 'Tis not death, but a glimpse of *paradise* ye give to me."

In the end he did not leave her. He couldn't, and it was not a question of control. It was a question of knowing that he must give everything he could to her at that moment. There would be nothing more after this, never another time, and for now, at least, he must give the totality of himself. There was no doubt that this should be a complete act of sharing. This was not mere coupling, not an act of taking, but lovemaking in its purest sense, and he let his body speak what he could not admit aloud.

Tenderly, he held her through the night, and when

the first blush of dawn filtered through the shutters, they made love again. It was a lingering, passionate union, neither of them, however, deceiving themselves that it was anything more than a bittersweet finale. These past hours would be the memory, the treasure. The flecks of gold from a rushing mountain stream.

Toward midday they rose from the bed to break their fast with fruit and fresh bread. They bathed one another with cool water from the laver, and dressed in silence, pretending all the while they were the same people they had always been.

"I will be taking Aislinn to Annacurragh," Bébinn informed her son the next morning when Bláth was brought into the yard. "Ye need not come."

"Ye do not trust me with her."

"In part," she conceded. "But it is more than that. I want to revisit my youth." Actually, she wanted more time to devise how she might change the course that Bran had set for himself. It was her hope that Marga might be willing to aid her in this endeavor.

"I will allow ye to go with her, and shall send Tadhg as an escort. Can ye be leaving within the hour?"

"Sooner. I need only a few minutes to prepare." Bébinn left to gather up what she would need while she was away.

Bran dawdled in the yard outside the entrance to the hall, feigning interest in the litter of pups one of his nieces was tending in a basket, and when his mother reappeared and called for her mount, he entered the tower to fetch Aislinn from his chamber.

"It is time," he said when she opened the door. He observed how the color upon her cheeks faded. The glimmer in her eyes dimmed. "My mother is waiting for ye below. She wishes to go with ye and see yer grandmother."

Aislinn nodded, forcing herself not to reveal her sadness. The end was at hand, and as there was no reason to delay, she simply followed Bran out the door. She said nothing, feeling as gray as the winding stone stairs she descended. In the silence of the stairwell, their footsteps sounded brittle. A chill enveloped her, and she knew it might be with her from this moment onward.

Halfway down the stairs, Bran stopped. He was a coward, and could not go into the bailey to stand before the clan, to bid her a cool farewell, and watch her ride away. He had, as she had accused, made a spectacle of their arrival, and he had no wish to risk the same with her departure. He was standing one step below her, and when he turned to her, they were at eye level. It surprised him. He had never gazed so fully, so completely into those dark sultry eyes, and for a moment, he thought they were a whirlpool into which he might be swept for eternity. They were so close and yet so far, he thought with a skirl of uncharacteristic nervousness.

"Before ye part, I must tell ye how I regret the times I was not kind or gentle with ye." *Feeble, stupid oaf,* he thought of himself, and reached out to trail a finger down her pale cheek. A curl fell across her face, and he brushed it away with all the tenderness of a lover.

Aislinn's heart leapt. She was back on the wharf at Wicklow, and in this last moment, he might understand, might relent, and open his heart to the truth. He had failed to do so before, but this time could be different.

"May God's hand guide ye and shield ye," he paraphrased "The Deer's Cry." "May ye be safe from all who might wish ye ill, afar and anear."

"Ná déan dearmud," she whispered, willing, fusing herself into his hooded, dragon-green gaze. *"Do not forget."*

"Ní hea. Aislinn, my lovely dream," he said her name easily. His heart was warmed with the righteousness of it. *"Nay.* I will never forget, and while it may be against the laws of man to keep ye, there is no law that will shut ye out of a place in my heart. *Do la agus d'oidce,* ye will always be there. *By day and by night.* Now be off with ye."

He gave her a gentle shove of encouragement to continue the rest of the way without him, and Aislinn's heart shattered into a thousand little mismatched pieces that could never make a whole again.

It was neither a long nor an arduous journey to the Aughrim, four to five hours at best, and through terrain that was more hilly than mountainous. They would reach Annacurragh before nightfall. Having left the safety of Glenmalur, they reached the head of the Vale of Avoca, and decided to rest above the river. It was a pleasant afternoon, alive with the song of birds, a bright sun, and gentle wind. They stopped at a grassy knoll situated between two hills.

Bébinn had not yet dismounted when the calm was destroyed. A thunderous battle charge rent the air, birds shrieked in fright, taking flight from the hedges and treetops, and then came the ruckus of horses snorting, the pounding of hooves, and the clang of metal as a heavily armed English troop charged down the two hills and surrounded them. Everything happened quickly. In an instant, Tadhg was dead, Bébinn was thrown to the ground by her frightened horse, and Aislinn rushed to help the stunned older woman as their horses ran into the forest, and the soldiers circled them.

"What do ye want? Who are ye?" Aislinn asked. She knew they were English, but in her distress she spoke Irish.

"Labair Bearla, ma tig leat," one of the soldiers commanded in harsh, stiff Irish. By his uniform, he was a captain, their leader, and he repeated the order in his own tongue, *"Speak English, if you can*. It is the law."

"Identify yourselves, sir," Aislinn demanded, fearing in her next breath that she had shown too much courage. She demurred. "We are merely women on a journey to visit our kin. Surely there is no reason for such ill treatment as you have shown us, nor the fatal wound you have inflicted upon our escort."

"We ride under the banners of the earl of Ormond, and the archbishop of Dublin. We are on a mission in search of hostages. O'Connor hostages, in particular."

"But why? What have any of the O'Connor clan done to offend Ormond, or his excellency, the archbishop? I beg you, pray tell."

"You are an impertinent native wench to ask so many questions. Who are you, woman? Speak."

Bébinn made as if to rise.

"Do not utter a word. *Bi do tost,"* Aislinn whispered urgently to Bébinn in Irish. *"Be silent*. Ye must let me do this."

Aislinn faced the young knight, and spoke clearly, slowly, "This is my serving woman, and I am Aislinn, Bran O'Connor's wife."

"Take her," the English captain ordered. An O'Connor hostage was, indeed, the prize they sought this day. The wife of the O'Connor chieftain was better then ten O'Nolans or Kavanaghs, and Ormond would be suitably impressed.

Someone grabbed Aislinn, jerked her away from Bébinn, and bound her hands before her, while the others cheered at their triumph. They all knew the importance of this particular hostage.

"A mission well done, eh, Gibbons?"

The soldiers gloated amongst themselves. No one would ever admit that it was more an act of chance than actual achievement, nor that there was not a man among them would ever have entered Glenmalur, no matter what their captain might have ordered.

"And a right pretty dove, she is. Do you think she knows how to coo soft and gentle for a man?" wondered the foot soldier, who had bound her hands.

"Don't get too close," warned the one called Gibbons. " 'Tis said they bite and fight like she-wolves."

Quickly, the foot soldier lengthened the rope between himself and his captive. The other English soldiers broke into ribald laughter.

"And ye, woman," the captain turned away from his men to address Bébinn, who was staring at him as if not able to fully comprehend what had taken place. He ordered Aislinn to translate as he spoke. "Go back to yer master and tell him the earl of Ormond and archbishop of Dublin hold his wife. If there are no raids upon any settlements to the north or south, she will be treated with all the courtesy due a hostage. If there is no trouble, and yer savage kin remain in yon mountains through the coming winter, she will be returned in the spring."

Then in a flurry of hooves and dust, twigs and leaves, they were gone.

Long after they had vanished, Bébinn lay with her ear to the ground, listening to the distant rumble of hooves, and even when the earth no longer spoke to her, she kept her ear to the dirt, straining for any sign that she was not alone. Bébinn wasn't certain how long she stayed on the forest floor, and when the light began to dim, she sat up. Her ankle was swollen out of proportion, and she unlaced the foot covering that had become uncomfortably tight.

The events of the afternoon were horribly clear to her. She remembered the sudden arrival of the English soldiers, their brutal slaughter of Tadhg, and how they had taken Aislinn away. It was not uncommon for the English to hold Irish wives and children, sometimes even a chieftain, hostage as a guarantee against unrest. It was also not uncommon for those hostages to be abused, if not killed. For only a minute or two, Bébinn rested against a tree, and stared at Tadhg's body, awash with guilt that she could not properly bury him. The night beasts would surely devour his corpse before anyone could retrieve him. But she must return to Baravore, and had only time to fashion a walking stick to support her weight, before she began to limp in the direction of Glenmalur.

Night fell. The forest darkened. Wolves howled in the hills. There was a stirring in the bracken, golden eyes peered through the thick foliage, following her, watching her. There was a painful stitch in her side, but Bébinn forced herself to limp onward.

By sheer force of will, she did not slow her pace, and only when she heard an owl hooting somewhere above her did Bébinn allow herself to slump to the ground.

It was her own chamber. The familiar scent of meadow-sweet and rushes comforted Bébinn, and she opened her eyes. Swimming in and out of focus, were the anxious faces of Bran, Niall, and her daughters. They were gathered about her, pale and whispering.

"Look, she awakens," Bébinn heard one of her daughters exclaim.

This was no dream. She was home and safe. Now

she must muster the strength to tell Bran what had happened.

Another daughter spoke, "Her eyelids flutter."

Bébinn sensed the crush of worried, grown children about her. She could almost feel their breath, hear their worried hearts beating.

"Stay back." It was Bran.

Slowly, her eyes opened, wider this time. The room came into focus as did the faces of her children hovering at a discreet distance from the bed.

"What happened? Was it bandits?"

"We found Tadhg's body."

"Where is Aislinn?" This was spoken almost at the same time by Bran and Niall.

"Not thieves," Bébinn began weakly. Someone brought her water, and after a cool drink she was able to go on, "It was the English riding under the banners of Ormond and the archbishop of Dublin. They were rounding up hostages. I can only deduce that they are alarmed by the extent of storm damage in their settlements, and do not know the tempest never reached our high hills." Here, her voice turned caustic, riddled with a sort of sarcastic self-mockery. "It seems there is great fear among the English that starving hordes of wild Irish will soon descend upon them, and thus, they must protect themselves from such barbarian assaults."

"But why did they take Aislinn, if they were in search of Irish hostages? Did she not tell them who she was?"

"She did not. Instead, she ordered me to be quiet. I was disoriented, ye must understand, otherwise I would not have let the bold, noble lass do such a foolish thing. But in my dizzy state, I did not stop her when she told them she was yer wife. Ye should have heard their cheers of success. Apparently, they had intended to come into Glenmalur, if need be, but she saved them the trouble. They believed they had captured the wife of Bran O'Connor, and were well pleased with themselves. They headed straight for Dublin with their valuable hostage."

For a brief instant, Bran was amused at the deception. "I suppose we should be grateful," he said, but in the next instant, his hands clenched into fists. He did not like the notion of the English thinking they had anything of his, even if it was not so.

"What do ye intend to do for her?" asked Niall.

"They do not always treat hostages badly." Bran was thinking out loud. "Besides she is not my wife."

"*Tá, cinnte,* she may not be yer wife. *Aye, certainly.* But she is the woman who sacrificed herself for our mother. Indeed, mayhap, for the security of Baravore." Every ounce of Niall's outrage rang clear in this denunciation of his older brother.

"That was low," Bran retorted.

" 'Tis naught but the truth, brother. Do ye not feel any sense of obligation?"

"Of course I do," he snapped, running both of his hands through his hair, frustrated and confused. "But what do ye propose I do about it? Attack Dublin Castle?"

"*Ní hea,*" Bébinn said. "I will go to Sir Roger."

"What? *Biodh ciall agat,*" shouted Bran. "Was it yer head, and not yer ankle that was injured in yer fall, Mam? *Have sense.* Ye cannot be going to Sir Roger."

"He is no stranger to me," she declared, undaunted, and not caring any longer if her secret came out after all this time. She must not fail Aislinn, and if they would not help her, she must.

The hairs on Bran's arms raised straight up. *He is no stranger to me.* Somehow his mother's statement did not surprise him. He did not, however, want to know how, or why it might be so. "It makes no difference, if Sir Roger is friend or foe. He will not believe such a story about his daughter. As far as he knows she is in England, or perhaps, by now he believes her to be dead."

"Sir Roger will believe me, if I tell him."

"Ye may not go, Mam. Ye've been injured, and even if ye were in perfect health, the danger is too great."

"Ye will go then?"

"I will not."

"What do ye propose to do in her behalf?"

But she got no answer. Bran had already turned and strode from the chamber, leaving his mother to the ministrations of his sisters.

He sought the privacy of the chapel built by Rourke and watched over by the guardian angels in stained glass. There, before the spent tallows his mother had lit, he did something he had not done in many years. He knelt upon the stones, and made his confession to Almighty God the Father, asking for forgiveness, and supplication, and His mercy that strength and wisdom might be his to know what path he must follow.

In the night, when her daughters had finally left her, Bébinn gathered into a small pack the necessities she would need to implement her plan. Quietly, she slipped from the postern gate at the rear of the walled enclave. Slowly, she made her way out of the valley, knowing how to go without being detected by the watch.

By dawn, Bébinn was on her way to Killoughter.

[illegible]

[illegible]

[illegible]

[illegible]

[illegible]

[illegible]

[illegible]

[illegible]

PART 3

THE HEART AND THE HOLLY

Chapter 15

Squads of English soldiers swept through the hills above *Uí Briúin Cualann* in search of hostages. The operation encountered little resistence, the captives being seized outside their respective enclaves. There were O'Tooles, Kavanaghs, O'Mores, O'Nolans, MacMurroughs, and O'Byrnes, mostly women and children. Some had been fishing or searching for mushrooms. The O'More women had been picking bog lilies; three Kavanagh youths had been booleying their cattle to a summer pasture. Melilot and bindweed, calamint, and swallow wort were in high bloom this last week of June, and the O'Byrne women had not imagined there was any reason to refrain from their usual herb-gathering expedition.

Four days after her capture, Aislinn was delivered to a storm-battered quince orchard near the archbishop's manor at Shankill. Converging upon the field, many of the Irish recognized kin among the other prisoners. The total count was forty-eight hostages. They were hungry, dirty, footsore, and frightened as they gathered about a spring to weep, and worry aloud as to their future.

Aislinn sat on a broken wall at the fringe of this

woeful gathering, trying to draw as little attention to herself as possible. She had seen her cousin Sean's younger brother, and several others from Annacurragh, but she did not reveal herself to them. She could not risk exposing her deception.

"Can ye be helping me?" someone spoke in Irish.

The urgency in this petition could not be ignored, and Aislinn looked up to see a young woman of about her own age standing before her. She was reed-thin, pale, and there was a watery, perhaps feverish light in her eyes. She held a bundle in her arms, and a small child was balanced on one bony hip.

"How can I help?"

The thin young woman leaned low, and whispered for Aislinn's ear only, "The soldiers have threatened to leave my babes on the roadside if I cannot keep up. Won't ye take my little girl? My granny already has charge of my sister's wee ones. Won't ye help me? With only the little one it will be easier for me. Go on, Eva." She slid the toddler to the ground, and gave her a gentle push toward Aislinn, but the little girl would have none of this. She clung ferociously to her mother and started to wail.

"We are almost to Dublin," replied Aislinn. Heads were turning their way, and she was afraid that the protective wall she'd erected around herself was about to be dismantled. "Surely the castle is our final destination. We can walk together. The three of us. Would ye hold my hand, Eva?" she asked. "*Tabair dam do lanu,*" she said in a tranquil voice. *Give me yer hand*. But the little girl was not reassured by Aislinn's kindly tone, and answered with an even louder scream of protest.

"I warned you about those brats," barked an English soldier. He seemed to have appeared out of nowhere, and glared at the young mother, his cruel expression mirrored by his ugly tone of voice. He had the flat nose and puffy face of a pig. "Shut them up, or I'll do it for you." He spoke English, of course, and in case they did not understand he pantomimed along with his speech, concluding with a mock strangulation.

This frightened Eva into silence. The young mother began to tremble.

"Please, if not Eva, then watch the wee one for me. Her name is Onóra, and she is too little to be giving ye any trouble," she whispered as she pressed the bundle into Aislinn's arms. In the next instant, she had hoisted Eva back onto her hip, and moved away to rejoin the group that was being ordered to rise.

"On your feet." The pig soldier prodded Aislinn. "We're to be on our way. And the same warning goes to you. Keep the brat quiet, or we leave it behind."

Aislinn's immediate instinct was to call after the mother and make her keep the babe, but the soldier's words induced a distinctly different reaction. Her hold about the bundle tightened until it was nothing less than possessive, and she cast an anxious glance downward. She knew little about tending a child so young, but she knew enough to get by for the time being, she told herself. The child was sound asleep. They were safe for now.

From Shankill, the hostages proceeded to Dublin town, entering through Dame's Gate in the eastern wall between the Liffey and the castle. For those who had never seen an English fortress, let alone been to Dublin, Dame's Gate, though a narrow passage, was an imposing sight. It consisted of two towers and a massive portcullis, and captivity assumed a stark reality when the hostages walked beneath the raised iron grillework. The women began to keen, a long, thin wail rising up and down the line like the mournful cry of the *bean sidhe*. Surely, death was at hand. An old woman began to recite backward the "Pater-noster," and only when someone pointed out the statue of the Blessed Virgin in a niche over the gate was there a vague semblance of calm.

Aislinn walked with her head down, her face hidden by a thick fall of hair. Now that they had entered the heavily populated town there was the remote chance someone might recognize her. But no one of her acquaintance would take a second notice of an Irish hostage cooing at her baby.

Onóra had opened her eyes. She was a pretty little thing with bright blue eyes, and a sweet disposition that tugged at Aislinn's heart. The baby made fretful noises, most likely owing to hunger, but smiled when Aislinn whispered, "Onóra, *math an cailín, good girl,*" and loudly suckled upon two chubby fingers she'd thrust into her mouth.

Aislinn suspected this wouldn't satisfy her for long. What the child needed was milk, and soon her little lungs would support a clamor that would not cease unless she got what she wanted. She must find Onóra's mother, and quickened her pace, threading between the clusters of women and children, working toward the front of the group.

They were herded a short distance along Palace Street before turning up Castle Street. Aislinn had almost reached the head of the line as they were going over the drawbridge into the castle itself.

Although Dublin Castle boasted seven towers, they were not all suitable for housing prisoners, and the soldiers briskly began to separate the men from the women. For a moment, Aislinn thought she had found Onóra's mother, but the atmosphere in the yard was becoming chaotic. A new wave of panic erupted through the hostages, and Aislinn was cut off from the young woman. The call went forth for males over the age of twelve to step forward, and while a handful of men obliged, the soldiers were not satisfied with their number, and took it upon themselves to pass judgment on the age of the others. The panic heightened. Eighteen men, mostly boys, in truth, were separated from the group, and this set the women to wailing anew as lads were taken from mothers, brothers from sisters, to be led into Bermingham Tower, the traditional and most secure keep for prisoners.

"You there, mistress!" a knight approached Aislinn, and guided her a few feet away from the others. He had not been in the orchard, and was dressed in the colors of the castle command, but Aislinn had never seen him before. "I am told you are one of the chieftain's wives. Is this so?"

"Yes." She had spotted the young mother again. She was several yards away, and Aislinn tried to move sideways in her direction.

"You are to come away from the others and stay there." The knight pointed to the stairs that led into the great hall. A woman with yellow hair was already seated on the top step. There was a guard posted by her side. "Come with me." He set a hand beneath her elbow.

Aislinn felt a rush of panic. "Quickly, now," she called to the young mother, intending to give back the baby as she passed on her way to the stairs. "Over here."

The mother made as if to move toward Aislinn, but another woman held her back, whispering something to her.

"Now." Aislinn held out the bundle.

The young mother looked between Aislinn and the woman beside her. "*Ní hea,* my granny says she is better off with ye," she said as Aislinn neared, and did not take her baby. "Perhaps they'll be treating ye better than the rest of us."

Aislinn was not sure this was the motivation behind her separation from the others, but it made no difference. She was by now several feet away, and had been ordered to stop speaking as the women and children were forced in another direction. They were being taken to Black Tower, a circular, three-storied tower with walls that were ten feet thick. A fortified door at the base of the tower opened, through which they entered one at a time.

Before the young mother entered, she cast a backward glance at Aislinn, who held her babe. Tears were streaming down her face, and with what must have surely been her greatest act of bravery, she called out in Irish, "Make sure my Onóra lives." Then she ducked beneath the lintel, and disappeared into Black Tower.

The door was closed behind the last hostage. An awful silence settled over the yard.

"With God's will," Aislinn whispered on a soft hush. She looked down at Onóra, and for the first time, experienced a blood-chilling fear. The Irish women were horror-stricken by the unknown, but it was what Aislinn knew about the English that terrified her. Her feet were cold, and her legs numb, as she continued the final distance to the stairs, where she sat beside the fair-haired woman.

Aislinn recognized the bride from Dysert. This was Broinninn, Bran's sister and wife of Dallán O'Byrne, but she did not speak to her. Instead, she sat as Broinninn did, finding strength in a shield of affected fearlessness. They were a portrait of womanly, Irish pride with slender backs straight, their gazes focused directly ahead, hands folded upon their laps, and chins tilted slightly upward, appearing altogether undaunted, and with a restrained hint of defiance.

An official came out of the hall with the knight. He was garbed in a black houpland, crossed from one shoulder and over the chest with a richly ornamented baldric that supported a dagger sheathed in matching green leather. Aislinn averted her face from his regard as he lifted a cloved pomander to his nose, and inquired on a sniff, "These are the chieftains' wives?"

"O'Connor and O'Byrne," the knight replied.

"Very good. Very good," the official said. He sniffed again, and had not noticed either of the women in particular, except that they were dirty and dressed like savages. It was impossible to fathom that these creatures were the wives of powerful men. "Arrangements have been made for them?"

The knight made some reply, and the two went back inside the hall while the guard stood over Aislinn and Broinninn.

"O'Connor?" Broinninn managed to say without her lips moving. She maintained her erect pose, but angled her head to stare at Aislinn, curious and suspicious. "Ye're not my brother's wife."

"Hush, please say nothing." Aislinn pleaded with her eyes. Onóra chose this moment to begin fretting. "Do not betray me," she said as she rocked the baby, but it did not have the calming affect she had hoped.

"Would ye like me to take the babe?" asked Broinninn. "I have some practice."

Of a sudden, Aislinn recalled that Dallán O'Byrne's bride had been a widow with children. Her heart skipped a beat as she looked toward Black Tower. She had to know, and asked, "Where are yer children?"

"At home with my husband, *buíochas le Dia*." Broinninn made the sign of the cross, *Thank God,* then reached out as if to take the babe from Aislinn.

"Nay, she was given into my care. I will be seeing to her needs."

Broinninn nodded, and decided that whoever this young woman was, she liked her. Indeed, her brother probably would, too. Gladly, she offered the suggestion, "Give her a bit of yer finger to chew upon."

Aislinn put a finger to Onóra's mouth, and was surprised when she quieted. She was surprised, too, at the presence of two tiny teeth.

The knight, who had gone into the hall with the official, returned with water for the women, a crust of dark bread, and two apples. The bread was rock hard, and the overripe apples were bruised, but it was food, and the knight displayed some courtesy when he offered them. "When you are finished eating, I will take you to your quarters."

Broinninn accepted the food with a polite nod. She was not certain what the knight had said except for something about eating, and she was more than willing to comply. She gave one of the apples to the woman beside her. "Who are ye?" she whispered as her lips closed over her apple.

"Yer mother and I were in the forest when soldiers surrounded us. They took me instead of her when I said I was the chieftain's wife."

"But who are ye?"

"My name is Aislinn . . ." she hesitated, and used the moment to bite off a piece of apple for Onóra. The baby was able to hold it in her hands and gnaw upon it, probably not actually eating much of it, but satisfied with the sweet moist taste. Aislinn looked at Broinninn and spoke, very softly so that no one else would be able to hear. "I am Aislinn Clare."

Aislinn Clare. The name tumbled through Broinninn's brain. She gaped at the black-haired beauty as her mind tried to make sense of this information, and then it came to her. This was Sir Roger Clare's infamous daughter. Even at Baravore they had heard gossip of the half-English, half-Irish girl. "But yer father is a knight—"

"*Ní hea,*" Aislinn cut her off. "Ye must not speak of it."

"But why do ye not tell the truth?"

"And put yer family in jeopardy? If the English discovered my deception, they would surely return for a real O'Connor. Plus, I am selfish. If my true identity was discovered, they would punish me, and I do not want that."

"Punish ye? But why, if ye're not really Bran's wife?"

"The statute. I've been among the natives. I've spoken Irish, and I am not dressed in the requisite English fashion. I know how they think, and they would wish to make an example of me." Her voice trembled. She knew too much not to be terrified by the consequences of what she had done. Her father was not here to intervene in her behalf, and even if he was, he could not help her anymore. "'Tis likely they would force me to stand with the penitents at the High Cross, where Skinners Row intersects with Christ Church Lane, and after several days and nights of exposure to the elements, they would probably flog me as well. I may be foolish enough to believe I can survive the adversities of being a hostage, but the mere prospect of punishment weakens me."

"Weak? Ye seem extraordinarily brave to me."

Aislinn bowed her head and confessed, "I am terrified."

"As am I." Broinninn set a sympathetic hand on Aislinn's forearm.

"Ye do not show it," said Aislinn.

"Nor do ye."

"We will help each other then to keep the truth from them. Yes?"

"Yes," Broinninn agreed. After awhile, she asked, "But why is it ye were with my mother in the first place?"

"We were on our way to Annacurragh."

"Which answers nothing. My brother has never kept contact with the MacMurroughs. None of this makes sense, let alone why ye would let them take ye instead of my mother."

"Bébinn was a special friend of my mother's, which is why after so many years she was coming with me to Annacurragh. She had been there many times as a girl, and wished to visit her old friends. As for letting the soldiers take me in yer mother's place, I had no choice. It was the right and only thing to do."

Broinninn almost laughed. She did smile. "Do ye have any idea how much ye sound like my brother, Bran? Remarkable. Do ye know him?"

"*Ó tá,*" she said as the memories and emotions she had tried to suppress these past few days rushed back to her. At first, her prayers had been for Bébinn's safe return to Baravore, then she had begun to wonder at Bran's reaction to what had transpired, and she could not help wondering if he had said a prayer for her. She could not help wondering if she had gained an ounce of his respect for what she had done. While that had never been her intention, it was impossible for Aislinn to stop hoping that he might be proud of her. She could not prevent her heart from wishing that because of this Bran O'Connor would not forget her as the years passed, that he would remember her in naught but a glowing light.

"But how is it that the daughter of an English knight comes to know my brother?"

Oh, there were a thousand answers to that, but Aislinn merely replied, "He saved my life."

Again, Broinninn smiled. "Ye have the uncanny ability of being able to answer my questions without telling me much of anything in particular. What are ye hiding?"

"Nothing," she said, while she thought, *Everything, including abiding, unrequited love, and an irreparably shattered heart.*

A few moment of silence passed between them. They shared the water. Broinninn helped Aislinn give some to Onóra, and then she asked, "Tell me, how did ye leave my family? Were they well?"

"Tá, cinnte. They were preparing for Niall and Ceara's wedding."

The knight returned. He dismissed the guard, who had been hovering over them. "Follow me, if you please."

They proceeded to the castle gate, where an escort was waiting. With two guards in front, one on either side, and two to the rear, the knight led them through the town. This escort was, perhaps, more for their protection than to prevent them from trying to flee. The narrow streets were filled with hostile, angry citizens.

"Savage Irish," someone jeered.

"Did they bring the tempest?"

"Witches!" The cry was taken up by several women.

Broinninn clung to Aislinn's arm.

"There is nothing to be frightened of," said Aislinn as much to reassure herself. This rabble was far worse than the crowd in Wicklow. They were looking for someone to blame for their misfortune.

"My English is not perfect, but I can understand enough of what they say." Broinninn was close to tears. "I did not know they hated us so. What have we done? We have not taken their lands or destroyed their homes. We have not imprisoned or killed their kings."

"Send them back to the hills." A man, his ears jutting through matted, greasy hair, dared to approach and wave a fist at them. "They'll only bring disaster on us."

"Step back," the knight instructed. "Or answer to the archbishop. Step back."

Although the crowd did not disperse, they fell quiet, and the man with greasy hair lowered his hand as they passed.

"Where do they take us?" Broinninn asked. They were heading down a hill.

The narrow streets were familiar to Aislinn. They were walking north down a very steep street toward the Liffey. "We are probably going to one of the towers on the town wall. 'Tis likely they fear someone will try to rescue us, and this is their way of foiling such an attempt. 'Tis also their way of offering us the respect they believe we are due; the English would expect the wives of their earls to be treated differently from other hostages. The English make a distinction between ladies and women, ye see, and to them we are ladies while the others were merely women. Although the English would not be outraged to have their servant girls tossed into a dank prison keep, they would be appalled if a lady were treated in that careless manner. We may be savages in their eyes, but the English conscience cannot forget we are the wives of chieftains. What the English do not realize is that the Irish hold every one of their hostages' lives in equal value, and they will try to rescue every one of their people, not just the chieftains' wives."

"Ye merely confirm what I have always believed," said Broinninn. "The English are a peculiar, cold-blooded race, and it was a good thing, I think, not to fully comprehend how their minds work."

Aislinn grinned at this, but said nothing more. Onóra was sleeping, and they continued in silence to one of the towers along the town wall above the Liffey.

The tower at the botton of Fishamble Street was four stories tall, and it was called Wood Castle because of its grand design and location at Wood Quay. Wood Castle had been granted to a citizen of standing, a wool merchant, whose wife opened the door at their approach.

"This is my sister-in-law, Mistress Picot," said the knight. "She has agreed to house you in her tower."

The escort remained outside on the street while Aislinn, Broinninn, and the knight entered the ground level that was a combination armory, storeroom, and work place. The air was heavy with the scent of unwashed wool. Two young scribes sat on high benches at a table making notations into ledgers.

"Treat Mistress Picot with respect," the knight said to Aislinn. "There will be guards posted outside on the street, so do not try to flee while you are guests in her home."

"They do not appear to be savages," Mistress Picot said to her brother-in-law as she accepted a coin purse from him. She studied the two women. They were dirty from days of travel, but of fine feature and poise. The baby appeared to be healthy. "We will be fine."

"That is good to hear."

"Although I am certain they are hungry and tired, and would appreciate some privacy." Mistress Picot cast a lingering gaze upon the baby. "Be off with you, so they can get about settling in."

The knight made a bow to all three women. "I will check upon you daily," he said in parting.

"Come with me, please." Mistress Picot indicated

that Aislinn and Broinninn should follow her to a stairs. "John. William. Do not ogle. Back to work," she spoke with authority to the scribes, and as the women ascended to the next level she continued, "I am Catherine Picot. My husband, Geoffrey, is the head of the wool merchants guild, but he is away. He was due to return the day of the great storm, but his ship has not yet arrived, and my brother-in-law thought I needed a distraction. He thinks I worry overmuch."

The second level was a spacious great room with a fire hearth built into the wall. There was pale green glass stamped with bottle seals on the three windows that were hinged and opened to let in fresh air. Rugs made from animal skins and finished about the edges with colorful braiding covered the floor, and the furnishings were plentiful and comfortable in appearance, being oversized and draped with velvet and brocade cloths or piled with velvet cushions. The wall hangings were vibrant in color, and rich in detail, depicting scenes of mythical creatures in splendid gardens and maidens in flowing gowns dancing round fountains. There were candles, many candles of varying shapes and sizes, instead of rushes or tallow dips.

"Such riches," marveled Broinninn in Irish.

"What does she say?" asked Catherine Picot.

"Your home is very luxurious to our eye, Mistress Picot," Aislinn said. She had heard gossip that there were people in Ireland, merchants and money lenders, who had more wealth than even the high lord justiciar, and here, she saw the reason for those stories. They were true.

"Please, call me Catherine." While there was genuine kindness in Mistress Picot's demeanor, she was painfully self-conscious, especially when she added, "My husband is an older man, you see, and has enjoyed many years of prosperity." She cast a longing eye at Onóra. "But we have not been blessed with children."

They continued upward through a third floor to the top level, which was a single, low-ceilinged chamber. In a former time before the bridges across the Liffey had been burned, it had probably served as a shelter for the watch. Now it was furnished as a sleeping chamber with a bed, a table with two benches, and a chest with a laver and pitcher. There were only two windows, very small and very high that let in almost no light.

"It is a small chamber, I know, but it will be better than anything at the castle, and I will be glad for your company. My brother-in-law is right. I have been doing naught but worrying since the storm."

"Thank you," Broinninn said in stilted English. Although she didn't comprehend everything Mistress Picot had said, she did perceive kindness, and the great good fortune that had befallen her.

"While you may not go onto the first level, where my husband's employees work, nor go into the street or rear garden, there is a rampart here that circles the tower, and it is not a bad place for fresh air." Catherine opened a tiny door. A wonderful salt breeze swirled around the chamber, sunlight streamed inside, the noises of the waterfront drifted skyward, and Catherine smiled to see the two Irishwomen relax. "I will ask my neighbor for the loan of a cradle. And any other things that may be necessary for the baby. Please tell me what you need. I have nothing, you must understand, but we will get whatever you need. Do not worry."

"Thank you." This time, it was Aislinn who spoke as she sat upon the edge of the bed. If it had been hard as a rock it would have been just fine, but it was heavenly. She knew in an instant that the mattress was not filled with rushes, but with goose down, and the prospect of sinking into that softness and sleeping through the night without the howl of wolves or the snoring of English soldiers was nothing less than a miracle. "Och, Broinninn, 'tis made of down, not straw. Come and see for yerself. 'Tis a fair wonder, it is." And while Broinninn was marveling at the wonders of English mattresses, Aislinn noticed the way Catherine watched Onóra.

"Would you like to hold the baby?" she asked.

"Oh, yes. May I? You would let me?"

"Aye. Her name is Onóra."

And when Mistress Catherine Picot took little Onóra into her arms, Aislinn knew that no matter what might happen to her, the baby was going to survive. There was a prickle at the nape of her neck. Indeed, the child was likely to live an entirely blessed life.

Chapter 16

Bébinn's progress toward Killoughter was ponderous, owing to her injured ankle and the frequent necessity to hide from English patrols, and as she neared the coast the storm wreckage made her headway even slower. The sights were sobering. Everything that had once been green was dead, and she began to understand why the settlers were fearful. She had never imagined wind and rain could cause such destruction, and her only comfort was the thought that this hardship would aid her plan.

After three days she arrived at a farmstead. Its garden and fields were in ruin. A woman was tending chickens in a muddy, rutted yard. Bébinn approached the housewife.

"I have need of a good horse and saddle, and can pay well," she told the woman.

At the mention of payment, the housewife beckoned the stranger to pass through the stile into the yard. It was obvious the traveler was Irish, but the woman would not care if she were the devil himself. She was recently widowed, and living alone at the devastated farm with a surly Irish farmhand, whom she greatly feared. The prospect of profit was irresistible; at least, she might not starve this winter, at best, she might be able to move out of *Uí Briúin Cualann* and return to town. Her name was Jehane, and she had not always lived here, she told the Irish woman as she led her to the house.

"Come inside, where my farmhand will not hear us. It is cooler out of the sun."

The abode was, indeed, cool. It was dank and shabby. Scrawny hounds lay upon soiled rushes scratching at their fleas. The sharp stench of mildew was overpowering, and the walls were stained with patches of the graying white substance. Bébinn sat on a bench by the door, where the light was best. She accepted some water, then unrolled the pack upon her lap as the housewife watched.

Bébinn had brought from Baravore three items necessary to her plan. One was a necklace of amber beads. They had been part of her dowry, and her grandmother's, and before that her great-great-grandmother's; she had been saving it for Bran's daughter, her grandchild. A long-ago ancestress, her great-great-grandmother's mother, had found the necklace buried at an ancient faerie ring. When Bébinn had been small she'd believed they held powerful magic. As she grew older, she'd come to believe they were the world's most magnificent jewels, being the color of the sun at the end of a hot summer day with each of the graduated beads being absolutely, perfectly rounded. Now Bébinn held both their antiquity and beauty in equal value, and as she had hoped the housewife agreed to trade them for her finest horse and saddle.

The housewife encouraged Bébinn to rest while she went outside to have the horse saddled. Once she was alone, Bébinn unrolled the second and third items she had brought. They were her finest linen kirtle dyed a vibrant blue to match her eyes, and a bright scarlet cloak. She changed out of her soiled tunic and into them. She coiled her hair in what she imagined was an English style, then went outside. In the yard, she handed the amber beads to the housewife, who handed her the reins.

The transaction was complete. The women bid one another farewell and good luck, and then, making certain to use the stirrup, Bébinn mounted the horse, perching uncertainly upon the peculiar sidesaddle. The housewife gave directions to Killoughter.

Bébinn was less than a mile from her final destination.

The ploy worked.

The watch commander at Killoughter listened to the beautiful, well-dressed woman's tale of having been beset by thieves. Her escort had been killed, she said tearfully, and she had barely escaped with her life, let alone with her horse. She required shelter, and wished an interview with Sir Roger, who was an acquaintance of her husband's. Without question, Bébinn was admitted into Killoughter, her mount was stabled, and she was shown to a chamber to await Sir Roger.

Although she was exhausted, Bébinn paced about the room. She was nervous about what was going to happen when Sir Roger walked through the door. In a few seconds, her past raced before her, more than twenty-four years' worth in a panorama of vivid details. But the future was murky. There was much at stake here, and while Aislinn's life was the most important thing to be addressed, that did not quell the expectations in Bébinn's heart. What if Sir Roger didn't recognize her? The possibility was awful, yet real, and while Bébinn would be willing to accept personal disappointment, she did not want to admit failure where Aislinn was concerned.

Bébinn collapsed in a chair and looked about her. The chamber was, perhaps, what the English called a solar, and the Irish called a women's bower. There were, however, no signs of a feminine hand in its care or contents. There were no baskets of embroidery, nor shelves of herbs or medicinals. It was dark and drab and cold, and although Bébinn imagined the oversized and ornately carved furnishings were expensive, she experienced a pang of sorrow. She could not picture Étaín spending a winter afternoon in this chamber, nor Aislinn, and she wondered if the rest of Killoughter was as somber as this.

"I am sorry to have kept you waiting, mistress. Welcome to Killoughter," Sir Roger spoke as he entered the solar. He did not see his visitor at first, then he spotted her in the great chair positioned in the opposite direction. He watched a feminine hand grasp the arm of the chair. The slender fingers seemed so white against the dark wood, so delicate against the elaborate design of larger-than-life thistles.

Bébinn trembled at the timbre of the male voice. Her hands gripped the arms of the chair for extra support as she made to rise and face him. She would have known that voice anywhere. It was as low and smooth as the deep masculine tones she heard every night in her dreams. Sir Roger was a knight and warrior, but she knew how gentle he could be, and she thrilled at the trace of tenderness in his voice. Her heart beat a reckless tattoo against her chest.

"I am told you still have your horse. That is good news. But I would be reassured that the felons did not harm your person in any way, and you must give me a description of the culprits so that proper measures can—"

Abruptly, Sir Roger ceased speaking. His breath caught in his throat at the sight of the woman who had stood and turned to face him. She was tall and slender with pale yellow hair that was coming undone from a coil about her face. He remembered stories of Irish faeries with long, golden hair sweeping the ground, and he wondered if he was to be haunted for what had happened to his wife. Could the faeries be so cruel to torment him with this vision from his youth, long ago and far away, but never forgotten?

"Bébinn?" He felt his lips move, but wasn't aware of any sound emanating forth. He had never used her name. He hardly dared to do so now. What if she wasn't real? When they had been in the forest he had not known her name except to call her *ceistean graidhean, sweetheart,* and *mo leanan, my beloved.*

When he had found her at Baravore, wedded to an O'Connor, he had not dared to utter her name aloud. And when she had come up to him with Étaín at Black Castle, he had known from the expression in her eyes that she hadn't told her friend about him. There was no way he could have known her name, and he had treated her with nothing more than the courtesy one extends to a stranger. Not a hint of recognition, nothing to betray them.

"Bébinn," he said her name now, and the word vibrated with all the wonder in his heart. How could it be that she was here?

"Roger," came her hushed reply. There was a thrumming in her ears as blood coursed through her, and she held a hand to her heart. How many times she had whispered that to herself in the long darkness of a lonely night, but she had never thought to stand before him, and call him by name.

"How?" he asked in English, and then forgetting himself, he repeated in Irish. *"Cén fáth. Why?"*

He was coming toward her. Bébinn took in the sight of his tall figure, his broad shoulders, the handsome nose that had been broken. She remembered how muscled his arms were, how tender his strength, how he had tasted like salt and smelled like leather and the forest. The years of dreaming caught up with her, and Bébinn swooned.

Sir Roger barely reached her in time. He caught her, scooping her into his arms, and he carried her to the massive thistle-carved chair, where he sat down, holding her like a lover holds his bride, her head resting in the crook of his arm, her slender body upon his lap, folded against his hard chest. He gazed at her face, finding it impossible to believe it had been so many years.

There were no lines of age about her mouth or eyes, and her color was as petal pink as a maiden's. Her face was the almost perfect oval he had remembered with golden lashes like downy feathers resting against her cheek, a straight nose, skin that was flawless, and a mouth that was the same plump, perfect bow of his dreams. To look at her made him ache with loss and longing and jealousy. He imagined that she must have had many lovers over the years. He had heard she was a widow, but he never imagined her bed had been empty.

Bébinn regained consciousness. She blushed beneath his intent regard, but did not drop her gaze.

"It is really you?" He wanted to reach up and run a hand down her cheek, but dared not.

She gave a little nod, all but mesmerized by the sound of his voice. The manner in which he cradled her allowed his arm to brush against her face, and she couldn't resist closing her eyes and inhaling the masculine smell of him. Leather and forest. "Aye," she said, breathless, and more alive than she had been in a very long time.

"Is the story you told the guard true? You were waylaid by bandits?"

"Nay, there were no bandits. I am sorry for the lie, but I could think of no other way to get in to see you. I am here because of yer daughter. Because of Aislinn. She needs yer help."

"You must be mistaken." He frowned and looked off at nothing in particular. "My daughter is in England with my wife's family. Though they may send her back when they hear what has happened to Lady Alyson. Barely three months my wife, and she is dead. Lady Alyson was with child, but there was something wrong. She had not been well for days, and her suffering turned to agony during the height of the tempest. The midwife could not get here from the village," he said, although he suspected it would not have made any difference. "She died during the tempest."

"I am sorry."

"It is for the best," he was speaking as if from far away. His voice was stark and dull, revealing not so much sadness as weariness, and guilt. "She was not suited to Ireland, and I was not the right husband for her. She deserved a less cynical man than myself." He almost said, *A man whose heart was free*, but stopped himself with a quick shake of his head. His heart had never been free, he thought as he looked back at Bébinn resting against his arm.

For a moment, Bébinn lost track of her thoughts. Sir Roger's words were almost a confession. The expression in his eyes was haunted and full of regret, but she did not think he would appreciate her sympathy. She found her voice. "Aislinn is not in England as ye believe her to be. I speak the truth. Please, listen."

Bébinn related what she knew of Aislinn's treatment on the ship at the hands of the Windsor brothers, how she had jumped into the sea, been washed back upon the shore, and rescued by her eldest son, who had brought her to Baravore.

Sir Roger cursed the Windsors and himself. "Do you think me a wicked father? Aislinn accused me of that more than once. Wicked and heartless. She thought I didn't understand."

"I am sure ye did what ye believed was best."

This time, he did not stay the impulse to caress her face. With the back of his hand Sir Roger brushed along her cheek, and, staring into her eyes, he had the look of a man who has been troubled for a long time, but only now has been able to accept all that has happened to him. "Do you know that every one of my decisions since coming to Killoughter was made because I believed it was right? I married Étaín because I thought it was the right and beneficial choice for a young lord with a castle beneath his command. The decision was easy, for she was lovely and passionate and devoted, but I did not marry for love. Oh, how many decisions I made and adhered to over the years even though deep down inside some little voice argued to the contrary. Some might say that my constancy was noble, honorable. But, in truth, it was cowardly and wrong. For in the end, those decisions have been my greatest, most regrettable mistakes. Too late have I learned that sometimes it is better to listen to one's heart than to one's mind. I know how it wounded my daughter when I called her Johanna Elizabeth, yet each time I did so, I told myself it was right. It was right to obey the statute even though it meant denying her Irish heritage; it was right, my ever-calculating mind reasoned, because it protected that long line of other decisions I'd made about wealth and rank and material security. I did not want to put into jeopardy everything I had worked so hard to acquire." He closed his eyes as if his thoughts had drifted to someplace far away. "Tell me about my daughter. Tell me about Aislinn."

"Ye believe me then?"

"I would never doubt you, *mo leanan*." Her stroked her cheek. *My beloved*. His other hand entwined with hers upon her lap. "Tell me, what is this trouble she faces?"

Bébinn blinked as unbidden tears pooled in her eyes. He had called her *mo leanan* as he had called that young girl in the forest, and her fingers entwined with his. She had a sudden memory of Aislinn's wish that one day she—Bébinn—might see her father again. Bébinn found herself wishing that this moment would last forever. But it wouldn't. She was here for one reason, and must make certain she did not fail.

"Aislinn was returning to Annacurragh when English soldiers surrounded us, and I had accompanied her—which is another story altogether and can wait until later. Anyway, the soldiers were looking for hostages, and Aislinn lied to save me, telling them she was the chieftain's wife. They took her instead of me. Can ye not send a message and explain the mistake? They will release her then, yes?"

"It is not that simple. 'Tis already widely known that she tried to run off with one of the O'Connor men. But the greatest problem is the statute. The king is angry that his subjects flaunt it. With every passing day, there are more transgressors, each bolder than another. It is a direct assault on royal power in Ireland, and there is even talk of his majesty dispatching his army to enforce the statute. She would be punished if they knew she had been living in the hills. It does not make any difference that she was not married to an Irishman, or that she is my daughter. No mercy would be shown my child, especially because she is the daughter of a knight, and a ruthless example would be made of her. She is in far more danger than you can possibly imagine."

"What can we do? I would do whatever ye ask of me to help Aislinn." She had heard the paternal concern in his voice, and held his hand tighter. "Your daughter has become very dear to me."

"There is no question that we must get her out of Dublin. It is only a matter of time before her deception is uncovered. There are many officials at the castle who will recognize her. Additionally, supplies are uncommonly low because of the storm, and if there is unrest in Dublin, the hostages could be at risk. But how to get her out is a dilemma. I must think about this. Your help will be needed, for you may be the only living soul I can trust." He rose, and set her back upon the cushioned chair. "You must eat now while I think."

A servant brought several trays, and placed them on the table. Sir Roger dismissed the woman, then pulled up a chair beside Bébinn to help her with the food. There were trenchers of rye bread filled with melted cheese, pickled eels, baked apples, and something that looked like peas doused in cream.

Bébinn laughed. "Aislinn warned me about English food."

"Ah, she did, did she?" There was a twinkle in his dark eyes. "And what else did my daughter tell you?"

"Aislinn answered every question I asked of her," came Bébinn's elusive, almost flirtatious reply.

Sir Roger cleared his throat. "Ah, yes, I see," he said, but he didn't, nor did he know what to say. After a short pause, he said, "Tell me about your son."

"The one who was going to elope with Aislinn, or the one who brought her to Baravore?"

"The eldest one. I exchanged a few words with him on the quay at Wicklow. He struck me as a courageous, honorable, and entirely unemotional Irishman."

"Och, ye've got part of Bran right. He is generous, handsome, and brave. There is no more honorable an Irishman in the hills. But as to the unemotional, it is only a pretense. He is a liar, and a bad one, too. Which brings us round to why it was I was going with Aislinn to Annacurragh. They're in love, ye see, but he won't admit it, and even if he were to do so, there's the accursed O'Connor tradition about keeping the Celtic blood pure. He clings to that as if it were the very air needed to sustain life."

"I take it from the frustration in your voice that you have tried to talk to him about this."

"Aye, and failed to make any impression. Indeed, I was shocked, ye have to know, when I told him that Aislinn had been taken hostage, and he did not break at that point. I was stunned."

Sir Roger rubbed his chin. "Does Bran know you're here?"

"I am sure he has guessed by now."

"And does he know about—"

"The past," she finished with a tremulous smile. "I have hinted."

He grinned in return. "Do not be afraid, Bébinn. It will all be concluded as it should, I promise. Everything. Aislinn. Bran. You. Me. I would do anything for you. Indeed, you must tell me what your wish is this very night."

She had finished eating, and pushed the trencher to the center of the table. She did not have to think long to know what she wanted. "I would like to walk in Étaín's garden."

"Then so you shall." He stood and offered her an arm as the courtiers did their ladies. He escorted her from the solar, down a series of torch-lit corridors, and out through a side door to the walled garden.

The moon was full in a cloudless sky, the seashell path was bright beneath their feet, and Bébinn thought of Niall's spoiled wedding. "My younger son had planned to marry this night. Och, Roger, tell me, have ye wondered how many times it is that events spin beyond our control?"

"Like the day we met," he said, softly.

"Do ye think of it?" she asked.

"Often."

That one word triggered a pang deep inside her, and she could not speak. How painfully aware she was of the sensual force that emanated from him. She was responding to him as a woman reacts to a man, and she wanted to be taken in those arms, to feel his lips upon hers. But this was not right, a little voice cried out inside her. His wife had recently died. She must get control of herself.

Bébinn walked ahead of him, afraid that he would know what she was feeling, what she was thinking. She went toward the graveslabs in the corner of the garden that was nearest to the hills.

Sir Roger watched. He wondered if he had offended her in some way. She was upset about something. Was he to blame?

In the moonlight, Bébinn saw the carved stones. A slender woman in an English kirtle with a fancy girdle resting on her hips, in her hands, she was holding flowers, and some had fallen loose, caught for eternity by the stone carver in mid-air as they tumbled past her skirt to gather at her feet. There were five smaller graveslabs, two to the right of their mother, three to the left, and each was depicted with something that told a little bit about them. A falcon perched on a small leather-clad arm. A bow and quiver of arrows proudly held. A sword and shield newly acquired. Hounds barking at one's side, ready for a run in the hills. And a book, a roll of parchment, and a quill.

"They are as perfect as Aislinn described," said Bébinn. With one hand she wiped at the tears that had started to fall down her cheek. With the other, she reached out to touch the high cheekbones of the woman, the curls about her serene face. "I see my childhood friend in this woman. It is a lovely tribute you have done for her."

"She was a wonderful wife." Sir Roger stood beside her, his hand coming to rest atop Bébinn's on the graveslab.

"As was my husband."

"But—," they both whispered at the same moment.

He reached out, and turned her to face him.

Bébinn finished, "But it was never the same as between us."

"How about the others?"

"What others?" She looked into his eyes.

"Surely a woman as lovely as yourself must have had many lovers."

"There has been no one else, Roger." She felt herself blushing. "Too late did I realize what a mistake I'd made in marrying. But I was young and did not understand. I thought the feelings that I had would pass, and I did what my parents told me was right. After Echrí died, they were not there to guide me, and I only knew that I didn't want to repeat my mistake with anyone else."

Roger stared at her, stunned by her words. It was as if she had snatched them from him. "You are a far wiser and better person than I ever will be. I understood, but twice went ahead with the wrong choice because I thought it was the right thing to do." He stared into her eyes, and saw a reflection of his need, his loneliness, and the passion that knew only one mate. He caressed her face with sad, trembling fingers. The powerful, physical pull that had overcome him so many years ago was back. "Do you feel that between us?"

She nodded. There was a fire in her eyes that spoke more than any word could, and he bent his head. Their lips met. She sighed, he moaned.

That first tentative kiss fused into another, then another, and another. Soon she was breathless and quivering. She was being carried back in time to that clearing in the forest when he had touched her for the first and only time, and all the years of dreaming were melting away.

"If I asked would you come with me to my chamber?" he murmured against her lips.

"Aye." Their mouths were barely touching, but there was an intensely pleasurable sensation vibrating between them. She brushed her lips against his.

"Would you let me make love to you?"

She swallowed in a dry throat, staring at him with wide, passion-clouded eyes.

A flicker of panic seized Sir Roger. Had he gone too fast? Assumed too much? He took her hand, and raising it to his mouth, kissed the tip of each finger, all the while his eyes locked with hers, then he turned her hand over, and his tongue drew a moist circle on the palm. He felt her tremble, heard her sharp little intake of breath. Closing his eyes, he dared to ask again, "Would you let me make love to you?"

"Aye," she whispered as her softly parted lips sought his. "And I will love ye in return."

Arm in arm, they strolled toward the castle, so absorbed in each other, and the promise of passion to come that neither of them was aware of the man who had slipped over the wall and into the garden.

Bran pressed against the tree trunk, his fingers digging between the ridges of rough bark. When he had first noticed the lovers it had been easy to hide himself and remain quiet. But when they walked past, and he had seen his mother with Sir Roger, he had nearly leapt out into their path like an avenging angel. A war cry had risen in his throat, but he had forced himself to swallow it, directing all his energy and anger to his hands, his fingers digging into the tree until the pressure was so great that they started to bleed.

Sir Roger and his mother had reached the garden gate. Bran went after them, staying in the shadows. They entered the castle, and he followed, finding himself in a dim corridor. There were no guards in sight. He heard their voices above him, and made his way up a narrow, winding stairs that ended at a closed door.

There he stood, awkward and uncertain, feeling like a complete fool. Why was he here? To rescue his mother? From whom? Sir Roger or herself? Or was he here because of Aislinn—who did not seem to be on her father's mind this night, Bran thought with an uncharacteristic bite of sarcasm. Bran was angry. He was furious. He was confused.

He opened the door, and entered with his dagger drawn. A loud noise shattered the quiet of the chamber as he kicked the door closed behind him. He didn't see his mother, but Sir Roger, who was bending over a brazier, quickly straightened, and turned toward him.

"So we meet again," said Sir Roger evenly, cautiously. He recognized the intruder right away. So, too, did he see the drawn dagger, and the thinly controlled anger upon the young man's face. No doubt the young Irishman imagined himself in the role of protector, come to rescue his mother from an unscrupulous, lusty English bastard. "What brings you to Killoughter, Bran O'Connor?" he inquired as much in greeting as to warn Bébinn, who was behind the bedcurtains, of her son's arrival.

"Where is she, damn ye? *Go de an donas a duine*!" Bran cursed Sir Roger. *What the plague, man*! "My mother, may the Blessed Virgin protect her soul, where is she? What have ye done to her?"

"Your mother is in no harm. My daughter, on the other hand, could be in grave peril. I hope that you have come to help her, for there is little I can do for her on my own."

"First, I want to see my mother."

"I am here, Bran," said Bébinn. She drew back the bedcurtains, and looked out. She had never seen her son so angry, and while she accepted that his reaction was normal, she could not help being saddened by it. Granted it went against reality, still she did not want Roger and Bran to be enemies. She saw the dagger. "Sheath yer dagger, Bran. Ye do not need it here. I am not a captive in need of rescue, nor is there any need for ye to avenge me. I have not been dishonored."

"Get off that bed," Bran ordered his mother. He did not sheath the weapon, but used it to gesticulate. "Come here."

Bébinn moved. She wanted to calm Bran.

"No," said Sir Roger. "Stay."

Bran moved toward the bed.

Roger blocked his way. "Do not order your mother

like that, nor pass judgment on things you do not understand."

"Please, Bran," Bébinn pleaded. "Listen to me. Listen to Sir Roger. Please, if ye truly care about me this is what I want of ye. Not anger and recriminations. I want ye to try and understand."

He sheathed the dagger. "Explain yerselves then."

"We are playing out something that started long before you were born, Bran. Something that has been unfinished for many years." It was sir Roger who spoke. "I had never dreamed of being offered a second chance, but thanks to my daughter, and a strange twist of Fate, I have that chance. And this time, I intend to see it finished properly."

" 'Tis a lot of clever words, Sir Roger, but what does that mean?"

"It means that I intend to marry your mother."

Bébinn gasped. Marriage. She had not dreamed, never thought beyond this night. "But the statute," she reminded him. "We cannot. Ye cannot."

" 'Tis not possible," Bran agreed. "Ye mutter nonsense."

"Ah, but it is not nonsense, and it is not impossible. Anything is possible if only one is willing to pay the price. To lose you a second time, Bébinn, would be unbearable, and I will not let you return to Baravore because someone else tells me it is the right thing to do. This time, I will listen to my heart. I will give it all up. Killoughter, my lands, my rank. I have no son to inherit, and for an English lord all of this is worth nothing without an heir. I will give it up, and we can go to a place where there is no statute."

Bébinn thought she was supposed to say, *Och, but ye mustn't be making such a sacrifice for me.* But she knew that it would be insincere.

"A place where the statute does not prevail?" Bran

scoffed. "And where might that be?" he asked, skeptical, sarcastic.

"Scotland. France," replied Sir Roger. "We will decide after we have a plan for Aislinn. She must come first. So I ask you again why you came here, Bran O'Connor. Was it only for your mother, or also for my daughter?"

There was a long, awkward silence. It was so silent the lick of flames in the brazier could be heard above the night wind circling the castle. Bran ran a weary hand across his eyes. There was much truth being revealed this night, and he could do no less. He had never lied to his mother. "I came for both of them. They are the two most important women in my life."

"Good," Sir Roger replied with the terse approbation common to a warrior. "Then I am sure you will do the right thing by both of them. We will work together to get Aislinn out of harm's way, and afterwards, ye will give me yer mother, and I will give ye my daughter."

"What!" Bran stared at Sir Roger.

"As I am soon to be your mother's husband, may I recommend that you do not repeat our mistakes. Marry my daughter. I will be gone from Ireland, and will depend upon you to take care of her. Indeed, I hope you will cherish her better than I ever did."

Bran looked from Sir Roger to his mother. What an unholy, unsettling, united front they presented. He wanted to resist. "What if she won't have me?"

"Don't argue," said Bébinn. "Listen to Sir Roger. He's soon to be yer stepfather."

At that, Bran had another one of his bizarre images of the world gone upside down. He had landed in a realm of lunatics, and the strangest thing about it was that he knew they were right. Indeed, somehow despite everything he had always believed, it was obvious that they were right, and he was wrong.

Chapter 17

"A castle on the quay," one leper whispered to another as they drifted past each other, slow apparitions of decay. Having delivered his message, the leper hunkered down near a pond. The other moved toward a great oak.

They were on the common land outside St. Stephen's Hospital, and their shrouds were a perfect disguise. There was no better way for persons wishing to remain anonymous to slip into Dublin, for soldiers and residents alike kept their distance from the wraithlike creatures. Who would dare to get close enough to inspect beneath the moldy, gray tatters? Sir Roger and Bran had agreed it was the perfect disguise for Irish warriors intent upon liberating their kin from Dublin Castle.

A castle on the quay. It did not make sense to Bran. As far as he knew there was only one castle in Dublin, and he sought out Sir Roger, who was seated in the shade of an oak tree.

In the past forty-eight hours, some dozen lepers had joined the wretched mass, who were not infirm enough to warrant admission to the hospital, and were thus encamped upon the adjacent common land.

This was one of the few places in English-held Ireland where the poor souls might receive daily sustenance in the way of food and kindly human word from the good brethren of St. Stephen's.

It was a quiet assembly, knowing better than to draw the attention of the healthy. Bébinn and Sir Roger, enshrouded in gray rags, generous cowls draped about their faces, were sitting in the shadows of a stand of trees. It was a hot afternoon. There was an unhealthy stench in the air. Bran squatted beside them.

"A castle on the quay," he repeated. "Do ye know what it means?"

"Indeed, I do," Sir Roger whispered in reply. He explained about Wood Castle. This was the final information they had needed—the location of the two wives who had been removed from the castle—and Sir Roger motioned for the others to draw near.

The dozen lepers gathered in the shadows of the oak were warriors, who had responded to Bran's appeal. When he, his mother, and Sir Roger had departed Killoughter for Dublin, several runners—degenerate English foot soldiers in Sir Roger's command who were ultimately more loyal to their Irish kin than to the English—had been dispatched into the hills with Bran's message.

Travel as lepers. Destination: St. Stephen's Green. Hurry, the message had implored. *We must be ready to act when the mayor rides the fringes.*

They had begun arriving almost immediately. Dallán O'Byrne. Sean MacMurrough. Kavanaghs, O'Mores, and O'Nolans. And Rian O'Toole, who knew better than the rest how perilous was this plan, but who would rather die any day trying to free the women and children of his clan than to sit and wait, trusting the English to return them in the spring.

It was a bold plan, audacious and risky, conceived jointly by two most unlikely allies, Rian O'Toole and Sir Roger Clare. That Bébinn and Bran O'Connor had vouched for Sir Roger had been most persuasive for the Irish chieftain, but that both men had a daughter being held hostage had struck an even deeper chord. For once, they faced a common enemy, shared a common goal, and felt the fierce determination that they must succeed. Indeed, Rian O'Toole's integrity was beyond doubt, for in addition to his only daughter, his grandchildren and mother-in-law were among the hostages.

Already luck was with them: they had gathered in sufficient number with time to spare before the riding of the fringes commenced; they knew the locations of the hostages, and the precise size of the guard that would be posted this night. These days there were willing accomplices everywhere. Not just at Killoughter.

Rian O'Toole had divided them into several groups. Six men were assigned to the castle, where the garrison would be empty, if not intoxicated, owing to the celebration about to commence. It would be those six who would subdue the meager tower guards, release the hostages, and lead them out of the city in small groups. Two other men were assigned respectively to Gormond's Gate and Dame's Gate, where they would do whatever might be necessary to make certain every hostage was on the other side of walled Dublin before the mayor's procession returned. Bran and Dallán would go downhill toward Wood Castle, while Sir Roger and Bébinn would proceed to the rear entrance of a substantial residence on St. Nicholas Street. It was the home of Sir William Sedgrave. He was a distant cousin of Sir Roger's, his mother had been a Clare, and by coincidence, Sir William had once been wed to a MacMurrough. Sir William could be trusted, and having been contacted the previous day, he had agreed to arrange passage for Sir Roger and Bébinn on a ship out of Dublin upon this eve's high tide.

The leper warriors waited in clusters about the pond, and beneath the trees. Some found strength in prayers for Divine Guidance, others by reaching beneath their shrouds to grasp their dagger handles, and still others closed their eyes to envision the loved ones with whom they soon hoped to be reunited.

For Bran, this was a moment of farewell. It was incredible, yet right, how easily he had come to accept his mother's decision to go with Sir Roger. It was hard to conceive of never seeing her again, and to cover his sadness, he focused on Bébinn's concerns, instead of his own.

"Have I ever lied to ye, Mam?"

"Nay," she whispered, the prickle of tears burned her eyes and nose. When she had slipped out of Baravore for Killoughter, she had never thought it was forever. She had not dreamed that she wouldn't return to the valley, or that there wouldn't be another afternoon when she sat with her daughters in the women's bower, teaching their children to make baskets, or showing the little ones how to spin wool about a tiny child-sized distaff. With the exception of Étaín's departure, all of the farewells in Bébinn's life had come upon her without warning. This was the first time that she was confronting the act of saying good-bye to someone, and she was overwhelmed with the images of everything she was going to miss. How hard it was not to shed a mother's tears.

" 'Tis true, my dearest mam, I've never lied to ye." Bran leaned down to peek beneath her cowl and smile for the both of them. "And I would not do so now. Ye must not fear a thing. We will be finding the both of them, Broinninn and Aislinn. I swear it to ye. Upon my life. My freedom. I will not leave Dublin without them."

"Ye've always been a good son." She tried to return his smile. "Ye're going to be a wonderful husband."

"Och, now, are ye certain I'm so irresistible as all that? The lass has a reputation for her willful, independent demeanor, ye must not be forgetting."

Sir Roger muffled his laughter. Lepers did not laugh.

"*Tá, cinnte,*" said Bébinn. "She will be yer wife. Not only have ye made me and her father a promise, but ye must not forget that willful and independent means nothing in the greater scheme of things. It was meant to be."

Fate. Destiny. Bran nodded, then turned to Sir Roger. "There is something that I want ye to have, sir." He reached beneath his tattered garment and pulled out the talisman that he wore about his neck. He worked the cord over his head and handed the upper half of the crucifix to Sir Roger. "This will guarantee yer welcome in the Highlands, for that is where the owner of the other half resides. He is a cousin by the name of Kirkpatrick and lives at a place called Loch Awe."

Sir Roger took the broken crucifix, and stared at the small sculpture cast in silver of Christ's drooping head with the crown of thorns. It was solid, heavy, and a magnificent, detailed work of art. He could only guess its value, but not so much in coin, rather as an heirloom of great antiquity.

It was easy now for Bébinn to smile at her son. There was nothing he could have said that would have meant more to her than this gesture. She knew beyond any doubt that Bran had accepted Sir Roger.

* * *

In the past few minutes, the populace of Dublin had begun swarming through the streets. Their voices, enlivened by ale and piment, competed with the music of flutes and cymbals. There were horses neighing, bridles jingling, and bells a-ringing. The English in their flamboyant clothes of blue and red, yellow and green, with pointed hats and pointed shoes, were headed for Dame's Gate, where they would exit the walled town to join in a massive procession behind the Mayor and Commons, who would be riding at their head, well-horsed, armed, and in full array.

It was called Riding the Fringes, and its purpose was to mark the city limits outside of the wall. From Dame's Gate, the procession would go first to St. Mary's Abbey, thence to Our Lady Church of Osmany, and from there, past the many orchards, hospitals, mills, market gardens, and monasteries that were part of the development outside the town walls. The extent to which the fringes had expanded was evident by the gateways of Coombe and Crocker's Bar to the south and west, and Whitefriars to the east that guarded the main approach roads. Riding the Fringes was a lengthy undertaking with numerous ceremonial stops along the way. Dublin would be all but deserted for the next several hours.

"It is time," Sir Roger said to Rian O'Toole. The chieftain agreed, and the word spread.

The warrior lepers began to rise.

Bébinn embraced her son one final time. She whispered for him alone, "Remember this always, my son. We cannot help the circumstances of our birth. We can only be responsible for the daily conduct of our lives. I learned that from Rourke, and I have seen the proof of it today in Sir Roger's aid to our kith and kin, and Aislinn has proven it on many an occasion. Never forget that." Her lips touched his cheek. She had a fleeting memory of a baby's soft skin. Her warm tears fell on his manly jaw, then she was gone toward St. Nicholas Street.

Slowly, quietly, the lepers began to drift away from the green commons of St. Stephen's, taking care to keep their distance from the healthy, knowing that good lepers did not beg or allow their poison breath to mingle with the pure. Quietly, discreetly, they made their way to their respective destinations.

Aislinn, Broinninn, Catherine, and Onóra were seated on the floor of the luxurious great room. Over the past few days a friendship had begun to develop between the three women. For both Aislinn and Catherine the companionship of a woman their own age was a novelty. Aislinn enjoyed helping Catherine with her daily chores while they talked of the kinds of things about which young women everywhere are curious. Catherine, for her part, was fascinated by Aislinn's dual childhood, and through Aislinn and Broinninn, she came to learn that everything her father, and then her husband, had taught her about the Irish and life beyond *terra pacis* was not quite true. Catherine saw a courage in Aislinn and Broinninn that she envied. As for Broinninn, she was astounded by the wealth and comfort that was a part of Catherine's everyday existence, and she was deeply touched by the utter, almost innocent goodness and generosity of Catherine Picot. But it was the books that truly captivated Broinninn, and this afternoon, she was seated upon the floor listening to Catherine read, while Aislinn translated, from a book that described the stars in the heavens, and how they had come to be in their particular patterns.

There came a heavy pounding at the door. The guards had been removed this day to march behind the mayor, and the scribes had left early to participate as had the two servants, who came in daily to work for the Picots. Catherine would have to answer.

"Stay here," said Catherine, handing the book to Aislinn. She descended the stairs. The pounding continued. Certain that it must be her brother-in-law, she called out that she was coming, and did not hesitate to unlatch the door and push it open. It was not him, however, but two lepers. The sight alarmed her. Quickly, she pulled the door closed to a mere sliver. She could not close it against any of God's children. Even lepers.

"What do you want?" Catherine spoke through the crack, noticing with a sense of wonder the calm tenor of her voice. She was certain this was how her two new friends would act, and that certainty gave her a courage she'd never before possessed. It was an empowering sensation, she'd noticed more than once of late. Indeed, only this morning, she'd started to think that she might survive even if—God bless him—her husband never returned to Dublin.

"Our wives," a man whispered in heavily accented English. His voice so low that Catherine was not certain she had heard correctly.

"Their names?" she asked, knowing that she could not turn these men away, if they were truly who they claimed. Even if she had wanted to deny them entrance, it would have been impossible without the guard to help her. But that was not why she acted as she did. It was because she knew the distress of separation from one's spouse, and if it was possible for her to prevent another soul from such suffering, she would do so.

"Aislinn and Broinninn."

Catherine opened the door and cast a hasty glance at the street. It appeared empty. "Come, quickly." She latched and bolted the door, then led them upstairs to the common room.

Broinninn gasped when her husband appeared, and threw herself into Dallán's embrace. They whispered fervent words of affection in Irish, she asked about the children, and he assured her all was well at home. She cried, and he kissed away her tears.

But Aislinn saw none of this. Her eyes were fixed upon Bran. He came to her side, so close she felt the warmth of him. But he did not touch her.

"Ye're fine?" he asked her.

She nodded. Her health was fine, if that was what he meant, but her heart was accelerating out of control.

Catherine picked up Onóra, and with characteristic sensitivity, excused herself from the great room to give the couples their privacy.

Aislinn looked into Bran's eyes, as green as the wild, hidden valley of Glenmalur. "How do I thank ye for coming after us? Did ye know yer sister was with me?" she wondered aloud, the unspoken question being, *Who were you really coming after? Was I only incidental*?

"I knew nothing of Broinninn when I set out." Bran stared at her, feasting upon the lovely sight of those soft black curls, the sultry eyes, and tempting red lips that beckoned him to kiss her. He could not imagine what his life might be like if twenty years were to separate him from this woman before he allowed himself to be honest with her. If he had learned anything these past few weeks, it was to respect, indeed, to accept the fluidity of existence, his existence. There was no such thing as perfection. Occasional snatches of happiness were fleeting at best, and through self-deception, he had already lost much. He must not hide anything from her, and he spoke the truth. "I came for ye."

"Thank ye. That is truly the most wonderful answer I could wish to hear." Aislinn wanted to laugh like a delighted child, but something about his expression stopped her. She gave him a tentative, quizzical smile, and tilted her head to one side as if asking him to explain.

"Do not thank me until we are out of the city. We may not survive the night."

Her insides jolted, her stomach colliding with her heart, at the realization of the full extent of what he was willing to do for her. "My security is not so important as knowing that ye came for me against such odds. Never so important as knowing that ye would die for me."

"Tá, cinnte, I would do that for ye, *cuileann."*

He raised his hands, palms open, hovering about her shoulders, and her heart contracted at the thought that he was going to take her into his arms with the same tenderness Dallán displayed for Broinninn. Her eyelashes fluttered down, but in the next instant they flew up as the piercing cries of the town watch shot through the opened green glass windows.

Bells were clanging, near and far. Voices, raised in alarm, echoed through the empty streets. Catherine returned to the great room, and at her suggestion, they went to the rampart.

"This is not the usual jollification for a Riding the Fringes," said Catherine.

"What does it mean?" asked Bran. "Fire?"

"I cannot say for certain." Catherine shook her head in confusion, then she spotted three youths dashing along the quay, and leaned over the rampart to call out to them, "Why do ye return so soon? What happens?"

"The Irish have attacked the castle!" cried the first.

"There were four hundred of them," added the next.

"Nay, five hundred," corrected the third.

"The entire castle guard is slaughtered!"

They disappeared up the narrow street.

This was the great dread in which the population lived. It had been more than one hundred years since the slaughter of Cullenswood, yet a repetition of Black Monday was a constant fear in the minds of the people of Dublin. Indeed, the murdering barbarians in the hills were the frightful stuff from which English children's nightmares had been spawned for generations.

"Five hundred?" said Aislinn. She spoke in English for Catherine's benefit. "Are there really that many of ye?"

"Nay, we are but a handful. Only six went to the castle."

Catherine could not stop herself from giggling, and the others joined in.

Then there came another knock from below.

They froze. The men pressed against the wall of the tower. Catherine glanced below again. "Soldiers," she said beneath her breath. Motioning the men to follow, she hid them in her chamber before going to the door.

This time, it was, indeed, her brother-in-law.

"You are all right?" the knight asked. "Everything is fine?"

"Of course. Why shouldn't it be?"

"The hostages have been freed from the castle, and we fear someone may soon come here. There is even a rumor the chieftains themselves have come for their wives."

"They are dangerous?"

"They are Irish," was the English knight's spontaneous reply. "I regret that I cannot come in and visit, but I must return to the castle. You are not afraid?"

Catherine noticed that the guards had resumed their posts. There were six of them standing shoulder to shoulder between the tower and anyone who might pass by in the street. "With my own garrison to protect me? I think not," she said with a sweet smile. "As always, you make certain I am safe. Thank you. Good night."

She shut the door, hoping that she had not appeared flustered or sounded rude, and having latched and bolted the door, she hurried upstairs.

Bran had not stayed hidden in Mistress Picot's chamber, but had hovered on the stairs, and he had heard everything the knight said. "We must leave while there is still confusion. That is our best chance. Otherwise we will be trapped, and our presence here will put ye in danger," said Bran. "Is there a back entrance?"

"Yes, but it is no good since the alley comes out at the front, where the guards are posted," replied Catherine. "There is a tunnel though. It goes east about a hundred yards beneath the quay, then uphill a small distance to exit into a shed in our garden plot on the other side of the town wall. I have not been down since the tempest, for it was badly flooded, and may not be passable. Come, I will unlock the door, and you can check."

Behind a heavy tapestry on the first level there was a small door. Bran took a candle and disappeared down a stairs carved out of earth. Several minutes elapsed before he returned. It was wet, but tolerable, he reported, and Catherine went to get the others.

Broinninn and Dallán went first. Bran held his candle as high as the low ceiling would permit to light Aislinn's entrance. She turned to take the baby.

Catherine, who was holding Onóra, looked down

at the child, every ounce of her concern apparent upon her kindly features. "Wait. I must wrap her more securely before you take her. It is certain to be cold down there."

Aislinn dropped her extended arms, and put voice now to what she had known in her heart since arriving at Wood Castle. "There is no need, Catherine. Onóra will not be coming with us. She was never mine, but entrusted to me. I was asked to make sure she lived, and since there is no guarantee for our safety this night, I entrust her to you, Catherine, with the same entreaty."

Tears welled in Catherine's eyes as she smiled. "Onóra will live and flourish, this I pledge to you on my own life. No daughter of my own could be more cherished than this child shall be. Onóra will know love and learning, honor and generosity, courage and kindness, and someday, I will tell her the most remarkable story of a miracle, and how the tempest changed our lives."

The two women embraced in farewell.

Onóra's charmed life had begun.

Bran clasped Aislinn's hand as they made their way through the tunnel. They were ankle-deep in mud, the water was up to their knees, and from all around came the scurry and squeal of rats. Upon reaching the shed, the women, suitably soiled from the tunnel, donned the lepers rags that Dallán had carried, after which the two couples parted company.

They walked in silence until dawn when they reached the hills. Morning mist rose from the ground, the treetops resonated with the racket of birds, and the familiar wind whistled soft and high about their ears. The bracken was moist beneath their feet. The air was crisp and clean, and as the sun rose they slipped into the shelter of the dense forest. They were going home.

Only when they had reached a sheperd's hut did they stop to rest. Only then did Bran allow himself to do what he had wanted since seeing Aislinn in the tower.

He pushed the leper's cowl off her head, swept the loose curls from her forehead, caressed her chin with his long fingers, and bent his head to kiss her. It was a slow, tender kiss. His warm lips moving over hers, thoroughly, adoringly, teasing and savoring the sweet taste of her, reveling in her response, which was as uninhibited as always.

"Have I told ye what an intoxicating creature ye are, *cuileann*?" he murmured against her mouth.

"Aye, ye have. But tell me, are ye not fearful of my powers?" she asked, indulging in a flirtatious series of little nips along his lower lip.

"*Tá, cinnte.* I'm as fearful as any man who knows how fragile the future before him can be." There was a sudden change in his tone. He kissed the end of her nose, but it was not a playful kiss, rather a lingering, almost meditative one to match his contemplative demeanor. He held her to him, kissed her brow in the same manner, and then looked deep into her eyes as if speaking to the farthest reaches of her soul. "I know why ye were spared in the pestilence."

"To save yer mother."

"Och, ye don't know the half of it." The hint of a smile softened his lean, angular features. "Yer purpose is much greater than ye could ever imagine."

"Tell me," she urged, sensing his wonder and feeling it transmit to her.

" 'Tis our parents."

"My father and yer mother? What do ye know of them?"

"Not as much as ye do, I suspect." He smiled fully. "They are the reason why ye were spared. Ye brought them back together."

"They've met again?"

"Aye, and 'tis all because of ye, *cuileann*. They have met again, and it was with their help that yer rescue and that of the other hostages was possible. My mother went to Killoughter to tell yer father what ye'd done in her behalf, and I went after her, having already decided that I must get yer father's help. Ye cannot guess what I discovered upon my arrival."

Aislinn did not hear the astonishment in his voice. She was thinking of something else, and wanted to know, "Where are they now?"

"They sailed for Scotland on the midnight tide. Yer father has given up Killoughter for my mother."

"But what of Lady Alyson?"

"She perished during the tempest."

Aislinn made the sign of the cross, experiencing a mingling of sorrow and joy. She remembered the quiet, kind-hearted Lady Alyson, and prayed that she had found a resting place among the angels. Then she thought of the girl with the spilled basket of mushrooms, and the sad, lonely man her father had become. "Together," she marveled. "I had a role in bringing them together."

"Indeed, ye did, *cuileann*. But that is not all. There is another reason why ye were spared."

"What else could there possibly be?"

"Ye were spared to be my wife. To teach this blind fool the powers of love and Fate, and make me see that there is something to be cherished beyond ideals."

She looked at him, and said nothing. If that was supposed to be a marriage proposal, it was certainly the most obscure one ever offered. He would have to do better.

"Teadam 'na baile," he said. *Let us go home.*

"Home?" she said with the intention of doing what she must to get him to declare himself. "But I will not be welcomed at Killoughter."

"I mean Baravore. That is yer home. Ye're my wife, or so ye claim, and yer home should be with yer husband."

"Is this a proposal?"

"I'm trying. But my words are sounding mighty pitiful, are they not? I think this should be making it clear to ye." He reached beneath his leper's shroud, brought out a pouch, and as she watched, he folded back the supple leather to reveal her holly enamel circlet.

"What have ye done?" she asked on a soft whisper of amazement. For while it was her circlet, it wasn't.

"See for yerself." He set the object in her hands.

Slowly, she turned it over. The enamel circlet of green leaves and red berries had been twisted into a sort of torc, but what was most startling was not this transfiguration, but what had been entwined between the stems to rest against a bed of holly leaves. It was the heart of polished green stone she had found in the chest in his chamber. *The pendant is for the woman who will be my wife.* Her hands began to tremble, and the heart and the holly shimmered through a veil of tears.

Bran's hands steadied hers, and together, they secured the torc about her neck.

"Och, 'tis as perfect as I dreamed it would be against yer lovely, fair skin," he murmured, his voice husky with emotions that he had never allowed himself to experience before. *"Go d'as a nguilean tu?"* he asked. *Why do ye cry?*

"I cry because there is nothing more precious that

either my mind, or my heart can conceive than being yer wife. This is the most wonderful gift." Her fingers skimmed over the leaves to rest at the smooth heart positioned in the middle of the torc. "It is, indeed, most eloquent, and for such tender consideration I cry. But I cry for another reason. I must know this, Bran O'Connor, do ye talk of marriage in repayment for what I did for yer mother, or because of some pledge ye may have made to my father?"

"It is for neither of those reasons, but because of love. *An bfuil a fios agad ca air a bfuil gean agam*?" he asked, feeling the pain of her words. *Do ye know whom I love*? He had given her every reason to be skeptical.

She stared at him, her great dark eyes wide with wonder and hope and the need to be reassured.

" 'Tis ye, Aislinn Clare. I love ye. *Ta mise mo buideac.* I love ye *with all my heart*. I could search to the edges of the earth, and I'll never find another woman like ye. I only want to be with ye. I dream of ye, and if I married another, I would never truly be that woman's husband, and it would be three people, instead of two, who had been cheated. 'Twas my Fate I saw that night in the castle yard, and 'tis trying to flee from it, I've been doing the past months. But to no avail. There is a bond between our souls, and while I could not see it, I sensed it from the first. It was fool's work to try to deny. We will be wed in the chapel at Baravore upon our return."

"But what of my English blood?"

"Och, that is something upon which I've been devoting much thought, and for a long time, I was telling myself, it was why I must be turning away from ye. But this is what I have come to realize. We will marry, and my seed will grow within ye. We will have children, and they will be like ye, *cuileann*. Brave and bold, beautiful and loyal. Like their mother, they will know good from bad, and they will grow up to defend our people. For ye believe in the same things that I do, and through us there will be another generation of O'Connors dedicated to Ireland, and to driving the English into the sea. And for those reasons, and for the yearnings of my heart, I want ye to be my wife. Will ye wed me, Aislinn Clare? Will ye give me yer love?"

"*Tá, cinnte,*" she replied. "*Aye, certainly,* I will gladly be marrying ye, Bran O'Connor, and my love is yers for always. *Ta locas agam go saiseaca me tu,*" she said with a radiant smile. *I hope I shall please ye.*

"Och, my darling, *cuileann,* ye've already pleased me beyond my greatest imagining."

This time, when his lips claimed hers their kiss was wild and hard, hungry and possessive, and thrumming with the passion that had always been there, and always would be.

"Tell me true, would ye be mine this night?" Bran asked.

"For this night and always," Aislinn whispered as he slipped the shroud off her shoulders, and she gave herself to the man who would cherish her for the unseen bonds between their souls.

Fate and Destiny were going to be fulfilled.

Epilogue

In the summer of the following year, a letter directed to the mistress of Baravore made its way to Glenmalur.

January 1, 1369

Dearest Daughter,

Upon our departure from Dublin, my darling Bébinn and I were wed at sea, and though our journey was not an easy one, we finally made our way to Eilean Fidra, the island stronghold of Bran O'Connor's Scottish cousins at Loch Awe. We have been most heartily welcomed by the current Kirkpatrick laird, who is the grandson of Alexander and Claricia, and thus, the great-nephew of Rourke and Viviane of Baravore.

The Kirkpatrick clan is an extensive one, generous and spirited, and Loch Awe is where we will make our home. The laird has bestowed upon us a small round tower on another island, quaintly referred to as the Old Believer's Isle. We hope to begin residence in our new home when the ice breaks and spring comes to the Highlands.

I am blessed beyond expectation to be afforded the privilege and enjoyment of Bébinn's company as my wife and life's companion, and it is our mutual hope that this missive finds you at Baravore, safe and healthy, and experiencing the abundant blessings bestowed upon a much beloved wife.

By the Grace of the Almighty, I am your loving father.

At Eilean Fidra, Loch Awe, Scotland.

Aislinn was, indeed, at Baravore, and as her father had hoped she was safe, in good health, and wed to Bran. Her letter in response to Sir Roger was dispatched immediately.

July 15, 1369

My Dear Father,

You cannot imagine the jubilation with which your missive was greeted by the inhabitants of this remote valley. You and Bébinn have been in the constant thoughts and prayers of your children, kith and kin. I speak for a multitude when I send congratulations for a journey safely concluded, and felicitations for your marriage and plans to settle at Loch Awe. Perhaps, there will be a time when we can visit you there. Or, perhaps, your grandchildren may do so one day.

Yes, Father, by that statement you may surmise that I am soon to be a mother. Indeed, I am told by the midwife sent from Annacurragh it is only a matter of days.

My husband enters our chamber as I write. His affection for his mother is abiding, and he asks that I remind you to honor her well. The sun sets behind the hills, the light dims, and Bran informs me a messenger is leaving for Wicklow. I must bid farewell. May you and Bébinn know that you will always remain in our hearts and minds.

With devotion and affection, Your Daughter.

At Baravore, Glenmalur.

Four years went by before another letter was able to make its way to Baravore. The political situation in Ireland was worsening. The Statute of Kilkenny was failing, and English determination to root out the offenders, to obliterate Irish ascendancy in their ancestral lands, and to punish those degenerate English who were becoming as Irish as the Irish themselves took on the zeal of fanaticism. English spies and henchmen were everywhere, and there was great peril for those who dared to move back and forth between the Irish in the high hills and foreign vessels at the Dublin and Wicklow quays. To be caught could turn an innocent communication into a death warrant.

June, 1373

Dearest Daughter,

With each unanswered missive, our concerns for our loved ones at Baravore mount considerably. May you know that you are in our daily prayers. We wish you good health, peace, and abundant happiness, and as long as the Good Lord allows, I will write regardless of reply.

As for this humble man, your father, and his dearest Bébinn, our news is of an extraordinary, if not miraculous, nature. We are parents, blessed not once, but doubly with the recent arrival of twins. An oc-

currence, we are assured, that is not uncommon to Loch Awe. Our son and daughter, named Rourke and Étaín by my most sentimental wife, are lusty bairns with fair hair like their mother, but temperaments, I am assured, similar to their eldest half-brother.

By the Grace of the Almighty, I remain your loving father.

At The Old Believer's Isle, Loch Awe, Scotland.

As summers faded into autumn, and winters into spring, sporadic missives found their way between Baravore and Loch Awe.

May, 1375

My Dear Father,

As is your practice, I, too, write, knowing that it is only the rare communication that completes the journey from these mountains to Loch Awe. How the years are passing. It is almost a decade since you departed Ireland, and I cannot help but wonder at how startling my news may sound given the gaps there must be in your knowledge of our lives.

Our family grows. You have four granddaughters at Baravore: yes, we have an Étaín, an Aislinn, a Bébinn, and even an Isobel, for your Clare ancestress. As for your wife, her grandchildren, widely scattered throughout the hills, total eighteen, the newest among them being Broinninn's three sons with Dallán O'Byrne.

There are deaths, too. While we were untouched in the pestilence of 1373, many at Annacurragh, including Marga, perished, and I have heard that our old friends at Llangony suffered mightily. And this spring, Rian O'Toole departed this earth. His was a warrior's death in battle against the English, who continue to seize the lands of those degenerate English who defy the statute to ride with the Irish. This time, it was a holding near Castlekevin that was seized. How near the fighting comes to us. But do not fear after our safety, for the English still believe the tales of evil faeries and seductive maidens lurking in our glen.

With hope and affection, Your Daughter.
At Baravore, Glenmalur.

1380, September

Dearest Daughter,

Still not a single reply from Ireland, and still I write most faithfully.

It is with great alarm we have received word that the English landed an army at Howth in May of this year. It appears you and I were both correct: you, in asserting the statute was doomed to failure, and I, for warning that its failure would bring war to Ireland.

Your husband's Kirkpatrick kin are incensed by this news, and nightly, our twins are treated to tales of the glorious time when the English were defeated at Bannockburn. Already our young Rourke speaks of the time he will be old enough to cross the sea to Ireland, and drive out the English.

Our children are the center of our lives, and although I cannot find adequate words to express the full extent of joy that being surrounded by family brings to me, I am certain your heart comprehends. Our days on the Old Believer's Isle ring with laughter and song; praise be that I was able to recognize where it is a man finds true value before it was too late for me. You must know that I do not experience a single shard of regret when I envision the lord justiciar seizing Killoughter in the name of the Crown.

By the Grace of the Almighty, I remain your loving father.

At The Old Believer's Isle, Loch Awe, Scotland.

December, 1391

My Dear Father,

At last, we have a son. He is called Brian after my mother's father, and while his name is Irish, there is a look about him that is pure Clare. He is a robust babe, and how odd it is after so many years to be holding an infant to my breast again. Odder yet, for our three eldest daughters are themselves married and mothers, making me a grandmother, and you and Bébinn great-grandparents. Our youngest, Isobel, is just turned sixteen and has an eye to marrying one of Dallán O'Byrne's nephews.

English authorities continue to enforce the statute. Their most recent seizure was the estate of the daughter of earl of Kildare; she had violated the statute by marrying an Irishman, none other than my young cousin, Art MacMurrough. Thus it is that the Wicklow clans are gathering to fight the English, and at last, O'Connor warriors will be standing alongside MacMurroughs.

With Much Affection, Your Daughter.

At Baravore, Glenmalure.

Nearly three years later this communication was sent from Baravore.

November, 1394

To Our Dearest Father and Mother,

This is, perhaps, the final letter you will receive from us. On October 2, King Richard landed at Waterford with an army of more than 34,000. They make their way toward Dublin, burning and killing as they march in their determination to expel the Irish from Leinster, and secure these hills for the English.

We have made the difficult decision to leave Baravore for the safety of a place, where the English do not wage war against women and children. Unlike the majority of chieftains, my husband does not intend to swear obeisance to the English crown, nor to relinquish his lands without a fight, and I stand firmly behind his decision. We are not alone, however, our greatest ally being Art MacMurrough.

My husband intends to fight Rourke's battle, and perhaps, after these two hundred years of bigotry and oppression, he will be among those to drive the English out of Ireland. Pray for us. Pray for Ireland, and for every noble warrior in the hills and bogs of this most beautiful land under the Heavens.

With devotion and affection, Your Daughter and Son.

At Baravore, Glenmalur.

When Aislinn left Baravore she carried a small hinged box. It was very old, crafted of metal, and engraved with Celtic birds, having been the container in which Bébinn's amber beads had been buried at the faerie mound. In that box, Aislinn put her treasures. Her father's letters from Loch Awe. And the heart and the holly.

That winter, Aislinn, her daughters and infant

grandchildren spent several nights in the ancient burial cairn where she and Bran had stayed during that tempest so many years before. There, in the chamber where her husband had prepared a feast fit for the old kings at Tara, Aislinn buried the little hinged box. She left it behind when a boat arrived to take them to an island in the west, where she and her daughters remained until it was safe to be reunited with their husbands.

As to the box and its contents, they are buried in that grave to this day. And if you stand on a certain spot above a strand on the Wicklow coast, where a tall man with black hair and dragon-green eyes jogs when the tide is out, you may be the one to find them yet.